ROBYN CARR

BLUE SKIES

MIRA

ISBN 0-7783-2042-1

BLUE SKIES

Copyright © 2004 by Robyn Carr.

MIRA and the Star Colophon are trademarks used under license and registered
in Australia, New Zealand, Philippines, United States Patent and Trademark
Office and in other countries.

www.MIRABooks.com

Printed in U.S.A.

For Jim, the strongest and kindest man I know.
And for the good people of National Airlines.

ACKNOWLEDGMENTS

The commercial airline industry is close to my heart. My husband has spent over twenty years as a pilot and executive in the business. He is now with his fourth airline—and two of them were start-ups. It is a business so competitive and unpredictable that it takes very special, very courageous people to get an airline off the ground and keep it flying.

The people in this edgy, exciting industry are nothing short of awesome. They can vie for each other's passengers with cutthroat enthusiasm, but when there's an emergency or disaster, this is an industry that becomes a small town in which everyone helps everyone else. You can count on airline people.

Needless to say, I have had the privilege to know the brightest and the best in the industry—my friends for life—so everything I needed to know to set a story against the backdrop of this fabulous industry was at my fingertips. I've taken a few liberties with minor details for the sake of storytelling, and the characters are all entirely fictional, but hopefully this world of a start-up airline rings true enough.

There is one gentleman I'd like to tell you about. Michael J. Conway, president and CEO of the former National Airlines, and before that America West Airlines, is one of the most remarkable leaders I have known. I watched him take money out of his own wallet to give to a ramp worker who was waiting for a paycheck before buying his required steel-toed boots. "Buy them now," Conway said. He encouraged a vice president to send his secretary home to take care of her desperately handicapped baby and paid her salary for whatever work she could manage at home. Mike Conway pulled strings to send a flight attendant to spend twenty-four hours with her soldier husband in Kuwait during Desert Storm, arranged free passage for veterans to Washington, D.C., for Memorial Day remembrances and was the creator of the policy of sick leave that went like this: You're sick? We'll pay you till you're well, no matter how long it takes.

But the events of 9/11, unsurprisingly, brought out his best. National Airlines, once profitable and successful, had been feeling the strain of a troubled economy and rising fuel prices. Dealing with a country terrified to fly, Mike Conway put the seats on sale for $1.00 one day a week for a month. Getting the country back in the air was the most important thing, because it was the right thing to do. He was not discouraged, nor did he change his plans when the chairmen of other commercial airlines refused to participate. And on every single one of those flights— full flights—Mike Conway and all of his corporate officers flew along, one on every flight, and thanked the people for being there, for supporting the commercial aviation industry and the United States.

One

Nikki stood at the grave of her ex-husband and thought, *This is the last way I expected to get custody.*

Beside her was her fourteen-year-old daughter, April, quietly weeping. On Nikki's other side, eleven-year-old Jared stared straight ahead, stoic. Nikki could sense her father, Buck, towering behind them. He would be scowling, she knew. Buck had hated Drake Cameron and probably considered his death just one more thing Drake had screwed up. Next to April stood Nikki's mother, and Buck's ex-wife, Opal, seriously soaking a hanky. Tucked into the crook of her arm was her fluffy white poodle, Precious, who was not. Opal had liked Drake very much; she probably thought marrying him had been one of the few things Nikki had done right. Opal was one to appreciate money and pedigree, both of which she believed Drake had.

Only forty-seven, Drake had appeared to be at the peak of health. Nikki couldn't remember when he'd last had a head cold. Yet April had come home from school and found him facedown on the floor in his bathrobe, apparently dead since morning. The medical examiner's preliminary finding was massive coronary.

About fifty mourners gathered at the cemetery in the quickly rising heat of a late May morning in Phoenix. Most were lawyers and secretaries from the firm that had employed Drake, a tax law specialist. The only one of them Nikki knew was his secretary, Mona, who had been with him for at least ten years, long before the divorce. Nikki had had to tangle with her every time she tried to make arrangements with Drake regarding the kids. A most unpleasant woman.

A couple of teachers from April's school had also come, as well as Jared's principal and one of the soccer coaches. A small knot of teenagers—April's friends—stood slightly off to one side, trying not to get too close to the adults.

It was not a big crowd. Like Nikki, Drake was an only child. His parents were deceased, and his rigid, domineering nature meant he didn't have a lot of friends. It was hard to cozy up to someone who insisted on control at any price. And then there was that business about grudges. Drake's anger had great stamina; he could stay mad forever.

Somewhere in the gathering were Nikki's two closest friends, Dixie McPherson and Carlisle Bartlett. Both were flight attendants at Aries Airlines, where Nikki was a pilot. They had worked together for the past ten years, starting when the company was still fairly new and small, and over the years there had been many times they'd have been lost without one another. Like now. Although Dixie and Carlisle were both involved in serious relationships, Nikki had been on her own since the divorce. Oddly, as she looked down at the black earth that would cover her dead ex-husband, an arm around each of her children, she felt *less* alone now.

The mourners filed past Nikki and the kids. "So sorry," they murmured. "He'll be missed." Or, "Hang in there, kids. Try to remember the good times you had with your dad." April excused herself and went to join her friends, who immediately embraced her. Jared's friends were probably considered too young by their parents to attend.

Nikki shook hands and thanked each person, but Opal accepted condolences as though Drake were her son, inviting everyone back to Drake's house for refreshments. Dixie and Carlisle waited till the last person had left, and April bid her friends goodbye and returned to Nikki's side.

"How're you holding up?" Dixie asked, while Carlisle simply filled his arms with April and Jared.

"She's doing very well, aren't you, Nicole?" Opal replied for her. Precious snarled.

"I'm doing okay. Are you coming over to the house?"

Before Dixie could answer, April pulled herself free of Carlisle's arms and, tears in her voice, asked, "Do we have to just keep doing this? Over and over and over?"

Nikki couldn't imagine her pain. The kids had had a hard time with their dad, but they had loved him. The hell of it was, she thought as she looked at Opal, you loved your parents even when you hated them. As for Jared, he just stared out at nothing, his detachment as troubling as April's tears.

"Oh, April," Opal said. "People are going to be there, sweet. It's the proper thing to do. Say a few kind words about the departed…offer sympathy… And your friends will be there."

"No, they won't, Grandma. I told them not to come."

"But we invited—"

"So? Do we *have* to?"

"It's your house, April," Nikki interjected. "I think Grandma's just trying to do the right thing…."

"What a pain," Jared muttered, giving the ground a kick.

"We don't want to seem rude," Opal said.

Buck grunted and turned away, heading for his car.

This whole reception thing her mother had planned was not for Opal, Nikki realized, and certainly not for herself. It was for April and Jared. And if they didn't want to do this...

"Um, guys," she said to Dixie and Carlisle, "can you take my mother to the house? We're going to beg off. I'll see you later."

"Thatta girl," Carlisle cheered.

"Nicole! You can't do that!"

"Of course I can, Mother. We'll be along later. Come on, kids. I have an idea."

With an arm around each, she walked them right past the funeral parlor's limo to her car.

Nikki had been born thirty-nine years before and named Nicole Evelyn Burgess. At that time, Buck Burgess was a twenty-seven-year-old aviator who worked a lot of part-time jobs. He dusted crops, flew cargo, gave lessons, took charters, sometimes buzzed the Grand Canyon. He also pumped gas, washed planes, swept out hangars, turned a wrench here and there—anything to be around the small municipal airport just outside Phoenix, Arizona. On the day of her birth he bought a twenty-year-old Stearman biplane and christened her the *Jazzie One*. It was the first plane Nikki learned to fly.

A few years later, rather than buying his wife jewelry or a larger house or new car, he bought into the fixed-base operation at the airport and became a partner. Still later, after Opal left him for a man without engine grease under his nails, Buck bought the rest of the operation. It then became Burgess Aviation and the place where Nikki grew up, because when Opal left Buck, she also left Nikki. "I'm not an idiot," she had said. "I know Nikki will be happier with you."

Although that was true, Nikki had been only nine at the time, and she felt as if her whole life had fallen apart. If not for the flying, she'd have been lost.

So that was where Nikki took her kids after the funeral—to Papa's airport. Buck was already there and helped her unleash the *Jazzie One* from her anchors.

"Me first, Mom," April said. "Please?"

Through the whole miserable ordeal of Drake's death, this one thing lifted Nikki's heart, that April would reach for the sky in an effort to come to terms with her grief. April was okay with flying and knew how. She could hardly escape it with her grandfather the owner of a large and successful fixed-base operation and her mother a Boeing 767 captain. But she didn't love it the way Nikki did, or Buck and Jared, so her eagerness was all the more precious to Nikki.

She'd take the kids out for a few loops over the desert, a little wild-horse chasing up where it was cool blue and clean and quiet. In all the tough times of her life— whether she'd been stood up for the Homecoming dance or going through a divorce—nothing could breathe new life into Nikki like the sun and wind on her face and the music of the biplane wires as she soared through the sky.

The instant she had traded her dark blue funeral suit and pumps for the mechanic's overalls and boots that she kept in a locker at the airport, Nikki had felt instantly more like herself. She'd found some sweats and tennis shoes in the same locker for April to use. Her daughter had sniffed them suspiciously and made a face, but she donned them quickly enough.

Nikki then fastened the leather flying helmet on April's head, pulling back her daughter's pretty blond hair to adjust the helmet over the earplugs attached to April's portable CD player. God, but the girl was beautiful, all pale flawless skin, large, luminous blue eyes and thick dusty-black lashes that fell softly against her cheeks as she glanced down. She had inherited her father's Nordic good looks and lean, sturdy body. Jared, freckled and already broad-shouldered, took after Nikki and Buck.

April climbed into the front of the Stearman, and Nikki into the back, while Buck stood ready on the tarmac with Jared. Nikki could have taken up the Bonanza or Cessna and had both kids in the air together, but flying outside with the wind on your face was so much more therapeutic.

She flipped a couple of switches, pulled the throttle back and yelled, "Contact!" Buck turned the prop, the plane sputtered, the engine caught, and they rumbled out to the runway. In just moments Nikki could feel that familiar lurch as the _Jazzie One_ lifted off the ground and began to soar. Up. Up. Up.

How ironic, she thought. This was where she'd met Drake. She'd fallen in love with him in the Stearman, or at least thought she had. She'd worked at getting over him in the Stearman, and now she was burying his memory in the same plane, flying over the same old ground.

Fifteen years ago, Nikki was a petite and sexy twenty-four year old with boundless energy, working for her dad at Burgess Aviation. She was a graduate of Embry-Riddle Aeronautical University with a degree in aerospace engineering, sigma cum laude. Plus, she could fly the hell out of just about any plane she climbed into. And she was in love with Paul, whom she had dated for a couple of years and expected to marry. They were both pilots looking for work in commercial aviation.

Paul got hired by Delta, left Phoenix to fly out of Dallas, met a flashy young flight attendant and broke up with Nikki over the phone. And that was when her life began to fall apart for the second time.

Her heart empty and aching, she took notice of a good-looking young lawyer who had signed up for flying lessons at Burgess. Drake was thirty-two and almost unbearably handsome. Nikki used to watch him when he went out with his instructor, but she didn't speak to him until the day she found him waiting for her, leaning against the hangar doors and looking devilishly sexy. "What would it cost me to have a ride in that thing?" he asked, pointing to the Stearman she'd just landed.

She shrugged. He looked like an even bigger risk than Paul, and she wasn't about to take that kind of chance again. Casually, she answered, "A cup of coffee?"

He grinned at her. "Say when!"

There were warning bells going off all over the place, but Nikki didn't pay much attention because after Paul, she wasn't about to take any chances on a guy, even if she was miserably lonely. She just loved an excuse to fly. "How about right now?"

It happened without her realizing it. Disinterested and detached as she was, she must have appeared a real challenge, because Drake wooed her vigorously. He flattered, showered her with attention, brought her gifts and flowers. Slowly she began to forget that Paul had ripped her heart out and handed it to her. With every ride she gave him in the biplane, she let go a little more and thought, what the hell? You only live once. The first time he kissed her, she felt hot and wild, and when he touched her breast she nearly died. In less than six months, she was pregnant and had married him. Not some of her best planning.

Drake never did get the knack of flying and gave up the notion in no time. It didn't take long before Nikki realized what a terrible mistake she'd made. He was impossible to please. He needled her about everything from her feeble housekeeping skills to her figure, which he found lacking, and he was furious at her refusal to take the name Cameron. But she was Nikki Burgess and planned to always be Nikki Burgess.

Had it not been for her father, things might have been worse. Buck, sweet old thing that he was, could look very threatening. In size alone he was intimidating. And he had not liked Drake from the first. Had Drake dared to so much as lay a hand on Nikki or the kids, Buck might have killed him.

She should have run for her life the moment she heard scorn in Drake's voice…but she was so stubborn. Plus, there was April. And as every abused and unhappy wife knew, once you stayed past the time you should've gone, you ended up staying far too long.

"Get out and don't look back," Buck kept saying.

"I'm sure you're being far too particular," said Opal. "After all, he makes a nice living."

It took her eleven years of unhappiness to leave him and she had no idea how high a price she'd have to pay.

Determined not to go quietly, Drake fought her every step of the way, right down to custody. Ultimately the issue came down to work. Nikki's job as a pilot for Aries Airlines took her out of town for three to four days a week; Drake's hours were nine to five, more or less, no nights away from the kids. It was very easy for his lawyer to convince a judge that Drake should have custodial guardianship and Nikki unlimited visitation. That meant she could spend as much time with the kids as she could manage to negotiate with Drake, which she quickly learned would be very challenging. And she paid child support.

She had moved in with Buck to save money. For four years she had done everything possible to be involved with the kids' education and activities, though Drake put — tremendous energy into screwing up their plans. Being divorced from him was nearly as emotionally draining as being married to him.

Nikki had only vague memories of that twenty-four-year-old hotshot, sexy pilot she'd once been—one hundred and fifteen pounds soaking wet, cheeks aglow and eyes sparkling with excitement and hope. She used to like what she saw in the mirror, but now she found that the woman staring back was plain of looks, her reddish brown hair dull, her figure shot and her eyes tired. She wondered if she would ever feel good about herself again. And as for having a loving relationship with a man who adored her...

Nikki pulled back on the stick, causing the biplane to soar upward, invert and execute a big loop. She might feel ordinary on the ground, but up here she was a goddess. Drake had done everything to make her feel dumpy and unattractive, but up here she felt sleek and quick and sexy. They had stopped having sex a long time before she left him; he said she just didn't do anything for him. But up here she was fast and hot and wild...

Thirty minutes or so later, Nikki landed the Stearman and taxied over to where Buck and Jared stood waiting. As April threw a leg over the side of the plane, she pulled off her leather helmet and shook out her hair. Nikki could see the dried streaks of tears on her chapped cheeks. April leaned toward her mom. "He wasn't real warm and fuzzy, but he wasn't a bad guy,'' she said. "Daddy worked really hard, sometimes all through the night. He meant well, you know. He just had his…you know…*issues.*''

The kids had loved their father, even though they had struggled with his sometimes arbitrary discipline and negative nature. And he had loved them. She was going to have to remind herself of that, make an effort not to malign the poor, dead, selfish bastard. "I know, honey," she said. "I know."

Fifteen crappy years of Drake, and because he'd given her two of the most awesome gifts a woman could ever want…April and Jared…she didn't dare indulge in regret.

Buck watched as his daughter took the Stearman up again, this time with Jared aboard. He couldn't shake the sensation that he had failed her, although he also couldn't imagine what he'd have done differently. He couldn't make Opal stay with them, couldn't change what had happened with Paul, couldn't keep Nikki from marrying Drake.

But she shouldn't have grown up at an airport with a bunch of guys who could teach her how to change points and plugs but didn't have a clue when it came to fixing her hair or putting on lipstick. So what if she could fly like a bird—she should have had someone other than a crusty old father to be her soft place to fall when she was weary.

Maybe if he hadn't raised her to fly she wouldn't have to struggle so much—a female pilot working and living in a world that still belonged to men. And wasn't that really why Drake had been such a dick? Because he'd envied Nikki's skill and intelligence and capability? Buck had always thought as much.

Her life had been too hard. But then, Nikki never did take the easy way.

Lucille Paxton approached him from behind, gazing up at the sky. She owned the café that was attached to the fixed-base hangar offices. In her sixties like Buck, Lucille had often been the stand-in mother and grandmother around Burgess Aviation. Heavy, gray-haired and rosy cheeked, she wore jeans and a T-shirt with an American flag on it and Support Our Troops printed underneath. "I fixed April up with a soda."

Trotting along behind her was Pistol, Buck's latest mutt. He was an odd-looking creature with the head of a Labrador, long curly ears like a cocker spaniel or poodle, the short legs of a dachshund, and the genitalia of a small buffalo. But by far his most endearing quality was that he adored Jared and despised Precious.

Buck squatted to pat the Labra-doodle-cocka-dachsie while watching the sky.

When Nikki came around and lined up to land, Lucille said, "She's due a break."

"Damn straight," Buck replied.

There were only two cars at Drake's house when Nikki, Buck and the kids returned—the housekeeper's old Camry and Dixie's Acura. Nikki breathed a huge sigh of relief. The open house was over and she didn't have to face anyone from Drake's firm. The mere thought of never having to deal with his secretary, Mona, again almost filled her with glee.

She found her friends in the living room, seated on the sofa, grim-faced. Dixie tilted her head toward the dining room and Nikki looked for the source of the problem. Ah, yes. Her mother. Who else? Opal sat in a straight-backed dining room chair, her expression dour, her poodle curled up on her lap. "Well, finally," she said by way of greeting. Precious stirred at her words.

The kids headed straight for the kitchen. Nikki dropped her leather shoulder bag on a living room chair and draped her funeral clothes over it. She hadn't bothered to change out of the greasy mechanic's jumpsuit and boots. "Sorry, Mother, but the kids just weren't up to any more. They'd had it."

Buck and Pistol sauntered in. Precious wriggled upright, and with his back legs on Opal's lap and front legs on the chair arm, snarled meaningfully. Pistol trotted toward him and snarled back, message received.

"You could have at least attempted to get here in time to say hello to a few of Drake's mourners," she scolded.

"Oh, for Pete's sake, Mother, he was my ex. If it weren't for the kids, *I* wouldn't even be here."

But Opal wasn't listening. She was transfixed by the ensemble Nikki wore, complete with unlaced steel-toed boots. "Good Lord, Nicole, what is that you have on? Merciful heavens." She stood slowly from her chair, holding Precious and clucking in disgust. "I believe I'll just go lie down. My head pounds."

Opal toddled down the hall with her poodle, past the master bedroom to the guest room. She went in and closed the door. Nikki, who had watched her departure, turned a stunned expression back to her friends.

"That's where I've been sleeping," she said. "I just couldn't make myself use Drake's room."

"I believe your mother knows that," Carlisle said. "She mentioned something about it being…what was it? Disheveled."

"Well, Christ."

"Cheer up. Maybe she'll tidy up while she's in there."

"I guess I probably owe you two for sticking it out with her all afternoon," Nikki said.

"Sometimes your friendship comes at a mighty fine price," Dixie drawled. "But Opal wasn't near as bad as that secretary of Drake's. Mona? She was all pissed that you and the kids weren't here." Dixie shook her head. "She's one black-hearted bitch." For Dixie to give a review that bleak was saying something. This sweet Texas beauty queen's greatest failing was not seeing the worst in people soon enough. Mostly men.

"A very unpleasant woman," Carlisle agreed, shaking his head. He stood up and stretched. "She completely ruined a perfectly nice funeral."

Buck's shoulders shook. He draped an arm around Carlisle. "Come on, cupcake. Let's see if old Drake left any decent whiskey in the liquor cabinet."

While the men went to the wet bar in the family room, Dixie followed Nikki to the kitchen to find the kids and Drake's housekeeper, Lydia. April and Jared sat at the kitchen table while Lydia fluttered around them, serving them sandwiches, drinks of soda, chips and cookies, all the while patting their heads affectionately and cooing to them in Spanish.

"Have you figured out what I owe you, Lydia?" Nikki asked.

Immediately a troubled expression clouded the woman's tanned and crinkled face, and she seemed to be wringing her hands on the dish towel she held. "Miss Nikki, Mr. Drake got a little behind for me."

"That's okay, Lydia. Just tell me how much."

The housekeeper moved closer to Nikki but didn't

make eye contact. She simply gazed down at the floor and whispered, "Twenty-five hundred."

"Twenty-five hundred?" Nikki replied in a near shout. Hoping it was pesos, she asked, "Dollars?"

The kids looked up from their food. Dixie clapped a hand over her heart. Buck and Carlisle entered the kitchen with a bottle of Scotch just in time to hear. Lydia actually flushed in embarrassment and began to fan her face.

"*Sí*. It was in dollars."

"How long has he been behind?"

"He say when the tax return come, but then—" That was all she could seem to get out.

"Oh, brother. I'm surprised you kept coming back."

"Sometimes he pay me," she said. She went to the laundry room on the other side of the kitchen where her purse and sweater hung on a hook. She got them both, then took a notebook from her purse and passed it to Nikki. "I keep track," she said.

Nikki ruffled the pages briefly. It was clear the woman had documented her earnings carefully. She was telling the truth. It looked as though Lydia worked for several families, and if she hadn't, she might have starved to death. Nikki handed back the small spiral notebook. "I'll get my checkbook," she said with resignation.

A little while later, Lydia left with her check and a promise from Nikki that she would be called to help with cleaning again once they got their bearings.

Drake had let himself get twenty-five hundred dollars behind in paying a Mexican woman of simple means whose entire family struggled to get by? What was he thinking? Did he have no consideration?

"You can repay yourself when the will is settled," Dixie suggested.

But something in the pit of Nikki's stomach tensed. Could there be a reason other than greed that Drake had not paid her? Could he have had, as April would say, financial *issues?* But why borrow trouble? She was seeing the lawyer the next day.

"Ice," she said, indicating the bottle Buck held. "We need some glasses and some ice. Right away."

The lawyer who handled Drake's will had also handled his divorce, and Nikki found it hard to be in the same room with him.

"You're not technically family," Richard Studbeck said in lieu of hello.

What a cold bastard. "I'm technically the parent of the minor children who will be represented in the will. Besides an estranged sister, they're his only family, as far as I know."

"Have a seat." He indicated the chair that faced his desk.

"Thanks...Dick."

He froze. "I prefer Richard."

"Of course. Now I remember." She smiled as prettily as she could. He was not fooled.

"I'm afraid I don't have much good news," he began.

She felt that tension in her stomach again and held her breath.

"Your ex-husband left only his personal effects. Clothing, furniture, linens, pots and pans, et cetera."

Nikki stared into his unblinking gray eyes, vaguely aware that her mouth hung open as she tried to understand. "Only?" she finally said.

"Unfortunately." He folded his hands primly. His deadpan expression did not convey any sympathy.

"But... The house, the car, the insurance...?"

"The house, of which you are co-owner, was mortgaged to more than one hundred percent of its value, the car is leased, the insurance canceled."

"That's impossible," she said, a little laugh escaping her as though this were all just a big, nasty joke.

"I wish it were, Nicole."

"When the house is sold, he owes me half the equity—it's part of our divorce agreement! And the firm he worked for *required* the insurance policy!"

"The firm is the beneficiary of one policy, for which it paid the premium. Drake let his personal policy lapse. And papers on file indicate you signed refinancing agreements."

"Not for more than one hundred per cent of the value of—" When she realized she was coming out of her chair, she slowly lowered herself again. Yes, she had signed refinancing papers, and there was something about an equity line of credit while the interest rates were so low and the stock market down. But the refinancing was only for the balance of the mortgage. Had he…? *Of course, you dolt!* Drake had either altered the amount on the papers or forged her signature. "He must have changed the numbers…or forged my signature."

Richard Studbeck shrugged. "It's going to be impossible to indict or prosecute him."

"Wait a minute, wait a minute! He didn't have planes or boats or beautiful women. He rarely traveled, rarely vacationed. I think I remember he spent a weekend in Las Vegas a couple of years ago, but that was before—" She swallowed hard. "I paid child support! It was supposed to be going into a trust for education! What the hell did he do with all the money?"

The lawyer paused at length before responding. "I'm afraid I have absolutely no idea."

* * *

Nothing. He left the kids nothing.

Nikki went home in a daze. How was she to tell them? Did she have to tell them? Maybe there was some mistake. Maybe when she could finally bring herself to go through Drake's personal effects and private papers, she would find a safe deposit box or secret stash somewhere. But no, she thought—it was more likely she would find he had given everything to a shelter for homeless cats, giving Nikki the shaft one last time from the grave. *Wham!* Take that, Nick!

Although she knew it wasn't justified, Nikki felt tempted to direct her anger at Opal. After all, her mother had had far more faith in Drake than in her own daughter.

Once Opal had married Mayer Gould, a neurosurgeon, and moved to San Francisco, Nikki had only seen her mother on her rare and brief visits to Phoenix. But after Nikki married Drake and moved into the big house in the gated community, Opal had visited more often. And in the last couple of years, since Mayer's death, Opal was constantly turning up, ostensibly visiting her grandchildren, but Nikki thought it just as likely she was visiting Drake.

And Drake, who couldn't get along with anyone, had allowed this. According to April, Opal fussed over him, constantly praising everything he said or did. It was as though she had finally found someone who cared as much about money and style as she did, and Drake had found a mother to worship him. Nikki hadn't cared a whit about that at the time, grateful not to have to deal with her mother herself. And Opal was good with the kids, probably because she was just about as mature.

But now Nikki had to get her life back together, which

would be hard enough without Opal questioning every decision she made. Her mother would have to go.

When she got back to the house, Nikki found Opal in the living room, cradling Precious and a magazine on her lap, her two-hundred-dollar shoes kicked off and her slim, pedicured feet up on the ottoman.

Nikki ignored the poodle's welcoming growl and sat down on the sofa opposite her. "Mother, I'm afraid you're going to have to go home and let me have some time alone with the kids."

"What?" she said, straightening.

"I know you'd like to stay, Mother, but we really need some time alone."

"But won't you be going back to work? I assumed I'd simply..."

Nikki shook her head. "I have a week off, then a couple of trips. The kids can stay with Buck, like they always have. They have bedrooms there. That's where I've lived the past four years."

Opal made a derisive sound, as though Buck's place was beneath them.

"I have to go through Drake's things, Mother, and I need privacy for that. You can visit again when our life is more organized, and stay as long as you like."

"I think April and Jared would like me to be here now," she argued. "And who knows how much time I actually have. I'm not getting any younger, you know. The last time I saw the doctor, he was concerned about a few things."

By sheer dint of will, Nikki kept from rolling her eyes. Her mother had been suggesting her impending death since she was in her thirties. "You seem very well. I'm sure you'll be around for many years to come."

"Don't be too sure. Carolyn Johanson was three years

younger than me, never had a sick day in her life, and—"

Nikki cut her off, unwilling to go down that path again. "I want the kids and I to make decisions about our life without any outside influence." Like whether we stay in this house or not, she thought, but didn't dare say that. Opal loved Drake's house. "I'll buy you a first-class upgrade to go with your pass," she bribed.

"Well…"

"And I don't want you to make this hard on the kids by complaining that I'm sending you away."

"Well, if the shoe—"

Nikki set her lips in a firm line and shook her head, brooking no argument. Opal traveled free on Aries Airlines at the courtesy of Nikki, a privilege that could be rescinded by Nikki at any time she chose. "Let's not make things any tougher on the kids than they already are. I'm sure you didn't bring enough luggage for a long visit, anyway."

"I did come rather quickly."

"You don't want to stick around and bake in this desert heat when you have a lovely home in California."

"I've never minded the heat—"

"And there's a flight tomorrow afternoon with plenty of room in first class."

"I much prefer first class," she admitted.

"Yes. I know."

Opal scooted to the edge of her chair and wiggled her feet around until they found her shoes. "You're in mourning," she said, hanging on to Precious. "You should be indulged right now. I've lost a husband, remember. I know what this is like. I wish Mayer's children from his first wife had left me alone to go through his belongings, but they were not nearly as considerate as I.''

That was Opal. Ousted with all the delicacy of a cattle prod and taking credit for being considerate.

I'm not in mourning! Nikki wanted to shout. *I'm enraged! I am so damn tired of getting screwed!*

Two

Nikki was back at work a week later—a week in which she had neither gone through Drake's things nor talked to the kids about their lack of legacy. Now, as she made her way to airport security, she forced her thoughts from her current problems and let her mind wander back to the days when she'd first fallen in love with the aviation industry.

When she was a little girl in the sixties, the airport was a mystical, magical fantasyland and the air crews were like movie stars—so exotic, so glamorous, so *beautiful*. The pilots were tall and handsome. Women would tilt their heads and gaze dreamily at them, and small children reached out to tentatively touch the silver bands on their sleeves. The "Stews," as they were called in those days, were slender beauties who showed up to work in narrow skirts and high-heeled shoes, each with a matching square makeup bag that held her cosmetics. The crew would enter the airport en masse—two or three stately, distinguished pilots and their gaggle of long-necked beauty queens—and glide down the concourse toward the big shiny planes. As they passed, the crowds would part like the Red Sea. They were magnificent.

"Do you want to be like one of them when you grow up?" Opal had asked her one day when they were at the airport together.

"Oh, yes," Nikki said with a deep sigh of longing. "Do you think they'll let girls be pilots of big heavies by then?"

Opal had groaned, but Buck had smiled down at her. "If they don't, you can be the first," he promised.

"You're *hopeless,*" said Opal.

It wasn't just the flight crews that were different, Nikki recalled, but the entire airport scene. And the industry was regulated. The government established the routes for the carriers and there wasn't much competition, so flights were expensive. Damned expensive. It cost more to fly from New York to Los Angeles in 1975 than it did in 2002. There was a certain formality to flying then. Women wore dresses, sometimes hats and gloves, and men were in their business suits.

Security in those days was almost nonexistent. Crews and passengers alike entered the airport and went quickly to their planes without being subjected to bomb-sniffing dogs and metal detectors. And passengers were extremely well-trained. They did as they were told. They were civil. Polite. No yelling at the gate agent, no demanding compensation for a delayed or canceled flight. Airlines were admired, pilots were revered. If a flight was delayed to repair a mechanical problem, your life had just been saved by their diligence, their skill. Through the flight, passengers were well-behaved. God forbid one of those beauties who served the meals—and they *were* meals, make no mistake—be abused in the commission of her duties.

There was no denying that times had changed. As Nikki passed through security in her pilot's uniform, complete with ID badge, she was curtly reminded to take her hat off her head and empty her pockets. Randomly chosen, she was told to step to the side, remove her shoes and extend her arms so she could be scanned with the magic wand. Now, it wasn't as if just wearing the flying costume should get you special treatment; she could as easily be a bad guy as anyone in civilian clothes. But—

"Hi, Virg," she said to the security agent with the wand.

"Hiya, Nick. You have the same trip this week?"

"Yup. Phoenix, Chicago, New York, again and again."

"Take off your shoes. Extend your arms. That a good trip?"

"Not bad."

Nikki saw these same people at least once a week. Did they really think she was packing a weapon or bomb? She had wondered aloud once why they didn't just move on to the next stranger in line when they saw she drew the random pick. It might give them a better chance of actually catching someone with something to hide. Virginia had replied that they just did it by the book.

While she was being wanded, Nikki watched as a very nervous man who seemed awfully protective of his briefcase went straight through the check while they detained and wanded a woman in her eighties. Nikki wondered why security didn't just adopt the JDLR method. *Just Doesn't Look Right.* But no. They kept checking little old ladies and pilots they talked to every week.

"Have a good flight, Nick."

"Thanks, Virg. You have a great day."

Another man with a briefcase, in a hurry and obviously disgruntled by the long security process, rammed into her and almost knocked her off her feet. He had both height and heft and smelled like a mixture of booze and perspiration. "'Scuse me," he muttered. Then, seeing she wore a pilot's uniform, he asked, "Any idea what time the nine o'clock flight's leaving for Denver?"

"Nine o'clock?" she ventured.

"That'd be a first," he grumbled, taking off down the concourse.

So much for the respect offered to pilots in days of yore.

Crowds didn't part for aircrews anymore, either, and Nikki stuck close to the wall to keep from getting knocked over again. Up ahead she spotted Dixie at the coffee kiosk and went to join her. "Hey," she said. "I didn't expect to run into you."

"Our inbound flight from San Diego is runnin' late. I should be servin' Bloody Marys over Albuquerque right now. Want a coffee?"

"Thanks. I'm a few minutes early. I'll meet you right over there," she said, pointing toward her gate.

Nikki crossed the concourse and sat in the almost empty gate area, watching the passengers. They were people in ragged jeans and flip-flops. Young families who would be trying to board with car seats, Cadillac-size strollers and half the nursery. Ah—and a pilot. Not one of those distinguished gentlemen of the past, this captain was about thirty-five years old, forty pounds overweight, no hat, scuffed shoes, loose tie and coffee stains on his shirt. He hadn't had a haircut in a while, either. What a wreck. His appearance didn't exactly inspire confidence.

Dixie handed her a cup of coffee and took the seat next to her.

"Remember the old days?" Nikki said. "When flight attendants showed up in high heels and pilots were like rock stars?"

Dixie took the lid off her paper cup and blew on the hot coffee. "And now they're just like rock heads?" Nikki turned her head to smile at her friend. "Present company excluded, of course."

"Remember when people dressed up to go on an airplane ride?" Nikki persisted. "They wore their Sunday best and behaved like they were in church. Even the hijackers were polite! They didn't want to hurt anyone— they just wanted to go to Cuba or someplace where you couldn't get a scheduled flight."

Dixie tilted her head and looked askance at Nikki. "Back in the days when flight attendants were Stews, had to weigh in before each flight, and were fired if they got married?"

"Okay, it wasn't flawless, but—"

"And the airplanes didn't have carts and the Stews carried their five-course meals on trays, up and down the aisles in their straight skirts and high heels and precious little hats?"

"Well…"

"And don't let us forget about girdles. Any decent woman wore a girdle then."

"Everyone?"

"It was required. And if you weren't bosomy enough, a little padding could be issued with the uniform."

"Nah-uh!" Nikki protested.

"Yes, ma'am. Got to have your girls right up there on your chest so Mr. Passengerman could appreciate the flight. And you better not bend over to pick up an olive off the floor because Mr. Well-Mannered Traveler would definitely put his hand right up your skirt." She blew on her coffee again. "He probably threw that old olive on the floor to start with. Mmm-mmm, those were some fine old days."

"You have to admit that the passengers were a lot less rude and demanding," Nikki said. "With the occasional exception."

"And the pilots were a lot more accommodatin'. They used to carry bags and pay for dinner, and… Well… They were much more accommodatin'." Dixie smiled suggestively.

Nikki grinned back at her. Dixie had been *accommodated* quite a few times. And vice versa. "So were the Stews," she said.

"Coffee, tea or me?" her friend replied, smile dazzling, lashes fluttering. All of Dixie sparkled. She could easily have been one of those airline beauties back in the sixties. Five-eight, blond, blue-eyed, slender as a reed except for "her girls," which were full and high and elegant. She had the kind of looks that had men crossing the room to ask if she was attached.

A very pregnant flight attendant pulled an overnight bag on its rollers toward a podium on the other side of the concourse.

"Now, there's something else you wouldn't have seen twenty-five years ago," Dixie pointed out. "In fact," she said, looking Nikki up and down, "it would've seemed pretty unladylike to ask to *fly* the plane."

"My God, she looks ready to pop!"

"She told a little fib about her due date. She can't afford to go on maternity leave, she needs the overtime. Her husband was activated reserve—Navy—gone to Kuwait. The family took a huge pay cut."

Almost everything about the industry had changed, all right. Back in the glamour days there was no real competition. Enter deregulation of the airline industry and the entrance of low-fare carriers. The large and established airlines found it increasingly difficult to compete.

The new entrants, often nonunion start-ups, had low costs, but the big guys had been around long enough so that with every union contract, the cost of labor went up, then up, then up some more. The cost of fuel kept rising, but competitive pricing meant ticket prices plummeted, and the business traveler took advantage, went global.

Before long the big airlines were making almost half their profit from the last-minute business traveler whose company paid the premium price. As for the rest of the travelers, they were no longer just the well-to-do. After deregulation it was cheaper to fly from New York City to Miami for the weekend than to go to a good restaurant and see a Broadway musical. It was frequently more expensive to travel by bus. Now the people waiting to board the airplanes were not wearing their hats and gloves, politely waiting for their flight, but clad in beach clothes or ragged jeans, complaining loudly about the degradation of the service.

The major airlines were losing millions a year, a month, some losing millions a day as they tried to compete with the start-ups. The start-ups would fail and disappear, but that did not put the money back in the coffers of the legacy carriers, and another start-up would appear with bargain-basement tickets, starting the whole process all over again.

Then the unfathomable happened.

Everyone remembered where they were that morning. Buck was hosing down tarmac outside the largest hangar at Burgess Aviation when one of the young maintenance techs came running, yelling for him to come to the office and see the TV. Carlisle was in New York on an overnight, due to fly out later that day. Dixie was in D.C., on the treadmill in the hotel's fitness center, watching CNN. At first, she thought she was seeing an Aries plane and she ran to the nearest phone and called Aries dispatch.

And Nikki was in Boston, sitting in the cockpit of an Aries 767, full of passengers, ready to push back. She was turned around in her seat, talking to a Delta pilot who was hitching a ride on an Aries jump seat.

An operations agent came aboard, stuck her head in the cockpit and said, "Did you hear what happened? An airplane hit the World Trade Center."

"What kind of airplane?" Nikki asked.

"A big airplane. Like a 737 or something."

"Whoa. How do you get that far off course?"

She shrugged. "Sit tight till the airport clears us," the agent said, and left.

Less than a minute passed when her first officer said, "Did you hear that? They closed the airport."

Nikki looked outside. "Why?" It was a beautiful morning. The sky was crystal clear.

Some other pilot at the airport keyed his mike and asked why the airport had been closed.

"The airport is closed for reasons of national security," came the reply.

The deafening silence that followed lasted for perhaps two full minutes. Alarm filled the air like static.

The operations agent came back a few minutes later. Her face had bleached so white that her lips were indistinguishable from her flesh. "Another plane flew into the second tower. Another big one."

"Holy Jesus," the copilot muttered.

"They're saying the airplanes are U.S. passenger planes. Hijacked," the agent said. She was visibly trembling.

The next announcement ordered all planes back to the gates. Passengers were deplaned, pilots and cabin crews were informed there had been several hijackings from Northeast airports and flights were canceled pending investigation. The airport was swiftly evacuated.

The unprecedented response was that every aircraft in the United States was grounded for several days. Nikki learned she had been sitting next to one of the planes that had been hijacked out of Boston.

That morning, trying to reach the kids on her cell phone, she couldn't get a signal. When she did get through, she found that the kids were with Buck, terrified for her safety because they couldn't reach her.

Her first reaction, like the rest of the world's, was shock and horror. But she had a bigger mission—she had a plane to get out of Boston and a crew that was shaken and needed her leadership.

They were put in a hotel where they sat glued to televisions, watching an unbelievable drama happening not very far away. Most of her crew didn't have enough money for days of meals and incidentals, so Nikki covered them. It didn't take long for the passengers to disappear from the airport to find alternative means of transportation. Some of them would never be back.

"Mama, I don't want you to fly!" April had wailed into the phone.

"April, flying is what I do, what I've always done, and no madman from an angry country is going to drive me away from it. But I promise you I'll be taking extra precautions."

"But what if it was you?"

"But it wasn't, April. We have to be strong now. Everyone in the U.S. has to be brave and strong now."

Days later Nikki and her copilot flew an empty plane

back to Phoenix. He had missed the birth of his first child. One of the flight attendants was sick as a dog all the way home, and the minute they landed she quit. When the industry was flying again, Aries canceled the majority of their flights, as did every airline in the industry; they flew approximately thirty percent of their schedule, and those flights were not half-full. Even the business traveler stayed home. When companies started sending their people on business trips again, a sagging economy necessitated prudence—they bought bargain fares, purchasing cheap, nonrefundable tickets in advance.

Nikki, her family, her friends and the rest of the country were consumed by pain and sorrow and anger that seemed to have no end.

Aries furloughed a fourth of its workforce in the first month after 9/11, then levied ten- to thirty-percent pay cuts across the board. Most of the other airlines did the same. Two small airlines simply ceased operations in that first week after the terrorist attacks, unable to sustain the losses.

Industrywide, the financial loss reached fifteen billion in that first year. The government came across with five billion in relief, but the bankruptcy filings of seven airlines proved it would not be adequate. Only a very small percentage of the ten-billion-dollar loan package approved by Congress reached a couple of airlines.

A year later the passenger-load factors were still not quite fifty percent of what they had been before 9/11. Dozens of airplanes, from puddle jumpers to huge jets, sat in storage, parked, unused. Their owners, the lessors that airlines leased the planes from, began laying off personnel and filing for Chapter Eleven protection, as well.

The average passenger didn't notice empty planes, missing planes or deserted airports; to Joe Six-pack it appeared business as usual, because airlines combined flights and canceled flights. The 8:00 a.m. and 9:00 a.m. flights to Philly became one flight, and it was almost full, and so on. And there was the hub-and-spoke operation—all the planes converged on the airline's hub several times a day and the passengers would deplane, filling up the airport, and reboard their connecting flight. These convergences were called "banks." Phoenix was Aries's hub—everything went through Phoenix, then out again, like the spokes of a bike wheel. In between banks you could fire a cannon through the deserted airport concourses, something the average traveler never saw.

Stricter security measures were put into place, but Nikki had no illusions about their effectiveness. She thought the airlines' greatest security assets were the passengers—they would never let a plane be taken over again.

And then the country went to war, determined to cripple, if not end, terrorism at its roots. Pain and strife and economic troubles spread wider.

Four small to moderately sized airlines shut down in the first year, and in the second year at least three huge airlines that had been around forever teetered on the brink of failure. Nikki's airline limped along, but had lost several hundred million and flirted with filing for bankruptcy protection.

Nikki was left with two overwhelming conclusions about her work and her world. One: we are no longer safe. And two: we must carry on.

When Nikki took her flight out of Phoenix, Dixie was still waiting for her inbound flight to arrive. She tapped her foot and crossed her fingers. Her trip had better not cancel; she had big plans for her layover. A sexy red teddy and a nice bottle of wine were tucked away in her suitcase, and she also had a very expensive man's watch wrapped in silver paper—much more money than she should spend, especially with all the recent pay cuts. But this was a very special man, and it was his birthday.

Branch Darnell, a pilot with Aries, was turning forty-seven, though Dixie didn't think he looked a day over thirty-five. He did have those sexy little crinkles at the corners of his eyes, but that was as much from his year-round tan as age. They'd been seeing each other for six months, and she couldn't help but think he was The One. At first she'd held off letting herself think that, but she was more convinced of it every day. Over the years Dixie had had quite a few love affairs, way too many of them with pilots, but this time felt different. It had the feel of permanence.

Branch was a Texan, and Dixie couldn't help but have a soft spot for the Longhorns. He commuted from San Antonio and had all but moved in with her in Phoenix when he came to town to fly. Every week, more and more of his belongings appeared in her closet and bathroom. She was senior enough to hold just about any flying line she wanted, and tried to bid his schedule so she could spend the night with him on layovers. The drawback was that he *wasn't* senior, and the lines he was awarded were usually awful—short hops, crappy layovers, working weekends. Branch was a retired air force colonel and had only been flying commercially for three years; he was still a first officer and not even a senior one. Dixie ended up working a lot harder than she had to just be able to spend time with him.

Fortunately tonight was a rarity—a long New York City layover. A nice birthday present in itself.

There was one minor complication—Branch wasn't divorced yet. He was separated, though, and when the divorce was complete, which he had warned her wouldn't be real fast, he wasn't going to relocate to Phoenix for a few years. There were still a couple of kids at home. So it wasn't perfect, but it was damn close.

Nikki was worried. "I don't know, Dixie. He's got that look. Like he's been around."

"Well, darlin', he's not the only one," Dixie had replied with a laugh.

"It's different with you," Nikki said.

Dixie didn't have to ask why. Nikki knew as well as she did that she never left a man she'd slept with. She was completely devoted. Completely naive, too. She fell fast, hard and completely.

So why hadn't she married at nineteen? It was all she'd ever wanted. From her first real date, Dixie had never stopped thinking church bells and altar. But time and the number of men she'd been through had too often left her brokenhearted and lonely. There was always a guy, even when she wished there wasn't. Men rushed to date her, to get her into bed, to take her on trips and buy her nice things. And then, *whoosh*—they were gone as fast as they appeared. She was thirty-five years old, had eleven tennis bracelets of varying value, when all she'd really like to have was a husband and baby.

"Maybe if you wouldn't jump into bed with them so fast..." Carlisle had suggested as gently as possible.

"I try to wait," Dixie told him. "But I fall in love, they swear it's forever, and then—"

"Well, at least you've gotten some nice jewelry out of it."

But she'd so much rather have a husband. Well, she'd been with Branch for six months, which was a bit of a record for Dixie.

He could have been put off by the number of men who had come before him, but he accepted her as she was. "How can I expect a woman as beautiful as you to be a virgin till she's thirty-five? So long as you're mine now, I've got no real complaint."

"I'm yours," she was quick to assure him. And it wasn't just pillow talk—she *was*.

She checked the inbound flights on the screen and saw that the one she was waiting for had finally landed. Pulling her cell phone out of her purse, she pecked off some numbers.

"Well, darlin', you gettin' tired of waiting for me?" he drawled.

"There's a rumor floatin' around that it's some tall Texan's birthday today."

He chuckled. "You got somethin' for me, ma'am?"

"I might be able to rustle something up," she said. "Tonight. In New York."

"Mmm, that sounds delicious, darlin'. See you on the plane."

Branch had had a layover the previous night and Dixie was hooking up with his trip here in Phoenix. Cockpit crews and cabin crews rarely flew full schedules together. The cabin crew that had been on this trip since yesterday was getting off in Phoenix, and a new set of flight attendants would go with the pilots to New York.

At least it was New York for Branch's birthday and not somewhere like Buffalo or Des Moines. Dixie wanted to be able to take him to a posh five-star restaurant later...if he'd let her out of bed long enough to go eat.

They weren't ridiculously secretive about their relationship, but they did play it cool at work. Branch was right—there was no point in having everyone talking. "It's your reputation I'm worried about, not mine," he had said. "Even though my marriage has been over for years, I'm still *officially* married."

She had dated so many pilots, there would be more than the usual amount of chatter when she let the cat out of the bag that she was dating yet another. Her coworkers were pretty quick to catch on, though. They knew the look, the glance, the little mating dance. If a very junior pilot and a very senior flight attendant always flew together…how discreet was that?

But if they came to work in the same car after Branch had spent the night at her house, Dixie would drop him at the terminal first and then go park. When they checked into a hotel on a layover, they went to their individual rooms and met in hers later. They never went to dinner together on layovers unless it was with the entire crew. Tonight they might just break that rule, though, since it was such a special occasion.

When Dixie got to the plane, Branch was doing a walk around out on the ramp, so she started checking meals and liquor in the galley.

Every flight was a little like a stage play, with a different cast of more than two-hundred-fifty every time. You never knew what would be in the script, and that was one of the things Dixie loved about her work.

She was the senior flight attendant on this trip and chose to work in the back cabin. Their Boeing 767 would be nearly full and they had four crew members in the back. The flight had a stop in Denver and they were getting a late start.

When Branch finished his walk around outside and

returned to the plane, he found Dixie in the forward galley. He looked around. The captain's back was to the door, there were no connecting passengers in first class, and there didn't seem to be any flight attendants nearby. He grabbed her and gave her a nice, long kiss, his large hand planted on her butt. "Missed you," he said against her lips.

The lav door opened and Bea, another crew member, stepped out. Smiling, she said, "Ha! I saw that."

Dixie put a finger to her lips to shush her and said to Branch, "Get to work." But Dixie was not upset. The truth was she'd be happy if people found out about them, because Branch was handsome, successful and sweet. What could be bad about finally falling in love with a great guy? So what if it complicated the work thing? They'd downplay it a little. But how long were they supposed to continue this ridiculous game of pretending not to know each other? Dixie was sure it showed all over her face every time she heard Branch's name.

Moments later the passengers started to stream aboard, and once everyone was safely seated, the plane pushed back and nosed toward the runway. Dixie and Bea sat in the first-class jump seat for takeoff. Bea was young, just a kid. Twenty-five and engaged. "So?" she asked Dixie. "How long has that been going on?"

"Shh. No reason to make a big deal out of it in the workplace. But we've been seeing each other for about six months."

"Is it serious?"

"Very. He doesn't want anyone to make a fuss over him, but today is his birthday. That's one reason I made sure to get this trip." She winked. "I have a little birthday party planned for F.O. Darnell."

"You're a bad, bad girl," Bea laughed. "You think there will be a little something to announce soon?"

"Marriage? Well, now, I don't like to count my chickens, but I was born and raised in Texas, and I know these Texas men. Kind of old-fashioned about their women. They like taking them off the market."

The flight went fast, dipping into Denver before Dixie knew it. Some passengers deplaned to catch connecting flights while others boarded for New York. Soon Dixie was serving dinner. The sun was going down and it was dark outside, even though her watch still said 3:00 p.m.

It was an hour prior to landing before the back-end crew could take a break, eat some leftover salads, exchange a little company gossip and sit down. Bea ventured back to the aft galley and poked her head through the blue curtain that separated them from the passengers. "Dixie? Do you have a second to help me with something?"

"Don't worry," Karen said, "I'll go."

"I really need Dixie," Bea said nervously.

At the distressed sound of her voice, Dixie abandoned the salad she'd been picking at. She was senior on the flight, after all. "Sure," she said, and followed Bea to first class.

In the first-class galley, Bea whispered, "The lady in 4A, she's on my manifest as Mrs. Darnell."

Dixie frowned. She poked her head out of the blue curtain and looked at the seat Bea indicated. The woman there was attractive, with soft brown hair that fell gracefully to her shoulders. She was reading, head down, so Dixie couldn't see her face. She withdrew back into the galley. "So?" she asked Bea.

"She said the copilot is her husband."

"I reckon that could be Branch's wife. They have two

teenagers. They haven't lived together for a long time, like a couple of years, and I think they're just waitin' on another Christmas before they—''

Bea was shaking her head. ''She says it's her husband's birthday and she's flying to New York to surprise him. She told me she has reservations at the Four Seasons for nine o'clock and wanted to know if we'd get there in plenty of time.''

Dixie was very well trained at staying cool and in control, no matter what. She had won beauty pageants, after all. And unfortunately, this was not the first time something like this had happened to her. But inside she was dying. *No! This isn't happening! Not again!*

But very calmly she said to Bea, ''Oh, the poor thing.''

''She says she has a negligee in her suitcase and left his mother in charge of the kids. If it weren't for all the charity boards she sits on, she'd like to stay in New York a couple of—''

''Oh, God, Branch warned me something like this might happen. She doesn't want the divorce even though she was the one who originally asked him to leave a couple of years ago. This is just so sad.'' If she didn't hurt so much inside, Dixie might marvel at how quickly she could make up a cover story. Who said she was a dumb blonde?

''What are you going to do?'' Bea asked.

''I'd hate if there was a scene. The best thing would be if Branch took her off somewhere quiet and let her down easily.''

''She still loves him, then?''

Dixie shrugged. ''Or maybe it just didn't work out with the other man, but whatever, Branch has moved on. I should warn him so he doesn't humiliate her…or himself...or *me,* for that matter. Can you, um, trade places with me? Tell the girls in the back that I'm lookin' over your paperwork as a favor or something? And when we're taxiing in, I'll give Branch fair warnin'. The less anyone knows about this, the better for everyone.''

"I guess so," she said. "You going to be all right?"

"Me?" she asked with a laugh. "This doesn't really have anything to do with me. Just another one of those difficult divorces. When have you ever seen an easy one?"

But she didn't warn him. She served the first-class cabin coffee and thought about striking up a conversation with Mrs. Darnell, but in the end stuck to the professional courtesies. It wasn't necessary to gather any more information—the truth was obvious. Mrs. Darnell was very confident about her birthday surprise.

They weren't separated. Branch was just getting a little on the side.

The passengers poured out of the plane, but Mrs. Darnell lingered. When the pilots came out of the cockpit, Branch second, he saw Dixie in the forward galley alone. "Well, angel, you have a good flight?"

"I did, cowboy. And there's a little birthday surprise for you in 4A."

He grinned stupidly, confused, and looked down the aisle. Dixie couldn't see his face, but she heard him. "Darlin', what in thunder you doin' here?"

Dixie peeked out. Mrs. Darnell was *so* happy, grinning from ear to ear, eyes sparkling, arms outstretched as she embraced her husband and kissed him. And he returned the favor.

Except for a sheepish glance over his shoulder to see if Dixie had drawn a bead on the back of his head, Branch made no attempt to communicate with her. First

Officer and Mrs. Darnell took a cab to the hotel rather than ride with the rest of the crew in the hotel van. F.O. Darnell must have been a tish nervous about the prospect of his wife and girlfriend getting to know each other better.

The captain and five flight attendants stood curbside, waiting for the van, when Dixie came up behind them. She heard Karen say, "Well, what the hell does she expect? God, she's such a ditz."

"Karen!" Bea warned, looking over her shoulder at Dixie, who stood there frozen.

"Oh. Sorry, Dixie. But, you know…" She shrugged lamely.

Dixie said nothing. She *did* know.

Unwilling to face her coworkers' curiosity and censure, Dixie skipped dinner, which she shouldn't have done. She opened the very good bottle of wine she'd brought with her and sat cross-legged on the bed and drank. She couldn't afford to have a good cry; her eyes would be all puffy and everyone would know the extent of her misery, including Branch, who would be on tomorrow's flight. She'd be damned if he would find out she'd cried over him.

It was about eleven when a knock sounded at her door. Discreet tapping. No surprise there. Empty bottle in hand and wearing only navy blue panty hose and her striped uniform shirt, she opened the door. There he stood, pilot shirt open at the neck, ice bucket in hand— his obvious excuse to leave his wife in their room—and a lame expression on his stupid face. He lifted his arms in helplessness. "Well, darlin'," he drawled. "You coulda knocked me over with a feather. What can I say?"

She stared at him for a minute, stricken by the fact

that even under these circumstances, she was tempted to embrace him, draw him to her and love every long, tall inch of him. How humiliating! Before she could reconsider, she rammed the empty wine bottle bottom first into his gut. "Ugh," he grunted, bending over in pain and grabbing the bottle as he did so. She backed into her room and slammed the door on him. There was a loud thud, which, she acknowledged with a wince, must have been his head.

Well, she thought, you could've knocked him over with a feather...or whatever.

Three

Dixie sat in the airport with the rest of her crew. She lazily filed one of her perfect red nails when her cell phone chirped from inside her purse. She pulled it out, identified Nikki's number on the caller ID, and answered, "Yes, Captain."

"Hey. Where are you?"

"We're sitting in Kennedy. How about you?"

"Chicago. About to push back. I heard the craziest thing. Did you guys have a pilot fall down the stairs and crack his head open?"

"We did hear that," Dixie said, "but I don't think anyone's talked to him. It was supposedly the first officer—Darnell. Do you know him?"

There was a moment of stunned silence. "Oh, shit, Dixie."

"I guess he was after a bucket of ice, slipped on the stairs and whacked his head. He couldn't remember exactly what happened so his wife called a cab and took him to the emergency room. We hear he has a slight concussion. Nothing bad, but he spent the night in the hospital for observation and can't fly until his flight surgeon clears him."

"His *wife?*"

"Yeah, poor thing. She got on in Denver and was gonna surprise him for his birthday with a special night in New York City. I just can't imagine their disappointment."

Dixie could feel the eyes of her fellow crew members on her. They might not know what had really happened, but from their looks and whispers, they knew there was more to the story. So, screw 'em. Dixie was beyond caring. Karen had called it the evening before at the curb—Dixie had been a stupid fool. About a hundred times.

"Dixie…"

"Hmm?"

"Are you sure someone didn't…*push* him down the stairs?"

"For heaven's sake, what a thought," she replied with the blandness of a yawn.

"When do you get back to Phoenix?" Nikki asked.

"Our flight was canceled because of the first officer's injury, which screwed up the rest of the segment. They had to deadhead a cockpit crew out here, so we're going to work the next flight back to Phoenix and then quit. I don't work again until Sunday. How about you?"

"I'll be back tomorrow night. Maybe I should swing by and see you on my way home?"

"You know you're always welcome," she said. "All I have planned is to clean out the closets. High time I got rid of all those old clothes just clutterin' up the place."

"Are you all right?" Nikki asked.

"'Course," she replied coolly.

"And he doesn't remember what happened?"

"Isn't that fortunate?" Dixie cleared her throat. "I'm sure his wife's very grateful."

She clicked off, slipped the phone back into her purse

and asked, in her very sweetest and most innocent drawl, "Can I get anyone a latte?"

"Great idea," Bea said. "I'll go with you."

"Don't get up, darlin'," Dixie said. "My treat. Anyone else?"

There were no other takers. Dixie walked to the coffee kiosk, allowing the rest of the crew the privacy to talk about her behind her back. *Lost his memory, huh? Forgot he was married for a while? How does she let herself get into these situations? All she'd have to do is make one phone call to check him out. What does she use for brains? Ah, she's just thinking below the waist, as usual. Lots of miles on that chick.* They would be quite entertained. They would also be quite accurate.

Dixie, whose given name was Helen, came from real brainy stock. Her father was a CPA with an MBA, and her mother had her doctorate and taught anatomy and physiology in a nursing college. Her older brother was a pediatric oncologist and her younger sister was in computers—the vice president of Information Systems for a large corporation. And Dixie had been the Homecoming Queen and the Fiesta Queen and the Oktoberfest Queen and Miss Temple, Texas.

At twenty-one she had dropped out of college to become a flight attendant, and there was no question this disappointed her parents, if not her entire family.

There was a very familiar pattern to what she'd just been through with Branch, Dixie realized. The only wonder was that she never saw it coming. Her denial must have been powerful. Over and over again she kept falling in love and getting lied to, cheated on and dumped.

She wished she'd been as brilliant as the rest of her

family, but what bothered her even more was that she'd apparently missed out on the meaningful-relationship gene, as well. The rest of them, Mom and Dad, her brother and sister, were all very happily married and had wonderful family lives. From high school through her short college career and every year since, all Dixie had wanted was to have a partner she could love, count on and have children with, like the rest of the McPhersons had.

Her brother, Hal, was a wonderful husband and father, as well as a big-shot doctor in Houston; her sister, Sue, was married with two kids who went to the day care in her Dallas office building, but Dixie just limped along looking for love, getting jewelry instead. She had been kicked in the teeth so many times it was a surprise she didn't need dentures. And not just by pilots. She had been used and then jilted in nearly every profession. She couldn't count the number of times she'd had to go get tested for STDs after discovering the man of her dreams had been cheating on her. In fact, she couldn't count how many men she'd had sex with—and she'd tried. Suddenly she was terrified.

Still, despite the brevity of her college education and the lunacy of her romantic life, Dixie knew she was intelligent. Maybe not brilliant like the rest of the McPhersons, but damned smart enough in other ways.

Although it might not seem like much to the Ph.D.s in her family, at thirty-thousand feet, her kind of skill could be priceless. No one could get control of a cabin or calm a ruffled passenger better than Dixie. She was good with people and she was excellent with safety procedures. She had administered CPR along with an onboard physician, had blown a slide to safely evacuate an aircraft after an engine fire, and had even once calmed the hysteria of a crew member who was suffering some form of posttraumatic stress disorder after the 9/11 attacks.

For fifteen years she had performed at the top of her game, and now she was tired and disappointed. She wasn't going any further in her job, even if she did rack up seniority, which translated into a little more pay and a little less work each year. But the challenge was gone and her personal life was in tatters. She was lonely, her heart hurt, and her coworkers didn't respect her.

How did Nikki do it? Nikki hadn't had a guy since her divorce. She didn't appear to want one or need one. But then Nikki had those two fabulous kids; maybe that was what sustained her. As for Dixie, disappointment that she had no one special had left her feeling bitter. She had just resorted to violence, for God's sake!

She felt like such a loser. Not only had she failed to find The One, but she'd let that be the most important thing in her life for the past fifteen years.

Now she was on her way home from one of the worst trips of her career. Branch was simply the last in a long line of failures, and the fact that he had lied to her didn't let her off the hook—she should have done some investigating. She was, as her sister flight attendant so coldly pointed out, a ditz.

Well, all that was about to change.

Dixie lived in a quaint little town house at the edge of the city in the shadow of the mountains. The complex was gated and secure and featured a community room, fitness center, pool, tennis courts and a drop-dead view. There were four town houses to a building, all with garages. When she'd bought the place she thought it would be temporary. Something to keep the rain off her head until she found Mr. Right, married, got pregnant and bought a nice little house near good schools.

Her friend Carlisle and his partner, Robert, lived right around the corner; she had told them about the unit when she saw the For Sale sign go up three years ago.

Now she found herself driving past her own town house, around the corner to Carlisle's place. It wasn't late. Maybe she could talk Robert and him into dinner, or at least a drink, because she just didn't feel like being alone. As she turned into their cul-de-sac, her headlights strafed the front of his house, and she saw something very strange. Carlisle was sitting on the front step of his town house, wearing his flight attendant uniform, his overnight bag parked upright on the sidewalk in front of him. The garage door was open, and his car sat next to Robert's inside. There was a nice little BMW parked on the street, and the lights were on in the house.

Dixie parked and got out of the car, then walked up the sidewalk to the steps. Hands on hips, she looked down at him. "Hey, you. You goin' to work?"

"I just got home," he said, standing up. He tossed a look over his shoulder at his house and there was no mistaking his sad expression. "My trip was cancelled. I came home unexpectedly and I found Robert... entertaining."

"Oh, damn, Carlisle. That's awful."

He shrugged, his hands shoved into his pockets. "I could've called. But I didn't."

Smarter than me, Dixie thought. *I never had a clue.* "What are you gonna do?"

"I've been trying to decide. Yell and break things? No. That's unlike me. Too messy. Get drunk? Exact revenge of some kind? I could dip his toothbrush in the toilet every morning."

"Very passive-aggressive," she observed. "You could hit him in the head with somethin'."

Carlisle stretched his back. "I doubt he'd hold still for that."

She chuckled in spite of herself. "Carlisle, the idea is to do it real fast, surprise the critter, get off one good shot like that whack-a-mole game, before—" She stopped talking as the front door slowly opened.

A pudgy young man around twenty-five poked his head outside, checking for danger. He paused as though listening for the cocking of a rifle. Dixie and Carlisle both glared. The young man sheepishly came out the door, down the steps past Carlisle, and, head down, made his way cautiously along the sidewalk to his BMW.

"I'll be hanged," Dixie said as the man got into his car. "He's a baby! Not exactly what I'd call fetchin'. And he's all swishy."

"And a little squishy, too," Carlisle said.

By contrast, Carlisle was quite handsome and solid. Thirty-eight, a *real* blond, he had classically handsome features—high cheekbones, strong chin, great smile. They always were the cute ones.

"All right, Carlisle," Robert said from inside the house. "He's gone. Come inside."

Robert stood in the doorway, very much at ease and unembarrassed. As if he'd been caught picking his nose, not screwing around on his partner. Even knowing he was gay, a woman could be stirred by the Latino's strong good looks. While Carlisle sometimes exhibited that telltale effeminate affectation, Robert—or Roberto—was what they liked to teasingly call "a man's man."

Carlisle's going to do what he says, Dixie thought in near despair.

"I don't think so, Robert. I'm going to help myself to some 'think time.'"

Yay!

"Let's not drag this out," Robert said. "That'll only make it worse."

Carlisle grabbed his overnight bag and began to pull it down the sidewalk toward the street. Dixie happily trotted along behind him.

"If you leave now, you might not be welcomed back!"

Without turning around, Carlisle lifted his hand in the air and gave him the middle-finger salute. Behind him the door slammed shut.

He didn't look back. After stowing his suitcase in Dixie's back seat, he climbed in front.

Dixie got in beside him. "I know that was hard for you, buddy. I'm proud of you."

He shrugged. "Now what?"

"My house," she said. "We'll have a couple of drinks, something to eat and maybe a little bonfire in the backyard grill. I have some pilot clothes I'm thinkin' of lightin' up."

It wasn't until the very last leg of Nikki's three-day trip that the work started to get interesting, and not just the flying part. It was Chicago to Phoenix, the sky was a crystal, unmoving blue, and she was ready to put this trip behind her. She had kids to get back to, a dead ex-husband's personal effects to sort through, and she was more than a little worried about Dixie. The hollow sound in her friend's voice had alarmed her, and she knew there was more to the injured-first-officer story than she had heard so far. She sincerely hoped Dixie wasn't homicidal. And to add to her worries, Nikki's first officer, Bob Riddle, was driving her nuts.

Bob was one of those distinguished-looking men in his early fifties with a deep voice that took on a slightly Southern drawl when he was on the radio and PA. It was a condition often referred to as *sky drawl,* when a pilot without a Southern accent turned into Chuck Yaeger whenever he got on the radio. Bob was tall and tanned, salt and pepper at the temples, full head of thick dark hair and a strong chin. Upon close inspection it appeared he colored his hair and used tanning cream on his face— those telltale orange stains on his cuticles and in the creases of his palms were dead giveaways. But you had to get close.

His mannerisms were laid back and slow-moving, aping Chuck Yaeger's loose yet deliberate movements. Except on Bob it was all just affectation, and he had a tendency to look and sound more like that hapless Ted Knight, the anchorman on the *Mary Tyler Moore Show*. Although married, he was flirtatious and suggestive, and their cabin crew for the last day and a half was all female and seemed to enjoy him a lot more than Nikki did.

Nikki supposed that if the only time you saw him was when you brought a cup of coffee or meal to the flight deck, you might be impressed with his style, but a couple of days alone in the cockpit with him revealed a copilot who was arrogant and barely competent. He acted as though he'd just brought in the space shuttle when, in fact, he had squeaked by his last two check rides, the evaluation of flying ability judged by the company's check airmen every six months. Nikki had to watch him every second, but so far his stupid oversights had not put them in mortal peril.

This lack of skill seemed incongruous with his background. He'd been flying for thirty years and had held significant management positions along the way, including chief pilot or something at a small regional airline that had been driven under by the economic crises following 9/11. But he was used to smaller and less-complicated aircraft, and this jumbo jet was a lot of airplane for the guy. He'd been flying F.O. for a good year and a half now and still he struggled.

Yet he had the temerity to seem surprised that Nikki was capable of handling a 767. When they met in the cockpit for their first flight together, he had said to her, "Well, let's see what you got, little lady."

She had leveled him with her iciest stare. When she finally found her voice, she said, "Look, Bob, I'm not one of those touchy women who overreact to every little sexist remark, but I would like to explain one important thing to you. I have been a check airman and training captain in this aircraft for more years than you've been flying it, and I am your captain, not your little lady. If there's any show-and-tell going on here, you're the one on stage. Are we clear?"

That had put a burr under his saddle for a while, but now he limited himself to occasional grumbling comments about having held positions a lot more stressful and challenging in the business than she had. Too bad he couldn't limit his arrogance and incompetence, as well. Nikki wondered for the millionth time why the two always went together. But at least this trip was nearly over.

There was one bright spot, however. He had a hilarious habit of using words that didn't exist, and did so with typical overconfidence. Nikki found herself mentally repeating them over and over so she wouldn't forget, and it took all her willpower not to laugh out loud.

"The pilots in this company are facing a *madrid* of problems with our management," Bob would complain, when he obviously meant *myriad*. Or, "I wouldn't have any *quelms* about participating in a slowdown if it came to that."

But any humor she felt was quickly disappearing at this moment. While Nikki was in the cockpit, tapping her fingers impatiently on her knee, Bob slowly, oh so slowly, completed the outside walk around preflight inspection of the aircraft. If he were any slower, he'd be going backward, she thought. She finally heard him in the forward galley. "Well, I guess I better strap this baby to my butt and get you ladies back to Phoenix," he said to the flight attendants. Then he sauntered into the cockpit and took his place…as second in command.

"Mind if I come along, Bob?" Nikki asked.

He looked at her crossly, but forced his lips into a smile. "You've got the cutest little sense of humor, Nikki. I love flying with you."

Yeah, you love it because I keep saving your life, she thought. But she didn't say anything. This trip was almost over and there was no need to make the last leg miserable.

The ops supervisor came aboard and stuck her head in the cockpit doorway. "Captain, I have two air marshals preboarded and waiting in first class. As soon as you're ready, we'll board the rest of the passengers."

"I'm more than ready," she said. "I don't want a late push back. I'll go talk to them and you can tell the gate agent to get the passenger preboards ready." She jumped out of her seat. "Bob, prepare to run the checklist while I brief the air marshals and crew."

Ever since the tragedy of 9/11 and the impending threat to future commercial flights, the undercover armed air marshals were part of the new routine. They were only on random flights, and the crew didn't know if they were coming until they showed up and flashed their credentials. Dressed as ordinary passengers, they would preboard via the air stairs from the ground outside, not through the jetway at the gate where all the passengers waited. They would be seated close to the cockpit, either in the first class section or the first rows if there was no first class.

The captain's job was to check their IDs and badges, make sure the numbers matched, and then they would go through a little briefing with the cabin crew. The air marshals would advise the crew that they weren't on board to handle passenger disruptions, since that could obviously be a tactic to breach the cockpit, and that their positions should not be disclosed to passengers, even if they asked about undercover marshals on the flight.

These two looked like a couple of ordinary guys stashing their carry-ons in the overhead bin. "Welcome aboard, gentlemen," she said. "IDs, please?"

The first man produced his picture ID and his badge. She turned over the badge and confirmed the numbers were the same as those on the ID. "Sir?" she said to the second.

He opened his wallet and flashed her the ID, then tapped his chest and said, "I'm wearing my badge on a chain around my neck."

"I'll have to see it, sir."

"I can vouch for him," the other said.

"Sorry. Rules are rules."

The air marshal got a disgruntled look on his face and then began to slowly thread the chain out of the neck of his polo shirt. Finally the plastic-encased badge popped through the neckline and smacked him in the jaw. "Ow! Jesus!" he exclaimed.

Nikki gave him a second. Another. She did not roll her eyes, though the temptation was powerful. Finally he removed the chain from around his neck and handed it to her. She compared the numbers and handed it back. "You seem to have...uh...nicked yourself. You might want to step into the lav and dab it or something." It was all she could do not to add, *I sure hope you don't have to draw your weapon!*

This whole security initiative since 9/11 did not fill Nikki with comfort. It would probably be more cost-effective and safer to give the World Wrestling Federation free first-class travel.

Nikki decided to take a pit stop herself before settling in for the flight. When she got to the cockpit, she found Bob was turned around in his seat, talking to one of the flight attendants. Her hands rested on the back of his chair and he was caressing her forearm. "You know we're behind you all the way, right?"

"Absolutely," she said. "And we appreciate it, too."

"Then you just do what you have to do."

"Thanks, Bob. We could use more like you." The woman didn't stare Nikki down or anything when she spoke, but the implication was pretty clear. The flight attendants were in contract negotiations and there had been a lot of disruptive stuff going on, like sick-outs and slowdowns and a little exercise called CHAOS—Create Havoc Around Our System. All this was meant to hold the company's feet to the fire so they would realize it made better sense to pay happy employees more money than to put up with these expensive job actions. Nikki did not endorse this behavior, especially now, when the entire industry was a wreck.

But she and Bob had already had a couple of these conversations, and she would prefer a more peaceful ride home and pleasant end to this miserable trip.

That's what she would have preferred, but not what she got. Bob was flying this leg and landing in Phoenix. Nikki kept a closer eye on him than she would the average F.O., and he seemed to be doing okay. Until they were on final approach and he was cleared to land. He was too high and his airspeed too fast, but he wasn't correcting.

"Bob, you're high and hot," she said.

"I'm okay," he shot back, not correcting.

"Go around, Bob. You're high and hot."

"Naw, we can make this work out," he said, bringing the aircraft down sharply, still too fast.

From somewhere on the ground—probably a pilot at a gate who noticed the inbound Aries 767 come barreling out of the sky like a rocket ship—a mike was keyed and a deep male voice said, "That's gonna leave a hole."

Nikki took the controls. "I have the airplane," she said. "Aries Flight 492 is going around."

"Thank God—" came an anonymous endorsement.

"Aries Flight 492, maintain runway heading, climb and maintain 4,000, contact departure control—"

She could feel the heat coming off her first officer as she took the jet up, but she wasn't sure if it was embarrassment or anger. "Make a PA," she instructed.

"Ladies and gentlemen, we're going to go around the pattern one more time and let them clear the runway for us," Bob informed the cabin in his calm, lazy drawl. "Sit tight, we're almost home."

Man, even Nikki had to admit he talked a good game. He was convincing as hell.

"You want to line this up and try it again, Bob? Or would you like me to do it."

"Give me a break, Nikki. We would've been just fine."

"By consensus, it was horseshit."

"We could've made that landing."

"Was that a yes?"

"*Yes.* I've *got* it."

Bob brought the jet around the pattern, lined it up again, and with a little needling from Nikki to "bring it down, bring it down, slow it down," he managed to get the plane on the ground, but not gently. He slammed it on pretty good; a half-dozen masks dropped. She would have to write up a maintenance report to inspect the aircraft for a hard landing.

They taxied into the gate and Nikki said, "*You* can say goodbye to the passengers while I write up the maintenance request."

"If you'd just let me do it the way I—"

"It was your landing that got us that rubber jungle back there, so don't push me," she snapped. "I mean it."

Exercising rare intelligence, he held his tongue. While Nikki worked on her log, she heard a couple of the comments, and they gave her perverse pleasure.

"Did we land or were we shot down?"

"Fifteen midgets in the back would like to compliment your landing, sir."

By the time she left the cockpit, all the passengers had deplaned, the cleaners were aboard and the food-service truck was already at the galley bay. Then she heard something she really didn't want to hear—Bob's low, seductive voice. "If you go out, you know we'll go out with you."

"We're counting on that." It was their senior flight attendant.

Nikki waited. She didn't want to get into it with the flight attendant, but she couldn't just let this go. Instead, she followed Bob through dispatch and upstairs. He was headed toward the airport doors, where he would probably pick up the crew bus to the employee parking lot. "Bob?" she called.

He stopped and turned, obviously unhappy to see her. He probably thought she was going to chew him out for that landing.

"Did I hear you right?" she asked. "Were you telling Stephanie you'd support them in a strike?"

He shrugged. "They're talking about a strike vote next month...or the month after."

"Bob, have you lost your mind? A strike now could be a death knell for this company!"

"That's what they'd like you to think. The flight attendants haven't had a raise in four years."

"Aries lost more than a hundred million dollars last quarter! Where do you think they're going to get the money for a raise?"

"That's what they'd like you to think," he repeated. "It's all smoke and mirrors—they're *indinuated* with money."

That took her a second. Inundated? *Indinuated?* "You sure about that?" she finally asked. "Do you read *Business Week* and *Aviation Week?* It's a pretty bleak world for airlines, Bob. All of them. Since 9/11 and the war, the industry has lost three times what it earned since Wilbur and Orville took off."

He looked at her as though he was very tired of her idiocy. "Look, the employees made pay concessions with 9/11, the government has given the company millions of dollars, and it's time the management of this company got the message that they'll have to cut costs somewhere else—their big fat paychecks, perhaps? Or deal with the consequences.''

"Bob..."

"Not all airlines are losing money, which tells me that the Aries management should take a look at profitable companies and learn from them."

"Bob, *two* airlines didn't lose money. One is a low-fare carrier that has a legislative monopoly out of Texas, and the other is a start-up that hasn't made a single airplane lease payment yet."

He sighed heavily. "Drastic measures for drastic times."

No matter how many times she heard this rhetoric, Nikki couldn't believe it. "Look, I'm not saying management is right or the union is right, but there is a basic tenet of logic that it just doesn't make sense to draw a line in the sand now, when the entire industry is struggling. Why not just hunker down and wait until there are signs of a recovery, and then turn the screws? That's when getting tough has a chance of actually paying off. A strike now could shut the company down."

"Exactly!" he said, as though finally getting through to her. "With that kind of threat, you think the company would let us stay out long?"

"Oh, man. You could end up in the unemployment line."

He smiled at her, turned and started walking again. "I've already got my résumé out there floating around. There are lots of possibilities."

"That's just it, Bob, there *aren't*," she said to his back. "Everyone is still trying to get their furloughed employees back. Some airlines are laying off even more."

He turned and spoke while taking a few steps backward. "I'm not worried. I have a ton of hours and lots of experience. I think I'm pretty competitive."

Nikki just stared at him in wonder. "Not if they see you land."

Four

When Nikki got to Dixie's, she walked in on an impressive pity party. Carlisle and Dixie were drinking mai tais with black rum floating on top, eating cheesecake and sorting through a big pile of men's and women's clothing that was heaped on the sofa.

"Oh, you are going to hate yourselves in the morning," she predicted.

"Want one, Nick? We can call you a cab...."

"How about a small glass of wine and an explanation."

Both were served up quickly. Dixie had whacked Branch in the head with the hotel door, and even though she'd done so unintentionally, she hadn't made any attempt to help him. She'd heard him moan and stumble away, and at least briefly hoped he was dead.

Nikki sank onto a kitchen stool and leaned her head on her hand, listening.

"I think I might've had fifty boyfriends," Dixie said. "Or a hundred. Do ya'll know I have eleven tennis bracelets? Plus a good many necklaces, earrings and miscellaneous jewelry. And look at this here," she said, going to the huge mound of clothes on the sofa. She lifted a fistful of sheer and lacy lingerie. Red, black, silver, gold, white, yellow—*leopard?* "Negligees, teddies and peekaboos—some I've fetched for myself, some given to me. All so that I can look sexy for whichever guy I pinned my hopes on.''

''What are you going to do with all that stuff?''

''Putting it out on the curb for giveaway. I'm getting Bali bras and Jockey For Her briefs from now on, and I'm going to start sleeping in a T-shirt like the rest of the female human race. And the next guy who gives me a teddy is going to be strangled with it.''

Nikki took a sip of her wine. Not only had she never been given a teddy, she had never bought one for herself. She'd worn cotton undies for ten years at least. And if she was honest, she didn't really need a bra.

''The homeless are going to look *très chic*,'' Carlisle said, slurring just slightly.

''I've heard you swear off men before…'' Nikki began.

''Oh, no, this time I'm through. I hate all men.''

''That is *s-o-o-o* unkind,'' Carlisle whined.

''Not all men, precious,'' she said. ''I still love all gay men. Well, not all,'' she amended.

''You're both shit-faced,'' Nikki told them.

''It might seem so to you, Nicole,'' Carlisle said, ''but we have been so badly bruised by love.''

She looked at him seriously for a moment before she burst into laughter, and with the slightest lisp, said, ''Carlisle, you get *s-o-o-o* gay when you're drunk.''

''Thanks, Butch,'' he shot back, taking another pull on his mai tai.

''So what's your story?'' she asked. ''What's driven you to drink? And are you giving up your sexy underwear, too?''

''It's just Robert, the bastard. He's chronically unfaithful and nasty to me. And I don't *wear* underwear.'' Then he began to sing ''Alone Again, Naturally.'' By the end of the first stanza they were on the floor in uncontrollable laughter.

Nikki indulged herself with another half glass of wine, just because her friends were so hysterically funny in their misery. "As much as I'd love to stay until you two get sick, I really do have to go," she said at last. "I have two kids, a cranky father and a dead ex-husband to tend to." But she made a pass by the sofa full of clothes. The men's had belonged to Branch Darnell, but the sexy girlie stuff was all Dixie's. She lifted a black shortie nightie that was totally transparent. "I have never owned anything like this," she said mournfully.

"It's just as well, sugar," Dixie assured her. "That stuff'll get you into trouble."

Nikki held the nightie up to her, over her pilot shirt, of course. "Do you know what I'd give to look good in one of these things? The hell with men, I'd just wear it on Saturday nights and stare at myself in the mirror." She waved it toward Dixie. "At least you can console yourself that you're gorgeous."

"I'd rather have two kids," Dixie said.

That gave Nikki pause. She thought for a moment. "There's absolutely no question that I'd ever give them up, not at the point of a gun, but I would like to have sex again. At least once before I die."

"Well, then," Carlisle said, "get down to the Salvation Army first thing Monday morning and you'll find all that striking *boudoir* gear on sale."

Carlisle had a headache the size of Texas when the ringing of the phone in the next room woke him. Dixie was already up, loading all the clothes into large yellow bags for the Salvation Army. She had turned some developmental corner. Five years ago, even one year ago, she'd have laundered everything and had her ex-lover come for it. There might have even been a tearful roll in the hay for old time's sake. No more, she said. Meet the new Dixie.

Well, Carlisle thought, I am the same old me—starving for affection. And sometimes, he thought, needing to be abused. Why else would he put up with so much? What had Robert ever done for him but make him miserable? Robert wasn't the least self-conscious about cheating; in fact, he became more open about it all the time.

The dark, depressing cloud that hung in the air at Dixie's town house was caused by the absence of phone calls. Branch hadn't phoned to beg forgiveness and profess his undying love, and Robert had certainly not bothered them. Neither Carlisle nor Dixie had dared venture around the corner to see if the BMW was back at the curb.

"You'd think that sorry bastard of a pilot would call," Dixie had said.

"You put him in the hospital," Carlisle reminder her. "It might have pissed him off. But Roberto…"

"Is very clever. He waits until he knows you'll be miserably lonely, then he calls, and you're the big dope who gives him one more chance. It's happened…what? Twenty or thirty times? At least I always move on to a new man." She cleared her throat. "Or I used to. I'm not gonna do that anymore. No more men! I just can't figure out what I'm going to do about sex. I'm awful fond of sex."

But this time it was neither Branch nor Robert on the phone. It was Nikki, offering an opportunity to keep them from just licking their wounds and medicating their hangovers. She asked if they were up to helping her go through Drake's clothes and other personal items. "I dread it," she told them. "School's going to be out soon and I have to get this behind us. I could use the company."

"You sure we won't just be in the way?" Dixie asked. "It's a mighty emotional thing for kids."

"I told the kids to think about what they'd like to keep—sentimental things, like watches and cuff links and stuff. The rest, they understand, is going to go to people who can use it. I'm going to get as much of it cleared out as possible while they're at school."

"Of course we'll help you, sugar," Dixie said. "The three of us. Just like old times. We'll meet you over there in an hour." When she hung up, she said to Carlisle, "She needs us more than we need to feel sorry for ourselves. Now, are you going to stay here with me for a while?"

"If you're sure it's okay…"

"It's not only okay, if you go back home I'll be very disappointed in you."

So Carlisle went around the corner to his town house to pack a bag while Robert was at work. He looked around the home they'd shared these past three years. You'd think Robert would have left a note or something, but he hadn't even picked up his dirty clothes or wiped out the sink. He left the scut work for Carlisle…and Carlisle always did it.

He drove his car around the corner to store in Dixie's garage, and when he pulled into her drive, she was putting the bags full of clothes out on the curb for pickup. This had been the fourth time in the past year that Carlisle had packed a bag to leave Robert. In his heart he hoped he would be strong enough and smart enough not to go back this time.

Of course, he had a long history of running away. Once he got to college, he had gone home to Anoka, Minnesota, as seldom as possible. He had no siblings, and his straitlaced religious parents were not just openly disapproving of gays, they were downright hostile. Carlisle was afraid they'd pick up on clues that would have been obvious years before to anyone else.

But they hadn't. Carlisle was a twenty-six-year-old fifth-grade teacher when he finally told them the truth, and they acted exactly as he had feared—stunned and angry. "But you went to the prom!" was his mother's first shocked and disbelieving cry. Mothers who were worried that their sons were gay always hung on to that prom date as confirmation that their worst fears were unfounded.

Then they told him not to discuss that filth around them again until he had examined all his options. Options? Like rehabilitation. There was a church in Minneapolis that was having great success helping gays return to a straight life.

Carlisle often wondered how you could "return" to a straight life. When had he ever been straight? He had no memory of it.

He seemed to be able to have a superficial, somewhat loving relationship with his mother, Ethel, as long as they never broached the subject of homosexuality. But this was hard for Ethel, who always wanted to know if he was *still* gay.

His father, on the other hand, was barely civil. It was with great sadness that Carlisle had left his teaching job and the Midwest ten years ago to fly for Aries, but he got the distinct impression that his parents were relieved to have him so far away. He visited rarely, and when he did, his father had nothing to say to him. There was no way he would ever introduce anyone in his family to a partner. Carlisle knew he was referred to as the Gay Cousin, and while a couple of his aunts sent Christmas cards and occasional notes, no one bothered to keep him posted on family events, probably fearful he might attend.

But then came the real deal breaker, the events of 9/11. Although there had not been an Aries jet involved, airline employees often traveled on other airlines using nonrevenue passes—a professional courtesy. His parents couldn't know for certain that he wasn't on one of the hijacked planes, whereas Carlisle had talked to his mother the previous month and knew they had no travel plans and were tucked safely away in Anoka.

As it happened, Carlisle had been in New York on a layover and was stranded by the grounding of all aircraft. He had watched the plume of smoke that grayed the city and wept his heart out at what was happening to the world. Dixie had been in D.C. and Nikki in Boston, and it had taken a couple of days for their cell phones to work properly so they could be certain of one another's safety.

When his parents saw those huge planes smash into the towers, killing thousands of people, did they not think, ''Where is Carlisle? Could he have been on one of those planes? Is he okay?''

They had never called. No one had called. Not his parents, aunts or cousins.

That's when he realized they weren't just annoyed with him for being gay. They simply didn't care about him at all.

Because of that, whenever he and his two best friends groused about their loneliness, Carlisle felt he was the most alone of all.

* * *

Ever since Nikki had left the house she'd lived in as Drake's wife, she had felt a little strange driving up to it. The feeling was even more pronounced now that he was dead and she was a guest in this house that belonged to the bank.

Buck had convinced the children to stay at his house while Nikki was away on her flight, and he had driven them to and from school. It was just too much to expect him to move into Drake's house; Buck used to seethe each time he had to pick up the kids there. But today after school they would return to this house that had been their home.

Dixie and Carlisle were parked at the curb, waiting for her. They had several hours left before the kids would be home from school.

"I really don't know what to do with this house," Nikki said to her friends as they met on the driveway. "There's not a dime of equity in it and the kids really like the neighborhood and schools, so it makes sense to just live here with them. But for me...?"

"Too many bad memories?" Carlisle asked.

"More than I can count. Plus, thanks to Drake's poor planning, the mortgage payment is horrendous."

"They say don't make any big changes right after a death," Dixie advised.

"If *they* had been needled and ridiculed by Drake for a dozen or so years, *they* might not have said that."

"I know, sugar, but if you're patient, just hang around here a little while, and maybe somethin' will turn up nearby. It might be easier for the kids if you didn't have to change neighborhoods, at least."

Since Drake's death, the master bedroom had been closed off. Now she had to go in there and sort out the remains of his life. She left the clothes to Dixie and Carlisle, while she bit the bullet and opened up his desk, filing cabinets, strongbox and safe. Although she had nurtured the secret hope that she would find some hidden stash that would take care of educations, at least, so far there was nothing. What she did find was debt, and evidence of stock trading. The market hadn't been good to Drake, and he'd borrowed against his 401K and house. He bought on the margin, sold short and lost his shirt.

With Dixie and Carlisle helping, it didn't take all that long to get rid of Drake's personal effects, but going through his paperwork was something Nikki had to do on her own, and it would take more than a couple of days. Resigning herself to that fact, Nikki hunkered down for a long, hot summer in her ex's house.

But after a couple of weeks, it became harder, rather than easier, to be at the house. Nikki took the kids out for most of their meals rather than cook in Drake's kitchen. And no way could she move back into the master bedroom.

Then April said the magic words. "I hate being here because Dad died here. I wish there was a way we could start over completely."

Oh, boy, was there ever. Nikki had the kids pack up their favorite things plus clothes, computer, books and games. She called the real estate agent and listed the house, and they all moved to Buck's.

"As soon as it sells," Nikki promised April and Jared, "we'll get rid of the furniture and start over. Completely. New house, new furniture, new pots and pans. A new life for everyone."

The only person in the family who wasn't happy about the sale of the house was Opal. "I was so looking forward to coming back—I've always loved that particular guest room.''

Nikki made a note to find a house with a guest room that was not quite as accommodating.

Carlisle had stayed with Dixie for a month, and his restlessness was growing more obvious to her by the day. He was cooking special dinners and complaining that she didn't have the necessary equipment for his gourmet cuisine. He kept tidying up rooms that were already immaculate, and often she noticed that he never turned the page on the book he was reading.

It was with some concern that Dixie prepared to leave Carlisle at home while she went to work a three-day trip. There was no question he was depressed. And Dixie's house was not far enough away from Robert to give her any peace of mind. She tried to convince Carlisle to go somewhere for the weekend. Or maybe stay at Buck's with Nikki and the kids.

''Oh, I couldn't do that.''

''Why not?''

''You know. When it comes to housekeeping, they're pretty…''

''Relaxed? Laid-back? Easygoing?''

Carlisle rolled his eyes. ''More devil-may-care. Or perhaps Early Vandalism.''

She whacked him with a dish towel. ''Stop. She's not that bad.''

''She's trying to be.''

''Well, just stay away from you-know-who while I'm gone.''

''Just worry about your own you-know-who,'' he replied, making her fear the inevitable even more.

''Huh. I'm not even tempted,'' she said, a little surprised that it was true. "And I hate to see you go through any more of those humiliating scenes."

"But why? I'm so good at humiliation!"

As much as she loved him, Dixie conceded it was a good thing she was getting a little break. While she was preparing to transform her whole life, Carlisle appeared wretched. The situation at home was just getting too heavy. A couple of days away would do wonders for her, and she actually looked forward to the work.

She'd done a little trip trading to get a schedule better than the one she'd had while following Branch around, and she'd pulled a Phoenix-Seattle-San Francisco with a nice long layover the first night. She was looking forward to a little seafood dinner, and a cool ocean breeze as opposed to the desert heat.

But the Trip Gods had conspired against Dixie Mc-Pherson. She was supposed to be flying with Captain Danny Adams and F.O. Mike McGee. At least, that's what it said on her printout when she checked in for her flight. But when she boarded and looked out at the ramp, the F.O. doing the preflight walk-around was not McGee. She'd know that long, lanky, arrogant swagger anywhere.

God, what kind of karma had her constantly drawn to men like Branch? Had she, in a former life, been a cruel queen who took young male paramours and then hacked them to bits once she'd had her fun? She hoped so. She sincerely hoped so.

Since Dixie wasn't senior on the trip, she couldn't escape first class, the hardest serving job on the airplane, which meant she had to serve the cockpit, as well as the cabin. Given her lack of desire to fraternize, it didn't look as if the pilots would be well nourished this trip. But long before she could think about beverage revenge, he poked his head into her galley on his way to the cockpit. Branch Darnell, his hat sitting jauntily back on his head, a roguish grin on his lips, and there at his hairline, a devilish-looking bright red gash. Somehow the wound only added to his good looks, which was par for the course. Anyone else would have been disfigured.

The extent of his injury took some of the bluster out of her sails. She let out a long, slow breath and gave her head a slight shake. "Um, I'm awful sorry about that. It was completely unintentional...."

"Aw, don't beat yourself up, darlin'. I like my women feisty."

Her mouth fell open slightly and she stared at him for a stunned, silent moment. Then she said, "Oh, you can't be flirting with me!" He gave a little shrug and headed for the cockpit. "I don't believe it!" she said to herself.

Dixie took a few deep breaths, counted to ten and decided to fake composure until the urge to put a matching dent on the other side of his forehead passed.

She was a professional. She wouldn't let a little thing like a ruined love affair and attempted murder prevent her from doing her job. She poured drinks, fluffed pillows, took dinner orders and spread good cheer through the first-class cabin. Until she heard his familiar silky drawl, she had almost forgotten how angry Branch had made her.

"Welcome aboard Flight 217 to Seattle, ladies and gentlemen. It looks like smooth skies and sunshine all the way to the Pacific Northwest, where you'll find the temperature to be around sixty-five degrees. We're cruising at thirty-one thousand feet and the seat belt sign is off. Now, if ya'll are up and about, take care not to clog up the aisles. We don't want to make life tough for our

flight attendants, five of Aries Airlines' most beautiful.
They're also the sweetest we got, so you just let them
know if there's anything you need. And when you're
sittin' down, you keep that seat belt fastened. We thank
you for choosing…''

Branch knew that she came from a family of overachievers who teased that ''Dixie majored in beauty,'' a
line that always hurt her. He could have made that announcement to purposely needle her. Then again, it was
just as likely he hadn't listened to her when she'd bared
her soul to him. Either way, it was a chancy thing he
did, considering that in first class she had access to all
those wine bottles and might just lose control and punch
him in the stomach with one. Or maybe just whack him
in the head to save time.

She settled her people with their food and their movie,
then fixed up a tray with two meals and drinks for the
cockpit.

Captain Adams greeted her. ''Dixie, you must have
read my mind…I was just wondering if there was any
food.''

''Coming right up,'' she said. ''One beef, one
chicken.''

''What's your preference, Branch?'' he asked.

The cockpit crew ate different entrées on the off
chance there was tainted food on board. But it was the
captain's call and Danny was a gentleman. ''Well now,
let's see.'' Branch made a slow appraisal of each entrée.
His answer should have been, ''Whatever you don't
want, sir.'' But instead it was, ''Believe I'll take the
chicken, if that's all right. I hate what a caterer does to
good old Texas beef.''

''Thanks, Dixie,'' Danny said.

"Captain, I have a small favor to ask, if you'd be so kind."

"Sure thing. What can I do?"

"I'd sure appreciate it if you'd have a little chat with your second in command, sir, and tell him we're not hired to be pretty or sweet. By FAA regulation, we're trained to open the door of this 767 upside down, in the dark, underwater, and get the people out safely. And we're mighty good at it, too."

Danny chuckled. "Be happy to, Dixie," he said, taking the tray from her.

The ride into Seattle was smooth and uneventful, and they were under way to San Francisco in no time. Because it was a good city for a layover and the layover was long, the whole crew was planning to go out together for dinner. This would definitely include Branch, who was very popular with the flight attendants. But before anyone even asked her, Dixie had an excuse ready. She was right in the middle of a very good book and would just grab a bite to eat at the hotel coffee shop or get a sandwich in the bar.

"Welcome aboard Flight 982 to San Francisco, ladies and gentlemen," the Texan drawled in his lazy, sultry voice. He gave the weather, the cruising altitude, the instructions about seat belts. Then, unbelievably, Dixie heard, "You're gonna want to stay out of the aisles while our flight attendants are serving. They might not be the prettiest we got here at Aries, but they can be mean as junkyard dogs. But you gotta admit, they're workin' like a pack a mules back there, aren't they?"

Danny Adams had seen her come into the hotel bar at about nine o'clock, just in time to order dinner before the place stopped serving hot food. She had a book in her hand and took a corner booth with a hanging Tiffany lamp over the table. In her jeans and knit shirt, her usual fluffy blond hair pulled into a clip at the nape of her neck, she looked like a young girl, though he knew she must be at least in her mid-thirties.

So, she hadn't gone out with the crew. Probably because of Branch. The first officer wasn't specific, but Danny got the impression he and Dixie had had some sort of misunderstanding. Tiff. Lover's quarrel?

At the age of thirty-eight, Danny had never been in a serious relationship. He was shy around women, which might be one explanation. Another would be height (short), weight (more than necessary), hair (very little) and general features—bland. Homely, he was homely. Each time he faced that reality, which was every morning as he shaved, he heard his mother's voice: "Now, Danny, you are not! You're simply average-looking, that's all." But Danny knew the truth—he was pretty ugly. His eyes were too small, his nose too big, no chin, large ears. His teeth were at least straight, thanks to Dr. Ward, with whom he'd spent the second Tuesday of every month for the majority of his adolescence.

Even though he'd known Dixie McPherson for years, Danny still felt that familiar old anxiety creeping over him at the thought of striking up a conversation with her in a social setting. He was great at work, especially as the captain in charge, but after hours he was a putz, and he knew it. Especially around a woman like Dixie. She was so incredibly beautiful, so poised and confident, so unattainable.

He was going to have to just suck it up and go to her, because he was on a mission. Picking up his glass of beer, he walked across the bar to her booth. "Dixie?" he said, looking down at her.

She glanced up from her book. "Hey, Danny. You didn't go out with the others?"

"No, I'm more the quiet-evening type."

"I'm sure your wife appreciates that," she said, closing her book.

"Huh?" he answered, then laughed in amusement that she might think that. "I'm not married."

"You sure? I hear that a lot and it's usually not true."

Without asking permission, he slid into the booth across from her. "Oh, man, do you? That's terrible. No, I mean it—I've never been married. Or even engaged." He cleared his throat. "Ah, Dixie, I owe you an apology. I had absolutely no idea Branch was going to make that PA about the mules. I told him I was going to check with you and see if you were planning to write it up. I'll support you if you decide to. That was uncalled-for."

"I'm not gonna write him up," she said.

"He said you wouldn't. You two must have had some kind of— Sorry, Dixie. It's none of my business."

"We were seein' each other," Dixie told him, then suddenly realized how Branch had contrived her silence—she had been protecting him by being discreet, not the other way around. Who cared if she was dating a pilot? She was single, over twenty-one. "He said he was going through a divorce. He was lying."

It took Danny a moment to absorb that. His experience with the volatility of love affairs was limited to the movies. "Why do people do things like that?"

"To get laid, Danny," she said with a note of irritation.

"I know, but I mean *why?*" Before Dixie could snap back, *Orgasms, Danny,* he said, "Doesn't he know how lucky he is to have a wife, a family? Why would you threaten that? There are people in the world who would give anything to have what he has."

And I'm one of them, came instantly to Dixie's mind. She was saved from comment by the arrival of her food. "Have you eaten, Danny?" she asked.

"Yeah. A couple of hours ago."

"Well, have a French fry so I don't feel self-conscious eating alone."

"Thanks," he said, taking one. "I'm really sorry, Dixie. About all of it."

Dixie gazed at him for a long, somber moment. She remembered what she had overheard the day of that fateful flight with F.O. and Mrs. Darnell. *What did she expect? She's such a ditz.* "I have to take some of the responsibility. I didn't check him out thoroughly, and I could have. I just believed him—the old smooth-talker." She sighed. "Sometimes I'm just a ditz."

He laughed outright. "You? Come on, Dixie, you were conned. It's not your fault. You're no ditz. I've worked with you a lot over the years. I know how smart you are." He grabbed the book she had been reading. "*John Adams* by David McCullough. Jeez," he laughed. "Who are you kidding?"

"I love John and Abigail Adams. Now, they were a real couple, a team. They checked everything with each other, gave each other advice and support. And that was not the typical way of marriages back then."

"The last time I flew with you, you were reading *The Lexus and the Olive Tree.*"

Her eyes lit up. "That's right! We had a big discussion about it! I forgot, you're an avid reader, too."

"Have to have something to do on these layovers," he said, then instantly wished he could withdraw the remark. No point broadcasting to the world that he was always alone.

"Do you ever get so sick of this?" she asked. "Sometimes it's hard, boring and just plain lonely."

Dixie? Lonely? Not from what he'd witnessed. She always had someone to spend the night with when she was out on the road.

"I've wanted to fly since I was a little kid," he said. "It gives me a rush every time. I still can't believe they let me check out a hundred-and-sixty-ton 767 and take it out for a spin every time I come to work. It's the one thing in life that never lets me down. In fact, it's one of those things that when it's a challenge, when it's just a little bit scary, it gets even better." He took another French fry off her plate. "Do you remember Joe Riordan? He was at Aries briefly, about twelve years ago— when the company was still pretty young and real small. In fact, he was responsible for a lot of the growth."

"Sure I remember him," she said. "But my friend Nikki knows him real well."

"Yeah, Nikki would've known him—she did something in management. Training or something. He left here for TWA, closed that one down, consulted for a couple of years, and now he's in Las Vegas starting a new airline."

"Oh, so he's certifiable?"

Danny laughed. "Actually, it's not as crazy as you might think. The really big companies are having a hard time getting costs down—like Aries. The odds favor a new start-up to the old dinosaurs that are bleeding millions a day. I'm thinking of calling him. I'd love to get in on the ground floor of something new."

She almost choked. "Danny! Are you crazy? You were in on the ground floor of *this* company."

"Sort of. The company was a few years old, but we only had three jets. But, God, it was fun. We were a bunch of kids and scabs and crop dusters and ex-patriots.... We did anything we were told. We swept up, dispatched, hauled trash, washed planes, cleaned up the cabin after every flight. And every single one of us would have paid Aries to fly their planes. Now? Hardly anyone is happy. They complain constantly. They'd turn their backs on Aries in a second. I have a feeling this company isn't going to make it."

"But you'd start over? At your age? That's a pretty big risk...."

"There's only me," he said, shrugging. "If I had a family to worry about, I might be more cautious.... But there's only me. And I want to be in a place where I'm having a great time. Like I had when this outfit started."

Five

Carlisle was pulling freshly dried and fragrant clothes from Dixie's dryer when he heard his cell phone twittering upstairs. He held a hopeful, fearful breath while it flipped onto voice mail. Then he went upstairs to check the message.

Ah! Him! Now what?

"Carlisle, let's stop this nonsense, you're not fooling me a bit," came Robert's voice. "If you were really leaving me, you wouldn't be right around the corner at Dixie's. You want me to find you. I'm giving you till 6:00 p.m. and then I'm coming for you. This is ridiculous. You've tried before and you just can't do it. We're meant to be together and you know it."

That was one of the first things he'd said to win Carlisle over. *We're meant to be together and you know it.* That one sentence had irrevocably changed Carlisle's life. At first he'd thought it had been to the good. Now he knew better.

When he'd met Robert, Carlisle had been in a dull, albeit stable, relationship. He was thirty-five then and had been "out" for about the same length of time he'd been at Aries. His partner, Alex, was fifteen years his senior, and they'd been together for just over six years. Had Carlisle given in to the seven-year itch?

Alex was a university professor with a Ph.D. in Renaissance literature. He tried to get Carlisle involved with his academic friends but had no interest in Carlisle's airline buddies or even the Phoenix gay community. Alex preferred a quiet, intellectual life, while Carlisle wanted to have a little fun.

Along came Robert, a flashy wine-and-spirits sales rep who put the moves on Carlisle. To his shame, Carlisle was swept away a little too easily. It wasn't true that gay meant easy. Carlisle had always been very discriminating; his good looks and sharp wit set him apart from the crowd and he did the choosing. But Robert was even more handsome, and they made a fetching couple.

After a brief and passionate fling with Robert, Carlisle left Alex. His friends endorsed the move. Robert was charming, funny, sexy. Men and women alike fell for him. "You have to be happy," they would tell Carlisle. "You've outgrown Alex." And "You have to follow your bliss."

The only person who had not encouraged his breakup was Nikki. "You just don't know how wonderful dull can be, Carlisle." But why in the world would he have taken her advice? She never encouraged anyone in romance, probably because of the mess she'd made of her own love life.

It was amazing how short that "bliss" turned out to be. Robert was a fraud. He wasn't charming, he was manipulative. Mean. Controlling and unfaithful and possessive. At first, Robert easily convinced Carlisle that their problems stemmed from the craziness of dealing with Alex, who'd become hysterical after Carlisle left.

But within a few months Alex had found someone new and left his ex alone. By then, Carlisle and Robert had had at least a dozen blistering fights, and Carlisle had been hit twice. Robert had been devastated that he'd lost control and swore it would never happen again.

Of course, it had.

Nikki and Dixie knew that Robert was an asshole, but of course they didn't know all of it. It was Carlisle's dirty little secret. He couldn't stand the thought of being some sissy queer who couldn't...*wouldn't* fight back. It was killing him. Even Dixie had struck out at injustice. Why couldn't he? It wasn't as though Robert was so much bigger and stronger.

He folded up the last of his laundry, packed his bag, put it in the trunk of his car and drove out of the neighborhood. Thirty minutes later he was parked at the curb of an elegant neighborhood with large, expensive homes and tall, mature trees. He looked at the house, remembering every room, especially the huge gourmet kitchen. It was nearly five.

Alex's small silver sports car came down the street and turned into the drive. Even after traveling across town, Carlisle still wasn't sure he intended to talk to Alex, but when Alex stepped out of the car, briefcase in hand, he looked directly across the street at his former partner. As if he could sense his presence.

"Oh, well," Carlisle said to himself, getting out of the car. Hands in pockets, he slowly crossed the street.

Alex looked well. At five foot eight, he wasn't a big man, but he was well built and distinguished-looking, with a salt-and-pepper beard that set off his deep, penetrating aqua eyes. Had Carlisle really been worried about the age difference? Alex was fifty-three and appeared to be robust, in the peak of health. He nodded once toward Carlisle, holding his briefcase against his chest with both hands.

"Hi, Alex. I'm sorry to just show up without calling first."

Alex shrugged.

"I won't stay or get in the way. I wanted to say I'm sorry. For what I did to you."

Alex simply lifted his brows and cocked his head to one side, as if asking without asking.

"I realized before much time had passed what a terrible…no, tragic mistake I had made. But I couldn't do anything about it by the time I knew."

"Why not?" Alex asked.

Carlisle just shook his head in a helpless way. "I just couldn't. But it has become important to me that you know I'm very sorry. Think you might ever forgive me?"

"It's not a matter of—"

"Hey," a voice called.

Both men turned. Standing in the doorway of the house was a slender young man with what appeared to be a dish towel in his hands. He was *very* young. Alex was robbing the cradle for sure this time. "Would you like me to open a bottle of wine and put out some cheese and crackers?" the young man asked.

"No— No, thank you," Carlisle called over to him quickly. "I have to run." And to Alex he said, "Take care, okay?"

"You, too. You don't have to be a stranger, you know."

"Thanks. That's decent. You always were so… classy." Carlisle went back to his car and drove to his own neighborhood, but instead of going to Dixie's house, he went to the one he had shared with Robert for the past three years.

Accepting his fate.

The next evening when Dixie came home from her trip, Carlisle wasn't there. She checked around for his belongings. And she knew.

She called Nikki. "He's gone. Again."

"Damn," Nikki said. "You'd think one of us would escape bad love before total humiliation forced it."

"He didn't even leave a note."

"He's embarrassed. He's right around the corner."

"Well, too bad. If he can't even tell me he's going back to Robert, he can just kiss my—"

"Don't be mad," Nikki begged. "Give yourself a little time, then call him. See if he's okay."

"I don't care if he's okay." Dixie sighed. "He's given up. But I'm not going to. I don't care if I have to be alone till I die, I'm not getting back to that mean old game."

Summer peaked, and the heat drove everyone indoors. Nikki divided her time between her job at the airline, the paperwork for the property sale and, gratefully, full-time motherhood. Buck chauffeured the kids around so they could keep their connections with friends from school and the old neighborhood.

Nikki saw little of Carlisle and Dixie, and she hadn't seen them together since the day they'd helped her sort through Drake's things. Neither of them would admit they weren't speaking, but they hadn't spoken.

Meanwhile, life at Buck's was crowded and complicated. There was a definite difference between having the kids there two to four days a week and having them all the time. While no one was given to anal-retentive housekeeping in their family, even Nikki was starting to get edgy because of the constant clutter. She knew it was time to start thinking about finding a place of her own for her and the kids. A place her father could visit. Although Buck didn't complain too loudly, he was sixty-six and set in his ways. The only real advantage to living with him was that Opal didn't visit.

She had just begun to tumble around ideas in her mind about what kind of fresh start they needed when a name floated up in front of her. "Do you remember Joe Riordan?" Dixie asked her.

"Yeah, of course. I know him real well. Why?"

"One of the captains I flew with a month or so ago said he's starting a new airline, in Las Vegas of all places. Danny Adams is thinking of leaving Aries to join Joe."

"Really?" Nikki asked. "Why would he do that? He's got a lot of seniority here."

"I know, but he says he hates all them bellyachin' pilots, whining about money all the time and threatenin' to go on strike. It's makin' him think fondly of those good old days when everyone was having a good time. Workin' hard but having some fun. Like back when Joe Riordan was runnin' it."

"That's when I was hired," Nikki reflected. "They brought him in to expand the company. He's a deal-maker, a closer. Aries was about six aircraft strong and losing money. Riordan came in and tripled the size of the company in a year, then did it again and again. I was hired in that first big expansion. Under him I got a chance to work in management, first in training and then in flight standards. Hmm. I agree with Danny. That's when it was fun. But starting an airline now? He must be crazy."

But Nikki couldn't stop thinking about it. It woke her up at night, preoccupied her at work, caused her to miss snatches of conversation. Five years ago, if anyone had suggested to her that she would even consider a job change when she had a perfectly good position as a 767 captain, she would have called him crazy. Even one year ago. Even six months ago.

But everything had changed—in her personal life and in the industry she had grown up loving.

When she told Buck the news about Riordan, he said, "Crazy like a fox. He's got a whole country full of equipment to shop from—all the airlines have been cutting back, not growing. Jumbo jets that leased for two to three hundred thousand a month are available for fifty. There must be a couple hundred thousand talented airline professionals looking for work. The major airlines can't compete—their costs have gotten too high while the ticket prices are too low for them to make any money. They're dropping like flies...."

"Like three-hundred-ton flies..." Nikki corrected him.

"But can you make money in the business? Now and then you can make a fortune. JetBlue did it when they went public."

Nikki looked at her dad. The thing about Buck Burgess was this—if you looked at him and didn't know anything about him, you might think he was a janitor. Or a mechanic, maybe, from the black engine oil that was always under his nails. He wore jeans and boots, and in cold weather a navy blue quilted vest that had seen better days. His hats—all from aircraft manufacturers—were dirty and had serious sweat rings around the bill. And when he spoke, his words weren't fancy and his grammar wasn't always the best, but he was smart as a whip. Buck Burgess was one shrewd businessman.

And Burgess Aviation was a lot like Buck. It looked

a little rough around the edges, but it was worth a fortune. Buck didn't talk about the value of his business, and Nikki had never asked. But he had been the sole owner for a long time, and he employed charter pilots, instructors, mechanics, fuellers—everyone necessary to run a small airport. He had even managed to keep those who worked for him employed when the FAA and Homeland Security practically closed down inland air training and charter facilities.

In the end Buck actually encouraged Nikki to call Riordan; she had to give him a lot of credit for not discouraging the idea. After all, he risked losing close proximity to his only family, his grandchildren. And they were all so dependent on one another, especially now. But he said, "Las Vegas is just up the road and I travel easily. Besides, I'm cutting back on my hours at ops. I'm really not part of this equation."

She decided not to talk to the kids about the possibility until she knew what Joe had going on. She might find the whole idea too risky. Besides, she'd never been very excited about Las Vegas and wasn't too charged up about living there. She was just going to talk to Joe to get this crazy notion out of her mind so she could sleep at night.

"What in God's name are you doing?" she asked him when she finally called.

He laughed at the sound of her voice, then said, "It's a little like smoking. Just when I think I'm through, I gotta have another one."

"I've heard the theory that it's actually a good time to start an airline, but that's just a theory. Give me one reason, one really solid, understandable reason why an otherwise intelligent man would take on something like this· at a time like this?"

There was a pregnant pause. "Because, Nick, even the threat of terrorism can't keep this from being a sexy business."

Dixie wouldn't call Carlisle. She was still angry with him for not calling her, too. There they were, at a stand-off, in twin town houses a few steps and a right turn from each other. And Nikki had decided to go to Las Vegas for a day to visit with Joe Riordan and look at his operation, so she was unavailable. Which meant neither of them knew that Dixie had gotten a notice from her supervisor to come in for a meeting on her day off.

She racked her brain. She hadn't called in sick, been late or cuffed a passenger. Supervisors didn't call you in for a chat unless there was trouble, and she couldn't imagine what she might have done.

"Hit him in the gut with a wine bottle?" Sonny asked her a few hours later. The director of Inflight Services was a perfectly nice woman whose job managing hundreds of flight attendants must be gruesome. "Gave him a concussion by slamming the door on his head? That ring any bells? Besides his, that is?"

This time Dixie had no chance to call on her beauty-queen training. Her face went scarlet. But the flush was as much from the shock of surprise as guilt. That was well over a month ago! She'd flown with Branch since then—and he'd had the gall to actually flirt with her.

"Remember?" Sonny prodded.

"Why, didn't he fall down the hotel stairs and crack his noggin?" she asked, feeling the heat burn her face and tingle her scalp. She hoped her hair wasn't standing straight up.

"He admits he was in a pickle," Sonny said.

"Pickle? That isn't what it's called in Temple, Texas."

"I'm not saying what he did to you was all right. But telling a lie in a relationship is certainly less dangerous than inflicting bodily harm."

"I guess that would depend on the lie," Dixie said sanguinely.

"Well, you're lucky he didn't call the police."

"Hah! He couldn't call the police!" she exclaimed, her voice rising a little wildly. "He would have had to tell his wife what he was up to!"

"So you did do that? Slam the hotel-room door on his head? Oh, Dixie, that's very—"

"I didn't say I did it. I said that if he said I did, and wanted to pursue that story by pressing some kind of charges, he would have had to tell his wife what would compel this single woman alone in a hotel room on a layover to slam the door on him. Could it be *unwelcome advances?*" Sonny was shaking her head. "When did he come to you with this complaint, Sonny? I've flown with him since his…*alleged* injury. And he came on to me like a bull. The slimeball."

"I'm not sure when the complaint was written. The chief pilot brought it to me a couple of days ago. I could have pulled you off your last trip, but… Well, I think we can handle this now without involving the chief pilot any further. Don't you?"

"Can I read it? His complaint?"

Sonny passed the sheet of paper to Dixie. She read slowly, carefully. Branch was completely shameless—it was all there. He admitted they were seeing each other, that he was married. *Ms. McPherson knew of my marriage, but it was a surprise to both of us that my wife showed up on our flight to New York. Thinking Ms. Mc-*

Pherson might be upset, I went to her hotel room to make sure she was all right, maybe to apologize or try to console her, but we did not exchange any words at all. She answered the door in her underwear and hit me in the gut with an empty wine bottle, which caused me to double over. She then slammed the door on me, striking my head, causing a laceration and slight concussion. I assume she had drunk all the wine.

"Oh, he is such a pig," Dixie said. "He told me he was going through a divorce. That he and his wife hadn't lived together in a long time."

"I believe you," Sonny said. "But that's not at issue."

"He put in here that I answered the door in my underwear and drank all the wine. A gentleman does *not* do that."

"That really doesn't concern me at all."

"I apologized to him. I thought this was behind us."

Sonny, a spindly woman in her fifties with fire-engine-red hair, folded her hands on top of her desk and looked at Dixie over the rims of her reading glasses. "Dixie, this is over the top. You could have killed him."

"Pffttt," she pooh-poohed. "He's a Texan. His head is made of lead."

"Seriously. I think it wouldn't hurt for you to talk to someone. Just in case there is a deeper issue going on here."

"I'll consider it," she said dismissively. But inside she was thinking perhaps she should see a shrink, because for the first time in all the years of bad breakups, she felt as though this once she'd gotten even. And it felt pretty good. It would feel a whole lot better if she wasn't being reprimanded for it.

"Well, you're going to have plenty of time to think

about it, Dixie. Thirty days on the beach,'' she said, meaning Dixie was being suspended. "Without pay."

"Sonny! Wait a minute—"

"I'm serious, kiddo. I know you were pissed off, and I don't really blame you, but we can't have one employee attacking another with a blunt object. Thirty days will encourage you to think of alternative solutions to your…uh…relationship problems. Of which, if you don't mind me saying so, you seem to have many."

Dixie stood abruptly. "I mind you saying so! You don't have to add insult to injury. You think I want it this way?"

"Can I make a suggestion, Dixie?"

"Can I stop you?"

"It might be time to take a break from men. Seriously. A significant break. Get some counseling. Work out some things. You're a beautiful girl—"

"A thirty-five-year-old girl!"

"Okay, woman, forgive me. But it's true—you're beautiful, bright, dedicated, loyal… You deserve better than this. It wouldn't hurt to try to figure out what it is that sets you on such a self-destructive path."

Despite Dixie's efforts, tears began to gather in her eyes. Did the fact that she was so often lied to automatically suggest she pursued liars? How in the world was this *her* fault?

"Perhaps you fall in love too easily, too naively…."

Okay, there was that little problem. But she was trying to quit!

"Because you really are far too wonderful a person to end up in so many of these situations, Dixie," Sonny said. And there was no question she was sincere.

"Thanks," Dixie replied weakly, feeling her nose grow pink and her eyes turn liquid. "Is that all?"

"I'm sorry, Dixie. It's what I have to do."

"Can I have a copy of this?" she said, holding the report written by F.O. Darnell.

"It's yours."

"Thanks. See you in a month, I guess."

A significant break from men? she asked herself as she left the Aries employee parking lot. Oh, yeah.

The flying time from Phoenix to Las Vegas was just under an hour. Nikki got a cockpit jump seat on Aries in the busy early-morning bank. She saw the captain in dispatch and he brought her on the airplane from the ramp rather than through the gate. She boarded right behind two air marshals who would ride in first class from Phoenix to Las Vegas to D.C.

Nikki was greeted by flight attendants she had worked with before. They gave her a freshly brewed cup of coffee and informed her there was plenty of room left in first class if she preferred that to the tight squeeze in the cockpit jump seat. Even though it was a short flight, the choice was an easy one. She let some of the passengers get settled before taking an aisle seat across from one of the marshals. These guys were not known to be chatty—she could probably count on a quiet ride—so she settled herself with a crossword puzzle from the inflight magazine and her coffee.

Not long before they pushed off the gate, a latecomer dashed into the cabin, stowed his bag overhead and squished past Nikki to take the window seat beside her, even though there were several empty seats to choose from. She knew immediately that he wasn't going to be a quiet seatmate. He might be having trouble slowing down after a mad rush to the airport...or else he had a lot of nervous energy. When he turned to her, he looked her over, and his smile had the hint of a leer to it. "How you doin'?" he asked with an accent laced heavily with Brooklyn Italian.

"Great," she said, going back to the crossword puzzle.

The flight attendant approached him. "We have just a few minutes, sir, but if you—"

"Yeah. Bloody Mary. Thanks." Then to Nikki he added, "Long night. Whoa, know what I mean. Name's Rocky."

Nikki just smiled briefly, then turned her head back to the puzzle. She wasn't going to ask about the long night.

"You got a name?" he asked her.

"Joan," she lied.

"Well, how do you do, Joan." He held out his hand to her and she gave it a brief shake. "You fly much?"

Apparently he wasn't going to make it easy to ignore him. "Pretty much, actually," she said.

"Me, too. Just part of the job." His drink arrived and he made fast work of it. "So, what do you do?" he asked her.

"I'm just going up to Las Vegas to spend the day with a friend who's starting a new business there. I haven't seen him in quite a while, so we have a lot of catching up to do." She was well aware that she hadn't answered his question. "And you?" she asked, turning his attention away from her. "What do you do?"

He gave a low and provocative chuckle and glanced around for eavesdroppers. "I fly for a living." He chuckled again, as though he'd let some cat out of the bag. "You're not married?"

"Ah, no. Not yet, anyway."

"And this guy in Las Vegas…?"

"We go way back," she said, already very annoyed. This one-hour flight was going to feel like a week.

The flight attendant came by to pick up glasses and cups as the jetway pulled back, the door was closed and the 767 jerked into motion. Mr. Chatterbox, aka Rocky, instructed the flight attendant to bring him another drink when they were airborne, then rattled on about the runway traffic, how long it was going to take to get clearance, the inefficiency of Air Traffic Control. Then he was on to different carriers and how they processed passengers, luggage and food.

The plane lifted off and rose, and once his second drink arrived, he went on to extol Aries Airline, which was one of his favorites. They were still young enough, he said, not to have old, jaded flight attendants who had forgotten how to smile. And they kept to their schedule more than some of the older and larger carriers.

Breakfast was a simple affair on a one-hour flight—a beverage, bagel, fruit and yogurt—but Rocky just drank his breakfast. Drank and talked. Finally she asked him, "Who do you fly for, then?"

He got that smirk again and glanced around before replying. "Well, I'm not supposed to mention this, but you seem pretty trustworthy. I fly for the government."

"Military?" she asked.

"TSA—that's Transportation Security Administration," he answered. "I'm...ah...an air marshal." He looked around furtively again.

"I see," she said. "How interesting. Do you have to carry a weapon at all times, then?"

"Well, that's the idea. But I'm not officially on duty at the moment."

"So that means you're not armed now?" she asked.

"Well, not *officially*. But believe me, if I were needed

in some official capacity, I wouldn't let you down." He patted her hand and she wanted to go wash it. Then he laughed. "Know what I mean, babe?"

Babe? Oh, he was going to so regret this behavior. "You must have a badge or something. Huh?"

"I wouldn't want to get that out…draw attention to myself… Y'know? Because I'm not working at the moment."

She wasn't sure if he was an idiot or a criminal. First of all, a person with a firearm was never served alcohol on a commercial flight, and this guy was getting loaded. Second, on duty or off, an undercover federal cop never identified himself to passengers—not even women he was trying to pick up.

This guy could be a fed doing things he shouldn't be doing, or he could be an impostor with fake ID. If the latter were true, he might have a weapon with him. And if he had a weapon, he might have plans for it.

So she made small talk. About how much flying he must do. About all the cities he must visit regularly. Did he have a family? Did he get tired of living out of a suitcase? Did he know the answer to one of her crossword clues? Would he like a magazine? Until finally she said, "You'll have to excuse me—all that coffee, you know."

"Sure thing, babe."

Babe again. Oh, he was going to be sorry.

She found the flight attendant cleaning up in the galley, whispered in her ear, then stepped into the bathroom. The flight attendant wrote notes on two napkins and took them with glasses of water to two men in the first-class cabin.

The flight was only about fifteen minutes out of Las Vegas. One marshal was across the aisle from where

Nikki had been seated and the other was a couple of rows up.

Nikki stepped out of the bathroom just as one of the marshals, an innocuous-looking middle-aged man with thinning gray hair and a cardigan sweater in a terrible pattern moved back to where Rocky sat. The one across the aisle was about thirty-five, had a ponytail and a leather vest, obviously playing the part of yuppie trash. But their choreography was delightful, and she ducked quickly into the galley, out of sight, to watch from behind the drawn curtain.

"Excuse me," the older marshal said to Rocky. "Could I impose on you for just one second?" He smiled engagingly, like a favorite uncle or harmless neighbor.

"Huh?"

"We're going to be going over Lake Mead in a second and I've never seen it. Mind if I look out that window there? You could sit here by the aisle while—"

"Someone's sitting there, man."

"I know. While she's in the lav, can I just look out that window? Just for a sec? Then when she comes back, I'll just get out of your hair and you two can have your seats back, before we land. Thanks, buddy. I'd sure appreciate it."

Rocky looked perturbed, but nonetheless hoisted himself up and moved into the aisle so the marshal could take the window seat. As the marshal lowered himself into the seat, eyes fixed on the window, he reached into his pocket. As soon as Rocky sat down again, he found his wrists clamped roughly to the armrests on either side of him. The marshals held him pinioned with one hand each, while with the other they produced badges.

"Federal air marshals," the older man said. "Are you carrying a weapon, sir?"

Rocky was stunned speechless for the first time this trip. He finally said, "No! What the hell!"

"Did you tell your seat partner you were a federal marshal, armed and flying off duty?"

"No!" he insisted, shaking his head. "She's lying! Why would she lie like that?"

Plastic restraints mysteriously appeared, and Rocky was lashed in place, while the marshals carefully patted him down in search of weapons. All the while he protested loudly that this was a mistake. He worked for a hotel chain, he traveled a lot, she must have misunderstood. The marshals repeatedly told him to shut up or there would be duct tape involved in quieting him down.

"I haven't got any gun, you can see that. Just untie me right now—I haven't done anything. What have I done?"

"You're going to see the federal judge, pal. And I bet you'll get some time to cool down and work on some new pickup lines."

"What makes you think she's telling the truth? She could just be lying!" He stretched his neck to see where Nikki had gone and found her across from the forward galley, sitting next to the flight attendant on the jump seat and talking on the interphone. What he didn't realize was that she was talking to the captain in the cockpit.

"She's telling the truth, pal," the marshal said. "She works for this airline. She's a 767 captain."

Rocky's face went dark. His eyes narrowed to slits as he glared in her direction. He'd been betrayed. "She could have told me,'' he said quietly. Angrily. ''That was a cheap play.''

''Oh, yeah? It had nothing to do with you, huh?'' And then they both laughed at him.

Six

For someone raised around airplanes, Nikki was surprised by the impact the newly painted jet had on her. It was more than the jet, it was the image it presented, the symbolism. New Century Air was painted across the fuselage, and NCA up the tail, underscored in black, gold and silver lines. A three-year-old Boeing 757, virtually new by aircraft standards, it was parked all the way across the runway. Behind the plane rose the pyramid-shaped Luxor hotel with its enormous replica of the Sphinx in front. It looked like New Century Air had been cleared for landing in Egypt.

The plane had snap and class. As did the plane's daddy, Joe Riordan.

That was why she was here, of course. Riordan. Pilots didn't follow planes or even airlines, but the men who built them. Joe Riordan was one of a kind. He was a young fifty and had been around airlines for almost thirty years. He had helped set up two, worked in senior management for one more, consulted for a few years, and now here he was—like a glutton for punishment—starting up again.

Riordan was a good-looking guy, tanned and fit, with a definite twinkle in his eyes. He was sexy, and his bad-boy charm caught the attention of the ladies, especially the impressionable young flight attendants who really went gaga over him. And he was a terrible flirt. Nikki liked getting a good banter going with him. He had a caustic wit and didn't like people who walked on eggshells—he preferred a woman with a spine, and a mouth.

What Nikki sometimes thought she saw in him was a younger version of Buck, polished up and on the make. Riordan was only about five-ten, but he had a real tall voice and a sharp tongue. Divorced three times—one child per marriage and what he called the meanest ex-wives in America—he was now being followed from company to company by a leggy blond named Jewel who worked as his assistant and had a reputation for iciness. The Gatekeeper, she was dubbed.

Riordan had two traits that most CEOs didn't. He was willing to take chances, not just in business, but on the people he chose to work with, and he valued people above money. Also, he had a gift for finding money when he needed it. In fact, you could spend ten minutes with the man and feel like giving him your life savings.

A small, loyal group had followed him wherever he went—a CPA named Paul DeLeon, who took charge of the finance department; LaVerne Peavy, an expert in the magic of fares and yield management; Gary Ray, marketing man and genius scheduler; and Mark Shows, whom Riordan called the Wrench, the VP of Maintenance. There were others, including pilots and flight attendants, who would love to work for Riordan again just because of his reputation. The fact that he'd left two airlines and closed down a third would not discourage his diehard fans, of whom Nikki was one.

There were three things that had brought her to Las Vegas to see him. A drastic need for change. An opportunity to take a position in the management of an airline from its first day of operation—a chance that might never come again. And the desire to work near someone as edgy and visionary as Riordan.

"In ten years you won't recognize this industry," Riordan had been quoted as saying in a national newspaper right after the 9/11 tragedy turned the airlines upside down. Since it was very clear the old system wasn't going to work, Nikki wanted to be around the people who were going to shape the new era of aviation.

She took a cab to the offices of New Century Air, just six miles off airport property, and eight or so miles from the Las Vegas strip. The freeway wound up a small hill so that the new office building sat slightly above the sparkling city. The airline occupied the entire second floor. Despite the fact that deliverymen in mint-green, tan and navy blue jumpsuits were everywhere, moving boxes and furniture on dollies into elevators, she was stopped by the security guard. After she produced ID and signed in, she was told to wait for an escort.

It was probably ten minutes before Jewel James appeared. Nikki had not had the pleasure before, but she'd certainly heard enough about this gorgeous but cold woman. There was speculation as to whether Riordan had finally found the perfect administrative assistant or simply given his lover a job.

"You're late," she said.

"Sorry. I had to have a man arrested," Nikki replied.

Anyone else would have asked what that was all about, or at least inquired about her flight, but not Jewel. She lifted one finely arched blond brow, looked down at the much shorter and unfortunately thicker Nikki, and allowed the slightest hint of curiosity to drift across her porcelain features. Nikki found herself looking right into the Gatekeeper's breasts. "Follow me," Jewel said, and instead of walking beside Nikki, led the way.

The elevators opened on the second floor to the chaos of moving. Furniture and boxes were pushed up against hallway walls and into the middle of offices, while techs with toolboxes hooked up computers, phones, printers, copiers and other miscellaneous equipment. It was hard to tell the employees from the movers and handymen—everyone was dressed casually, in jeans, khakis and sweats.

Nikki passed a conference room in which six men were conferring around a table covered with laptops, stacks of papers, manuals and coffee cups. Very likely this was the FAA meeting with employees working on the airline's certification. There would be more than thirty required manuals, ranging from flight operations and safety to weight and balance, fueling and emergency response. By the time this process was complete, four thousand man hours would have been invested to get a flying certificate worth roughly thirty million dollars. That FAA certificate would be New Century Air's greatest asset. In addition, there would be a veritable library of support manuals—all created by its founders and original staff, all approved by the feds.

The hall finally opened into a reception area, the only room completely decorated so far. There was a sofa and several chairs, a coffee table with potted plants, and art on the walls. The double doors to Riordan's office stood open, but outside was an expansive L-shaped desk with computer and printer—the Gatekeeper's post.

Jewel stopped at her desk, and with one long, slender arm, bedecked with gold bracelets, indicated the double doors. ''He's waiting'' was all she said.

Whew, Nikki thought. If Riordan is boinking her, he must be awful chilly below the belt by now.

She stood for a second in the open doors and looked

into the office, appreciating the sight of him standing before a wall of windows. Hands in his pockets, he was watching a Singapore Airlines 777 on its final approach into McCarran International Airport. The huge plane flew right down the center of town and looked as if it would land on Las Vegas Boulevard, right between the Bellagio and the Paris. In fact, it would land just south of the strip, but so close that the passengers would see the breathtaking panorama of the new casino resorts close up and personal.

From here, the city had a beautiful, freshly scrubbed appearance. Unlike any other city, Las Vegas was a cache of multicolored, sparkling shapes—not office buildings, but enormous, glittering hotels that were more like cities with stores, malls, restaurants, bars, movie theaters and amphitheaters. While it had been the mecca of buffets and three-dollar steak dinners fifteen years ago, Las Vegas now had more famous five-star chefs than Manhattan.

Yes, flying people in and out of the biggest tourist attraction in the United States was probably a good idea.

She let the triple seven pass out of Riordan's view before she spoke. "I saw your new plane."

He turned around, bright-eyed at the sound of her voice. "What did you think?"

"It's awesome. You know it's gorgeous. Who designed the paint job?"

"It was a group effort. A few rounds, pizza and genius, the usual combination. I'm trying to figure out how I can be here when the first flight comes in so I can see it on final approach.... But I'll have to be on the first flight. Tradition."

"You can stand right there for the FAA-proving flights. You can see your plane landing in the city while your senior check airmen are passing the final check rides required for your certificate.''

A smile began to spread across his lips. He hadn't thought of that, she could tell.

"Damn good to see you, Nick. You look great, despite the shit we've all been through.''

"You, too, Joe.''

"I heard about the ex. Kids okay?''

"It was tough on them, of course, but they're very okay now. My dad is with them when I fly. And while I'm up here.''

"Good. Kids shouldn't have to suffer like that.''

"How close are you to certification?'' she asked.

"Closer than it looks. Some of us have been up here working for almost a year, even though we just got into this office space. We hired a consulting firm out of L.A. to help with the manuals, and the FAA has been real flexible with us regarding substituting our principals on the certificate for the consultants. Mark Shows is our maintenance principal, and we just made an offer to a VP of Operations and he's going through the motions of getting approval from the feds. By the time everyone is approved, we'll be ready to hire our first classes of pilots and flight attendants to start training, mini-evacuation and proving flights.''

His reference to the final exams in the birth of an airline gave her a little rush; the enthusiasm and optimism of the entire employee group during these trials were always at fever pitch. The mini-evac was held at night on the edge of the airport when the FAA timed a random selection of flight attendants in emergency evacuation procedures. The proving flights had FAA-check airmen riding with a pilot and copilot, grading every second of their flight from preflight checklist to landing—the final test before the airline could load up the passengers. When that plane returned to the airport to land with a thumbs-up, every employee of New Century Air would be on hand to cheer the crew into the gate.

"You going to join us, Nick?" he asked her as he walked around his desk to sit down.

"It's tempting, but I have a lot of seniority at Aries." He made a face. "They're in trouble."

"Everyone's in trouble," she said, so sadly accurate. "How are you going to make this work?"

"We have some innovative ideas. I'll have Paul take you through the business plan item by item if you're interested, but the quick and dirty is that it's a damn good time to start an airline. The equipment is cheap and available, we're going to get really good people, and we've got some of the best marketing analysis and yield-management experts in the industry on our team. Plus, you got me. I'm still right more than I'm wrong."

"Who did you ask to be VP of Ops?" She wanted to know, because anyone in pilot management would ultimately be working for him.

"I'd rather not say—he hasn't signed the contract yet, but I think we've got him. Our executive search company highly recommends him. You might even know him, but—" He stopped himself. "Let me ask you this—is there anyone you'd refuse to work for?"

"Let's not get ahead of ourselves. I just wanted to talk to you about—"

"Can you think of anyone you'd run away from?"

She shrugged. "Not offhand."

"And you wanted to talk about...?"

"I'm just curious about your operation. What are you looking for?"

His lips curved slightly. He reached behind him to the

desk and lifted a piece of paper, handing it to her. "These are the positions in operations that haven't been filled."

She looked down the list—chief pilot, director of training, director of flight control, crew scheduling and a host of management positions in Maintenance. Once the first batch of pilots were hired, there would be lots of check-airman positions.

"Have you been interviewing for these?" she asked.

"We've had some calls. Some interest." He nodded toward the page. "Anything on that list spark your interest?"

Something came over her, and it was so spontaneous that she almost flushed in surprise. "Chief pilot," she said, handing him back the list.

He gave a short laugh. "A woman chief pilot, imagine that. What makes you think you're qualified?"

"I've either worked in or directed every department on your list, and I have a lot of experience. I'm current in your choice of aircraft, I have a degree in aerospace engineering and mechanics, and I have a very good relationship with the FAA—I've been a check airman and training captain for years."

"But you're a woman," he said.

"Yet another advantage."

"You think the boys will work for you?"

"Let's see. Are we going to hire boys who are looking for work? There's thousands of them out there, right?"

"They're usually a little, you know, indelicate...."

A laugh burst out of her. She'd been raised in an airport. She'd gotten a degree from a college dominated by men. She'd worked with the louts for years. Hah!

"What about Training?" he asked.

A year ago she might have settled for that. Even a

few months ago. But damn it all, those deals she hadn't screwed herself out of, she'd been screwed out of by some guy who had the balls she lacked. She couldn't believe what she was doing. It was a leap from where she was, but she wasn't sure if it was a leap into a great opportunity or off a cliff. What would Buck say? Would the kids go along with this?

But all she could think of was *going for it*.

"No way I'd come up here, move my family, give up my seniority at Aries for anything less than chief pilot. And that's only because you think you've filled VP of Ops."

A little voice inside her screamed, *Are you crazy? Taking on something like that before thinking it through? What if the men pound you into a bloody pulp before you even get this outfit airborne? What if the kids balk at moving?*

"You want to think about this?" he asked. "I've known the guys to be a little… Well… Sexist?"

"Hah!" she said aloud. "After ten years of having the cockpit called the box office when I'm in there, you're going to scare me off the boss's job with *sexism?* Shit, Joe. You must think I'm some kind of candy ass."

"You want it?"

A huge, insane grin broke over her face. "I'm going to be their worst nightmare," she heard herself say. Then she gathered her common sense, cleared her throat and said, "I'm sure the pilots and I will have an excellent relationship."

He looked at his watch. "All right, then. You should see Paul, say hello to some of the people who put this business plan together, and get a bona fide tour. Tell you what, I got a ten-thirty. It shouldn't take long. By the time you're done with Paul, I'll be free again and we can talk compensation.'' He stuck out his hand. ''Welcome aboard, Nick. You're going to like this New Century.''

''I bet I will,'' she said. But someone inside her, some woman who'd had more than her share of rotten luck, was screaming, *Holy shit! You're the chief pilot! How'd you pull that off?*

It didn't take much to sweep Nikki up in the energy of the place. Paul DeLeon gave her a brief explanation of their plan to offer a nonscheduled charter service in and out of Las Vegas to major U.S. cities and scheduled service to a few others. Included were presold seats to corporations that needed dependable, comfortable travel. Not only was Las Vegas the number-one tourist attraction in the United States, the Grand Canyon being second, but it was the number-one convention center.

After successfully launching that service and slowly adding planes, New Century would add cities to its scheduled air service. Their 757s, reconfigured to hold larger first-class sections for lower prices, would lure both the business traveler and group charters like professional ball teams, entertainment groups and political and governmental junkets. The airline also hoped to certify for international passenger carrying to be ready to launch any charter service out of the country.

Paul then walked her around the building, introducing her to people. The only one she knew was Mark Shows, the Wrench; she had met him at her dad's fixed-base operation in Phoenix many years ago. The minute Mark saw her, his ruddy face lit up. A burly man of about sixty, he chewed on an unlit cigar that looked like the same one he'd been chewing on for the last twenty years. He pulled her unceremoniously into his big, bearlike embrace and shook her a little, like an animal does to his catch before biting into it.

"Finally that good-for-nothing kid in the front office listened to me," he said. "Riordan called you, eh?"

"No," she said. "I called him."

"Either way—at least we got you on board."

"Well, that seems to be a fact," she said.

"What are you gonna do for us, Nick?"

"Chief pilot," she said almost weakly. She was going to have to practice saying that; she couldn't afford to sound unsure.

"That's fine, that's just *fine!*" he replied, no doubt in his voice. "And how's your old man?"

"Ornery. Where'd you come from?"

"I helped certify Universal and was there when Riordan came on board and had to shut her down. I took a little time off while he poked around, trying to decide what to do next. I figured it'd be something like this."

She took his ham paws into hers. He was the VP of Maintenance, not the mechanic, but like always, his big, callused hands looked like they'd been working on an engine.

Mark had been all over this industry, having started at American Airlines. He'd worked for at least three of the major airlines in different capacities under the maintenance umbrella, and had also put in time in smaller, deregulation start-ups. Of everyone she knew, next to her father and Riordan, this was the man she trusted the most. He had a down-to-earth, basic common-sense approach that always proved true.

"What kind of chance do you give this operation?" she asked him.

"I'd give us a better chance than any of the big guys right now. They can't even make their low-fare spin-off regional carriers work. They're so big and ungainly and have so many labor issues, every day's a struggle.'' He stuck the cigar back in his teeth. ''But that doesn't mean this'll be easy. It'll be tough.'' He grinned around the butt. ''It'll make you feel like you *did* something.''

Nikki had a folder full of confidential planning materials when she made her way back to Joe's office. The Gatekeeper's desk was abandoned and the doors to Joe's office stood open. She heard men's voices within and decided to wait for them to finish rather than to interrupt.

''I had someone else in mind for that position,'' she heard a man say, and she knew that voice. Deep, distinguished, the merest touch of the South... Who was that?

''Did I lead you to believe you'd be filling all those positions without input from me?'' Riordan asked the man.

''If she's going to report to me...''

''Shows will also report to you, and I hired him before I even talked to you. So will the director of flight control. I'm using the same airline-executive-search agency that I've used before, the one that recruited you. If you bring on anyone with promise, he or she will have a chance to move up the ranks.''

''Look, if you'll excuse my candor, this one could be a problem.''

Silence followed this last remark, Nikki drifted closer to the doorway. *This one could be a problem?* Who was this guy? He obviously knew her, though apparently not very well.

''First of all,'' he went on, ''I don't know how well you know pilots, but their *wilfulness* to work for a woman is questionable. And this one—well, I don't mean any disrespect—but she lacks that necessary air of command, if you know what I mean.''

''I hear nothing but praise about her air of command,'' Riordan said. ''And she worked in management when I was at Aries. She impressed everyone. She's smart, capable, experienced and loyal. You're the one I know very little about.''

Thank you, Joe! she thought, a smile coming to her lips. She looked around guiltily.

''I'm just saying, this could open up a *madrid* of problems with the boys,'' he said.

Riddle! It was Riddle! *Oh, God,* she thought. *I can't answer to Riddle! Can't can't can't!* She let her head drop soundlessly against the wall three times, as if bashing it.

''What about with the girls?'' she heard Riordan ask. ''Because we might be hiring some of them, too.''

''What I mean is—''

''I know what you mean,'' Joe said. ''The fact is, we need her kind of skill, experience and ethics. You see,'' he said patiently, ''I *think* you're what I want. You certainly have the qualifications on paper and that particular headhunter hasn't let me down before, but I happen to *know* Nikki Burgess is what I want. We clear on that?''

That's when she knew—he had played her. From the moment she called him, if not before, he meant to have her in that job. His slight hesitancy to give her the position was only to make her insist on it. Well, fine then. She'd show him.

''Just thinking about your interests, boss,'' Riddle said.

''That right? Well, rest easy. So am I.''

But there was no question, she would not have pitched for the job had she known Riddle was the VP. When

Joe had given her a chance to name any person she'd refuse to work for, it had never in a million years occurred to her that Riddle could be an executive here. Talk about making your bed...

A toilet flushed in the distance and Nikki looked around in confusion. The door behind Jewel's desk opened and the magnificent blond stepped out to spy Nikki, but she looked curiously unsurprised. "Does he know you're here?" she asked, one side of her mouth curling up suspiciously. For all Nikki knew, the Gatekeeper might have surveillance cameras in the john.

"Ah, no. He seems to be with someone...."

Jewel tapped on the open door and stuck her head in. "Captain Burgess is here."

"Send her in, send her in!" Nikki stepped through the portal and faked surprise at seeing Bob Riddle. She stuck out her hand and shook his. "I guess the cat's out of the bag, Nikki. Bob has agreed to take the position of VP of Operations. And according to him, you two are acquainted."

"Congratulations, Bob," she said.

"And to you," he returned. If she hadn't overheard him, she might almost think he welcomed her.

"Well, Nikki and I have a few things to discuss, so if you've concluded your business...?"

"Ah! Yes, sir. I guess I'll start getting settled in my office and see both of you later." With something that resembled a courtly flourish, he quit the room.

Then the doors were closed. Nikki had the distinct impression that opening or closing those doors was never accidental. During her time with Joe, they only opened once, when Jewel brought in a tray that bore coffee cups, glasses, cream, sugar and a bucket of ice. Nikki had a cup of coffee. After roughly two hours, they had ham-

mered out the bare bones of a deal that included her pay
and benefits. By pushing on Riordan a little here and
there, giving him one last chance to look further for his
chief pilot, she had ended up making a great deal for
herself. Her compromise was that she'd get back to Las
Vegas as quickly as possible to concentrate on complet-
ing the certification process and hiring the pilots.

Deal made, Joe went to a cabinet against the wall and
retrieved a bottle of Scotch from the lower cupboard. He
poured two fingers in each glass. Nikki helped herself to
a couple of half-melted ice cubes while he took his neat.
He raised a glass. "Welcome to the best experience of
your life."

"Thanks for the opportunity, Joe."

*The opportunity that will change my life, whether I
like it or not,* she thought.

On her way out, she passed by the office that would
be hers, and stood in the doorway. By the time she returned to Las Vegas, this room would hold a desk, credenza, small conference table and four chairs, computer
and phone. The reception area outside was for her yet-
to-be-hired administrative assistant, and soon would be
populated with everyone from pilots to job applicants to
vendors from aviation suppliers.

"Excuse me?"

She turned around to see an attractive man in his forties standing behind her. He held a folder in his large
hand. "Yes?"

"I read about this company in *Aviation Week* and
wondered if anyone could tell me when hiring would
begin."

"For what position?" she asked.

"Pilot. I'm qualified in the Seven-Five."

"Interviews should be starting in about four weeks.

Training will begin in about six weeks for a November 10 start date.''

"Is there anyone around to give my résumé to?"

"Yes," she said. "I'll take it from you."

"Thanks, but I was hoping to meet someone in pilot management."

She stuck out her hand. "Captain Burgess," she said. "Chief pilot."

He was startled for a moment, something she decided she'd better get used to. But then he broke into a big grin. "Awesome," he said. "That's awesome, a woman chief pilot." He shook her hand vigorously.

"Well, I wasn't expecting that reaction," she said. But his smile was infectious and she immediately found herself smiling back.

"I don't know that you'll always get that reaction, but I'm the father of two daughters, nineteen and twenty-three. We dads like to see our girls break the gender barrier."

"I suppose my dad feels exactly that way," she said. Then, thinking *This is going to be fine, absolutely fine,* she said, "How about a cup of coffee?"

They went to a restaurant around the corner, a place that would likely hold many impromptu meetings and lunches in the days and months to come. The pilot's name was Sam Landon, he was fifty, had worked for one of the smaller airlines that failed after 9/11 and had been out of work for a couple of years. He was a retired military pilot, a widower with one daughter recently married and the other a full-time college student, so he was very flexible about starting work. And he was very eager to get back into the cockpit.

He asked a lot of questions about New Century Air and Joe Riordan, and Nikki surprised herself by being able to answer them. In her very first official act as the chief pilot, she said, "I'll get in touch with you in a few weeks, Sam. I can't promise you a job, but I can promise you an interview."

"That's all I can ask," he said.

She went away from that brief meeting thinking that if she could hire about thirty guys like Sam, she'd be able to put together the perfect first class of pilots.

Back in Phoenix, Nikki drove out to Burgess Aviation. It was late in the day, the sun was low in the sky, and the devastating heat of the desert was lifting. She headed for the open hangar, where a couple of mechanics were at work on a corporate jet under Buck's watchful eye.

She stood in the frame of the huge double doors and cast a long shadow toward her dad. He turned to look at her, and she just tilted her head and lifted her hands in a helpless gesture. He walked toward her, looked down at her and said, "Good. It's time for you to take some chances, get on your own with the kids again. Make a life. What'd he offer you?"

"It wasn't so much his offer as what I said it would take to get me to move—chief pilot." Each time, it came out a little stronger.

To Buck's credit, he didn't register the least bit of surprise. But then he'd always had tremendous faith in his daughter's abilities. He had expected her to be an astronaut, but he wasn't disappointed with the path she'd taken. Now he nodded. "Good. Then only a couple of people have to die to make you CEO."

"Buck, shame on you!"

He grabbed her elbow. "Come on, let's find the kids, get a beer and celebrate."

"You're taking this awfully well."

"You're finally doing what I always expected you to do—run an airline. Besides, Vegas is just up the road."

Dixie had given the matter of Carlisle a lot of thought before she finally picked up the phone and called him. No one could sympathize more—when it came to romance, hadn't she been the biggest damn fool ever? She knew what it was like to make miserable choices and pay for them over and over again.

When he said hello, she asked, "Were you going to call me and tell me you were going home? Or just let me think you'd been kidnapped and murdered?"

Heavy sigh. "I just didn't feel like being lectured," he said.

"Really? I thought you enjoyed verbal abuse."

"See? You're doing it. Getting snotty."

"It's just so hard seeing you get hurt over and over again...."

"At least I keep getting hurt by the same man," he said meanly. "You've taken on half the male population."

"Ouch."

"Sorry. I might be a bit defensive."

She was quiet for a moment. "Well, you're right. I always get hurt by some new loser.... You just keep going back to the same loser. Carlisle, I'm afraid he's going to give you some disease. I can't stand it!"

"Dixie, you don't have to stand it. All you have to do is respect my choice."

"How can I? Tell me that! If I care about you, how can I watch you do this to yourself?"

"Just bite your tongue and be a pal."

"Let's go out for a drink and talk. Okay?"

"Can't. Robert is due home soon and I promised a nice dinner since I didn't fly today."

"Tomorrow, then?"

"Look, Dixie, let's give ourselves a little time to let the emotions settle down. Then we'll have that drink and that talk, okay?"

"You're brushing me off."

"I'm saving myself an argument," he told her. "Let me give you a call later. Hmm?"

"Sure," she said. "Talk to you later, then. Oh, and incidentally, I'm fine."

Silence answered her. "Sorry, chicklet. I never even asked. Are you? Really?"

No! I've been suspended without pay. I'm lonely. I'm scared...for both of us. We're just a couple of dopes who keep getting shat upon. But all she said was, "Yeah. Fine."

Seven

"Chief pilot," Nikki told Dixie.

She was answered by a gasp, followed by stunned silence on the phone line. Then Dixie whispered, "Chief pilot? Oh...my...God..."

"I know. I'm kind of fluctuating between feeling my wildest dreams just came true and wondering if they've slammed the door behind me in the lion's den."

"You'll knock 'em dead, sugar. You will."

"Or they'll eat me alive. Either way, I'm going for it. And I'm going for it fast. The kids and I are going up there right away to look the place over. If they approve of Las Vegas, we'll start looking for a place to rent or buy so they're ready to start school in, gosh, another month."

"How'd they take it?" Dixie asked.

"It was incredible. I had myself all set up to argue with them about how this opportunity could be good for all of us when they started squealing and jumping up and down in excitement. Their mom is going to run a flying operation in Las Vegas. You'd think I was being elected president."

"They're such good kids. *Smart* kids. Are we going to get together for a goodbye?" Dixie asked.

"No," she said. "There will be no goodbyes. It's a

forty-five-minute flight, for God's sake. You fly free. Come up next weekend and help me look at houses."

"Sure. Why not?" What Dixie didn't add was, *I don't have to go to work, after all.*

Although she totally deserved it, Nikki as the chief pilot of a new airline was a stunner! There were not a lot of women lined up to manage a fleet of commercial jets, and there weren't all that many in line to fly them. And leaving a company where she had so much seniority when seniority was God? Not to mention uprooting the kids and moving away from Buck.

"I just can't tell you what it feels like," Nikki said. "I must be crazy—I'm not the least bit afraid and I should be scared to death. I just want to leave all this behind, the mess Drake left, the grind of complaining pilots at Aries, my personal—" She stopped.

"Your personal what?" Dixie pushed.

She sighed. Fifteen years of feeling like a total drone. Eleven years in a bad marriage, four years in a bad divorce. But what she said was "I need a challenge and a change, but what I need even more is to feel alive and have a little fun. To enjoy my life more. I'm really hoping the kids and I can do that."

"Nobody deserves it more than you," Dixie said.

"I don't even have time to come over. I'm leaving Aries with my terminal vacation. Just say you'll come up and help me. We'll be starting from scratch because I'm getting rid of Drake's furniture and leaving our bedrooms intact at Buck's. You have some days off coming, don't you?"

Dixie laughed into the phone. "As a matter of fact, I do."

So Nikki and the kids left the following morning, with Buck's promise to fly up on the weekend. Thanks to cell phones and their package deals, Dixie talked to Nikki several times that week. And she talked to the kids, as well. Each time they told her about some new discovery they'd made in the suburbs of Las Vegas. They had all been to Las Vegas before, but none of them had ever been off the Strip. Just minutes away were hillsides blossoming with new homes, schools, rec centers, libraries, shopping, parks and parks and parks.

Dixie kept the sulk out of her voice and cheered them on. "How wonderful!" she exclaimed. "Awesome!" But inside she was so jealous she could spit.

I'm toast here, she thought. *I have a lousy reputation—people I work with think I'm a slut or an idiot and I don't know which is worse. I'm on suspension, one of my best friends is starting her life over, the other one isn't talking to me.... Oh, God, I need a fresh start as much as anyone!*

So...why not? I'll go, too. I'll leave Phoenix and get a job in Las Vegas—start over. At least I'll have one good friend there.

It was a totally impetuous decision, one Dixie didn't even share with her parents. For all she knew, her family felt the same about her as her coworkers—that she was either stupid or easy. When she got right down to it, she didn't care that much what people thought. The problem was that she was starting to wonder herself which was true.

Every time Nikki called, Dixie forced herself to sound upbeat. No, she said, she couldn't get up there that very first weekend Nikki was in Las Vegas...but maybe the next one. She kept her plans to herself and just kept packing.

A friend who was in real estate came over to look around the town house. Dixie didn't want to list it for

sale until she was sure the move was in her best interests—and the job and housing market in Las Vegas
would tell her that much pretty quickly.

Her essential household items were stored in boxes in
her garage, but Dixie left the furniture in the town house.
She could hire movers from Las Vegas if things worked
out there. Nikki and the kids were staying at a suites inn
in Henderson, so she called and made sure she could get
a room there, as well. Then she filled up her car with
luggage, a few linens, an emergency cooking kit and her
favorite potted plants.

Wait till Nick and the kids saw her drive up with her
car loaded! They wouldn't believe it!

Dixie felt the same way she had when she left college
at twenty-one to become a flight attendant, before com-
pleting her degree. Back then she'd fully intended to
travel the world and snag a husband and start a family.
Her own family was horrified, but she had been so sure
of what she was doing. This time, though, she wasn't
thinking husband or family, she was thinking of building
herself a life with herself for a change. No way did she
want to end up as pathetic as Carlisle—just not happy
unless she was being treated like pond scum by some
handsome and useless guy.

She would have to say goodbye to him of course.
They hadn't talked since he told her they should let their
emotions settle down awhile. Frankly, she was furious
with him, but that didn't keep her from loving him like
a brother. He and Nikki were her closest friends, and
even when she hated him, she loved him. She would
miss him desperately, but it had become increasingly
painful to watch Carlisle's self-image deteriorate because of Robert's bullying.

She just hoped she wouldn't sob all the way to Las Vegas.

The day she was to leave, she locked the door to her town house and closed the garage door, then drove her packed car around the bend to Carlisle's house. She left the engine running when she went to the door so she wouldn't be tempted to delay. But there was no answer. She rang, knocked, rang and knocked again. Trust Carlisle to screw up their sad farewell, she thought, even if he hadn't known she was leaving.

As she started back down the walk, she heard the door creak open behind her. When she turned, Carlisle was standing in the doorway. "So, you are home," she greeted him. "Were you not answering because it was me knocking?"

"No, of course not," he replied unconvincingly. He looked at his watch. "But I have to go get in the shower and change clothes. I…ah…picked up a trip. Can I give you a call tomorrow?"

"That's okay, Carlisle. I just came to say goodbye. I think I'm moving."

He wrinkled his brow in question. "You *think* you're moving?"

She stood in the middle of the sidewalk, trying not to go closer. "Did Nikki call you and tell you about Las Vegas? The new job she took?"

"Yes, but—"

"Well, she doesn't know this, but I'm moving up there, too," Dixie said. "I'm going to surprise her and the kids." She swallowed. "I need a fresh start, Carlisle. And I wanted to say goodbye, even though we're having this little… What would you call it, Carlisle? Standoff?"

He gave a huff of unamused laughter. "Something like that."

"So, don't tell them, okay? I didn't even ask her. Not that I need her permission. But I hate my life here, my life at Aries. You know what I mean. And…I'm the only one who can do anything about it, right?"

"Do you have a big job waiting for you at the new airline?" he asked her.

"I have *no* job waitin' for me there." She laughed, amazed at how okay that was. "But I bet I can get hired, and if not, I should be able to land a good waitressing job in one of the big casinos. I hear the tips are great." She grinned. "Think I'll be able to sling drinks if the ground isn't movin' beneath me? I might even go back to school. Finish my degree. I'm obviously never having a family, so I figure I better see if I can find a career where I can move up the ladder." She took a couple of steps toward him and saw him flinch uncomfortably. So, he was still pissed. "If I do apply to the airline, I bet I can get a good seniority number, though. I might even try to get into management—supervisor or training or something with a little more responsibility."

"You'd be a good supervisor," he said, but he was so distant, so detached.

"You're still so mad at me?" she asked.

"No," he said. "No, I'm just— Really, I have to get going."

"I know, Carlisle, and I hate goodbyes, so there's no need to drag this out." She walked toward him briskly. "I'm going to miss you so much," she said, her voice catching. "As soon as I get a place, you bid a Las Vegas layover, okay?" She reached for him then, and even though he kept his arms rigid at his sides, she embraced him. He felt stiff, uncomfortable, and he didn't hug her back. Dixie was filled with the pain of loss. It was so hard to believe that their tiff, about the twentieth on the same subject, could completely alienate them this way. "Come up to Vegas and spend a night or two, let me take you out on the town. I'll try to make up for being such an opinionated…"

She stopped talking and withdrew from him a bit, looking into his eyes, which were moist and sad and not making contact with hers. Dixie didn't know how she knew, but she did. Tugging on his lightweight shirt, she pulled it free of his waist and lifted it up.

His torso was covered with bruises. Very gently she let the shirt fall back down and waited for him to say something. But he just bit his lip and his eyes filled with tears.

Sweet Carlisle! Sweet, generous, loving Carlisle! Never before had Dixie felt such a murderous rage. She concentrated very hard on keeping her voice under control and fairly whispered, "Have you seen a doctor?"

"Yes," he said. "I had some X rays. I'm all right."

"Not exactly, but nothin's broken. Huh?" He nodded. She gently grabbed his chin in her thumb and finger. "You don't have a trip, do you?"

"No. I have a little time off to heal from my…fall."

She winced. "Come with me. Right now. Get your wallet, checkbook, keys and get in my car."

"I can't," he said.

"No, what you can't do is stay here another day. We'll stop at the police department and file a report, get an order of protection and be on our way. We'll put a couple of clothing changes on my charge card and take care of your car and things later. All that matters right now is that you get away from here and that Robert is never allowed to touch you again."

"He's due home any—"

"Carlisle, if you don't get in my car before he gets

here, he is in very grave danger, because I so want to kill him.''

''You just don't know—''

''I do so! This is it! This is the end of the line! Either come now or let him kill you. Because you know that's where it's going. You know it only gets worse and worse and—''

He kissed her forehead and, with a lame smile, turned and walked into his town house. The door clicked closed.

Dixie stood there numbly for a moment, then kicked the door with all her might. Fists clenched at her sides, she stomped like an angry two-year-old. ''Damn it, damn it, damn it!''

She sat down on the front step, not sure she could leave him bruised like that. Should she go back home and unpack—tell him she was still right around the corner? But hadn't she been right around the corner when this happened?

Maybe she should call the police. Have them come out and make a report whether Carlisle wanted to or not?

She could wait for Robert to come home and run him over when he was on his way down the street to the mailbox.

She covered her face with her hands and cried. Stupid, stupid, stupid jerk! How could Carlisle let this happen and not leave? Not fight back? Not even tell his best friend? Because this had not been the first time, and it would not be the last. It was never the last.

Fighting back her tears, she stood and wiped her hands down her jeans. All she could really do, she knew, was give up and leave. She'd go to Vegas and tell Nikki. Maybe she could get through to him. As much as Dixie wanted to kill Robert, she'd better go before he came home. Chances were if he found out she knew, it would just go harder on Carlisle.

But leaving him there was so hard! What if she never saw him again? She climbed into the car and drove into his cul-de-sac, her vision blurred by tears, and made a U-turn.

As she drove back to his house, she saw him walking toward the curb, pulling his suitcase on rollers behind him. She should have figured Carlisle would keep a bag packed for work.

Dixie slammed on the brakes and jumped out, but her driverless car almost ran her over as she rounded the front. She'd forgotten to put it in Park. As soon as she set the gear, she rushed over to Carlisle.

He put up a cautioning hand. "Easy."

"Yes! Yes, I know! Just get in, okay?" Grabbing his bag away from him, she shoved it onto the pile of stuff in the back seat while Carlisle settled himself in the front, a plant on the floor at his feet. She slammed the back door and jumped into the driver's seat. "Thank you," she said. "Leaving you there was one of the worst moments of my life."

"Well, being left could have been one of the *last* moments of mine."

The kids were wild about living in Las Vegas. They'd expected just another desert city like Phoenix, but Las Vegas was a fantasyland. Life-size pirate ships did battle right on Las Vegas Boulevard; brightly colored hot air balloons raced over the desert; choreographed fountains danced sixty feet in the air to the strains of Andrea Bocelli's "Con Te Partirò." Nikki took them to dinner in the Eiffel Tower and for gondola rides along the indoor canals of the Venetian resort.

She also showed them her office at New Century Air,

but it was hard for them to be impressed because of all the confusion and clutter. She introduced them to a few people, whose names they would no doubt forget before they got home—with one exception. Her clotheshorse, April, would never forget Jewel's Prada handbag. Then she called Mark Shows and asked if there was any way they could get on the airplane.

"Matter of fact," he told her, "we're working on the galleys. I'll pick you up outside Terminal One in fifteen minutes."

It was perfect. The sun was blinding bright on a hot day with a hot breeze when Mark showed up in his New Century truck. The airplane was parked on the far side of the airport near a group of hangars and other aircraft. All the doors were open with air stairs leading into the fuselage.

April and Jared stared gap-mouthed at the beautiful jet—resplendent in its fresh paint job, dazzling white with lines of silver, gold and black down the sides and up the tail.

"Cool," Jared said.

Mark stopped the truck near the stairs and they all just sat there for a moment, appreciating the magnificent aircraft.

"Is it really ours?" April asked.

April had no idea what feelings that question had provoked. *Ours.* Yes, it's ours. All of us who work to put it into the air. And our families, too, who feel the birthing process just as keenly as the CEO and pilots and dispatchers. *Ours.* We are its family.

"Good-lookin' piece a tin, ain't she?" Mark asked.

"Damn good-looking," Nikki said.

"Let's go aboard, then." He got out of the truck and headed for the stairs. Mark was a large man with a big stride, but in their excitement, Nikki and the kids had no trouble keeping up. They entered the fuselage to the sounds of drills, saws and hammers as maintenance techs worked on installing a new and enlarged forward galley.

The 757 was completely reconfigured to hold one hundred and fifty seats, approximately forty fewer than capacity. Not only were there more first-class seats, the coach section was far roomier. The seats were black with alternating gold and silver piping, and the carpet was patterned in diamond shapes the same colors. Gorgeous tapestries with the New Century Air logo covered the bulkheads, and the spotlessly clean interior smelled like a new car.

"Wow," Jared breathed, sitting down in one of the first-class seats.

April smoothed her hand over the rich black threads of the tapestry. "This is so beautiful."

"Haven't seen one this pretty in a long time," Mark said around his cigar.

"I haven't seen one this pretty ever," April said. "I can't believe it, Mom. You're really going to be the chief pilot of this airline?"

Mark put an arm around Nikki's shoulders as if he'd personally trained her for the job. "This here's the boss," he said.

Later, she would think about how bonding this experience was—taking her kids to the new airplane. *Our* airplane. No matter what else transpired, April and Jared were on her team, on the New Century team.

They had just come to look the place over. There was nothing that would make them go back.

"But Nicole," Opal said, "are you sure you want to take on that much responsibility?"

"Oh, yes, Mother. Do you know how many people work their whole flying careers without ever getting a chance like this?"

"I suppose. But the children... You'll need help with the children...."

Nikki smelled another extended visit coming on. She couldn't make Opal stay away forever, but she could stall her. "The kids are fine. They're helping *me*. Now, be a good mother and give me some time to get settled here before you come racing to Las Vegas. I'll let you know the minute I can handle a visit. All right?"

"You act as though I presume on—"

"Mother! Promise!"

"Why, Nicole..."

"I need a little time and space to settle into the town, the job, the new life. If you show up unannounced, I'll turn you right around and put you on the next plane home."

Opal sighed heavily. "I do hope you're not going to take too long. I never expected to see sixty, much less—"

I'm going to take as long as possible, she thought. "Of course not, Mother."

Sometimes April felt a little guilty. Was she allowed to be happy this soon after her dad's death? It was great to be able to spend time with her mom without the headache her dad would put everyone through. Everything was an issue with him, and he wouldn't stop until absolutely everyone was as miserable as he was.

Of course she wasn't glad he was dead. She missed him sometimes; she even found herself talking to him, reassuring him that everything was going all right. But now that she was older, she needed more time with her mother. Or more accurately, her mom needed more time with her, especially when it came to shopping.

The suites inn where they were staying was right off the Strip, one of the family places where there were no slot machines or smoky bars. They had a small suite with a large bedroom that held two double beds. There was also a living room with a pullout sofa and matching chair, and a kitchenette area that included a microwave, small fridge, table and four chairs. April and Nikki shared the bedroom; Jared kept his clothes in the bedroom and slept on the sofa bed at night. They hadn't packed much, so it was time to shop for new school clothes. What they'd left behind at Papa's would be shipped later, when they found a house.

After a couple of days of looking around the Las Vegas area, checking out the schools, neighborhoods and shopping, Nikki had to think about getting to work. "We've got to get you kids some new clothes," she announced. "I should probably buy some things for myself, too, since I'm now in an executive position."

April didn't think much about that statement until later. They left a sulky Jared in front of the TV in the suite; he'd rather have a tooth pulled than go shopping with a couple of girls. This suited April fine. She'd be more than happy to pick out a few things for him if it meant she wouldn't have to listen to him complain all day.

She was so much more like her father and maternal grandmother than her mom and Papa—she *loved* clothes, loved fashion. And the Vegas valley was proving itself up to her shopping standards.

After several hours with only a brief lunch break, Nikki and April were once again in side-by-side dressing rooms.

"Oh, Mom, wait till you see this," April said. "It is so-o-o-o cool."

"Show me," Nikki invited.

April opened the door to Nikki's room, and immediately forgot about the low-ride jeans and brief top she was wearing. Instead, she took one look at Nikki, slumped in the fitting room chair in a skirt, jacket and blouse, her socks still on her feet, and April suddenly knew she was now through shopping for herself, at least for a while.

"That's the thirtieth blue suit you've tried on today," April groaned. "And it's every bit as gross as the last twenty-nine."

"It doesn't do much for me, either. But I'm going to have to buy something. I've been wearing a uniform for the past ten years."

"Stand up," April ordered. Nikki obliged. "Mom, the skirt's too big, the jacket shoulders are too wide, and the blouse is too frilly. You basically look like you're wearing your mother's clothes."

"I have a funny shape."

"No, you don't. You're not trying the right sizes. I think you're a petite. You're kinda short…and short in the stride, too."

"I don't have the first idea what to try on."

"Well, let me give you a hint. Not another blue suit."

"I have to dress like a businesswoman."

"Really? I met a couple of businesswomen at your office, and they didn't look like that," April said, a tone of disgust creeping into her voice.

Nikki knew that April could only be thinking of Jewel and a couple of other women who seemed to be imitating her style. "I can't look like a flashy secretary. Believe me, there's no room for sex appeal in this position.

And I sure can't look like one of the guys. By the same token, I have to be taken seriously, and I won't garner much respect if I look like I'm wearing my mother's clothes.''

"You have to start with the right size. I don't think you've even noticed, but your jeans are *hanging* on you. You've lost weight since Daddy died."

Nikki pulled at the navy skirt. It was her usual size, but she was swimming in it. She thought back over the stress of the summer. If Drake's death wasn't enough, she had worked for weeks getting that house on the market. And then there'd been the excitement of taking on a dream job and moving the whole family. "Hmm," she said. "Maybe I did, huh?"

"Two sizes," April said. "On the bottom, anyway."

Slumping back down in the chair, Nikki removed the clip that had held her naturally curly mane out of her face for the past many years and gave her tired scalp a ruffle. Then she pulled her hair back again and reclipped it. She looked up at April and shrugged.

April shook her head. "You're going to need a little work."

"But is there much to work with?"

"Oh, come on. I *know* what to do. The question is, are you going to let me?"

"I have only one stipulation," Nikki said. "I'll try anything you pick out for me, as long as I don't look short and dumpy in it."

"Why do you always say that?" April asked in frustration. "You aren't short and dumpy. You're petite and have a nice shape. Even better since you've slimmed down around the hips." She gave her a sidelong appraisal. "You have a hot little figure."

"I do?" It couldn't be true.

"Who said otherwise?" April wanted to know.

Nikki didn't answer. First her mother and later her husband. Both of them commented so often on her short legs, flat chest and wide hips that that was all she saw in the mirror. Nikki thought of herself as short and dumpy with a freckled face and kinky hair.

"You have a great figure, and it's time to dress it," April said. "And you have great skin and hair. You just have lousy taste. But don't worry about it—I can't fly as good as you. Now, take off that ugly suit and I'll be right back."

And so the assembly line began. April enlisted the help of a saleswoman, and between them they reassembled Nikki. First, they made her get rid of the tennies and sweat socks and don a pair of slimming panty hose. A bra with a little more uplift and foundation appeared. Then skirts, slacks, shirts, blouses, jackets, sweaters, pumps and scarves. Not a single navy blue suit was allowed in the fitting room. In fact, the colors were fabulous—April had a real eye for what would look good with Nikki's red hair and light up her green eyes.

"And...as soon as we get your clothes for work, we're going to do something about that hair."

Nikki gulped. She imagined, fearfully, some punk cut with spikes. Since she'd never been able to control her hair, she'd been tucking it away under her captain's hat. What other option was there? It had to be off her collar—that had been the uniform dress code.

The option turned out to be a layered cut, highlighted blond, that barely reached her collar and curled softly, not tightly, around her face. It took hours out of the next day, but the result was worth it. Nikki wondered why it had never occurred to either her or the woman who had been cutting her hair for fifteen years to try something different. Of course, she also wondered if she'd ever be able to fix it like that herself.

Next, at April's insistence, came new makeup, along with lessons in applying eyeliner and lip liner and tips for keeping lipstick off your teeth, things Nikki had never gone to a lot of trouble about.

"That was before," April said. "If we're going to start a whole new life here, then we're going to start it by looking good."

"I can see your point," Nikki admitted. "But you know I've never had an aptitude for this sort of thing."

"I know," April assured her. "That's why you have me."

For the first time in maybe her entire life, Nikki felt passably attractive. Not beautiful like April or Dixie, but no hag. Almost forty and pretty at last? How had she missed all this? Obviously Buck wasn't the best person to teach her these refinements, but who had taught April?

"My peer group, teen magazines and MTV," she said with a shrug, as though it was unimportant. "Now, listen, you don't want to shock anyone at work, okay? You don't want it to look like you've had a big makeover. So what you do is this—dress casual and wear a little makeup, like base and light lips. And every day you'll upgrade a little. Go to the pantsuit with heels, then add eye makeup and wear a casual skirt. By the end of the first week, you're ready for your first suit, the sage with the slit in the skirt. Get me? Then you're where you want to be. Sort of like using Grecian Formula on your gray hair…slowly getting the gray out, so no one really sees it happening and they just learn to accept it. Got it?"

Nikki stared at her daughter, openmouthed. It was as much a science as this? She wasn't sure she was up to the job.

April grabbed her mother's biceps and gave her a little shake. "Mom! Snap out of it!"

"Sorry. I have to break them in to me looking good?"

"Yes. So they think that all that really happened is you got a haircut and you're wearing your real clothes and not your uniform to work. They'll be impressed by how beautiful you are and assume it was overlooked before on account of that manly uniform and barfy hat. And about uniforms... When you get the new ones at New Century, we're getting tailored pants for the women. The ones Aries had are cut for a man. No wonder you felt dumpy."

"You know, April, if you were as good at math as you are at fashion, I'd have to relent and admit you're a genius. A purebred genius."

Her daughter winked. "Some people wanna run the company, some people wanna dress the people who run the company."

Buck flew up for the weekend and announced that he had taken a week off from Burgess Aviation to spend a little time with the kids before school started. While Nikki began the process of acclimating herself to her new job, Buck got the kids enrolled in school and took them on day trips around the area—Lake Mead, Mount Charleston, Zion National Park, Mesquite, Hoover Dam, Nellis Air Force Base. Evenings, they looked at real estate with the relocation expert provided by New Century.

It took only days for April to say, "I think there's definitely a boat in my future. A nice big boat with plenty of skis."

"And a place in the mountains for me," Jared added. "For downhill skiing."

The first day of her new job, Nikki followed April's

directions to the letter when she got ready for work. Even if she'd wanted to cut corners, the little matter of sharing a bedroom with her daughter would have put a stop to that. April insisted on helping with things like eyeliner and lip liner, and Nikki had to pass inspection before going off to work.

She started her second week at New Century Air with company ID, a benefits package, a parking card for the airport, as well as a reserved spot at the office building. She no longer had to stop at a security station, but gave a high-five to the guard. Office furniture was delivered, including silk plants and trees and a couple of prints for the walls. There was a new computer on her desk and a laptop in her briefcase, and she'd been given a new cell phone and nameplate on the door. Bob Riddle told her to see Human Resources about getting a secretary for Flight Operations and to pick up any pilot applications that had been floating in with the mail.

If New Century was going to make a November start-up, they'd have to hire the first couple of pilot classes immediately. In addition, the training department, crew scheduling and dispatch would have to be staffed.

Shanna Norris, the head of Human Resources, looked like a Jewel James wannabe. Her hair was bleached and flouncy, and there was a slit up the thigh of her leather skirt. The heels on her shoes were uncomfortably high and her nails dangerously long. Plus, she was one cold fish. Nikki sincerely hoped this wasn't the kind of job where she'd be constantly dodging the nastiness of fancy women. All things told, she found them even less appetizing than chauvinistic men.

Upon request, Shanna handed over a folder containing the list and résumés of applicants for the job of department secretary who had passed the background checks and met the minimum requirements. ''There are more than thirty. It's my job to make sure they can work for this company and your job to make sure they can work for you. And Bob Riddle said you'd be asking for the pilot résumés that we've collected so far. Correct?''

''Yes. Thanks.'' Nikki scanned the names on the list.

''Come with me,'' Shanna said. She turned and walked ahead of Nikki down a corridor of cubicles in a manner she could only have copied from Jewel. When she finally stopped at one, she said, ''Help yourself.''

Nikki looked into the small room, but all she saw were several boxes. ''Where are they?'' she asked.

''Right there. Do you want me to have a desk moved in here, or would you like to take them to your office?''

''Wait a minute,'' Nikki said. ''Where are the pilot résumés?''

''Right *there*,'' she replied impatiently. ''Those boxes.''

Nikki experienced a moment of terrifying clarity. There were, after all, a couple of hundred thousand commercial airline employees out of work since 9/11, but New Century Air wasn't even certified to fly passengers yet!

''Have you any idea—''

''In the neighborhood of twelve thousand,'' Shanna said curtly. ''There's a dolly in the janitor's closet if you want to move them.''

''Holy God,'' Nikki breathed. For an instant she felt the individual agony of each person captured on paper in those boxes. Out-of-work pilots with families to feed. Unemployed in an industry that seemed to be shrinking because of terrorism, war and a weak economy. It was like having her life flash before her eyes, except in this case it was the lives of twelve thousand qualified pilots who needed jobs. And that was probably the tip of the iceberg.

"Shanna, when did these start coming in?"

"Joe had one box full by the time I was hired to build the human resources department. The minute word got out that there was funding for NCA, they started pouring in."

Nikki took the lid off one box and found it filled with stacked résumés. There were four huge boxes, all full, she assumed. She lifted the résumé on top and scanned it. "Amazing," she said. This guy was forty-five, so he had a good fifteen years of flying left before he would be forced to retire at age sixty by FAA regulation. He had more than ten thousand hours, four thousand of them captain time in a large wide-bodied jet. He had worked for three airlines, the first two big companies who had furloughed employees and the third a post-deregulation start-up that had been quite successful, then was forced out of business by the effects of 9/11. Married, he had two teenagers, both college age. She hoped his wife had a good job.

The next guy was fifty-five. He'd logged more than twenty thousand hours on the big jets, with plenty of international experience. He'd held positions as check airman, instructor, former assistant chief pilot and had not worked in three years. His company went under after the Air Transportation Stabilization Board turned them down for the loan guarantee promised by Congress after 9/11. This guy, so talented and experienced, must think he would never work again.

Ah, here was one, thirty years old, aeronautics degree from MIT, two thousand hours in cargo... She imagined him wanting to be a commercial pilot since he was a little kid, and now what were his chances? With all these pilots out of work, this guy was up against résumés with twenty thousand hours on them.

There were American pilots who had been flying in foreign countries and wanted to come home, retired military airmen, pilots who'd been out of work since 9/11, pilots who'd gone from airline to airline, moving on as each one crumbled. They had degrees, thousands of hours clocked, vast experience, high hopes and crushed dreams. There were strikers and those who had crossed picket lines, ex-patriots and retired military who had served the country faithfully through a war that followed the terrorist attacks. She kept looking for one man or woman she could say was less than desirable. *Available immediately,* the résumés said. *Will relocate anywhere.*

Travel and tourism was the largest industry in the world, and the industry was bankrupt.

The next résumé made her realize this box must be filled with recent submissions. It was from Danny Adams, Captain, Aries Airline. Nikki had known and respected Danny for years. He was a good, solid aviator, an ethical and honest man, intelligent, diligent, motivated. He was a little on the shy side, but that was preferable to the usual arrogance in the cockpit. One thing she could be certain of with Danny—if he accepted a job from her, she would have his unquestioned loyalty. As a woman in a man's job, she knew enough to start building her alliances. Like it or not, her gender was going to be outnumbered. And there was a male faction out there who would be just waiting for her to screw up.

She went back to Shanna's office and peeked in. The woman looked up from paperwork, unsmiling. This was going to get old, Nikki thought. All these ice maidens. "I ran across the résumé of a good friend. I'm going to give him a call and—"

''We have procedures,'' Shanna said, cutting her off. ''When you identify a candidate for hire, I'll make the call, set up an appointment for his interview, physical exam, psychological testing, et cetera.'' She was holding her hand out toward Nikki, her way of saying, *Hand the résumé over—I'm in charge here.* ''All hiring and firing is done through HR. We keep the employee files, you provide us with documentation. Understand?''

Nikki looked around, frowning. We? Us? As far as she could tell, Shanna had no staff.

''You know what?'' Nikki said. ''Forget this for now.'' Then she escaped before Shanna could attack her with a lot more rules and instructions. Nikki had stopped by as a courtesy; it had never occurred to her to ask Shanna's permission to hire someone she had known for years, someone who could actually use Nikki and Joe Riordan as references.

She made a fast break around the corner on her way to Joe's office, when she passed him in the hall. ''Hey, Joe—just the man I'm looking for. Do you remember Danny Adams? Captain at Aries?'' Joe frowned, thinking. ''Short guy—bald,'' she said, trying to jog his memory. ''He was a check airman...nicest man you'll ever meet. Good pilot, too.''

''Yeah, I think so. Why?''

''I ran across his résumé. I know him very well. He's smart and loyal and hardworking. I thought I'd get him up here to help me with hiring, if he'll come.''

''Good idea,'' Joe said, walking away.

''So you have no problem with that? You don't want me to have HR do it?''

He glanced over his shoulder. ''I don't care. HR is there to help you if you need them.''

''Yeah, thanks,'' Nikki said. Just as she thought. HR

is here to help us, we're not the HR support system. Then she smiled as she realized this was going to piss Shanna off.

Carrying Danny's résumé, she went back to her office, closed the door and called the phone number listed. "Danny? Hi, it's Nikki Burgess."

"Hey there! How are you?"

"Great, Danny. And you?"

"Never better, but what's that area code on my caller ID?"

"Las Vegas," she said.

He burst out laughing. "Then it's true? You left Aries for chief pilot of Riordan's new company?"

"Word travels fast," she observed. "It's called New Century Air, and one of my first official acts as chief pilot is placing this call. I came across your résumé, Danny, and I need some immediate help with hiring. Why don't you come up and look the place over?"

"I knew I wanted to get into Riordan's new company when I sent the résumé. And now that I know you're in charge, I'll just put in my notice and come up. How about two weeks?"

"Um, Danny, just so there's no misunderstanding, I'm not exactly in charge. I report to the vice president of operations, one Mr. Bob Riddle." She was answered by stunned silence. "Danny?"

"Bob Riddle?"

"He has a lot of management experience," she said. "An executive search company selected him as one of their prime recommendations to Joe."

Danny whistled. One thing Nikki knew about Danny was that he didn't seem to have the penchant for gossip and rumor that ran rampant through the cockpits of the world. In fact, she'd never heard him say a seriously negative thing about anyone. But after his whistle he said, "I'll see if I can cash in my accrued vacation and get up there right away, Nikki."

"I owe you."

Eight

While Nikki was getting into her second week at the new airline, Carlisle and Dixie were still trying to get out of Phoenix. Battery domestic violence, they both learned, was a crime taken very seriously by the police department. A report was filed, photos taken and an arrest made, something that couldn't have made Robert any happier with Carlisle.

The police might have just talked with Robert about the situation, but he made a tactical error—he admitted hitting Carlisle. But he said it had occurred in a physical fight in which both of them were involved. The problem with that version was that Robert was completely unscathed, and he had been the one to take Carlisle to the emergency room and insist that the injury had occurred when Carlisle fell down the stairs.

The emergency room staff should have made the call to the police, but they'd let the ball drop. "Bigotry," Dixie had snorted to the police. "If it had been a woman punched around by her husband, they'd have called."

"You're only making it worse," Carlisle said, mortified.

They were forced to stay at a hotel under assumed names for a couple of days while the business of this crime was settled. It would have been crazy to go back to Dixie's house; Robert was released on bond before twenty-four hours had lapsed. While an order of protection was procured through family court, Carlisle paid a visit to a friend of a friend, Mr. Ross Levine, an attorney who specialized in same-sex separations in which property was involved. Carlisle paid him a retainer to begin the process of negotiating with Robert about dividing their home equity.

"It may come to a civil suit," the attorney told Carlisle. "I'll know more in a couple of weeks, but this is going to take some time. You may as well go ahead and leave town—put some distance between you and your ex-partner. Let the lawyers handle this because there have been injuries involved."

Dixie and Carlisle talked about telling Nikki what was going on, but instead, they took her calls on their cell phones, getting updates while chuckling behind their hands. At long last they were on the road and a mere five hours later, Las Vegas spread before them.

It was about 7:00 p.m., so they drove directly to the suites inn where Nikki and the kids and Buck were staying.

"Look," Carlisle said, pointing to a gold SUV. "There she is."

Dixie squinted in the direction he indicated. "That's not her."

"It sure is," he insisted.

"That's not her hair."

"She said she had it cut and highlighted," he argued.

"But Nikki can't fix her hair, bless her heart, and that hair looks *good*."

"She said she got new clothes and new hair," Carlisle insisted. "She said we'd be proud of her."

"No way can we be *that* proud."

They followed the SUV, which turned into the suites

inn and parked. Dixie came to a halt across the lot. "We can find out pretty easily." She dialed her cell phone.

They watched as the woman in the gold SUV began to speak. "Hey, what timing," Nikki said. "I just finished work."

"That so? How's it going?"

"God, it's hard." A beat. "God, it's fun!"

"Really?"

Nikki got out of the car, cell phone earpiece dangling from her ear. She had a briefcase in one hand and laptop in the other, and in the crook of her arm she cradled a bag of groceries. "Wish you were here—I just bought a bottle of wine and some snacks."

Carlisle elbowed Dixie, whose mouth hung open. It was indeed a whole new Nikki, dressed in a beige pantsuit with black silk blouse and black pumps with gold accents. There was even a gold lapel pin on her jacket.

"Will you look at that," Carlisle muttered. "Nick's accessorizing. The world must be coming to an end." The early evening sun caught the highlights in her hair and she seemed to almost sparkle.

"It's hard work, Dix," Nikki continued. "Much more complicated than I anticipated, but with the help of consultants, we've somehow already managed to impress the FAA. I've got Danny on the way and we're going to get about the business of hiring. And—"

"What are you doin' now?" Dixie asked.

"Well, I'm going to read and edit some of the flight ops manuals before we give them to—"

No, I mean *now*. Right now."

Nikki bumped her car door closed with her butt. "I just pulled into the hotel. I'll get the kids and my dad and we'll grab a bite to eat, and, well, I'll probably get some work done later before I hit the sack...."

Across the parking lot, Dixie and Carlisle got out of their car. They started walking toward Nikki. "Think maybe we could tag along?"

"Huh?"

"I said…" Dixie clicked off the phone and raised her voice. "Think you could stand some company?"

Nikki turned and saw them walking toward her. "Oh, my God," she said. "You're here! You're both really here!" She struggled to hang on to all her possessions while she raced toward them. Laughing, they grabbed the groceries and laptop while giving her hugs. "What are you doing here?"

"Well, it's a couple of long stories," Dixie said. "But if it works out, we may be staying."

The kids were probably even more excited to see Dixie and Carlisle than Nikki had been. And gruff old Buck almost cracked his face smiling. The two of them booked a room just around the corner from Nikki and the kids, with Buck and Pistol in between. Buck's weekend had turned into a week, and even he didn't know how long he'd hang around.

There were still a couple of weeks until school started, and Nikki hadn't had much time to look for a house. Dixie and Carlisle could help Buck and the kids explore more of the suburbs and maybe preview a few houses for Nikki to look at in the evening or on the weekend.

Carlisle had some time off—medical leave to recover from his "fall." He had no intention of changing jobs, but then it wouldn't be hard for him to commute the forty-five minutes to Phoenix once a week. There were more than a dozen flights a day between the two cities.

As for Dixie, she wanted to take a look at the local job market and investigate housing for herself. And she would check out the university and see what she needed to finish her degree and teach school, which had begun to crystallize as her ultimate goal.

The next day when Nikki went to work, she found her desk buried under enough paper to sink a battleship.

"FAA manual requirements, drafts of manuals, positions that have to be filled in flight operations and aircraft-leasing agreements," Bob Riddle explained. "And we'd better start contacting potential pilots for the first class. You're going to need a director of training who can complete the manual that the consulting firm made a good start on, then set up classes and book simulator time. Get interviews rolling, and then get your own résumé over to the general counsel for his application to the Department of Transportation for a certificate of public conveyance."

"Convenience," she corrected him.

"Conveyance," he argued. "We don't convenience people, we *convey* them."

"Bob, I know it only makes sense that it would be conveyance, but it's actually convenience."

"Bullshit, Burgess. You better study up. And by the way, we're behind schedule."

"Well, Bob, I just got here," she said patiently. And she wasn't fooled by his effort to bury her in work she had never done before. She had heard him say he had someone else in mind for her job, but there was this one little thing he didn't know about her—she had grown up at an airport. She had already forgotten more about FAA certification than Bob Riddle had ever learned.

"Then get going," he said. "And I'd like to sit in on the pilot interviews when they start. Make sure you hire as many boys as girls."

"I wouldn't have it any other way," she said, sifting

through the paper on her desk and making piles. Fortunately, there wasn't anything there she didn't recognize or understand.

Riddle was standing in her doorway, watching. She looked up and saw confusion in his expression. Ah! All this was on her desk because *he* didn't know what to do with it! "Anything else?"

He cleared his throat. "Hmm. I'll check with you later to see if you have any questions."

"What will you be working on, if you don't mind my asking?"

"I do mind," he snapped back. "But I'll indulge you this once. I'm concentrating on the operations budget and pilot work rules."

She might have asked why he would spend time on that before they actually had pilots, but he turned and left.

Nikki called Danny Adams immediately, filling him in and asking when he'd be arriving in Las Vegas. At the end of the call he recommended another man. "His name is Eric Nowlin and we're old friends. He flew at American until he was laid off. He's had a lot of experience and would be a big help in hiring."

"What can he bring to the party?" she asked.

"For starters, he developed a hiring program that gives composite points to job candidates for each quality from experience to personality to reputation. It's complex yet simple."

"Really? When did he do this?"

"Years ago, when he flew for a corporate outfit, it was real important that the pilots be able to mingle with the executives, guests and investors they flew around."

"Call him," she said.

"I already did and he's faxing you his résumé. And I should be there in a couple of days, ready to work."

This was the way companies developed personalities—by combining word-of-mouth hiring with the leader's philosophy. Riordan's motto was "We're all in this together and we're going to do right by one another."

In an hour, Nikki had made sense of the stacks of paper on her desk. She'd only begun, and already had two key people on their way to town.

Next she focused on the manuals that the FAA would have to approve for flight operations, leaving the tons of résumés until she could get Danny and Eric on board to help. But that alone made for long days. She felt the pressure to have an assistant or secretary, but no time to hire one.

In the evening, her family and friends would gather, first in her room at the suites, then at one of the dozens of great little neighborhood restaurants in the suburbs, where they'd all compare notes. Nikki would fill them in on the progress at the company, and the others would fill her in on what they'd found by way of houses. It was as much an adventure for Dixie and Carlisle as for Nikki and her family, because, although they'd been to Las Vegas many times, usually on trip layovers while flying, they'd never been off the Strip.

Nikki's hours were long, but nervous energy kept her going. She got up before five so she could put in a full day and be home early enough to spend some time with the kids while everyone was still awake. Many nights she'd go back to the office for a couple of hours in the evening.

Riddle, on the other hand, didn't get in until 9:00 a.m. or later, and the light under his door was always out if

Nikki returned in the evening. On the weekends he always went home to Phoenix. Typically, Riordan's light was always on, and Nikki had begun to wonder if he slept there.

Danny and Eric arrived midweek and Nikki sent their completed applications to Shanna via company mail, with a request to have their employment date start the day they arrived. She attached a note promising they would drop by HR to get their IDs and make appointments for physicals as soon as possible.

Nikki and the two pilots were barely engaged in a meeting with Bob Riddle when Shanna opened the door without knocking and simply stood there. Gripped in her trembling hand was the interoffice mailer, and her glossy red lips were pursed in anger.

"Was there something about my instructions you didn't understand, Miss Burgess?" she barked. She shook the envelope. "We have very specific procedures when hiring people. Do I have to write them down for you?"

There was lipstick on her teeth. Nikki had to bite her lower lip to keep from laughing out loud. Though Shanna was very young, there was a frightening look about her. As if she could, with the tip of her pencil, change the entire hierarchy of the firm.

Nikki was feeling pressured, and a bit impatient. There was an obvious power struggle going on, and if a line had to be drawn in the sand, it was best not to put it off.

"Will you gentlemen excuse us?" Nikki asked with dangerous calm. The men fled the room, and it was not lost on Nikki how grateful they appeared. Big tough guys. They didn't want to mix it up with the HR goddess.

"Miss Norris?" Nikki invited, indicating a chair.

"I'm not sitting down, I'm just going to get this straight with you before it happens again. I gave you very—"

"Get in here and shut the door," Nikki commanded firmly but quietly. "We're not going to air this discussion for the whole building. I, too, would like to get this straight." When Shanna seemed to be frozen in place, Nikki stood up and braced her palms on the conference table. "Now."

Shanna entered, but she slammed the door. Nikki held her with an icy glare until she sat down, then took a seat herself.

"Let's talk about this calmly and respectfully," Nikki said. "It's already been a very long day."

"You— You—" Shanna sputtered. "Look, I told you exactly what the procedure is and you deliberately went around me to—"

"To hire two very capable men whom I need urgently. I called them, I told them to come on down. I personally checked their licenses and absence of violations with the FAA. Their medicals are current. All they need to do for you is get an ID badge and pee in a bottle. Now, what the hell is the problem?"

Shanna slammed the folder down on the conference table. "This isn't the way we do things!"

"Listen to me. The two men I've hired were approved by the president and CEO and we need them now—our deadline for certification with the FAA is fast approaching. All your squares will be filled eventually, but I can't afford to waste time by putting them through your paces first. I have no quarrel with your procedures, but in this case you can afford to be a little flexible with the schedule."

"You could have contacted me and requested—"

The word *requested* teed her off. "I don't have time to screw around," she said sharply. "I was given to understand that HR was here to support me in my hiring efforts, not that I was here to support HR's hiring procedures. And I most sincerely thank you for your help."

"And who exactly *gave* you to understand that?" she asked, her voice dripping sarcasm.

"Daddy," she said. Shanna looked at her stupidly. "Your boss. Joe Riordan."

"You're pulling rank!"

"I wanted to be sure I have the authority to hire the people I want, as long as they're not felons or terrorists, and Joe has assured me that I do. Now, as for your display, miss, if you ever throw a tantrum like that in front of other employees again, I will have your ass. Understand?"

"My— My— Huh!"

Nikki almost confided that she had a fourteen-year-old daughter and knew very well how to handle these little hissy fits, but she kept that to herself.

Shanna gathered her papers and stood.

"You'll see the newly hired gentlemen as soon as possible to complete their hiring requirements," Nikki told her. "And it's not *Miss* Burgess. It's *Captain* Burgess."

Without saying a word, Shanna whirled around, her back to Nikki.

"And you have lipstick on your teeth," Nikki said.

Shanna threw a glare over her shoulder and Nikki held her breath. If the younger woman slammed the door again, Nikki would be honor bound to chase her down and reprimand her. Shanna was ambitious and greedy for power, and that could make life horrible around here. Nikki knew she could not allow Shanna to overrule her.

But she simply left the door ajar.

Nikki glanced down at the notebook in front of her. The men must have gone in search of coffee. Within seconds, though, Danny peeked in the room. "Come in, come in—we can continue. Danny, you and Eric have to be diligent about getting that stuff done in HR. We don't want Shanna to feel she has to troop down here in search of it again."

"Oh, I don't think she'll be back," he said. "At least, not without reinforcements."

As the day was winding down, Nikki was called by the Gatekeeper. "Joe would like to see you before you leave for the day."

Nikki had already been to his office at least five times that day, but what was once more? She filled her briefcase and swung by the boss's house, where she was told to go on in.

Sleeves rolled up, glasses perched on the end of his nose, he glanced up from the papers spread out all over the desk. "You tell Shanna Norris you'd have her ass?"

Well, that was fast, she thought. "Big tattletale."

"How'd she take it?"

"Obviously it pissed her off."

"There's got to be a better way to resolve your differences."

Nikki shrugged, very annoyed to be taken to task over this when Shanna had clearly overstepped. "I could've decked her, I guess. But she looks like a hair-puller."

He slapped down his pen. "She's talking about filing a complaint against you. For harassment."

"Look, Joe, I—"

"She was in here for more than forty-five minutes ranting about her *procedures*. About your abusive tone."

"Oh, brother. If anyone has *tone*… Well, that's total bullshit. She burst into my conference room during a meeting, without knocking, and *berated* me for not following her hiring procedures. In front of a superior and two men who work for me. She was shouting at me. I couldn't let her get away with it. I can't have some twenty-five-year-old girl busting my chops in front of male pilots who wonder if I have the balls to run Flight Ops."

"More than forty-five minutes," he said again. *"Ranting."*

"Well, now it's starting to sound like a personal problem," she said. His expression did not soften; he did not find her amusing. "I'm sure that was very taxing."

"I hope that whatever you were trying to do by putting her in her place worked, because I don't want her in here ranting again. You do understand that, don't you?"

"Of course." But she was dying of curiosity. Couldn't Jewel have ejected her?

"And because, really, you can't have her ass."

"Well…" she said, on the verge of arguing that point.

"But I can have yours."

He wasn't really mad at her, Nikki knew. Because as the days passed and certification drew near, she could see he was increasingly relying on her. The more Bob Riddle talked about his "profencity" for getting things done and how "indinuated" he was with job applications, the more Joe worried that the VP choice had been the wrong one—she could see it in his eyes. This starting an airline was no cakewalk. But Joe also needed to assert that he was the Grand Poobah in this place, and Nikki could appreciate that.

This brought her other problems into specific relief. She needed a gatekeeper of her own. Someone with class and finesse and authority and experience. Someone who could head off the Shannas of the work world and act as her sentry, who wouldn't be intimidated by the onslaught of pilot applicants. Someone whose loyalty was unquestionable.

And someone to answer the phone. All day long her phone rang. The word was out that she was hiring, and those who didn't phone dropped in to visit. Though she didn't have the time, she tried to say hello, shake a hand whenever possible. She could understand the panic to make contact, to get an edge on the job.

And these applicants worked hard to stand out among the crowd. One candidate sent in a shoe, his résumé tucked inside with a note that read, "Now that I have my foot in the door…" Another put his résumé on a sheet cake, still another sent a shirt with a note saying, "I'll give you the shirt off my back for a job."

An old and time-honored method of getting in to see the chief pilot was to send the chief pilot's secretary gifts—flowers, candy, et cetera. Well, Nikki didn't have a secretary and she was a woman, so…these things started coming to *her*. The outer office was beginning to look like a funeral parlor. At least these guys were smart enough, almost to the last one, to have congratulatory and good-luck notes attached rather than pleas for an interview. Because really, flowers and candy were not making a favorable impression on a female chief pilot who wanted to be considered one of the guys, professionally speaking.

"I'm starting to get sick from the sticky-sweet smell in here, Burgess," Bob Riddle said.

"I can't get rid of them fast enough.... And I feel so guilty, throwing them away."

"Are you keeping track of who sent them?"

"No. Believe me, it's better for them if I don't."

At the end of the day she went home to the suites inn. She let herself in to the efficiency and found Carlisle helping Jared with a jigsaw puzzle on the coffee table, while Dixie and April chopped vegetables for a salad. She had noticed that, with the added attention the kids were getting from Dixie and Carlisle, they were doing so well. Even living on top of one another in the hotel as they were, and nervously anticipating starting brand-new schools, they seemed to be in high spirits.

Everyone looked up with contented smiles, said hello, then went back to their work. The picture of domestic tranquillity, she thought. What lovely families people created for themselves when the ones they came with weren't available. Or amenable.

And then it struck her. "Dixie, can you type?"

Dixie had never seen herself in the role of secretary or administrative assistant. It had always looked to her as if those drudges were tied to their desks and phones and boss's whimsies, without having the luxury of leaving the ground. As for problems in the workplace—hers had always deplaned at the end of the line.

But she would do anything for Nikki, and just hearing what her best friend was up against in the office, without a front man, as it were, was enough to cause Dixie to spring into action. And this was a plan that could serve her. She could take this full-time position long enough to qualify for a mortgage on a cozy suburban bungalow,

give Nikki the help she needed, and then find a way to
turn full-time into part-time so she could go back to
school. Perhaps by spring she'd be ready to start taking
classes.

She doubted her instincts about people, however. Especially since the wine bottle episode.

"Don't be ridiculous," Nikki had admonished. "In
love you might be blind, but in all other things you have
uncanny insight. Besides, where I really need your people instincts is with the women in the office. There's at
least one who's out to get me."

So Dixie said she'd do it.

Her first order of business was a call to her supervisor
at Aries and her real estate agent in Phoenix. The town
house was put on the market, but she did not turn in a
resignation to her old boss. Rather, she asked for an
unpaid leave of absence. With the huge number of lay-
offs industrywide, the Aries management welcomed the
offer. In fact, while it was usually the policy not to let
an employee have a leave to work for another airline,
especially a competing airline, these were hard times and
there were no questions asked. Dixie's leave might mean
someone else being called back.

Next, after fifteen years in a uniform, she had to outfit
herself for the job. This was not as hard for Dixie as it
had been for Nikki; Dixie loved clothes and had some
very nice ones. She pinned Nikki down and quizzed her
about both Jewel and the Jewel-wannabes' work ward-
robes. There was a very essential protocol here if Dixie
was to win them over—she would have to be up to their
standards but not a smidgen over.

Dressing was something she could really get into, and
the shopping in Las Vegas was *good.* She decided she'd

also book in for a manicure, pedicure and touch-up on the hair.

She made an appointment to see the lioness of HR, Ms. Shanna Norris. That in itself took some doing; Shanna was *very* busy, her *staff* was new. Nikki had confided that she hadn't seen any staff around there yet.

"My stars, it sounds like you're the one who could use an administrative assistant," Dixie cajoled.

It took a few days to get in to see Shanna, and Nikki was already in her third week at the airline and positively deluged with work. Dixie dressed carefully for her debut, hoping to be given the blessing immediately. She entered the HR domain, résumé and application in hand, and scoped out the target.

Ms. Norris sat at her neat desk in her mauve skirt and patterned sweater, her bottle-blond hair teased for fullness and falling to her shoulders. Her long nails were color-coordinated with her outfit, and a peek under the desk revealed her legs crossed at the ankles. On her feet she wore a pair of mauve-and-gold pumps. Nikki had described her pretty accurately.

But what Nikki would never realize and Dixie knew at once was that the skirt and sweater were both Jones of New York knockoffs, probably purchased at a discount outlet, and the shoes were absolutely The Shoe Factory. The bottle job was strictly over the counter, as were the makeup, lip gloss and manicure.

Dixie wore beige. She had had some lowlights mixed with the highlights in her blond hair and had pulled it back into a conservative clip, but it was still quite full. Her nails were done in a short French manicure, understated, and beneath her beige jacket she wore a black crepe blouse with a high collar. But *her* suit was Donna

Karan, her shoes Anne Klein, her make-up Bobbi Brown.

"Knock-knock," she said. Shanna looked up. "You must be Ms. Norris. I'm Dixie McPherson. Am I early?"

Shanna pursed her lips, looked her up and down very critically, then said, "Have a seat right there. Give me a few minutes to finish up."

"Sure. You take your time." Dixie sat at one of the three chairs that lined the wall just inside Shanna's office. There were two larger, more comfortable chairs right in front of the desk, but she was not invited to upgrade yet.

Then Dixie watched the woman. Her movements were precise but very slow. The wait was deliberate. Shanna moved her pen over a piece of paper, picked it up and took it to a file cabinet, then repeated the process with a second piece of paper, and a third. Anyone else would have courteously left these simple tasks until after the appointment. Dixie would not look at her watch and betray impatience, even though Shanna kept her waiting until twenty minutes past her appointment time. Just so Dixie knew who was in charge.

Dixie used the time to survey the room. Most of New Century Air was still in disarray, but not Shanna's office. There were a couple of prints on the wall—tense and rigid like her—and silk plants. No photos on her desk, though. Shanna looked to be about twenty-five—a woman alone, Dixie thought. She'd better loosen up and start being nice to people or there would never be pictures on her desk, Dixie predicted.

"Miss McPherson?" Shanna said. "Have a seat?"

Dixie moved forward, handing Shanna the folder containing her completed application and résumé.

"Oh!" she said, nonplussed. "You've already filled this out?"

"Yes. I thought that would make things easier."

"But how did you...?"

Dixie waited a beat. "Captain Burgess gave it to me, of course."

Shanna's mouth formed an unpleasant line. "Captain Burgess," she said derisively, and began looking over the paperwork.

"You sure have a nice office," Dixie said. "And wonderful art." She highly doubted Shanna referred to her prints as art. Or even prints. "You're all settled in. You must have come here with the first wave. The *founders*." Shanna looked up, sort of. She lifted her eyes slightly. "It must be real exciting to start an airline with Joe."

Now Dixie had her attention. "You know Mr. Riordan?"

"Yes, but I've known Captain Burgess much longer. She's the one who recruited me." Shanna's expression took on that closed look; she'd been had again. "I suppose there's lots of in-processing to do. I'm really anxious to get it taken care of so I can get to work. Captain Burgess told me she promised Joe that I would go through all the proper channels with HR before reporting to work, so—"

Shanna sat at attention, head cocked. She might as well have shouted, *Hallelujah! I've been heard! My orders are being followed!* She smiled and, oh God, there was lipstick on her teeth.

"I hope you don't consider this too forward," Dixie said, "but I was wondering, is that a Jones? The sweater? It looks absolutely *made* for you."

"Why...yes," Shanna told her.

It is not, you big liar, Dixie thought. But she smiled. "I knew it. I can spot Jones New York anywhere." She shook her head appreciatively. "You certainly have excellent taste. Joe must pay you well."

"Not yet," she said amicably. "But one day I'm sure he will."

Ah, foolish, foolish girl, Dixie thought. You've let your cat out of its bag. You're building an empire from the bottom up with a brand-new company. No wonder it's so important that people follow the rules!

"Well, you'll earn your keep in Human Resources. Humans can be a real handful."

"Tell me about it," sighed the grande dame of HR.

In-processing went a lot faster after the director was paid a few compliments, Dixie thought smugly. After a long but very fruitful afternoon, long enough that Nikki had already left the office, Dixie returned to the inn with her insurance card and ID for New Century Air. "Mission accomplished," she reported to Nikki. "I have delivered the enemy into your hands."

"You're awesome."

"She's a piece of work," Dixie said. "If she was half nice, I'd take her shopping. Show her where the real knockoffs are."

"Knockoffs?" Nikki asked.

Dixie and April exchanged glances. They both made silent oaths to never let Nikki out of the house before making sure she looked good.

Dixie had never thought she wanted to be tied to a desk, but there was something about this situation that excited her. First of all, she was in on the ground floor, and not as a flight attendant this time. As a flight attendant, her opportunities for promotion tended to be limited to managing other flight attendants, but as an executive assistant she could be promoted into other areas of airline management. Look at Shanna Norris! If she had started as the director of HR at Aries at age twenty-five, when there were only forty employees, she could possibly have risen to VP of HR in a twelve-thousand-employee company sixteen years later.

Being in the right place at the right time was crucial, and if you could perform…

Another weekend arrived. Saturday was spent shopping and looking at houses, activities from which Jared and Buck were happy to abstain. Since Dixie would start a new life on Monday, she went to the local nursery Sunday afternoon and bought herself a very attractive potted plant. After that, she stopped at the mall and picked up a couple of frames that complemented the planter. She would use them for pictures of her nieces and nephews. Then she went to the office. Even though it was Sunday, the parking lot was half-full and the office was astir with people trying to catch up on their work.

She used her ID to get into the building and went to Flight Ops. The hallway was quiet and darkened, but strips of light shone beneath the bottom of closed office doors. The hum of a vacuum cleaner sounded somewhere in the building, and a smoke detector running low on batteries was beeping. When she came around the corner to her office space, someone was leaning over her desk.

"I beg your pardon," she said, already territorial.

Danny Adams straightened in surprise and turned to her. "Dixie! I never expected to see you here today."

"I didn't expect you, either," she said warily.

"I'm going through résumés in the conference room. I…ah…had something for your…ah…desk," he said. Stepping aside, he revealed a black nameplate with gold letters with silver trim, the New Century colors. *Dixie McPherson.*

Her mouth dropped open in surprise.

"I know you go by Dixie," he said. "I wasn't sure if you'd prefer that or your given name. I can get it changed if—"

"Danny," she said, touched. "That might be one of the nicest things anyone's ever done for me."

He stepped back while she came toward him with her plant and frames. Hands in his pockets, he said, "I wanted to do something to welcome you aboard. It's great you're going to run this office."

"Oh, I'm just going to help out," she said, lifting the plaque and looking at it with admiration.

"No, you're going to run it. The chief pilot's assistant is a person with a lot of power. You'll see. And the way you handle people, Nikki couldn't possibly have made a better choice."

Suddenly Dixie felt large. Strong. Capable. Yes, she would be running this office. And maybe she wasn't the most brilliant person in the world, but she was brilliant with people.

"Thank you, Danny. That's very nice of you to say." Then she took her eyes off the plaque and looked at Danny, which made him blush uncomfortably. "Was there going to be a note with this?" she asked him.

He shrugged. "I was just going to leave it."

"And not even tell me?"

He took another step back. "A lot of the guys… There are going to be guys who want jobs, and think the way to the chief pilot is through you. And then there are going to be pilots who work here who want better jobs...like check airman...because they make more money that way. And they're going to... You know..."

"Suck up?" she asked, smiling.

He nodded and seemed to relax a little because she understood, but his hands stayed in his pockets.

"Well," she said, puffing up a little. "Finally."

"Finally?"

"It's high time this little old Texas gal had some leverage." She laughed. "But the only thing I care about is that Nikki is a total success in this."

That actually made Danny grin, and Dixie remembered that when he smiled, he looked kind of handsome. Good teeth. And his eyes, though a little small, fired up with happiness.

"But you should have left a note."

"I didn't want you to think I wanted anything."

"Not *anything*, Danny? Didn't you even want to be friends?"

"We're already friends. And it'll be good to work with you."

"And with you," she said, meaning it from the heart.

Nine

Dixie stood guard outside Nikki's office and sorted through the gifts from the pilot applicants. She circulated the flowers, candy, stationery, fruit baskets and, her personal favorite and most dangerous to her figure, chocolate-covered strawberries. She made sure that the best of the lot went to Shanna.

Settling in proved more challenging than she'd thought, but it was largely due to the fact that she absorbed all the interruptions formerly directed at the chief pilot. Additionally, she began to work on a job description for her position that went beyond answering the phone and taking delivery of flowers and candy.

Dixie wasn't the only new face at NCA. The population grew daily. A director of flight control appeared, along with a director of maintenance. The Web site was up, as was Reservations. Shanna had a couple of clerks shuffling paper for her and held a job fair at one of the hotels on the Strip. Interestingly, and almost predictably, the two young women she hired were both unattractive. One was well over two hundred pounds and the other, though painfully thin, was very homely. It was as though the goddess of HR feared competition.

The director of in-flight was interviewing potential flight attendants; marketing and sales expanded their work force; and a pass bureau was set up to begin negotiating interline travel agreements with other airlines for the employees and their families. That was just a fancy way of saying companies would trade low-cost stand-by travel.

Bob Riddle's office became more ornate by the day as he added pictures, models and other airline bric-a-brac given to him by airplane and engine manufacturers, and leasing companies and aviation vendors of all kinds. In fact, Bob's office had more aviation gear than Riordan's.

And Bob hired himself an administrative assistant. Ms. Crue Delue Boxley, six foot two, hard as a rock, with legs that went on forever. Her skin was the color of lightly creamed coffee, and long skinny braids wound around her head in turban fashion.

Crue was met with openmouthed stares, and not just because of her beauty, stature and imposing figure. Crue was gorgeous, no doubt about that, but no one had expected Bob to hire a black woman a half foot taller than himself. He seemed to prefer petite young blondes, like the ones he'd flirted with at Aries. But he had hired Crue, so like Jewel in height, looks and cool demeanor that his motivation seemed obvious—he was aping his boss's taste. And while Bob seemed to gloat over his new hire, Crue did not appear to be at all happy in her new position.

But Dixie, in that friendly down-Texas way, went straight to her. "Welcome aboard," she said, extending her hand.

Crue touched the tips of Dixie's fingers. "Thank you."

"I'm Dixie McPherson. I work for Nikki Burgess, the chief pilot."

Crue nodded.

"If you need anything," Dixie said. "Anything at all...just give a holler."

Crue looked her over, and Dixie didn't miss her obvious disdain. "Haven't you been here just a week?" she asked, her diction precise, haughty.

"Yes," Dixie said brightly. "But I know all the right people." She turned on her heel and walked away, headed straight for Nikki's office.

Dixie walked in and closed the door, then waited for Nikki to complete a telephone conversation. "Is it a requirement that all secretaries in this company be cold, mean and just superior enough to make you hate them?"

"It would seem that way."

"It's maddening, isn't it?"

"If there were time, it would be maddening. Here, you can start calling this list of pilot applicants and begin scheduling interviews."

This was probably the most rewarding part of Dixie's job—notifying these applicants of their interviews. In the good old days, every second phone call would find the applicant already employed elsewhere, but those days were over. Now every call she made was answered with an enthusiastic response and promise to get to Las Vegas right away. New Century Air provided travel vouchers, but the candidates were on their own for hotel accommodations.

Back at the ranch—or suites inn, as it were—Carlisle had returned to town after a three-day trip to find his favorite young people morose and twitchy. They'd been in the hotel for three weeks and were beginning to climb the walls. Nikki was too busy to house-hunt and now Dixie was working, too. Buck had taken a week off to entertain the kids and take care of chores such as school physicals and registration, but he'd gone back to Phoenix, leaving them to their own devices.

They played video games, rented pay-per-view movies, walked to the mall and called their mother seventy times a day.

"You people need a house," he said to April and Jared.

"No kidding?" April replied. "You noticed?"

"So, the holdup here is the time thing?" Carlisle asked.

"Yeah, Mom doesn't have much time to go out looking," April told him. "Plus, she said something about the house in Phoenix...."

If Nikki was waiting to find time to house-hunt these two were going to be in a hotel until Christmas. It was seriously affecting their enthusiasm for the move and the new airline.

Carlisle still didn't have a car in Las Vegas, so Dixie had taken to riding with Nikki to work so he could use her vehicle when he was in town. That way he could get himself and the kids around when he had days off in Vegas.

Over the next few days, the women were so overwhelmed by the demands of work that they didn't even ask about how Carlisle and the kids spent their time. They also didn't seem to notice how much improved the kids' moods were since Carlisle returned.

On Friday at noon, April called her mother. "I need you to see something, and it's lunchtime, so can you meet us somewhere?"

"Who? Where? And most important, why?"

"Me, Jared and Carlisle. At 3416 Paradise Court. Because we've found a house. Now, write down these directions. *Please.*"

When April took that tone, Nikki did as she was told. But once she hung up the phone, she just sat. And thought.

Nikki had grown up in an unpretentious rambler with a desert yard that was conveniently close to Burgess Aviation. After her mother left, there were few new decorator touches. Buck didn't care about such things and Nikki was just a kid, but both of them took an engine change on a Lear very seriously. The house Buck occupied now, which he had so generously shared with Nikki and the kids, was similar, though now he at least employed a cleaning lady twice a month. And Nikki had had nothing whatever to do with selecting and decorating the house that had become Drake's. She didn't have an affinity for these things. It was just not her department. And perhaps that was the real reason she'd put off house-hunting in earnest. It was easier to be the chief pilot than find the right place for her and the kids.

"Come on," she said to Dixie. "You have to come with me. Carlisle and the kids have found a house."

They drove for twelve minutes. Each day Nikki was growing more appreciative that Las Vegas was actually small. The city was surrounded by planned communities made up of planned neighborhoods. Following April's directions, they passed a couple of very large parks, a dog park and shopping center with restaurants and movie theaters, before arriving at a gated neighborhood. Nikki keyed in the numbers April had given her. They drove around the circle past lovely two-story homes with manicured lawns.

They knew the place by the car parked in front; it was Dixie's. The walk that led to the house wound up a small hill, so that the house itself sat above the street by a good ten feet. A gate stood open, leading into an outdoor courtyard that took Nikki's breath away. To the right of the courtyard was a two-car garage, and to the left, a single-car garage detached from the house. In the center of the courtyard stood a lovely water fountain surrounded by ferns and flowers. Nikki kept an emotional grip on her heart because she had already fallen in love.

The door was answered by the real estate agent, who introduced herself as June. They stepped into a marble-floored foyer that opened to a sunken living room on the left and staircase on the right. The house was spacious and empty of furniture. The walls that were not papered had been freshly painted, and the light beige carpets had the tracks of recent shampooing.

"As I told your decorator and nanny, the sale of this house fell through at the last minute. There's another interested buyer, and he and his wife are thinking it over this afternoon. I did warn him that I'd be showing the property—"

Nikki and Dixie were exchanging curious glances. Nikki looked back at June. "And where *is* the decorator and nanny?" she asked.

"I left him and the children to explore the walking path that runs behind the house and joins two parks. The middle school is within walking distance, but I'm afraid the high school is more than two miles. There's a bus. If you'll come this way, I'll show you the downstairs first...."

In the front of the house was a formal living room and dining room, and in the back the family room, kitchen and nook. The two-car garage could be entered by way of a short hall that divided a spacious laundry room from a powder room. And on the other side of the family room was a rather large bedroom with full bath.

But it was the backyard that must have won over the

kids, Nikki suspected. It wasn't large, but it was beautiful. The perimeter was richly landscaped with palms, shrubs, roses and ferns and a medium-size pool and spa dominated one side, while a built-in brick barbecue and patio sat to the right of the back door. There was room enough for chaise longues, a good-size table and outdoor furniture.

Buck may not have put much fuss into his house, but he'd been very particular about his yard and barbecue. Nikki had spent a great deal of time outside—taking her morning coffee and newspaper there, a book in the afternoon, that 5:00 p.m. glass of wine.

"The impact of this during the day may not be powerful, but at night it's breathtaking," June said. The house behind was built a story and a half lower, so that if you looked over the wall you would see down into the neighbor's backyard. But if you looked straight ahead, between the palms and over the rooftops, there was a panorama of beautiful Las Vegas. "You have absolutely no idea what this view is worth. Lots with a view in Seven Hills and Anthem cost more than this entire property. This house is incredibly underpriced."

Upstairs was a large master and three more bedrooms, a master bath and two full baths. There would be absolutely no squabbling over bathroom time. Nikki had been counting. One, two, three, *four* bathrooms? "And a powder room between the living room and family room," June supplied. "And of course there's another in the casita in front of the courtyard."

"Casita?" Nikki asked.

"The previous owners turned the free-standing garage into a guest house with bar-size refrigerator, microwave and bath with shower."

"Oh, my gosh," Nikki nearly gasped. "Really?"

"We'll look at it on our way out."

The house was only six years old and had been well maintained. There were walk-in closets, ceiling fans, plantation shutters, built-in bookcases and shelves. Fireplaces were in the family room and master bedroom, and there was a fire pit in the outdoor patio.

The casita was adorable—just enough room for a bedroom suite and perhaps a couple of chairs and ottomans.

By the time Nikki and June were standing in the courtyard again, Carlisle and the kids were back. Carlisle managed to rein in his enthusiasm, but there was no calming the kids. They were going on and on about the yard, the pool, the barbecue, the parks, the bike paths, and of course both of them had their eye on the casita. April would no doubt turn it into a place to entertain future boyfriends—*not!* While Jared would make it into a fort—over someone's dead body!

Nikki didn't have furniture, nor did she want to inherit any from Drake's house, and this place was going to need tons. There wasn't much in savings besides her 401K, and if she did scrounge enough together for a down payment, that money might already be committed to get out of the overmortgaged house that Drake left behind. This "incredibly underpriced" house carried a nice big sticker price with a very healthy monthly payment. She was sure it was out of her reach.

But it was perfect, and she loved it.

She pulled her checkbook out of her purse. "Tell that other buyer that he waited just a bit too long to make up his mind." She put a few zeros behind a number and handed June the check. "Will this hold it while we do the paperwork?"

"I think I can make this work for you, Mrs. Burgess."

The kids were jumping up and down, thrilled both by

the house itself and the fact that they could soon be out of the suites inn. Carlisle slipped an arm around Dixie's shoulders and sucked in a big breath, as though he'd just successfully performed cardiac resuscitation.

They all stood in the street, looking up at the beautiful house for a long time. April said, "Thank you, Mama, thank you," about a hundred times. Jared kept running up and down the driveway. "I can't believe it" was all Dixie could say. "I just can't believe it." And then to Carlisle she added, "You can get started on my house next week. It'll have to be a little smaller." Nikki said nothing. She was in shock. She wondered if the kids realized they'd be sleeping on the floor for about five years.

The alarm went off at 5:00 a.m. on Monday morning as usual and Nikki was up like a shot. She wondered how long it would feel like this—the energy. After working most of the weekend, she should be exhausted. But there it was—the sense of urgency to get to it. And today especially so. This was the day she began to assemble her primary team. Her first class of pilots.

Of all the different jobs she'd held in the airline business, she'd never participated in hiring. She'd done work in training and standards, in engineering and flight control; she'd been on scheduling and compensation and work-rules committees, but never hiring. And now the pilots she chose would be the first in this new airline...all captains...the leaders of this work force.

She sat on the edge of the bed, April still gently snoring in the bed across from her. She resisted the urge to reach out and gently brush her pretty brow.

She was counting the days until they could get into the new house; they were climbing all over one another in this little suite. It was impossible to keep the place neat, and Nikki had never been all that good at house-work under any circumstances. She could change the points and plugs on the Stearman with her eyes shut, but she'd never quite figured out how to fold sheets so they didn't look like they'd been rolled up in a ball.

After showering quickly, she stood in front of the mir-ror, smiling. She was getting pretty good with the blow dryer and curling iron, and even with her makeup. Ha! Who'd have thought?

When she went back to the bedroom, April was sitting up, holding a cup of coffee toward her. "Well," Nikki said, "what a nice surprise."

"I made it from the hotel pot instead of the one you brought," she said. "I can't screw up with those little packets."

"Delicious," she said, taking a sip.

"Your hair looks good—aren't you glad I made you do that?" her daughter asked.

"Absolutely. Without you I'd be a hag," she joked. "And I have to compete with the office dishes."

"Mom? How did you feel when Grandma left you and Papa?"

Nikki was brought up short. She stealthily glanced at the clock, hoping April wouldn't notice. Why was it her kids never had major life problems at a reasonable time of day? They either waited until after ten at night when she was nodding off, desperate for sleep, or caught her as she was walking out the door, already late.

"Honey, we've talked about that."

"I know. Just tell me."

Patience. Kids come first. Besides, she thought, sitting a little taller in her robe, they *will* wait for the chief pilot.

"Okay, here's the deal. Opal was not cut out to be

married to a guy like Papa. I might not have realized that until later, when I was much older, but even when I was nine I knew on some level that she wasn't happy. You know Papa—he's kind of gruff, not very fancy, and God knows he'd never think of taking her out for a nice meal. He wanted to fly, work on planes. Opal didn't even like taking a commercial flight. She still doesn't.

"And Opal is very fancy, very chi-chi. She's also very high-maintenance and…well, you know…she requires a lot of attention. She doesn't entertain herself very well. And ever since I can remember, she's been dying. 'I'll never make forty' and then 'I'll never make fifty' and 'The doctor didn't exactly say it was cancer, but he said I shouldn't start any serial novels.'"

"Yeah, what's that all about?" April asked.

"I'm not sure." Nikki shrugged. "Her mother did die young, but it's probably just an attention-getter. I called her doctor after one of these little comments and he said her health was great. And I don't know if you've noticed, but she's awfully spry for a dying woman."

"I noticed," April laughed. "She can shop me to death, and that's saying something."

"Well, Buck and I could be happy just messing around with the planes all day, every day, but Opal likes to have fun, to go dancing. Can you imagine Papa trying to dance? Lord," she said, and that even made April chuckle. "I must have been a huge disappointment to her. She couldn't get me in a dress at the point of a gun. And when—"

"But did that make you feel bad?" she asked.

Where is this going? Nikki wondered. "Well, no, *that* didn't. Did I feel bad when she left us? Yes, I remember being so angry with her that when she called, I wouldn't even talk to her. And then she came to visit," Nikki said with a laugh—a laugh she didn't have when she was nine, but one that came easily now. "She picked me up, took me straight to her hotel and told me to get in the tub and scrub. Then to the beauty shop to get my hair cut and styled, then to the department store for girl-clothes, then to the photographer to take a mother-daughter picture. I didn't smile for those pictures for at least the first five years. Later, we'd go out to dinner with Dr. Gould, my neurosurgeon stepfather, with whom I never did have a relationship. Finally, I'd go home to Buck, where I could fly, work on engines, play rough with the boys and have a great life."

She touched April's soft cheek. "If I had to be with one of my parents and not both, they picked the right one for me. In your case, I always felt you'd be better with me than your dad, but that might have just been selfishness on my part."

"No, you were right. We shouldn't have been with Dad. He was too strict and hard to please. But I understand there was nothing you could do about that. He wouldn't have had it any other way."

"That's nice of you to say, April. Letting me off the hook like that. I wonder if I'll ever let myself off the hook."

"Did you ever look forward to Grandma's visits?" she asked.

Nikki sighed deeply. "I missed her, I wanted to see her, I wanted a mother so badly sometimes... But Grandma and I have never had a single thing in common. The things I was most proud of appalled her. The things I cared the least about were very important to her. I don't know how else to explain it."

"I know," April said. "I miss Daddy. Sometimes I even cry about it, about him. But really, what a *load*," she groaned, making Nikki almost laugh. "So you love Grandma?"

"Of course, honey. All daughters love their mothers. Even when they can't stand them." She grabbed April's chin. "What's all this about, honey? Questions about Grandma so early in the morning?"

"Oh. I called her," she said. "I wanted to tell her all about the house. I invited her to come to Vegas as soon as we move in." Her lips curved into an innocent little smile.

Nikki's features froze. At that moment she felt like strangling her beautiful daughter. "Oh," she finally said. "And it never occurred to you to run it by me?"

"Heck no," April said, bounding out of bed and heading for the bathroom. She turned around. "Do I look dumb? You'd have said no."

"I might not have said no...."

April didn't bother closing the door. "No," she called out. "You'd have said something like, 'Let me get everything settled and then I'll phone her, honey.' But you would keep putting it off and off and off." She flushed the toilet then stuck her head out. "I don't blame you, Mom. But Grandma and I are alike. We like all that chi-chi foo-fooing. I want her to see our new place. I want her to take me shopping. She loves to dress me."

This was enough to ruin her day, Nikki thought. "Fine. You take care of her, then. Because I don't have time to answer to all her little whims and wants. Understand?"

"Oh, totally," she said. "And Mom?"

"What?" Nikki demanded, no longer feeling like putting her kids first.

"I think she's going to really like your hair."

"If she says one thing about my hair, I'll shave my head."

"Whew. I think you have some issues."

Yes, Nikki had issues. No one knew it better than she did. Simply put, she and Opal had nothing in common. Even the fact that they were both divorced women whose husbands got custody didn't give them any shared ground.

As far as Nikki was concerned, all the wrong things were important to Opal. When April was born, the very first words out of Opal's mouth were, "Oh, thank heavens, she has good skin." Was she concerned about the baby's health? Her mind? Her hopes and dreams? "Of course I'm concerned about all that," Opal had said. "If she has problems, I'm sure you'll tell me!"

Opal was superficial. Completely shallow. She wanted nice clothes, nice vacations, nice friends. It was clear to Nikki that you could have a fine appreciation for such things and still not come up empty. Both Carlisle and Dixie were good examples of that—people with good taste, great style and substance to boot. Not so with Opal. She had found herself someone with way more prestige and social standing than Buck and made the switch, never mind that Buck probably could have bought and sold Mayer Gould five times over.

But perhaps the deepest issue was this: Opal never could accept Buck and Nikki as they were. She never appreciated their gifts and talents, which were considerable.

"*I placed in the Reno Air Race in my category, Mom!*"

"*Oh, Nicole, when are you going to do something*

*about those nails! They might as well be on a boy's
hands!''*

But April loved her grandma; Opal was the only one
she had with Drake's mother and father long gone. So
why couldn't Nikki just suck it up and get along with
her mother for her daughter's sake?

Well, maybe she could. But it was so difficult...
because Nikki had these *issues.*

The six applicants were waiting in the first-floor
lobby, all looking obviously needy. The applicants were
all men in the first batch. Nikki had looked hard for some
highly competitive women pilots, but in that collection
of twelve thousand résumés, only a few had risen to the
surface, and they'd be interviewed tomorrow and the
next day. There were more in the pile, she had no doubt,
but as always the women were way outnumbered by the
guys.

One fellow wore a leather blazer with his hair in
something of a pompadour. Another was in a pin-striped
suit and wingtips, and a couple wore herringbone sport
coats with patches on the elbows—the pilot's civilian
uniform. One guy was so stiff and military-looking,
Nikki nearly saluted him. They ranged in age from thirty
to fifty-five. Taking on a fifty-five-year-old was not as
dicey as it seemed. At least he wouldn't go looking for
a better, higher-paying airline after New Century spent
twenty-thousand dollars training him. The thirty-year-old
with all that youth and vigor and years ahead of him, he
was the greater risk.

But that was old thinking. That was *back in the day*
thinking, when there was still a United Airlines paying
senior captains close to five hundred thousand to work
ten days a month.

The pilots assembled here did have one thing in common—they were all early for their morning interview.

Nikki checked with the security guard to make sure she hadn't falsely labeled anyone, and he confirmed they were all pilot applicants for New Century. So she cut them a break and went over, which was when she spotted Sam Landon.

"You're all here to interview with New Century Airline?" Nikki asked. Nods all around. "Hi," she said. "I'm Captain Nikki Burgess. Why don't you come upstairs with me and we'll get everyone started." She stuck her hand out to Sam. "Good to see you, Sam."

"And you, Captain."

A couple of the guys smiled, but a few looked confused—could it be? A woman chief pilot? And the stiff guy with the high-and-tight buzz cut looked like he'd just gone into shock.

Nikki shook hands with the men. A pilot name Dick Cleary pushed forward, all confidence and smiles. There was Chris Wagnon, Ken Spencer, Jeff Hayden and Rob Knowles.

"Glad to meet you all. Right this way."

She might have led them, but Dick was quick to get to her side and walk with her. "Is this still the first class hire?" he asked. And, "How close to certification is NCA? How many planes do you have to start? What's the projected expansion? How much was the initial funding?"

Here's a guy interested in starting with an airline that's going to last, Nikki thought. Ambitious. Strong. And kissing up a bunch.

Of the six, two were very talkative, almost giddy. Three were mute and appeared almost scared, but Sam seemed just plain easy in his skin. Comfortable. Almost like he could take it or leave it. He had the kind of confidence that came across as total peace of mind.

There was no mistaking their awe when they saw Dixie. She was in charge of their paperwork, which would include a five-year background check and an FAA research for valid licenses and any violations. Also, she would escort them down to Shanna's office, where the head of HR would have her procedural way with them. All through the morning Dixie would do what she did so well—make small talk with them, draw them out, get an idea what kind of pilot each was. Maybe the word was out that the chief pilot was a woman, but the fact that her right arm had been a flight attendant for fifteen years was surely not common knowledge. Perhaps if Dixie were looking for a guy to date, her judgment might not be so sterling, but she had plenty of experience when it came to judging a pilot's personality. She'd taken a lot of cups of coffee to the flight deck, after all.

Nikki, Danny, Eric and Bob Riddle assembled in the small conference room in Flight Ops. One at a time the men came in to be interviewed. "Why do you want to work here?" they were asked, and the answers were varied.

"I'm real impressed with the innovative business plan Joe Riordan has proposed."

"This is the best opportunity going in this business environment."

"Looks like this is going to be a great company."

"I've always wanted a chance to get into a new airline at the beginning, be there from the start."

"You're hiring."

This last came from Sam, and it brought a giant smile to Nikki's lips. It was impossible not to like him. She looked at his résumé. "Tell me about Pacific Air," she said.

He leaned forward, elbows on knees. "It was a good little company. It should have done well. But it faced 9/11, didn't get any of that promised government help from the ATSB and sank like a rock. It was gone in four weeks. A terrible loss. People loved flying Pacific Air."

"What have you been doing the last couple of years?" Danny asked him.

"Not a whole lot," he answered. "I put out a couple of résumés, but it was just as well I didn't get hired. I put the time to good use. I have my air force retirement…money wasn't the issue."

"What was?" Eric asked.

He took a breath. "Two years ago, when my daughters were aged seventeen and twenty-one, their mother…my wife…died suddenly. They needed me. I was actually on a leave from Pacific when they went under."

Everyone around the table expressed sympathy.

"Thank you. The three of us, we moved on pretty well, I think. My older daughter graduated and was recently married, the younger one is just getting started in college." He grinned. "They'd be very grateful if I'd move to Las Vegas. Or Hawaii."

"Are you ready to get back into the cockpit?" Danny asked him.

"Oh, yeah, I miss it way more than I thought I would."

"And what can you bring to New Century Air that makes you our ideal job candidate?" Eric asked.

"Gratitude and humility," he said without missing a beat. Nikki felt the warmth that he inspired spread through her as he spoke, his voice so gentle but deep, kind and strong. "I never thought I'd see the airline industry fall apart as it has. This company, and more like it, will reshape the whole commercial aviation industry. A lot of us who thought we were indispensable will be left behind. Those of us who have jobs at all should be very grateful. And I am humbled by what I've seen the last few years."

Nikki, Danny and Eric exchanged looks. They were all thinking the same thing—they hoped he could fly like a bird because they wanted thirty just like him.

Bob Riddle's phone chirped in his pocket. "I apologize," he said, "but I really can't turn the phone off. I'm basically on call twenty-four/seven." He flipped it open. "Riddle." He paused to listen.

Nikki grimaced unhappily. Her phone was turned off, as were Danny's and Eric's.

"You're right," Bob said. "You have a serious problem there. I'll get on it immediately. In fact, I'll set up a meeting with the president of Boeing and make sure we all understand one another. Don't worry about a thing. I know they'll see it our way." He flipped the phone closed and stood. "I'm going to have to take care of that aircraft issue or it could cost us millions." He shook Sam's hand dramatically. "Nice to meet you, Sam." He gave a half bow to the others. "Gentlemen. Captain Burgess."

Everyone waited while Bob left the room. No one said a word for a moment. Finally Nikki shook Sam's hand and thanked him for interviewing. She promised to call him within the week.

But what weighed on her mind was Riddle's phone call. She couldn't prove it, but in her gut she thought he had somehow contrived that call to make himself appear important. To what purpose, she couldn't imagine.

* * *

Nikki saw to it that Danny was awarded the director of training position, which he ecstatically accepted. This was exactly what he had hoped for. Eric was asked to select a couple of pilots from the first thirty hires to help him form a hiring committee. Both men would be check airmen if the FAA gave its blessing to their check rides.

Danny immediately set about the task of hiring instructors, both ground school and simulator. As in other areas of the industry, there was a surplus of talent available. He had the cream of the crop to choose from.

Once the interviewing process and background checks were complete, the training for both pilots and flight attendants commenced. The number of bodies in and around New Century was growing by dozens…dozens that soon would turn into hundreds.

The first class of pilots, no matter how vast their experience, had to go through FAA-approved training in every new company. That involved three weeks of ground school, two weeks of simulator training and twenty-five hours of IOE—Initial Operating Experience. That meant check airmen would ride along to observe how the pilot carried out operating procedures for that particular aircraft and airline. NCA didn't have simulators, so they booked their sim time at, of all places, Aries.

Before the first class of pilots was shipped off for their simulator training, the second class would be in ground school and the third class would be in the hiring process. And the potential future hires were still putting flowers, candy and other little gifts on Dixie's desk. Dixie in turn endeared herself to the other employees by making sure it was spread all over the building.

The kids had started school, and since they were not

yet in their house, Nikki had to take them and pick them up whenever Carlisle was working. Buck and Pistol were making a habit of their weekend visits, but as the kids began to go out with their new friends, Buck found himself making an occasional visit to one of the casinos' poker tables. Or craps. Or blackjack.

One Sunday as he was getting ready to return to Phoenix, he handed Nikki an envelope. She opened it and found a check for twenty-five thousand dollars. "What in the world…?"

"Rent," he said.

"What rent?"

"Rent you paid me when you moved back in with me. I never wanted it. I told you I never wanted it. You paid rent, you bought groceries, you gave that slimeball ex-husband child support, which he probably day-traded away, and you never once asked for help. Not with the lawyers or the kids or even the overmortgaged house he dumped on you. So just take it like a good daughter and put some halfway decent furniture in that new house."

She could have cried, it touched her so.

The next thing she did was sit Carlisle down for a chat.

"I'm going to close on the house in about ten days, Carlisle. I don't know what your plans are, exactly. You've been talking about renting an apartment or something until you can get things sorted out with Robert. Well, Dixie's already made it clear she's not interested in having a roommate—she wants her own place. She's going to borrow a guest room for as long as a couple of weeks, but that's it for her—she wants to go her own way. I'd like to offer you the casita, rent free, until you get your affairs in order."

"Rent free? But—"

"Well, it's not *really* free. It's sort of in exchange for all the things you already do without being asked. For helping with the kids' transportation and meals. For being the decorator and nanny even without being hired on. Just because. I want to say thank you, and you can use the break right now."

His eyes got a little misty and his chin quivered a bit. "My God, Nick, that is so generous of you!"

"Aw, really, it's nothing...."

"No, I mean it—I don't know what to say. People just don't do things that wonderful."

She began to feel a bit guilty. "Actually, you have a place with me and my kids for as long as you want it or need it, but I do have a bit of a selfish motive."

"Believe me, I can help out...."

"I mean, as long as you're in the casita, Opal can't get any ideas. Know what I mean?"

Ten

Nikki promised to go furniture-and-accessory shopping on the weekend, but first she had to run by the office and take care of a few things. Dixie was likewise drawn to the office, since her desk took on the overflow from Nikki's. Because April was itching to shop, she went along with the women to help out making copies, filing—anything to hurry them along.

The parking lot was as full as on any weekday. Danny and Eric were there, working on training manuals and curriculum. "The manual was bounced back from the FAA with several items noncompliant with the regulatory requirements," Danny said. "Minor, but they still have to be addressed before we meet with the FAA again on Wednesday."

"You going to make it by our deadline?" Nikki asked.

"Oh, yeah," he said confidently. "Eric offered to stay in town this weekend to help."

"Your family is in Texas, right?" Nikki asked.

He nodded. "My wife has the house on the market. We're planning to relocate."

"We really appreciate the dedication," she said.

"If this outfit gets a good start, I don't have to job-hunt ever again," he returned.

"God willing."

Training would start in another week, if the FAA smiled on the training manuals. If NCA were delayed in training, the airline might not make the certification deadline, and if that happened, they'd lose a ton of money by putting their ticketed passengers on other carriers at high-priced, last-minute ticket cost. The reservations department had been selling seats for a mid-November start-up to take advantage of the busy holiday travel season.

There were a lot of people in the NCA offices who were helping friends and coworkers in other departments, the way Eric was helping Danny in training rather that focusing on his own hiring department. Pitching in wherever necessary for the good of the company.

From one trip down the halls, it was plain to see that Flight Ops wasn't the only place where there was plenty of work to be done. Joe and Jewel were hard at work, most of the finance department was cranking away, and Nikki had seen the Wrench's truck in the lot. For as much as Shanna annoyed her, she was at work with her clerks, probably trying to catch up on the dozens of HR tasks that had to be completed to staff the company.

But one person Nikki never saw after five or on a weekend was Riddle.

She walked around the corner and down the hall. Riddle's door was closed and Crue's desk was clean as a whistle. She tried the door and it swung open. Riddle's desk was clean, too.

The certification process required so much paperwork, so many meetings and conferences, there was only one way Riddle could manage this. He was giving all the work to everyone else. And there was nothing Nikki could do about it.

She went back to her office. Dixie was bent over a

large stack of personnel files while April was humming away on the copier. "Let's wrap it up before lunch," Nikki said.

What, she thought as she sat down at her own cluttered desk, was Riddle doing this weekend? She thought about pulling up her roster and calling his cell phone, but quickly put that idea from her mind. She tried to put *him* from her mind. She knew the certification of this airline wasn't going to happen because of Riddle's contribution—she had always really known that. He talked a good game, but his performance was sorely lacking, just like in the cockpit.

He must really look good on paper, she thought resentfully.

Grabbing her purse and briefcase, she stood up and left the office. "Are you at a spot where you can quit?" she asked April and Dixie. "Because I'm too distracted by that totally empty house I'm buying to get anything done in here today." That was only partially true. She was more distracted by the way she seemed to work constantly while Bob Riddle was never around. Buying things for the new house might take her mind off him. For now, anyway.

Carlisle had finished up a short trip on Saturday evening and taken a commute right to Las Vegas. His head ached and he was tired. Nikki and Dixie had been shopping all day and were doing show-and-tell, but he begged off, claiming he had a headache.

They were going shopping again on Sunday, but he wasn't up to it. Much as he thought he should be helping Nikki with the furniture and decorating so she didn't bring home anything too tacky, he just couldn't bring himself to concentrate on it. Instead he darkened his room and lay on the bed all afternoon. Jared called his room once and tried to interest him in a movie or a trip to the park, but he declined. Buck was up for the weekend, so it wasn't as though Jared was abandoned.

Then the phone began trilling again. He looked at his watch. It was almost six—the girls, back from shopping.

"Come on," Dixie said, calling from Nikki's room. "Come down, have a glass of wine before dinner and see what we've got."

"I have a headache," he said.

"What crock is this?" she demanded. "You'd never pass up a bunch of paint and wallpaper samples because of a stupid headache."

"It's a pretty bad one."

"Jared said you don't have a headache at all—you're just a little moody, like usual. This wouldn't have anything to do with Robert, would it?"

"Oh, you're so psychic," he said. "Big deal."

"You gonna sit down there by yourself and pout, or are you gonna come down and join the family? We could all hear the latest instalment—"

"I haven't seen Robert," he said. Then he sighed. "I'll be right down. Give me a minute."

When he got to Nikki's room, April had spread pictures of furniture, paint and paper samples, fabric swatches and window-treatment brochures on the small table for her grandfather to look at. Buck seemed to be doing well at pretending to be interested in these things. Jared sat in front of the TV working some video game, with Pistol at attention beside him. He didn't even turn around as Carlisle entered, but said, "Hi," without missing a beat on his game.

Dixie put a glass of wine in his hand. "What's the matter, sunshine? Tell Aunt Dixie."

"It's not as though it should come as a surprise. Robert is angry with me." He shrugged. "What else is new? I spoke to him and he told me that the locks have all been changed and I'll get my things back and the money I have invested in the house over his dead body."

"Oh, well," Buck said, perfectly resigned.

Everyone turned and looked at him.

"I never liked that little fairy, anyway," he said.

"Don't you ever worry that I'll be offended by your remarks?" Carlisle asked him.

"I don't know why you would be," Buck said. "I like you."

"Papa," April lightly admonished.

"What does it mean?" Nikki asked Carlisle. "I don't know the law, but if that's your house and you have stuff there, can't you force your way in?"

"In a way," he said. "The law gives co-owners thirty days to go, with a locksmith, and get their belongings, provided there's a certain amount of evidence it's yours. I have a car title, no problem there. I might even have some furniture receipts. And my clothes would never fit him."

"So is that what gave you your headache?" Jared asked without turning around from the TV.

"No. What gave me my headache is that my thirty days is nearly up. I'm going to have to go do it. And I dread the hell out of it."

"Oohh," Nikki and Dixie said together.

Carlisle sipped his wine. "I'm going to Phoenix to fly on Monday afternoon. I'll get back on Wednesday afternoon, so on Thursday I'll attempt to get my car and move my stuff out of the town house."

"You're not going alone, I hope," Dixie said.

"No. Mr. Levine is coming with me to be sure I have

some kind of legal representation in case the police are called or whatever. But Robert should be at work. I'll try to get a couple of friends from work to help. I'll just put the stuff in storage down there for now. I can have it moved up here later. But I'm going to drive my car back.'' He smiled a small smile. ''That should help, huh, Dix? You can have your wheels back.''

''That's not a big deal, Carlisle.''

He knew it wasn't. The big deal was that he didn't want to do this—go back into that house, pack up his things, separate his life from Robert's, for good this time. Not that he was even slightly tempted to move back with him—he wasn't. But no matter how convinced he was that this move was the best thing he could do for himself, the process was painful. And frightening, damned frightening. What if Robert beat the crap out of him again?

He shuddered.

''The sooner this is over, the better,'' he said.

As a rule, crews liked flying with Carlisle. He was good at entertaining the passengers and had a cutting sense of humor. Helpful by nature, he fluffed pillows for little old ladies, walked the aisles with crying babies and was so quick on his feet that he did the work of two flight attendants, which made the flight easier on everyone.

But on the two-day flight preceding his visit to his former house, he was off. Impatient, testy and distracted.

Conditions for air travel were likewise off. A cold front had blown in and there were storms all over the country, particularly in the Midwest. The terminals were full of disgruntled passengers who just didn't understand why blustery winds and snow flurries in Minneapolis would make the flight from San Francisco to Phoenix late, or cancel the run from Dallas to L.A. It brought out the worst in everyone. Of course, the reason was both simple and rational—the inbound to San Francisco came out of Minneapolis, and the Dallas airplane was being switched over to a New York trip because there were twice as many passengers up there stranded by storms.

Carlisle was just checking first-class seating on one of the gate computers when one such crazed passenger began screaming at the agent. "What do you *mean* you can't get me on any flight to Atlanta! I've had this reservation for *months!*"

"Unfortunately Mother Nature picked today to pepper the Midwest with low visibility, high winds and snow and sleet, which has grounded the flight that was inbound to pick up this leg and take you to Atlanta."

"Well, you'd just better come up with something, young lady. Do you know who I *am?*"

Carlisle glanced at the agent and could see that, despite her best effort, her skin was beginning to mottle and she was close to coming unglued. He pulled the mike toward him and said, "Your attention please, ladies and gentlemen. We have a gentleman here who can't remember who he is. This is not uncommon during a rapid drop in barometric pressure. If anyone here knows this gentleman's identity, please come to the podium immediately."

The man grew bright red under the chuckles of passengers in the gate area. He shook his finger at Carlisle. "You're going to pay for that imbecilic remark!" he choked. He turned in a huff and stomped away. His fellow passengers rewarded him with applause and laughter.

The low-pressure system and tense crowds also

brought out the pervs. Carlisle was standing at the jetway door taking tickets from passengers. The plane was almost completely boarded and the gate area nearly empty when an older man sauntered toward Carlisle. He stopped in front of him and opened his coat to expose his naked self. Carlisle wished he could say it was the first time that had happened, but airports were getting more and more like the circus. Without missing a beat Carlisle said, "I'm afraid I'm going to need to see the whole ticket, sir, and not just the stub."

The man turned and ran. Just another exhibitionist. At least he wasn't a traveling exhibitionist.

"Gayle," Carlisle called to the agent at the podium across the concourse. He pointed at the quickly departing man. "Peeper. Call Security!"

"Gotcha," she said, picking up the phone.

Things didn't get a whole lot better in the air. He found he was working the first-class cabin with a lovely and personable woman affectionately nicknamed Salads Over St. Louis, because she was so slow it would take her all the way from Phoenix to St. Louis to get the first course out. She was a delight to talk to, but Carlisle was going to have to work his butt off to keep things rolling, and by the end of the flight he'd probably want to kill her.

And the passengers were a surly lot, a condition no doubt caused by the tension of being late, bouncing around the sky and just the general unease of flying. It was a state of anxiety the industry had been stuck with since 9/11 and didn't seem to be easing up.

"What can I get you to drink, ma'am?" Carlisle asked an elderly woman with thin pink hair and bright red lips.

"I'll have a ginger ale," she said.

"I'm terribly sorry, but we've run out. I can get you a cola, a lemon-lime soda or perhaps a juice?"

"I want a ginger ale," she said in a shrill, angry voice. "Can't you at least go look back there in the closet?"

Heavy sigh. "I don't have a closet back there, dear. I have all the available drinks right here."

"Well ask someone else!" she snapped.

"Ma'am, I simply don't have one. What's your second choice?"

"For what I paid for this ticket, with no meal to speak of, I should at least be able to get a ginger ale!"

"For what you paid for your ticket, I should be pushing you out over Albuquerque." He turned to the man across the aisle and asked him what he'd like. Behind him the woman was loudly yapping that she'd been insulted, and demanded to know his name at once.

He wrote it on a cocktail napkin for her, thinking, *Swell—on top of egomaniacs demanding a flight in the middle of a windstorm and a perv showing me his bobo, I'm going to get written up by this malcontent with the voice box.* "There you go, madam. Now, have you changed your mind about a beverage, or do you choose to be unhappy *and* thirsty? Hm?"

She snatched the napkin out of his hand. "Give me a cola," she said. "Not diet."

"God forbid," he replied, snapping the top of the can and pouring the bubbly drink over ice.

A while later, strapped in for landing in the flight attendant jump seat, Salads said, "You're a little short today, huh?"

"I know it," Carlisle sighed, as if exasperated with himself. "They all think they're the only ones who get a little bent out of shape when the flights are late or oversold or like riding a bronco through the sky. And that one," he said, jutting his chin toward the planeload of passengers. "The woman with the candy floss on her head? Did you hear that voice? That demanding, demeaning voice?"

"They heard it in Buffalo," she agreed. "But if anyone can handle that type, it's usually you."

"Yeah. But not when we're going up and down, up and down, two hundred and fifty people on board, all either pissed or—"

The thought had no sooner crossed his mind than he heard a terrible retching noise followed by a *splat*. He didn't want to look. He leaned to the side and glanced past the bulkhead down the aisle. Ew, not good. "It's 2A," he said to Salads.

"Damn. That's gonna start a chain puke. I'm just not good with things like vomit."

"Oh, how does that not surprise me?" Carlisle said.

Bing, bing, bing went the flight attendant call buttons; people started rustling around. There was the telltale sound of seat belts unsnapping, and Carlisle grabbed the PA speaker.

"Ladies and gentlemen, we'll be landing momentarily and taxiing to the gate. Please use your flight attendant call buttons for emergencies only. And remain seated. The flight attendants will come back into the cabin to help you as soon as it's safe to do so." He clicked off. "I hate wind," he muttered.

As the 767 eased into its parking spot and the jetway moved toward the door, passengers sprang to their feet, popped open overheads and filled the aisles before the captain had turned off the seat belt sign. It just infuriated him. He was already in a bad mood that was getting worse by the second. He grabbed the speaker again. "Clear the aisle so that flight attendants can assist the sick passengers!'' he ordered. No one moved. ''Please!'' he nearly shouted into the PA. No one moved.

''Bastards,'' he muttered.

''Come on,'' Salads said. ''It'll be easier to get them off the plane and then help any sick passengers. You get the club soda and paper towels, I'll get the door.''

''Swell. That'll be such a great help,'' he said sarcastically.

Salads patted his knee. ''No problem, sweetie.''

''People are just so damned inconsiderate,'' he pointed out.

''We better load more club soda,'' she said, ignoring his futile bitching. ''We're going to be bouncing all over the country.''

''And ginger ale,'' he added tiredly.

Carlisle was getting himself a little more worked up with every leg of the trip, until finally Thursday morning came and he was headed for the town house he had shared with Robert. His attorney was to drive him there; Ross Levine was just a little guy in his sixties—not exactly what Carlisle would term protection. And he'd only found one person to help, a guy he worked with who promised to show up at about noon.

''Have you decided exactly what you want to take?'' Ross asked him. ''Because I really don't plan to stay all day while you pack your house. I just want to be certain Robert understands the legal situation and isn't likely to give you any trouble.''

''Likely,'' Carlisle said. He felt sick to his stomach.

''As long as you feel vulnerable, I'll stay,'' he said. ''But I have other—''

''It's all right, I understand. You have other clients. And I'm not as prepared as I should—''

"Try not to worry too much. It's been my experience that once the boundaries are established and the law is clear…"

He continued talking, but Carlisle wasn't really listening. Hang experience, this was battery, domestic violence. Once you finally named it and came to terms with it, you knew the beast for what it was. Robert was dangerous.

He knew he should have had a plan. He should have hired a moving company to meet him at the town house. What had stopped him was frazzled nerves and denial. He was watching the clock tick, the calendar pages slip off one by one, knowing he was running out of time. He was going to end up doing what so many before him had done—he'd leave much of his stuff behind just to get away clean. He'd probably never get his half of the equity….

His thoughts were distracted as they pulled into the neighborhood and found it as crowded as a block party. There was a big U-Haul truck backed into the drive, though the garage door was not open. He'd booked a U-Haul for later, after his friend arrived to help, so where'd this one come from? Cars and pickups were parked along the curb; people were standing around. Carlisle was totally confused. His first thought was that Robert was moving, stealing the furniture. But then he recognized Buck. Buck? A man of equal size stood on either side of him. And Nikki? And there was Dixie talking to some women. Mexican women? Who the devil were they?

His legs were like lead as he experienced that dreamlike inability to move. The scene started to slowly come into focus as he recognized Lydia, Drake's former cleaning lady. Nikki started to walk toward Carlisle.

"Hi. We thought two things could be accomplished here today, with some help. One—we can get everything that belongs to you out of here and up to Las Vegas, where you'll need it, and two, Robert will come to understand you're not kidding, and you're not alone. Not by a long shot."

"You all came? How did you manage it? You work days, nights and weekends as it is."

"Yeah, I know. This is going to be a treat. I called Lydia and she brought some friends. We'll get them packing. Dad brought a couple of guys from Burgess Aviation to help load up the furniture. I'm guessing we're out of here in two hours. After we get in, that is. That might be the most time-consuming part of this event."

Carlisle glanced at the house. Ross Levine was walking up to the front door with his briefcase in hand.

"He's home," Nikki said. "He's seen us all."

"We had to tell him when we were coming," Carlisle said. And then a slow smile spread across his lips as he saw the front door open and Ross begin a conversation with Robert. "Why do these things never occur to me?" he asked himself aloud. "Why didn't I just do this myself? Gather up a small army to converge on him? Because if I end up suing him, which I will surely have to do, all these people will have witnessed him denying me entry to my own house. Denying me my possessions, which I have a legal right to." The front door closed, Ross Levine came back down the walk, and within seconds the garage door lifted. "Why don't I think of these things?"

But he knew the answer. The pathetic answer. When it came to this relationship, he acted like a victim.

But here were ten people backing him up. It gave him tremendous confidence. He walked into the open garage and through the door into the kitchen, where he found Robert. He couldn't deny a slight wave of fearful nausea, but he was determined that it wouldn't show. Nikki was beside him, and Buck quickly brought up the rear to stand behind him.

"Thanks for letting us in, Robert," Carlisle said. "We'll be out of here in no time and I promise we won't leave a mess."

Robert snorted and turned away. He took the cordless phone out onto the patio.

"That wasn't too bad," Nikki said.

"I so hope he stays on the phone out there till we're ready to leave," Carlisle told her.

"Why? He doesn't seem too surly."

"I'd like my last act to be plucking it out of his hand as I wave goodbye. It's my phone."

In a choreographed dance, Carlisle's presence was removed from the town house. He pulled kitchen items that belonged to him out of cupboards and placed them on the table for Lydia and her friends to pack. In the bedroom, Nikki and Dixie packed his clothes in boxes. Given Robert's meanness, it was amazing that he hadn't thrown away these things, but then he never expected Carlisle to show up with a team and a truck. Truth be told, if this move had been up to Carlisle, it wouldn't have happened with such smooth efficiency. In these circumstances, he had no objectivity, no courage.

It was not yet noon when the furniture and boxes were in the truck, which they also used to tow Carlisle's car. Lydia and her friends left, and one of the guys from Burgess Aviation would drop Dixie and Nikki at the airport so they could get right back to Las Vegas. Behind the wheel of the truck was Buck.

Carlisle looked around the interior of the town house from the kitchen. He had taken the living room furniture, big-screen television, pictures, bedroom suite, most of the kitchen accoutrements.

Robert came in from the patio, a hangdog expression on his handsome face. Carlisle held out his hand for the cordless. He placed it on its base, unplugged it from the wall and wound the cord around it.

Robert's hands were plunged deeply into his pockets, and that errant lock of dark brown hair flopped onto his brow. "Well," he said. "Looks like you've taken almost everything. Even my heart."

Carlisle surprised himself by laughing out loud. "Oh, kiss my ass, Robert. There's a lien on the house." And then he got the heck out of there.

He jumped in the truck beside Buck. "You know, I can get to Las Vegas just fine. You don't have to—"

"I promised the girls," he said, putting the truck in gear and moving slowly forward.

"It's really nice of you," he said. "I know where they're coming from. Even I would have expected me to be falling apart, a basket case, but oddly enough, I've never felt more—"

"Listen, buttercup," Buck said, cutting him off. "Don't tell me too much, okay? Because... You know."

It was a five-hour drive. Carlisle was going to make him say it. "Because what?"

Buck let out a ragged sigh. "I'm sixty-six. Not only don't I get the whole gay thing, I don't much get the regular stuff."

"That a fact?"

"Here's what I get. You're Nikki's good friend, you

treat the kids like they're special, you have that occasional drink of Scotch with me and you seem to be a good person. Good people should catch a break now and then. That asshole should never have hit you, and you need to go to Las Vegas with your friends.''

Hmm, Carlisle thought. And he says he doesn't get much.

Dixie and Nikki were using a couple of old standby passes for perfect attendance that Dixie hadn't given away before taking her leave of absence from Aries. Because of this, they couldn't travel in the jeans and tennis shoes they'd worn to help Carlisle move. They headed for the airport bathroom to change into the required business attire.

While Nikki finished fluffing her hair and putting on new makeup, Dixie waited in the gate area for the standby's to be called. A man sat down beside her.

''How you doin'?'' he asked in a thick New York accent.

She edged away a little. ''Fine.''

''Heading for Vegas?''

''As a matter of fact.''

''Small world, ain't it? I was just thinking about getting a drink. This flight isn't going to board for a long time. Wanna join me?''

''Ah, thanks, but no. I'm travelin' with someone.''

He chuckled. ''Don't it just figure? I finally get to fly for pleasure, and the most beautiful woman on the flight is already with someone.''

''You're a pilot?'' she asked.

He nodded. ''Triple seven,'' he said smugly. ''American.''

She half smiled. He thought his prowess as a pilot

was going to get him laid. Ha-ha-ha-ha. Boy, had he got a wrong number.

"Any chance I can get you to ditch him?"

Amazing. That was more brazen than the worst block-head pilots she knew. It made her laugh. "Oh, my, does your wife know what you do when you're out on the road?"

"I see you've met Rocky," Nikki said. She'd come upon them without either of them noticing her. He looked up at her, his mouth hanging open in confusion. He clearly didn't remember her, but then she had an entirely new look. "I thought you weren't allowed to fly this airline, Rocky," she said, still standing and looking down at him.

It took him quite a while, then his eyes slowly grew wide as he came to recognize her. Once he was sure, he simply stood and made his getaway. Not to the bar, but down the concourse and past Security at a very fast pace.

"You know that man?" Dixie asked.

"Remember that guy I told you about who was impersonating an air marshal?"

"No way!"

"Way. He's not supposed to be able to get a ticket on Aries," she said. "I don't know if he did any time, but I'm sure there was a hefty fine and his name is on the watch list. I wonder how he managed it."

"Well," Dixie said thoughtfully. "He wasn't an air marshal today. He was a triple-seven pilot for American Airlines."

Eleven

Bob Riddle was the original meeting man. By keeping her ears open and instructing Dixie to do the same, Nikki soon learned that when Bob arrived in the morning, he handed Crue a list of calls to make and meetings to schedule. He met with pilots who had just been hired; he met with in-flight personnel—flight attendant managers—individually and in small groups; he spent a lot of time wandering around the corporate and finance end of the office building; and he had meetings with vendors who supplied everything from airplanes to airplane coffeepots. Nikki had no idea what he was doing, but he was doing it very busily.

Then one of his little projects saw the light of day. A fashion show was scheduled to be put on by a uniform vendor for flight ops and in-flight senior staff. They would have to make a selection for pilot and flight attendant uniforms immediately if they were to be ready for the first flight.

Ordinarily Nikki would not trust herself to choose anything dealing with fashion, but these were uniforms. They had hardly changed over the past forty years, with the exception of the occasional avant garde look—like hot pants and boots. So, how hard could it be?

Harder than she'd dared fear.

"Our objective at New Century Air is to accentuate

the new,'' said Reese, flight attendant and head of the uniform committee. "We want to be innovative. We want to *stand out*.''

That's where the trouble started. The whole point was that pilots *not* stand out. Pilots were cool, detached, in control behind the scenes. At least that's what the airline preferred the flying public to believe. The truth might not be good for ticket sales.

Bob Riddle had joined forces with Charles, the head of in-flight, and his committee of four flight attendants, who apparently had been longing to go to Mardi Gras for some time. Between them they had come up with some rather interesting ideas. The manufacturer had both sketches and mannequin models set up in the conference room when Nikki arrived.

The first outfit she saw was a turquoise suit for pilots with gold filigree on the sleeves and gold piping along the edges. There was a complementary one-piece fitted jumpsuit made of spandex for the flight attendants, including a wide belt with a large gold buckle. It reminded Nikki of something that might be worn by the crew of the *Starship Enterprise*.

"Um, have you taken into consideration that there is no longer a weight standard for flight attendants?'' Nikki asked. She mentally noted that there were about three people she knew who would look good in that leotard— Dixie and two men. "And then there's the maternity issue,'' she added.

"We can find a way to deal with maternity, but we don't intend to let our flight attendants get fat,'' Reese said.

"Ah, then you intend to be sued?'' Nikki asked. "I believe that's an EEO issue.''

"It *can't* be!'' she argued, aghast.

"Let's just move along," said Charles. "There's plenty here to see."

Next they viewed a mannequin wearing a tan suit with red-and-black shoulder boards and gold buttons.

"That's a favorite of mine," Bob said.

"He looks like an Iraqi general!" Nikki protested.

"Look at the sketches for the coordinating flight attendant uniforms," Reese urged. "They're striking!"

"They look like female generals!" Nikki exclaimed. "Look, you have to know pilots, especially the men. They don't like to get all trussed up. They tend toward conservative and comfortable clothing that's easy to maintain."

"I beg to differ, Nikki," Bob said. "I'm a pilot and I very much favor a snappy appearance."

"Bob," Nikki said pleadingly, "turquoise spandex is way beyond snappy. That'll get a union in here faster than low pay."

"Let's not get ahead of ourselves," Charles said. "We have more sketches and actual mock-ups to look at."

Nikki held her tongue. She sat quietly while being shown sketches of low-rider, bell-bottomed pants with paisley vests, multicolored layover shirts with Nehru collars, and her personal favorite pilot's uniform, very loosely pleated pants, silk shirt and leather bomber jacket. Vintage forties. And for the flight attendants? One-piece, tightly belted silk jumpsuits with extra-large shoulder pads. If there'd been a rag tied around the woman's head, she would have been Rosie the Riveter.

"What does Joe say about these ideas?" she finally asked.

"He hasn't been involved. Well, he had this idea that he wanted the first-class flight attendant uniform to differ somehow from the coach—but when we vetoed that idea he didn't argue.''

"But you're going to show him?''

"Eventually.''

"No, you have to show him now!'' she insisted. "I don't know that much about fashion, but—''

"That seems painfully obvious,'' Reese said, a very superior edge to her voice.

"But,'' Nikki went on sharply, "I believe these ideas stray too far from the public expectation, and that can't be a good thing.''

"Let me show you one that was mocked up for me, so you can see what a real classy pilot looks like,'' Bob said, exiting to change. "This one is a little more conservative.''

Nikki took advantage of his absence and dashed out of the room to summon Dixie. "Pilot costuming has gone out of control,'' she said. "Call Riordan's office, and if you can't get him to make an appearance, at least see if you can get the Gatekeeper. And see if you can find Danny and Eric. I'm in trouble in there.''

When she got back to the room she fessed up. "I called Riordan's office.''

"Now, what the hell did you do that for?'' Reese demanded. "This job was delegated to us and we're getting it done.''

Bob entered the room in a dark suit with gold accents, but Nikki didn't really take it in.

"Sorry. If the boss goes for this, I stand corrected and will apologize—but this stuff is too far over the top for me to be comfortable with. I'm not dressing my pilots up in these costumes unless Riordan insists. And I am going to fight it.''

She then looked at Bob. He was right—he wore the

most conservative uniform thus far, and even it was beyond belief. The double-breasted jacket was black, with two rows of large gold buttons running up the front—eight in total. Swirling gold piping made decorative loops up the sleeves, and there were gold stripes on the shoulder boards.

Riordan walked in. The look on his face suggested he wasn't thrilled to be interrupted for this. His dress shirt was open at the neck, sleeves rolled up. Nikki thought it was yesterday's shirt, and yesterday's circles under his eyes. He took one sweeping look at the uniformed mannequins and sketches laid out on the conference table. "D'you have to wear drag to get in here?"

Jewel stepped into the room behind him. She looked at the uniforms casually, crossing her arms over her chest.

"Bob," he said, poking at one of the gold buttons running up his chest. "I'm not sure whether you're going to fly a plane or lay down and feed your puppies." He frowned at the sketches, then at the flight attendant committee. "What the hell is this? Gimme a navy blue suit. Put some skirts and slacks and blouses together. The fanciest thing I wanna see is a vest. Jesus, this shit looks like a fucking Cher concert!" He pointed to the tan suit with the filigree and shoulder boards. "Who the hell is that supposed to be? That guy looks like a friggin' Iraqi general."

He turned and left the room. Jewel pulled the door closed behind them both. "Do they have bad taste or what?" Riordan could be heard saying as they walked away.

"Okay," Nikki said, breathing a huge sigh of relief. "Back to the drawing board?"

''What's the point,'' Reese said angrily, slapping her notebook closed with an angry snap.

Nikki stood up. ''The point, I believe, is uniforms for a professional airline crew. Let's keep that in mind. Hmm?''

Thirty new pilot hires were assembled in a leased training facility in a hangar at the airport. The first two days of their training was orientation, during which time they would hear a list of speakers from the roster of corporate officers, including Joe, Bob and Nikki. Then ground school and aircraft systems would begin in earnest for three weeks, followed by two weeks of simulator training.

Until Danny could hire a full-time teaching staff, he'd get help from Nikki, Eric and consultants.

Nikki had to go to ground school, too, as did Riddle. She'd also be teaching some of her own classes, which her degree and experience definitely qualified her to do. In the meantime, she was up to her eyeballs in work that had a very short deadline. Riddle had saddled her with the emergency-procedures manual, and she was trying to get ready for proving flights. And while there was a flight scheduler to plan the movement of the airplanes around the system, there was no crew scheduler as yet. She could do it—three airplanes, thirty pilots, sixty flight attendants. But when would she sleep? And there was the Med Link rep coming in for a meeting; that onboard communication would put a crew member in direct contact with a physician in the case of an ill passenger during flight. Nikki considered getting this contract high priority.

And the aircraft lessors were at the door. So many planes were scattered around the country, sitting idle, costing their owners millions. When a new airline started up, the leasing companies competed for business, and they wooed prospective clients with golf, fancy dinners and gifts. Riddle was taking on most of that, with Nikki's total good wishes; she simply couldn't fit any superfluous entertainment into her schedule. But it did feel as if his job was fine dining while hers was the hard work of getting an airline certified.

And the closing on her house was drawing near. Next week, she hoped. Thank God for Carlisle. Feeling more secure and safer now, he had thrown himself into helping the kids shop for their bedroom furnishings. The closets, as well as every inch of floor space, were filling up with new purchases from towels to bedding to kitchen items. How in the world she was going to find time to move into the house was beyond her. She desperately needed a wife.

Loaded down with accordion files, Nikki passed Crue's desk. Bob's office door was open, the light on, but no Bob. And Crue's desk was, as usual, neat. She appeared to be working at her computer at a leisurely pace.

Nikki stopped and looked at Crue until the woman turned her head. Nikki was unconsciously frowning, deep in thought. Crue gave an impatient snigger and Nikki shook herself. "Where did you work before coming here?" she asked. "TWA?"

"US Airways. TWA before that."

"A secretary?"

Crue shook her head but didn't offer anything more.

"Well? What?" Nikki pushed.

"Scheduling."

"Aircraft?"

She shook her head. "Cabin crews."

Nikki started to chuckle. She went around the corner and ducked into the conference room. Sitting down in a chair with wheels, the heavy files resting in her lap, she scooted out the door and down the hall until she sat right in front of Crue's desk. "You're going to wear me out with all that chatter," she said. Crue did not crack a smile. "Come on! Cripes." She sighed. "Crew scheduling at both airlines?"

Crue nodded.

"In what capacity?"

"What difference does it make?"

Nikki leaned a little over Crue's desk. "I need *help*."

Crue looked back at her computer, her fingers drifting to the keyboard. "He has someone in mind."

"What?"

"He said he has someone in mind for that job."

"Well, he hasn't told me that. In what capacity were you scheduling?"

"I was a manager at TWA, and after they folded I worked as a scheduler at USAir, then got laid off after 9/11."

"What systems did you use?"

Her lips pursed, as if she was getting angrier and angrier. But she answered, "Years ago it was a computer program made by SDI, then the Bornneman system, and... Well, there was pencil and paper."

Nikki grinned. "I'm only checked out on pencil and paper. You...ah...real busy with Bob's work?"

She took her time on that one. "Positively worn out," she said.

"Where is he?"

"Over at the airport, with the pilot class."

Nikki looked at her watch. "Damn. I gotta get over

there. Quick—why'd you take this job if you're a scheduler?''

"Lashawn is nine, Lincoln is eleven. And like I said, he has someone in mind for scheduling."

"Ha! Me," she said, standing. "Will you help me?"

"Will you pay me extra?"

"No. But if you do a decent job, I'll put my head to the task of trying to utilize your skills more effectively than this."

"And then he might just say he has someone in mind...."

"Look, I have thirty more seconds to screw around with this. You want the chance, or you want to do this forever?"

"Okay. But don't tell him," she said, tilting her head toward Riddle's office.

"Why not?"

"Don't make me say why. Just don't."

"He's not giving you a hard time, is he? He seems good with employees, especially women."

"He's not giving me a hard time." She held out her two very large, capable-looking hands. Nikki leafed through the stacks of files and found the one for crew scheduling. "Where's the manual?" Crue asked.

"I'll have Dixie scare it up for you before the end of the day. Thanks, Crue. Maybe if we churn this up a little, we can make butter."

As the workday drew to a close, Dixie organized her desktop and prepared to leave. The airline offices were beginning to quiet down. The receptionist had left and was no longer fielding calls—only those people with the direct numbers would get through. She took a fistful of messages to leave in Nikki's office, along with an updated list of the background checks she had completed. Nikki was simply amazing—spending all day teaching her own aircraft-systems training, leaving to have dinner with the kids, then back to the office to catch up on work that had accumulated during the day while she was in training.

Of course, Dixie's contribution was even more necessary now. And Dixie had surprised herself; she hadn't realized the extent of her capabilities. She was virtually running Flight Ops in conjunction with Nikki. She didn't need anyone to tell her—she was doing a great job. This was just the shot in the arm she needed.

She answered the ringing phone one more time, after which she'd switch it over to voice mail. To her absolute delight, it was the Phoenix real estate agent—Dixie had a buyer for her town house! A very interested buyer who wanted a fast closing. Now she could get about the business of house-hunting here in Las Vegas. She'd been in that town house for ten years and it was going to turn a nice little profit.

Before leaving the office, she visited the ladies room. On her way back to her desk, she was slowed by the sound of male voices, male laughter.

"Have you seen her? She's gorgeous!"

"Yeah, I've seen her. I heard we got her from Aries."

"Yeah, that's what I heard, too. She's in pretty good shape for being manhandled by those morons," came a third voice, followed by laughter. There must have been three men standing around her desk. "Just leave her a note, Sam. We can stop by tomorrow before training."

"Yeah, okay. So, how old you think that little honey is?"

"That I couldn't tell you. She's got a lot of miles on her, though."

"Who cares? I can't wait to get my hands on her."

"Yeah? Well, get in line. I'm senior to you."

"I just wanna get inside her. I'll bet I can make her purr like a kitten."

"You?" More laughter. "Yeah, right. You need help to find your zipper."

They moved away from her desk and down the hall. Sam was the only name she recognized; she didn't even know who the others were. But Dixie felt like the wind had been knocked out of her. Tears stung her eyes and she walked weakly to her desk. Through clouded vision she looked down at the note on her tidy desktop. "Dixie—what's the procedure for recommending a pilot applicant? Sam Landon."

Sam, joking with the guys about getting his hands on her? She'd thought he was such a gentleman. But that was the way of it—they always seemed so much nicer and more honest than they turned out to be.

She should have known her reputation would follow her. Airlines were just like small towns. Everyone knew someone who knew someone who had heard something. It was a business in which you either heard a rumor by noon or were required to start one.

Dixie sniffed, a deep and ragged sniff. Oh, God, she was so filled with regret! She could hardly breathe. It felt like a lifetime ago that she was at Aries, falling in love all the time and love never working out. She hadn't even realized how often it had happened, how many men she'd had, until the episode with Branch, when her supervisor pointed out her many failed relationships.

But Dixie had always practiced total fidelity. *Never* had there been more than one man in her life at a time. And yet she was clearly considered a slut. A tramp. *I heard she's got a lot of miles on her.*

She couldn't keep from crying. Not just crying, but snuffling and hiccupping, too. Tears were pouring out of her eyes, her nose began to run, and it was too late to stop. She grabbed a box of tissues out of her bottom desk drawer. No way was she going to hide in the bathroom and be found by one of the secretaries or, God forbid, Shanna or Crue. And she couldn't go back to the suites inn and face everyone there with a red nose and puffy eyes.

Sneaking around the corner, past Nikki's office door, Dixie let herself into the Flight Ops conference room. There wouldn't be any meetings tonight. She closed the door behind her and sat in the corner, in the dark, her purse and tissue box on her lap, and wept.

Just when she thought her life had changed for the better, she found instead that her old life had simply followed her. It hurt so deeply. Burying her face in her hands, her sobs muffled by tissue, she let it all go.

Without warning, the door flew open and the light flicked on. Danny didn't see her as he entered in a rush. He walked all the way around the table to the credenza at the end of the room where a stack of paper and a couple of manuals sat, obviously left behind after an FAA meeting.

He picked up a manual and began paging through it as he headed out of the conference room. Dixie sat frozen, praying he would turn off the light and leave without ever noticing her.

But no. He glanced up from the manual and saw her there, so small and pathetic in the corner, her face streaked and red.

"Dixie?" he said. He dropped the book on the conference table and went to her. "What in the world...?"

That only brought a new flood of tears. "I...need...to be...alone...."

He crouched down in front of her. "No way. What on earth happened?"

"Please..." she begged piteously. She couldn't remember ever crying like this before. Through all the breakups and broken hearts, nothing matched the pain she felt now.

Danny glanced over his shoulder at the open conference door and got up to close it. He then pulled a chair from the table and positioned himself directly in front of her, their knees touching.

"I can't leave you like this, Dixie. You're going to have to tell me what happened. Did someone die?"

A bubble of rueful laughter broke through her tears. "Just my reputation," she said. "I guess it was dead a long time ago."

A black frown covered his features. "What is this? Did someone say something mean to you?"

"I overheard," she said with a hiccup. "I was coming out of the ladies' room and there were some pilots gathered around my desk. They didn't know I was there."

Danny reached for her, grabbing her upper arms. "What, Dixie? What was said? Tell me."

She shook her head. "Why? What difference does it make now? There's nothing you can do."

"We don't know that. Maybe there is something. Just tell me."

"They said they heard I'd come from Aries. That I had a lot of miles on me, but one of them couldn't wait to get his hands on me. Then another one said—I couldn't believe this—he said he couldn't wait to get inside me and he could make me purr like a kitten. And then—oh, I don't really remember—they were laughing.

Said I was in pretty good shape after being manhandled by those morons at Aries.''

"Jesus," he said in disgust. "That's awful. Do you have any idea who they were?''

"One of them was Sam Landon, whom I thought was such a gentleman.''

"I thought so, too," Danny said, perplexed. "You're sure it was him?''

"I know for a fact because he left me a note. I think he was the one who said, 'Well, get in line—I'm senior to you.'''

"He said that? In reference to what?''

"The one who couldn't wait to get inside me and make me purr like a kitten.''

A dumbfounded look came over his face and he studied the wall behind her, thinking. Then his gaze came back to her face. "Dixie, did you hear any of them mention you by name?''

"No. But one of them said, just leave her a note. And the note was left by Sam.''

"And the note said?''

She shrugged. "What is the procedure for recommending pilot applicants?''

His face broke into a broad grin. "Dixie, I don't think they were talking about you. I think they were talking about our new airplane.''

"Huh?''

"Yeah. A sweet little honey that Aries dumped when they downsized. It's been sitting in storage in the desert for almost a year—the lessor is giving her to us at an incredible price.''

"No way," she said, and hiccuped.

"That's the only way I can explain the comment

about seniority. I mean, you don't date by seniority, do you?''

"Very funny!" She blew her nose. "Is it possible?"

He nodded. "Dixie, I'm not exactly a charter member of the boys' club, but I don't know you to have a bad reputation," he said. "Truthfully, I've never heard any but the nicest things about you."

"You're just saying that."

"No, I'm not. It's true—the men comment about you because you're very beautiful. But I haven't heard anyone say anything disrespectful. You have to know I wouldn't stand for it. What put this idea in your head?"

"Oh. It was probably what my supervisor at Aries said when she put me on suspension. Something about how I'd had far too many failed relationships for a nice girl…"

"That was a crappy thing to say."

"I think she was trying to help."

"Ah. She thought she'd help by saying something as demeaning as that. I'm sure glad she didn't want to hurt your feelings or anything."

Dixie laughed a little.

"You're a mess," he said. He wiped a tear off her cheek.

"Tell me about it. I don't know when I've ever cried so hard. Not since I was a kid. High school, maybe."

"And you're probably tired. You've been putting in some long days here."

"Everyone has…but it usually feels pretty gratifying."

"Why don't you go wash your face, blow your nose and let's go get something to eat."

"You don't have to do that, Danny—"

"Yes, I do. I'm starving. And I have to come back here and work tonight."

"I don't know...."

"Go wash your face. Hurry up now." He pulled her to her feet and gave her a little push out of the room.

Three hours later, when they were back in the NCA parking lot so she could hook up with her car, Dixie still didn't want the evening to end. "God, what a night. First I cry harder than I've ever cried, then I laugh like a fool all night."

"It felt good, didn't it?" he said.

"It sure did, but it's late. You were going to work some more."

"Don't worry," he said, indicating Nikki's car. "The boss is still here. I'll go in and make a good impression."

"Danny, thanks. You're a really good guy. A good friend."

"Aw. I'm just glad you feel better. I thought I was going to have to challenge someone to a duel."

That made her laugh all the more. She had always known Danny was a nice guy, but she had no idea he could be so much fun. So entertaining. She moved toward him and had to lean down a little to kiss his cheek. "Thanks. Don't work too hard, now."

As she headed toward her car, Danny retreated just a bit more into the shadows. He didn't want her to see how deeply he was blushing.

It was 9:00 p.m. and Sam didn't really expect Nikki to be in the office. He wanted to slip a note under her door explaining that he'd made a mistake reporting his flying hours. He'd been off by several hundred, but it shouldn't make too much difference, since he had thousands. Still, he wanted to be precise in all the paperwork that was kept on file.

Her light was on, the door open, so he leaned into the frame and tapped lightly a couple of times. He stopped himself. Her head was down on her desk. "Captain?" he asked quietly. She didn't move. Her hair fell in soft curls over her left arm.

He looked down the hall toward Riddle's office. All was dark at that end of the hall. In fact, only a faint light shone from around the corner in the opposite direction. This was probably not the best idea, sleeping on one's desk late at night in a mostly abandoned office building.

Her back rose and fell gently. She was probably dead on her feet. And she had said something in class about getting her kids settled in her new home before taking off to Phoenix for simulator training at Aries, her old stomping ground.

He went into her office and sat in the chair across from her desk. Now, this, he knew, was presumptuous. It might even piss her off, but he wasn't going to leave her alone in her office, asleep, vulnerable. And he'd wake her in a minute, but first he wanted to just sit here with her. While she was quiet.

Nikki was always on the move. She didn't look anything like Sam's late wife, but she had some of the same qualities—energy, a ready smile, intelligence, a quick wit. And like Leanne, when the energy ran out, she'd just conk out. Wham.

Leanne had been tall, dark and lean. Nikki was small, compact, fair and freckled. He wasn't sure of her age, somewhere around forty, he guessed. But she had such a girl-next-door look about her that she'd be one of those women who never seemed to age. Sometimes it was hard to concentrate on the material she was teaching in their training sessions. He was so easily taken by the way her green eyes danced in humor or snapped in quick response to a question.

Nikki Burgess was something of a legend. She'd been raised around aircraft of all kinds and had been a pilot since she was a young girl. An accomplished racer, she was also an engineer with a degree in aeronautics. And then there was that hard-won reputation—he'd heard she could fly the hell out of an airplane, a compliment that came grudgingly from the men who'd issued it.

It startled him to realize he hadn't had thoughts of any kind about a woman since Leanne's death. In fact, it threw him so off guard that he got up out of the chair and gently touched Nikki's shoulder. "Hey," he said softly. "Nick. Wake up."

She stirred slowly, sitting up, blinking. She wiped her mouth and looked at her watch, then at the crew schedule spread out on her desk. "Damn. Sam."

He stood in front of her desk, and when she looked up at him, he couldn't help but burst out laughing.

"What? Did I drool?" she asked.

"Not exactly. You have a cheek full of schedule."

She dug under her desk for her purse, found a mirror inside and checked it out for herself. "Great," she said, rubbing at the offending imprint. It was not going to come off easily.

"You've been asleep awhile."

"I must have hit the wall," she said. "What are you doing here?"

He shrugged. "It could have waited, but I had been studying and was restless. I thought I'd slip a note under your door—a correction on my hours." He pulled the paper out of his pocket and put it on her desk. "I don't know if this is a good idea, Nikki."

She looked at the page, the number of hours. "This is okay, Sam. There would only be an issue if you were close to the minimum. But thanks…"

"That's not what I meant. I mean, it's kind of late. Almost everyone is gone. You're practically alone."

She gave him a lopsided smile. "How 'guy' of you. We have security."

"Yeah, but—" He was going to say that there was enough security if she was awake, but sound asleep on her desk was another matter. "Okay, let's go have some pie."

"Pie?"

"Yeah. Right over at Appleby's. A cup of coffee, piece of pie, and then you'll be right to drive home."

"That does sound kind of good…."

He scratched at his own cheek. "You, ah, think that'll come off? Or maybe you could lay your other cheek on the page so you'll match."

Training had been clipping along at a nice pace, but today on her lunch break, Nikki was besieged by people in need. Everyone had learned that she'd be in class from eight to noon and would take a one-hour break in her office to return calls, sign letters and throw a deli sandwich, thoughtfully provided by Dixie, into her mouth.

Crue was waiting with a rough draft schedule for crews, along with some questions about seniority and how many reserve crews Nikki thought necessary in the first month of operation. There was also a guy from Rolls-Royce with the Wrench, who had been chasing her for days to talk about an engine replacement on one of the planes. She looked at her watch—she was more than an hour late for class.

"I am *so* sorry," she said when she finally flew into

the room. "It's the downside of being predictable. Everyone knew where to find me on my lunch break—and everyone did, I think." She put her books down on the table at the front of the room and took a breath. Then she looked at the pilots. There were barely concealed sniggers, some red faces, a couple of uncomfortable coughs. "Did I tuck my skirt in my girdle?" she asked.

Chuckles. She looked down at herself, making sure she didn't have toilet paper stuck to her shoe.

"All right," she said. "You're all looking very guilty. Have you been dipping braids in inkwells? What's going on?"

No one responded, so she focused on Bob Riddle. He shrugged.

Sam Landon eased himself away from his study table and went to the back of the room. He pulled some poster-size sketches from the trash can and held them up for Nikki to see. The attempt at pilot uniforms. He shuffled them, putting the turquoise spandex ensemble on top. There were some whoops and claps.

"Oh," she chuckled. "You like that one, huh? Want me to make a recommendation on behalf of this group?"

"It was suggested that this is the kind of stuff you get when you have a woman for a chief pilot," Sam said.

"Is that right?" she asked. She looked right at Bob.

"I told them all I'd never make them dress like that," he said, feigning innocence.

"And did you also tell them that I threw myself on those land mines at the risk of being pummeled to death by a roomful of transvestite dress designers?" There were a few chuckles, a couple of pointed and questioning looks at Bob, but Nikki didn't indulge any more speculation. She knew what had gone on. If Bob hadn't actually dug up and planted the sketches, he'd at least jumped on the opportunity to paint himself in a better light while doing what he could to damage her credibility. "Girl chief pilot, huh? Don't kid yourselves. Let's get right into chapter nine, the hydraulic system."

Twelve

Nikki had been looking forward to and dreading this day for weeks. She longed to get out of the suites inn, but she shuddered to think what it was going to take to settle into her new house. It would easily require three trips with a full SUV to empty out the two-room suite she and the kids had shared. She'd filled up every nook and cranny with weekend acquisitions.

Then there was the truck from her dad's place in Phoenix. A relatively small load, true, because she was leaving the three bedrooms of furniture there for herself and the kids when they visited. Visited? Hah! She hadn't taken a full day off since arriving in Las Vegas! And when she bought bedroom furniture for the new house, she'd furnished a room for Buck, as well, since his weekend visits would no doubt continue to be regular.

Furniture was also arriving for the family room, dining room and kitchen, and had been purchased from three different stores. Then there was Carlisle's U-Haul. Some of his furnishings would be moved into his new casita, and the rest he would put in long-term storage until he decided to strike out on his own again. He was driving everyone crazy with his concern over using that truck as storage for the past ten days. He was convinced his belongings would be stolen or damaged or maybe even bored to death, sitting in an RV rental park, waiting for the big day.

Nikki was going to have to buy cleaning supplies, groceries, pool chemicals and make those inevitable trips to Home Depot. And she wasn't exactly talented in this arena. But that was all right—Carlisle would be there, bossing everyone around. She had already decided that if they just did what Carlisle told them to do, everything would be fine.

Fortunately, the October weather was decent—temperature in the seventies, dry, pleasant, not too windy. Whoever had named Chicago the windy city hadn't been to Las Vegas. You could always tell the new residents by their lightweight lawn furniture and picnic umbrellas blowing down the street.

No prodding was necessary to get the kids going that morning; if anyone was more sick of the suites inn than Nikki, they were. The kids were determined to get everything thrown into their new rooms in time to use the pool. Carlisle had already made an early getaway with Dixie in tow.

Nikki had signed her life away for this house—far more house than she had ever aspired to. That Riordan better make this airline work, she thought. And the little voice that bounced back said, *Isn't that why he hired you, Captain Burgess?*

Her new neighborhood was crowded for an early Saturday morning. She spotted the U-Haul and several vehicles lined up around her house. It looked as though more than one family was moving. Then, to her astonishment, she saw that Dixie and Carlisle were standing in the drive, talking to a group of men—men she had not expected to see. They were holding court around a very large white cooler. Danny and Eric and three of their new pilots, Sam Landon, Ken Spencer and Jeff Hayden.

"So, boss," Sam said with a grin. "We heard it was moving day."

There was beer, sodas, water and juice in the cooler. With so many able hands to pitch in, Nikki no longer had to worry about Buck and Carlisle having to haul the heavier loads on their own. There were also errand runners galore—Danny took Dixie to fetch her car and check out of the suites inn, Jeff and Ken made a Home Depot run and returned with the requisite picture hangers, chair coasters, dryer-vent tubing and a few other incidentals. Sam picked up lunch at the sub shop, and later, while Nikki shopped for her cleaning supplies and groceries, the rest of the moving crew were back at the house doing as they were told by Carlisle.

Because of the size of the team, by six, the house was habitable. Beds were put together and made up. Shelf paper had been laid down and kitchen cupboards filled. The washer and dryer were installed and the computer hooked up. The phone company had been out, and the security alarm—new to Nikki and the kids—had been accidentally set off at least three times.

As evening came, the lights of the city glittered in the distance. There was nothing in the world like the view from their patio. The illuminated resorts actually glowed in the center of the valley—black, gold, bright emerald-green, red and purple. The beam from the top of the Luxor pyramid shot into the sky, while incoming planes lined up over the mountains like beacons, headed straight down the center of town to land right at the edge of the Las Vegas Strip.

Eric and Danny had taken off in late afternoon. Dixie

was helping Carlisle settle in his casita, while Nikki and her pilots pulled out cold beers and sodas from the cooler. In the absence of patio furniture, they dragged dining room chairs outside. But for now this was perfect—Jared splashing around in the pool, the sound of April's radio from her bedroom window, Buck tinkering around with something or other in the garage, and here in the back, above the lights of the beautiful city, Nikki and her friends.

She had never dared envision this life.

"Well, boss, I think we have you fixed up pretty good," Sam said.

"I'm not used to that... Being called 'boss' all the time."

"I think you like it," he said.

"Yeah, she doesn't have any *quelms* about it," Ken said, drawing laughter from them all.

"She has a real *profencity* for it," said Jeff.

Nikki just smiled. She wanted to laugh with them, but she had to remember her position. And pilots talked. Theirs were some of the loosest lips in recorded history. But she was glad, relieved in fact, that they had noticed Riddle's funny vocabulary. It meant that there was a good chance other things about him might be noticed. Like the fact that he didn't appear to be doing any work.

"She's not laughing, guys."

"She can't laugh. She works for him."

Nikki's smile just grew a bit wider, but still she said nothing.

"That right, boss?"

"Have you seen the company's organizational chart?" Nikki queried. "The chief pilot works under the VP of Operations who works under the president."

"Yeah," Jeff said. "And laughing at him could create a whole *madrid* of problems."

By now the men were laughing so hard that Nikki couldn't help but give in to a snigger or two.

"As great as it would be to hang around and drink myself stupid with you guys, I have to study," Sam said at last.

"You haven't had anything but Diet Coke all day," Ken said.

"I can't afford to," Sam said. "I haven't flown in two years. I have to study."

"Yeah, all right," Ken relented. "Come on, Jeff. We probably could get a little smarter, too."

"Surely not much," Nikki said, then had to listen to their protests. She stood to see them to the door. "Listen, it was really smart of you guys to come over here and help me move in. Now when I'm looking for management people, I'll be influenced."

"Well, that was easy," Jeff said.

"I do appreciate it."

Within a few days of moving into her new house, Nikki was headed back to Phoenix for simulator training. Not all airlines had simulators for pilot training, but Aries had three 757/767 sims and leased time to other airlines. In such a harsh economic environment, the simulators were better moneymakers than the planes.

She'd only been gone for six weeks, so it wasn't exactly like a reunion, but she did find that many of the pilots she'd flown with over the years were seeking her out between simulator sessions to ask about the new operation.

But for Riddle, who was there, too, it was like a victory lap. "Yes, I'm spearheading the certification process, and I must say, I've assembled an *exemplatory* team."

Nikki winced visibly when she heard him tell that to a couple of Aries pilots and his simulator instructor.

As the chief pilot, she'd worked with the training department to set up the sim schedule, and even though Riddle was number one on the seniority list and Nikki was number two, she arranged that they would *not* go into the box together. She was afraid she'd have to carry him the whole time, and twice as afraid that if he had serious problems, he'd somehow manage to blame her. So she had Danny take him, and Nikki paired up with tall, quiet Eric from Texas.

Also in Phoenix was a third of the first class—ten pilots. They stayed at a downtown Tempe hotel, right on the university campus, close to the airport. Nikki could have stayed at Buck's—it would have been close, familiar and free, and would save NCA a few dollars—but she thought it best to stay with her group and, if possible, continue the bonding.

In addition to regular sim training, Nikki, Danny and Bob were being given an extra two-day course that would qualify them as check airmen at the start of operation. That way they wouldn't have to go through the twenty-five hours of Initial Operating Experience with a check airman that would be required of the other pilots. The three of them could then provide the training of the other check airmen during proving flights with the FAA.

Nikki said nothing. This was what Riddle wanted, and it was his prerogative, being the boss and a pilot. But the facts were simple—he'd had trouble flying as a first officer at Aries. He wasn't check airman material. He wasn't even captain material.

That aside, they hoped to get at least six check airmen

out of their initial group of thirty pilots. Nikki would take recommendations from Bob, Danny and Eric, but the decision was ultimately hers.

For a week they worked like dogs, taking four-hour sessions in the box with a one-hour briefing on each side of that. The FAA inspectors were all over them; they wouldn't let anything slide by. It wasn't just the standard operating procedures that were being thrown at them, but the most challenging problems—engine fires, clear air turbulence, loss of hydraulics, rapid fuel leaks, sudden cabin decompression and, literally, the cause of every fatal aircraft accident known to the FAA. The simulator, a cockpit inside a box that stood up on four hydraulic legs, rocked like a carnival ride while the pilots inside struggled to manage every possible flying situation. They would frequently come out soaking wet.

But they all did pretty well. Almost all.

Nikki found Danny in the hotel coffee shop at 6:00 a.m. He was just returning to the hotel after a sim session that took place in the middle of the night, while Nikki was getting ready for hers. He sat in a corner booth nursing a cup of coffee. "That's gonna keep you awake," she said.

"This isn't what's going to keep me awake," he said. "Riddle can't do it, Nick. Forget check airman, the FAA isn't going to sign him off as captain."

Thank God, she thought in utter relief. She was afraid that by some miracle he'd make it and the FAA would pass him.

She slid into the booth across from Danny. "The FAA could make our lives real easy. We flew with him at Aries—we all know what we know. Does he get it now?"

Danny slowly shook his head. "He thinks he's *exemplatory*. He wants more training time before he takes a check ride."

"What have you said to him?"

"That if I were his training captain, I wouldn't recommend him for a check ride. He told me I didn't know what I was talking about."

Nikki shook her head slowly, mystified. She had the opposite problem. She could come out of the sim feeling that she just hadn't performed to her standards, and the inspector would tell her she was brilliant with the airplane. "He's amazing," she said. "He can barely keep the greasy side down and he thinks he's Sky King."

"I know. Based on what I've seen this past week, I would not hire him if I were in charge. Not as a first officer."

"Damn him, why doesn't he have any concept of his limitations? The only way I'd put my kids on his plane is if he had a really strong captain in charge. I'm not saying he shouldn't fly—but he's just not up to this equipment. He can't handle it. It's too fast a horse."

"Well, whether he sees it or not, there's no way the FAA is going to bless him as a check airman."

"That's only half my problem. They might pass him over for captain and let him fly copilot. And I don't like it. That leaves too big a margin for error."

"What are your options?"

"I'm going to go at him. Are you comfortable backing me up?"

His expression was pained. Going up against the boss? Telling him he sucked at flying? Oh, man, Danny hated the idea. "I don't think *comfortable* is the right word... but I'll do it."

They decided on four o'clock that afternoon. Nikki

and Danny went to Riddle's hotel room as opposed to a public setting. When Bob opened the door, the look on his face suggested maybe he actually did understand reality, but just didn't like it.

"Can we talk?" she asked.

"I don't have a lot of time."

"Make time," she said. "It's really urgent."

He held the door open. "Get straight to the point."

Nikki was determined that this was not going to be a replay of the last time she'd flown with him, when he simply ignored her opinion of his technique and walked away from the situation as quickly as possible. She entered his room and went to a chair by the window. Danny followed her and took the other one, leaving Bob to sit on his bed and face them.

"Danny tells me the box is challenging you."

He shrugged. "It challenges everyone."

"You're having trouble, Bob," Danny said. "The FAA inspector said he wouldn't recommend you for a check."

"Hell, that happens with regularity," he said, brushing it off.

"It hasn't happened to anyone else we've got in the sim," Danny pointed out. "In fact, the FAA has been pretty impressed over all."

"Maybe it's my sim partner more than me," he suggested.

Nikki scooted forward in her chair. "Bob, I've been a check airman for years. You had trouble when you and I flew together. Cut your losses. Save face. You don't have to fly in your job. As long as one of us is qualified and on the certificate, the FAA will give its blessing."

"*What?*" he reeled, standing abruptly. Even Danny

started, swiveling his head toward Nikki in surprise. He'd had no idea she was going to do that.

But Nikki didn't startle. "If you pursue this, there's a good chance the FAA will fail you. It's almost guaranteed they're not going to give you check airman status. Before you have to live with that on your reputation, call time out. You're too busy and you manage the entire operation," she pointed out, giving him way more credit than he was due. "You'll be ahead of the game—when too many pilots call in sick on Christmas, you won't have to fill in. Make this your decision, not ours."

"Ours?" he demanded, still standing.

"Yes," she said coolly.

"Yes, ours," said Danny.

"I'm as disappointed as you," Nikki went on, "but the 757 doesn't appear to be your strong suit. Let it go before it gets taken away from you."

"I can't believe you dare to do this, to suggest this. Who the hell do you think you are?"

She stood so she could meet his eyes levelly. "I'm the chief pilot and I'm charged with the safety of this flying operation. Think about this. It makes sense."

"You'd better go."

"Believe me, this is not fun for me," she said.

Bob stood aside, stone-faced, waiting for them to leave. As they were walking down the hotel hallway, he called to Danny's back, "I'm going to be switching a few things around tonight. I'm going to fly with someone else."

Danny nodded. "Suit yourself."

That night it was Sam Landon who met Riddle at the sim. Of all the people there for training, he'd picked the one guy who hadn't flown in a long time. Nikki suspected it was to divert attention from his own incompetence if the session didn't go well. She hung around the training building until they came out. They were both drenched in sweat. The FAA inspector had a cut on his forehead that she later learned was the result of hitting the sharp corner of the exit sign inside the sim during a particularly tumultuous ride.

Two days later, Bob Riddle went back to Las Vegas without taking a check ride. He was hanging his wings.

In the outdoor section of a small bar and restaurant right in the middle of the little college town, Nikki saw Sam reading a propped-up newspaper while eating a hamburger. She leaned over the railing. "Sam?" When he saw who it was, there was no mistaking the pleased look in his eyes. "Have room for one more?" she asked.

"Absolutely."

She sat across from him. "Well, I'm relieved to see you're still speaking to me."

"Why wouldn't I be?"

"That fiasco with Riddle. You must have thought that was my doing. Or Danny's."

"Riddle called me himself. Said Danny was not up to his standards and asked if I'd fly copilot for him. I said I thought he might be making a mistake—I've heard Danny's very good."

"He's the best. New Century got very lucky there. But you certainly didn't embarrass yourself. I heard you did a great job. And Bob has decided he just doesn't have the time to devote to both flying and running operations."

"Is that the party line?" he asked, picking up his hamburger and taking a healthy bite.

"That's just what I've been told," she said. The

waiter approached their table and she pointed to Sam's plate. "Bring me one of those, and a Coke."

Sam took his time finishing that big mouthful of hamburger. He wiped his greasy fingers, then took a drink of water. Finally he said, "Riddle can't fly."

"Is that so?" she returned.

"Look, I know you have to be political, and I can appreciate that, but if you let pilots of his caliber slip by, this company is going to be in big trouble."

"I didn't hire Bob," she said.

He put his elbows on the table and laced his hands under his chin, studying her for a moment. "But you know all about him."

Nikki assumed he held her gaze to measure the honesty of whatever she said next, but something unrelated to this discussion was going on with her, just as it always did when she was with Sam. She felt herself growing warm, and it was not the balmy October afternoon or the sun. It was Sam. That rugged face, strong, square jaw, gorgeous big brown eyes under bushy brows. When he grinned, it sliced through her with a searing heat. He was going to think she was lying because she began to fidget and she could feel her cheeks start to glow. When was the last time she'd blushed? In 1980? "I know about him," she said. "Don't let your burger get cold."

He let a little smile slip through before picking up the sandwich again.

"Based on what the FAA inspector said about your performance, I was wondering if you're interested in the check airman program. It pays a little extra, but you'll earn it."

His mouth was full. This time she had surprised him; he couldn't even chew. The corners of her lips turned up in a smile. This was kind of fun—dropping a bomb just as he bit into a big, sloppy burger.

After a moment he said, "Wow. I wasn't expecting that."

"Why not? I hear you're an excellent pilot."

"That so? They don't lavish the praise on you in the box. They're afraid it'll make you weak."

"They told the right person. You want to think it over?"

"Yeah, maybe I better. Thanks."

"It is a good deal, however. We haven't nailed down all the pay issues yet, but Danny and I have been talking to Riordan about a twelve thousand dollar a year bump in pay. In a start-up, that's decent."

"In a start-up it takes you above the poverty level," he joked.

Her cola arrived and she took a drink. He dived into that burger again and she just couldn't resist. "I bet you want to know what they said about your sim with Riddle."

Caught with his mouth full again, he peered at her over the large bun. But this time he chewed slowly and swallowed. As the waiter passed, Sam beckoned him.

"Yes, sir?"

"Are you going to bring her food pretty soon?"

"I'll check on that, sir."

"Thanks," he said. He sat back in his chair and looked at Nikki curiously. "Were you a dentist in another life?"

Nikki was attracted to Sam in a very big way, and if she was honest, she had been since that first cup of coffee. It was something she was just going to have to live with, because there was no way she could let herself get involved with him. He worked for her. She wouldn't risk it.

But a little over a week in the same hotel and training center threw them into each other's company quite often, and she grew to like him more and more. She loved his sense of humor, the easy camaraderie he seemed to have with his fellow pilots, and the way those few wild gray hairs defied the proper shape of his eyebrows. Then there was the strength of his forearms and the size of his hands; it seemed as if a plane…a *person*…would be so safe with him. Sometimes when she watched him, it really did feel as though the ground shifted just slightly under her feet.

This hadn't happened to Nikki in forever. There was that childhood romance with Paul, the disastrous rebound with Drake, which, if not for the kids, she would regret till the end of time. Once or twice over the years she had felt the stirring of attraction, but never at work. Nikki had never been big on flirting, either, so if a man didn't make a move, no moves were made. But she wasn't a total mannequin. She had managed a near affair with one of the soccer coaches after the divorce, but he was much younger than she was, and though he wasn't April or Jared's coach, it had felt a little too close for comfort.

She tried not to look at Sam too often or too hard for fear someone would pick up the clues—for fear *Sam* would pick up the vibes. No way would she complicate an already-complicated career position by introducing an office romance.

Not that such relationships were discouraged. On the contrary, if ever there was an industry in which work-related romances were common, it was the airlines. On the plus side, a lot of people had relationships or marriages and worked together successfully in the same air-line for years. They had a great deal in common, after all.

On the minus side, there were the inevitable affairs that resulted from sending small groups of men and women out on the road together, where they worked in a very tight space and then spent their off-time in hotels.

But as long as the romances were between consenting adults and not destructive, the administration didn't have a problem. So that aspect had nothing to do with Nikki's hesitation. She had two very clear reservations. She did not want the men who worked for her to think she was just another girl. And she did not want to risk her heart and have it broken. Again.

So she looked at Sam now and then, felt that little lift in her heart, that unsteadiness in her stance, and covered it with a laugh. She might have the odd dream in which he was present, but as far as the other pilots knew, as far as Sam knew, their relationship was strictly professional.

She didn't even tell Dixie.

As for Dixie, Nikki had known that the room she was using at the new house was just temporary, but she had no idea how temporary. While she was in Phoenix, Dixie had found what she described as an adorable little house with an adorable little pool just a few neighborhoods away. "Within walking distance, if you can believe that," she had said over the phone. "Carlisle and I are staying here with April and Jared until you get back, but we're going to make up my room for Buck so it'll be ready for him."

"I can't wait to get home," Nikki said. "Really, my first house."

She was fortunate to be returning on a Saturday morning so she could spend a day or two with the kids, getting to know her new house. If it were a weekday, she'd be haunted by the piles of work in her office, but after ten days away, she was more than due a break.

The closer Nikki got to Las Vegas, the more excited she became. As she drove to her new neighborhood, her heart pounded with enthusiasm.

It would feel so good to organize her house. To do laundry in her own laundry room. To wander into the kitchen late at night and find some tasty leftovers in the fridge.

She entered the kitchen through the garage and was greeted with the mind-bending aroma of freshly baked cookies. They were cooling on the cutting board next to the oven. She glanced around. The family room was immaculate with fresh vacuum tracks lined up perfectly on the carpet, and several magazines were neatly arranged on the coffee table.

In the living room, a vase held fresh flowers, and a couple of potted plants and a ficus in a brass pot were new additions. The sun slanted in through the shuttered windows, and the ceiling fan lazily circulated the air. A new area rug graced the marble foyer.

Nikki took her suitcase up the stairs to the master bedroom, where she found everything she owned put away in perfect order. There was even a shoe tree in one of the walk-in closets, obviously purchased by Carlisle. In fact, everything new must have been purchased by Carlisle, and she would have to make him whole.

She put her suitcase in the extra closet; she'd deal with it another time. The alarm made its beeping signal that a door had been opened and she heard Jared call, "Mom?"

"Up here," she yelled, then ran toward him. They

met on the stairs. Both kids were hugging her, yammering about school, sports teams and concerts and friends, even though they'd talked at least once every day. They pulled her along to their bedrooms, which were now completely settled.

The phone in April's room was ringing by the time Nikki had toured both rooms. Soon she would probably resent that ringing phone, but right now it symbolized her daughter's budding friendships, her acceptance into her new community, and for that Nikki was enormously grateful.

April lay on her bed, legs crossed, chatting and laughing. Jared had already fled—she heard the front door slam—so she went to the kitchen, where she found Carlisle sitting at the breakfast bar with a glass of iced tea and a magazine in front of him. She looked at him with utter gratitude and affection. "Will you marry me?"

He let the magazine flop closed. "I don't think so, Nick. You're just not my type."

Joe Riordan called her cell phone on Sunday evening and asked her to stop by his office first thing Monday morning. When she got there, he handed her a piece of paper, a printed e-mail.

Subject: Chief Pilot
Date: 10/28/04 1:44:42 p.m. Pacific Daylight Time
From: BRiddle
NCA.com (Riddle, Bob)
To: JRiordan
NCA.com (Riordan, Joe)
To the President:
It has come to the attention of several of the

pilots hired in the first class, the majority of thirty of us, that the choice of chief pilot is causing problems. Most of us have tried to keep an open mind and not base any of our judgments on the fact that she's a woman and just thinks differently than a man. But the fact is, she's a poor communicator, she has an attitude of superiority, and worst of all, she isn't good in the cockpit and isn't good at deciding who is—yet she has appointed herself as someone who will arbitrarily select all check airmen. I'd hate to see a company this good start to falter before it even gets started, but nothing will get a union in here faster than an incompetent female leader.

Anonymous

Nikki looked up from the page to Riordan. She was a little confused. Not by what Riddle said in his e-mail; that was painfully clear.

"What the fuck is that?" Joe said, not in a patient tone.

She shook her head. "It looks like an e-mail from someone who doesn't know how to send an anonymous e-mail."

"Nobody is that stupid. Maybe someone hijacked his computer over the weekend."

"We have locks on our doors. We have passwords."

"You think it's him?"

"I know he feels this way about me. Frankly, I could give a rat's ass."

"He feels that way about you because you're a woman?" Joe asked.

"Partly. And partly because I took the airplane away

from him once and told him he was about to make a horseshit landing. And partly because the FAA wasn't going to pass him for check airman and it was looking iffy for Captain, and he'd like everyone to believe it's because I paid them large sums of money and had sex with them rather than because he's a limp stick.''

"Oh, Jesus Christ…"

"I wasn't even close to the situation. Danny Adams, director of training and head of the check airman group, came to me with serious concerns. I wouldn't have been doing my job if I hadn't said something to Riddle.''

"Goddamn it…"

"I suggested that rather than being failed, he take the opportunity to save face. Choosing not to fly is an option. I'll stay current, have my name on the FAA certificate.''

"Son of a bitch…"

"I think he's wrong about the pilots in the first class, Joe. I have good rapport with them. A few of them surprised me by helping me move into my house. The sim went well for everyone but Riddle. I don't think I lack credibility with them because I'm female.''

"Jesus, Mary and Joseph," he said, rubbing a hand along the back of his neck.

"Well, what the hell do you want me to say?" she demanded rather more hotly than she had intended.

"You don't have to say anything!" he shouted back. "I have a goddamn vice president who can't even send an anonymous e-mail! You can be goddamn sure *that* wasn't on his fancy résumé!"

"Yeah, well, I can't—"

"If he hadn't delivered three excellent manuals into the hands of the FAA just last week, I'd fire the snotty dipshit.''

Nikki's eyes grew huge. She was speechless. "What manuals?" she asked quietly.

"I don't know. I think it was emergency procedures, cockpit check lists and something else."

Her cheeks were on fire. *Her* manuals. He'd taken them from her office while she was at the simulator and handed them in, taking credit for them.

"At least he's not a total—" Riordan noticed her grim expression. "What? You have something to tell me?"

He said, she said? The chances were pretty good Riordan would believe her over Riddle, especially after this ridiculous e-mail, but she just wasn't sure she wanted to go there. "No," she said.

He wore a disbelieving smirk and began to nod his head facetiously. "If you have something to say, you'd better say it before the opportunity passes."

"I have a very sick feeling the opportunity will come again."

Thirteen

Nikki put a note with instructions on how to send an anonymous e-mail on top of the printed sheet Riordan had given her and handed it to Crue. "Put this on Bob's desk for me, please," she said.

Crue glanced at the page very quickly and shot a startled look at Nikki.

"Yeah, I know. Kind of hard to believe, isn't it? By the way, I went over the schedule you put together and I think it might be flawless. You're very good. I'll keep my promise, Crue. But one battle at a time, okay?"

The secretary only nodded, dumbstruck by her boss's e-mail fiasco.

"Did you know about the manuals?" Nikki said.

Crue looked down at her desk.

"I see. Well, there was nothing you could do, I suppose."

"I was going to tell you," she said very quietly. "As soon as you got in."

"That would have been risky for you," Nikki said.

Crue took on a fiercely proud yet pleading expression. "You understand, I need this job."

Nikki nodded. "One battle at a time."

The airline was rapidly taking on weight; the countdown to flying paying passengers had begun. The pace around the office, particularly in reservations, marketing, accounting and among Riordan's staff was picking up speed. Bookings were coming in faster as the date of the inaugural flights approached. Every department fleshed out and grew in size. Nikki, Danny and Eric were ready to begin proving flights with the FAA as soon as the flight attendants passed their aircraft evacuation check.

Another airplane at a bargain price was located, so Nikki prepared to hire another class of ten pilots. Once an operation was up and running, it took two to three months to crew an airplane. If they could get all thirty of their first pilots qualified, Eric could find among them a competent hiring committee, and that would be one more job she could delegate.

Even in the throes of certification, it was personnel issues that kept the chief pilot's office busy. A little background checking, which Dixie was getting very good at, showed one of their new pilots to be saddled with a conniving ex-wife who liked to get on the phone and accuse him of unspeakable things for which there were no police records. For some reason, a lot of pilots had complicated and melodramatic personal lives. Another of their lads had made a rather large blunder in his reported flying hours. He'd also exaggerated his previous employment, adding an awful lot of time with an employer to make himself look more desirable. It was Nikki's first experience with firing someone. Then Danny called to say he was sending a new hire to see her. "He started training really strong, then something happened. He fell apart in the sim, like he couldn't focus. I'm convinced it's a personal problem."

Blake Thompson, forty, sat in her office staring down at his lap.

"If you're worried about confidentiality, I can do my best to keep whatever you tell me between us," she said.

He looked up slowly. "Do your best?"

"Obviously, if you have a problem that has to be reported to the FAA…"

"It's nothing like that," he said. "Look, I've been out of work awhile. I just got this job, just got back in the cockpit, and I can't afford to go another few years without flying."

"Don't get ahead of yourself. You sure you're going to lose your job? It must be serious if—"

"My brother's in kidney failure," he said flatly.

Nikki was confused. Brow wrinkled, she waited.

"He needs a kidney."

"You need some time off?" she asked.

"I just started training," he said. "And I'm a match."

"Blake, spit it out. I don't see the problem—other than this isn't a real good time, personally, for you to take a check ride, worrying about your brother the way you are."

He gave a hollow laugh. "Don't you get it? I have to choose between keeping this job and saving my brother's life."

She looked at him a long moment. "Why?" she finally asked.

"It'll take months before I'm medically approved to get back in the cockpit! I've worked here three weeks! You gonna let me take three months off after working here for three weeks?"

She folded her hands on top of her desk. "Blake, have you talked to the flight surgeon about your medical? Are you okay to fly with one kidney?"

"Yeah, that's not the issue. It's the time off."

"No, the time off is not the issue. Haven't you looked

at your benefits package? We don't do sick leave here. If you're sick, you get your base pay until you're well. Your seniority number is not affected.''

The shock registered on his face. "I figured that was for, you know, your basic illnesses. Like the flu."

"No, it's for any illness or injury. If we couldn't support you helping your brother, would you want to work for us?"

"But how can you do that? How can NCA afford to do that?"

"It's actually more cost effective. Studies have shown that people who don't have, say, six days a year of sick leave don't take time off unless they're really sick, but when employees get a certain number of days, they regard them as vacation. In the end, those long-term absences are few—and Joe would rather you have actual vacation than sick leave. So, the vacation is more than average, the sick leave less." She smiled at him. "He's not stupid, Blake. Not only is it cheaper in the long run, but happy and healthy employees do better work."

He shook his head and laughed. "I'm dreaming, aren't I?"

"Go take care of your family business. Let us know what's going on, like where the surgery will take place."

They both stood and he put out a hand. "Captain Burgess, I don't know how to thank you."

"Just come back well and ready to get to work."

It was that piece of business that made her feel all the hard work was worth every second. She knew of no other airline with such a policy.

The days were still long, but Nikki was not going back to the office after dinner so much anymore. What she couldn't do in eight to ten hours would have to wait for the next day; she wasn't going to risk her family or let herself get exhausted this close to the start-up of the operation. The kids had been such great sports about her heavy schedule, and getting home to them at the end of the day was something she looked forward to.

Plus, she *loved* that house. Sitting outside by the pool in the comfortable October evenings as the lights of the city came up was more rejuvenating than a full body massage. She didn't think things like houses mattered to her, so she was surprised by how excited she was about this one. Buck's house was large and perfectly fine, and he kept it in good repair, but it wasn't what she'd call beautiful. The house she'd had her children in had been chosen by Drake, and he'd approved all the furnishings and decor. Sometimes she had felt he only let her live there.

But this house felt like *hers.* Even though Carlisle and the kids had found it, she was the one who brought them all to Nevada. Giving Carlisle and April a free hand with the furnishings didn't make the house feel any less like her haven from the world. Her haven with her loved ones.

She could actually feel her spirits lifting as she pulled into the drive, then into the garage. But as she entered the house through the garage door, she stopped suddenly.

Something was different.

She was afraid to move. The hair at the nape of her neck prickled and her pulse picked up speed. She took two cautious steps toward the kitchen, praying it was not so.

"Well, there you are, Nicole," Opal said.

Oh, God, it *was* her and her obnoxious white poodle. Her cologne scented the air—gaggingly sweet. It would be a year before that cloying smell would be out of the walls. Nikki knew when Opal was in the same city, much less her own house. Damn. April must have known Opal was coming and kept it from her.

"Mother," she said. "When did you get here?"

"Just this afternoon, maybe two hours ago. April wanted to call you at the office and tell you we'd arrived, but I wouldn't let her. I wanted to be a surprise." She cradled Precious in the crook of her arm, stroking him.

"And so you are," Nikki said. There stood Opal in the kitchen, with Jared and April at the breakfast bar. April had that wild-eyed, perplexed look on her face that said, *I didn't know!* But Nikki didn't believe it for one second.

"That charming young homosexual fixed up a guest bed for me. I must say you have surprised and impressed me, Nicole. I am astonished at your good taste and sense of style." She let her gaze drift about in appreciation of the house and its decor.

Jared rolled his eyes and April looked petrified, as though Nikki might beat her later.

"Where is Carlisle?" she asked tentatively.

"I believe he's in his little guest house. He said something about work."

"Well, since you're in good hands, let me go tell him I'm home. I'll be right back."

Nikki went to the casita, muttering under her breath that she was not going to be able to do this. She could not have Opal here for long; it would give her gastroenteritis. In fact, she felt her stomach begin to rumble at the thought. Why hadn't she forbidden April from inviting Opal to visit? Because A, Opal was her grandmother and she deserved to have a grandmother who loved her, even if it was Opal; and B, April probably would have encouraged her visit, anyway. Nikki just hoped she could hold her tongue; she had a tendency to confront her mother and turn an unpleasant situation into an all-out bloody fight, which made her feel worse in the end.

She tapped on Carlisle's door and waited. "Coming," he called. When he finally got there, he was shirtless and in his uniform pants, a towel around his neck and his hair wet from the shower.

"Do you have to work or are you running away from home?" she asked.

He laughed and held the door open for her. "I do have to work, actually. I was called in because of a shortage. I think the feisty union devils are throwing their weight around. Just a two-day trip."

"I apologize for Opal. I can't do anything about her."

"Not to worry, Nick. She doesn't bother me as much as she bothers you."

"Oh, come on. She's even more offensive than Buck. At least Buck is joking around, but I know in his heart he loves you like a son. Opal…?"

"She did ask me if I thought it wise to have someone of my homosexual persuasion minding the children."

"No!" Nikki almost shouted, amazed at the things Opal would say. "I hope you slapped her."

He shrugged. "I just told her that if Rosie O'Donnell could manage, I could." He grinned. "Your mother *loves* Rosie."

"Maybe she won't stay long," Nikki said hopefully.

Carlisle lifted one brow in a devilish gesture. "She likes your house, Nikki. She mentioned that she likes Vegas in the wintertime."

Nikki thought about that for a moment and said, "I'm going to kill myself."

When she went back to the kitchen, her mother was not there, but April was. Jared had obviously escaped; he was not inclined to hang out with his grandmother and sister. "Mom, I had absolutely no idea...." April whispered this, looking around guiltily. Nikki saw the shifting shadows of her mother's shape on the patio. She was outside; the door was ajar.

"But you told me you invited her."

"Yes, but I didn't think she'd just *come*. Without calling. Without asking. She's never done anything like that before."

"Yes, she has. The whole time I was growing up she would just appear, out of the blue. It was only with your father that she was cautious, because she didn't want to make him angry and lose her nice accommodations. But..."

Had Opal really appeared out of the blue when Nikki was growing up, or had Buck not warned her because for years after Opal left them, Nikki would throw a holy fit at the mere thought of her visit. She was an incorrigible monster where her mother was concerned. Even though Opal probably deserved her behavior, Nikki had to concede she'd been a horrid kid.

Then when she was about sixteen, there had been a shift in her behavior. Just when other teenage girls were beginning to rebel, Nikki straightened up and bore Opal's visits more stoically. Lucille, who owned the café at the airport, had said to her, "One day you're going to realize she could have taken you with her. Buck wouldn't have had a prayer of getting custody of you, the way he is, raising you at an airport, never making curfews, feeding you every meal at my lunch counter, letting you go to school in your pajamas if it suits you.

If you don't start being nice to Opal, she's going to think Buck's lost control of you and take you home with her.''

Nikki had nightmare visions of charm school, froufrou clothes and no airplanes. She cleaned up her act then and there. Her mother got on her every nerve, but she was as polite as possible.

''But what?'' April whispered.

''I was just remembering. I wonder if she paid surprise visits or if Papa didn't tell me she was coming because I was so hateful to everyone when I faced my annual makeover and photo session and dinners out with Opal and Mayer.''

''Grandpa,'' April said, for though he was a stepgrandfather, April had considered Mayer Gould as one of her grandpas.

''But you know, she stayed in a hotel when she came to town, because she'd never stay with your papa. After I married your dad, she'd stay with us for a few days if she visited alone, but if Mayer was along, it was always a hotel. This is her first visit since I've had a house of my own. I have a sinking feeling her routine is going to—''

The door swung open. ''You have a most marvelous view of the city, Nicole,'' she said.

''Would you like to have a glass of wine, Mother? On the patio?''

''I would be delighted. And what are we doing for dinner?''

''Well, since I wasn't expecting you, I haven't made any plans and—''

''I'll bet that nice young homosexual man—''

''*Mother!*'' she snapped. She took a breath. ''I don't want to fight with you the very moment you've arrived, but you must stop referring to Carlisle that way. Use his *name*."

"Well. Gracious. Do you think I don't know what's what? I live in San Francisco, you know. And I don't dislike homosexuals. Though I find some of them tiresome. But not George or Frank—I rely on them for everything...."

"When you speak of Carlisle, use his name. Please."

Opal made some pooh-poohing sounds, but she didn't argue.

Nikki went for the wine, and in the refrigerator she found that Carlisle had indeed left something. It appeared to be his famous chicken pesto on penne. What a peach.

She poured two glasses. "And another thing, Mother. I'm sure you know this but hadn't considered it when you made your plans. Dad comes up every weekend. He looks forward to it and has his own room."

"Of course I know that, Nicole. Your father and I talk, you know."

"You do?" she asked stupidly. "You do not," she argued.

"We do indeed. Always have."

"No way," she said. She looked at April. "Have you ever heard that?" April shrugged helplessly.

"Yes, we've always kept in touch. Not so often as to pester each other, but regularly. At first I wanted to be sure you were fine, and later it was force of habit."

Nikki handed her mother a glass of wine and took a couple of gulps from hers. *I am too tired for any more of her surprises,* she thought. But she was determined to call Buck later and check this out. It would turn out that Opal called him once a year, she was sure of it. Her mother had a tendency to stretch the truth.

''Well,'' Nikki said. ''Should I call Dixie and invite her to join us for dinner?''

''Yes, do,'' Opal said. ''She's such a fabulous dresser. I am always so anxious to see what she's wearing. The same as that charming young ho—'' She cleared her throat under Nikki's threatening glare. ''The same is true of Carlisle. Such a clotheshorse.'' Then she smiled conspiratorially. ''But then, they all are, you know.''

Dixie kept asking herself why she had felt it necessary to lie. She could have told the truth. But she was too afraid Nikki would caution her. ''Remember, Dixie, what we decided. No dating, especially pilots.'' Although Dixie might have considered this dating, she was certain Danny did not. He was as warm and darling and sweet as could be, but kept her at arm's length. Just a friend.

So she had said to Nikki, ''Oh, gosh, I'm sorry! I can't! I have…ah… I have to go to my neighbor's house. They're welcoming me to the neighborhood. Isn't that nice?''

''Which neighbors?''

''On the left. You know. That two-story.''

''Oh. What's their names?''

''Um. Johnson? Jacobson? God, I can't remember. Barb and John, I think. But I'll get acquainted and tell you all about it tomorrow. Sorry, Nick.''

''Maybe you could come over after? For a coffee? Say hello to Opal and show her what you're wearing?''

''Huh?''

''She just *loves* your clothes. You know Opal. Deep.''

''Oh,'' Dixie said with a laugh. ''I think I'd better pass. My boss has been working me to death and I'm tired. Tell your mom I'll see her tomorrow, or at least on the weekend. And thanks for the invitation." The doorbell rang. "Oops, there's the doorbell. Probably some school kid selling something. Have a nice dinner."

"You, too," Nikki said.

Dixie put down the phone and hurried to the door. Danny stood there, flowers in one hand and wine in the other. "Welcoming committee," he said.

"You're too sweet! You shouldn't have!"

"You're cooking," he said. "Of course I should have."

"You're right, you should have. But I owe you big time. You've been such a great…" She looked for the right words. She didn't want him to turn and run. He could be so easygoing and fun, then so shy and kind of withdrawn. "Support system," she decided. "Here, let's put these in water and let the wine breathe."

Dixie felt at a complete loss. She was used to being pursued, and now she found she had very little talent for pursuing.

Danny looked around and whistled in appreciation. Pictures on the walls, books on the shelves, photos and potted plants in place. "You've been in here, what, less than two weeks, worked full-time and got all this done?"

"And helped look after April and Jared, Nikki's kids, when I was the only one around. Let me open this wine and then I'll show you the rest."

The rest was a perfect little house for a single woman. Three bedrooms, one of them a large master with adjoining bath, and another made into another den for her desk and computer. There was a living room with fireplace, a dining room, kitchen and nook. The backyard was very small with what was known as a "spool" sunk into the ground at one end—a little bigger than a spa, a little smaller than a pool.

As they passed by the dining room on this short tour, Danny noted that the table was set formally, with candles. After Dixie had arranged the flowers he'd brought, she'd added them to the table. Now she settled him in the living room with a glass of the merlot he'd brought, along with some hors d'oeuvres she'd prepared.

"Dinner's ready, but there's no rush," she said.

So they talked, which was something they'd been doing, their conversations growing and becoming more and more personal. After that day Danny caught her hiding in the conference room crying, he'd started giving her a call to see how she was doing. He'd usually open the conversation by asking her if she'd heard any gossip about new planes lately.

When he went off to Phoenix for training, he'd called every day. He'd give one excuse or another, asking for airline news or the number of calls from potential new hires, but after that sixty seconds of conversation they would talk about each other's lives. And histories. For *hours.*

A couple of times she'd called him. And she hadn't used any excuses. She just said, Hi, and, How's it going down there, we miss you up here.

By now he knew how Dixie and Nikki had become friends, that Dixie was the youngest in her family, and her brother and sister were quite a bit older. He knew her family were all overachievers and she had very little interest in such intellectual pursuits. "I would teach school, if I had the chance," she said. "But that has more to do with my love of children than a career goal."

And Danny had told her about his life, dull though he thought it was. High school, college, his degree in business for no particular reason—something to do while he pursued flying, his first love. He'd lost his father very young and his mother just a few years ago. No, there had never been any serious women.

"I find that so unbelievable," she said over dinner. "I would have thought you'd have been married or at least had a long-term relationship."

"Why would you think so?"

"You're so sensitive. So easy to talk to. So... I don't know. Charming?"

"Dixie," he said, "you're the one who's easy to talk to. You're so guileless and open that you bring out the best in others and make *them* seem charming. But it's you."

"Oh, don't be so self-effacing," she chided. "You know you're charming. And funny. When you're not being tremendously kind and serious, you're hilarious."

"What about you? You should be married...."

"That was my plan," she said. "Now I finally realize how stupid that was as a goal."

"Why?" he asked.

"You have to plan a life and fit your relationships into it. You can't just plan to have relationships. I've wanted to be married since forever. It was the first thing I thought about when I started seein' a man. No wonder I kept gettin' hurt. I probably ran them off."

Of course she knew better; you couldn't run off a married man. Her problem was that in her desperation to find the right guy, she could make herself believe that every guy who seduced her was The One. She never looked at their motives carefully enough.

"But you should be able to want something like that," Danny said. "Marriage and children. It shouldn't be considered old-fashioned to have that ideal as a dream."

She looked at him through the candlelight and just

smiled. "See what I mean, Danny? That's so sweet. I'm amazed no one has caught you."

Finally, Danny learned that Dixie had come to this town, this job, to get away from the life that had so disappointed her. One of the first things she told him about herself was that she was taking a hiatus from men, from dating, from the whole circus it had become. She was going to think about herself for a while.

He was glad of that. It gave him this chance to be her friend. He'd never aspire to be her partner, but their friendship was bringing him more happiness than he'd had in years.

They cleaned up the dishes together, and then with decaf and dessert, talked late into the evening. It was midnight before he finally said, "I'd better go and let you get some sleep."

"Yeah, I promised Nikki I'd go over to her house tomorrow and say hello to her mother, who's visiting."

"And I'm going to drop by the office," he told her. "See if I can get a little work done. The simulator put me way behind." She walked him to the door. "Dinner was awesome, Dixie. You're an incredible cook."

"We'll do it again. Very soon."

"You have to let me take you out to dinner first."

"I accept!" she said enthusiastically.

He gave her a little peck on the cheek, turned quickly and went down the walk to his car. She stood in the doorway and watched him go, lifting her hand to wave.

I wonder, she thought. Will he *ever* be attracted to me as more than just a friend?

Nikki left the office a little early on Friday. She went to the small municipal airport in Henderson to await Buck's arrival. You could set a watch by Buck, he was such a creature of habit. Four-thirty on the nose, the Cessna 310 lined up for landing. He bounced around in the wind but put her down nicely, taxied in and cut the engines.

Before he got out, he reached around behind him and opened the kennel door, letting Pistol loose. Then the two of them deplaned and tied the plane down.

Pistol didn't wait. When he caught sight of Nikki, his short little legs wound up and he charged toward the fixed-base office. She bent down and scooped him up. "Hey, Pistol. How was your flight?"

He answered by licking her face.

"Well, to what do I owe this special honor?" he asked.

"Opal is here," she said. "She's at my house."

Surprise registered on Buck's face, much to Nikki's relief.

"So. You didn't know."

"No. Should I have known?"

"She said you two talk. That you've always talked. She knew you came up every weekend."

"Aw, Jesus," he groaned. "That isn't exactly so."

"Well? Do you or don't you? Talk? Because I have a few other questions."

"Nikki…"

"She drives me crazy, Dad. Now, if you two have some relationship that—"

"Let's just get a cup of coffee," he relented. On the patio at Starbucks, where Pistol was welcome as long as he behaved, Nikki had a latte and Buck had his straight. "What can of worms has Opal opened now?" he asked.

"Let's start with her showing up, unannounced, with her suitcase, as though we should all have been expecting her. And acting as though she's just part of one big happy family. And talking as if she has this chummy little relationship with you, and—''

''I imagine she thinks she does,'' he said, exasperated. ''When she was nineteen, I found that quality so adorable.'' He made a grunting noise. ''It's like this, Nick. She calls whenever she wants something, but she never asks for anything. The calls have come more often since Mayer died and she's alone, and I have to admit, I let her talk without paying much attention to what she's saying. Now and then I'll even nod off, but that's never really bothered Opal.

''She does things and then makes out like it was your idea. She shows up and has fourteen reasons why you invited her and should have been expecting her. She talks too much, she's meddlesome, and she exaggerates the truth....''

''She *lies!*''

''She isn't a malicious liar. Like her saying we talk all the time. It's not a malicious lie, because for her, all the time is whenever she wants to—but I've called her three times. When the kids were born and when Drake died.''

''Really?'' she asked, strangely mollified.

''What's got your undies all in a knot about this?'' he asked.

''God,'' she said, annoyed. ''Everything.'' And nothing. There was nothing any different about Opal's behavior now than during Nikki's entire life. ''If we had something a little harder than this coffee, it would be easier to articulate. She ran out on us, Dad. She left us but she won't stay away. She keeps showing up to criticize and manipulate, and annoy the shit out of me. She calls Carlisle that charming young homosexual—''

''I call him Tinkerbell.''

"But you do that with affection, and he knows it."

"Has he complained about Opal calling him that?"

She didn't answer because the answer was no. "Why am I the only one who is completely bent out of shape by her?"

"She annoys everyone, Nick, but you just cave in and let it drive you crazy."

"She complimented my taste and style when she saw the new house, but has she said one goddamn word about me being the chief pilot of an airline?"

Her dad leaned toward her. "You think she has any idea what the chief pilot of an airline *is?*"

Well, there. Of course not. Besides all the annoying things Opal was, she was also somewhat simple-minded. "What am I supposed to do with her?"

"Let her stay awhile and spend some money on April and Jared. Don't let her get too comfortable. She'll get bored soon and go home where there's bridge and mah-jongg, her friends and shopping."

"I suppose."

"And I'll be staying at the Station Casino right down the street. A little bit of Opal goes a long way."

She glared at him for a moment.

"I'll come to dinner and drop off Pistol for Jared. I'm a good sport, but I'm not crazy."

Fourteen

Crucial to NCA's certification was the flight attendants' mini-evacuation, which would be timed and evaluated by the FAA. It took place after training was completed and before the pilots started their proving flights, and was one of the final hurdles before the airline could take on passengers.

The test was done at night, and the purpose was to ensure that any group of randomly chosen flight attendants could find unblocked aircraft doors in the dark and blow the slides for passenger evacuation. The FAA required that all the flight attendants who had been hired and trained in the first class gather at dusk in a prearranged area at the airport. Two pilots, also evaluated by the FAA, would bring one of New Century's 757s to the designated place, out of the range of airport ground traffic. The FAA would draw names to select four flight attendants from the gathering to board the aircraft, go through their checklists and do their demonstrations with safety cards, seat belts and oxygen masks, just as if this were a typical commercial flight full of paying passengers. They would secure the doors to close up the aircraft and take their seats. The pilots would likewise simulate a takeoff by doing all of their preflight work.

The FAA inspectors would then take their places— two would already be in the cockpit examining the pilots' performances, and eight positioned themselves in the cabin, one by each of the 757s exit doors. The inspectors each had a large peel-and-stick circle—four white, signifying an unblocked door, and four black, for a simulated blocked exit. When the pilots shut the engines down and killed the lights, simulating an emergency requiring an evacuation, each inspector would slap a sticker on his exit. With the aid of the emergency flashlights and floorboard running lights, the flight attendants had to find four unblocked doors, open them—not the easiest thing to do quickly—and blow the slides.

All in *eleven seconds*.

It was something of a tradition among start-up airlines for the entire employee group to show up for the event, and NCA was no exception. There was a carnivallike atmosphere in the air, and despite the fact that security was heavy, people arrived in droves, electric with anticipation. Nikki brought the kids, Carlisle was in town and wouldn't miss it, and thankfully Opal could care less. The sun had not yet set when the crowd began to gather on the far side of the airport between two hangars.

Some sixty flight attendants, dressed casually in jeans or sweatsuits and tennis shoes, were broken up into smaller groups, where they grilled one another on checklists, demo speeches and emergency procedure. They ranged in age from twenty-one-year-old kids with no previous airline experience to fifty-year-old, seasoned flight attendants furloughed from other carriers. The groups would occasionally burst into a cheer, not unlike team huddles at championship football games.

The stakes were high. This test had to be passed, no matter how many times it took, and if the slides were blown, but the task exceeded the time limit, the cost of repacking them was four to five thousand dollars each, and couldn't be done quickly. Twenty thousand dollars and another day delay for each failure.

Nikki noticed that many of the pilots were present, including all her movers, Ken, Jeff and Sam. Dixie found them and joined the group, as did the Wrench, Mark Shows. When Crue arrived with her boys in tow, Nikki waved her over so the kids could be introduced to her two.

The sun was lowering in the sky as still more people arrived. A group of FAA inspectors gathered and stood in a tight knot at the edge of the gathering.

"Why aren't you bringing the plane over, boss?" Jeff asked.

"Danny and Eric are doing the honors. I wanted to be out here with my own stopwatch and my kids. They've never seen one of these mini-evacs."

"What about the inaugural flight?" Sam asked.

"I'm doing that, with Danny as copilot, and these two in the back." She put an arm around each of her kids. "I didn't do this alone. April and Jared have really made it possible."

Someone shouted, "Here comes the plane!"

Lumbering across the ramp, its new paint job shining in the dusk, the rotating beacons, wing and taxi lights bouncing brightly along, the 757 approached—forty-four feet high and one hundred fifty-five feet long, able to hold as many as one hundred and ninety-five passengers. The cheers that rose from the crowd were loud and proud.

Nikki cheered, as well, but for her, the greatest charge of excitement came from being with these people, the starters, all gathered in one place, rooting for the airline's success. She felt a huge swell of emotion in her breast that she'd never experienced before. Even Crue, usually so reserved, was jumping up and down, hooting in excitement.

"God, this is amazing," Sam said, and Nikki realized he was standing beside her. She wanted to grab on to him, but resisted.

"It's infectious, isn't it?" she said. "Indescribable, really."

He bent a little so that his head was at Jared's level. "I've never seen anything like this, either. Pretty awesome."

"After they blow the slides, we can get on the airplane and go down 'em," Jared informed him. "They'll be thirteen feet from the ground. I can't wait."

"The only way I'm going down one of those slides is if there's an engine fire," April said.

Sam traded glances with Nikki. Jared knew every detail about this plane and many others. He was already flying with his papa. April knew her share, but the details of the plane were not nearly as important to her as, say, what the flight attendants would be wearing.

"Hey, look who's slumming," Dixie said, sidling up to Nikki.

Nikki glanced over to find Joe Riordan mingling with the troops, and beside him, in boots and rather snug jeans, was Jewel. She also wore something else they never saw much of—a smile. Not a big smile, but nonetheless...

Before the airplane stopped and the chocks were placed behind the wheels, the first flight attendant was chosen—a female who looked to be in her thirties. Nikki hoped that meant she was experienced. The next was a young man who jumped around in a Rocky imitation to the cheers of his peers. Then came a very young woman, who was immediately enveloped in a group hug. And

finally, a woman who was surely tipping the calendar at
fifty and might even be the oldest new hire they had.
She must have been laid off from another airline and
very experienced, because at her selection, wild cheering
rose up, as if she was their ringer.

A flight attendant supervisor gave them last-minute
instructions while the air stairs were brought to the
plane. By the time the inspectors had boarded, the crowd
was vibrating with energy. The selected group and their
supervisor held hands in a tight circle and did some kind
of prayer or motivational affirmation that ended with a
shout—"Yes!"

Joe Riordan's voice came from behind Nikki. "The
last time I was at one of these, it was imperative that we
pass because we had just enough time to complete proving flights and start boarding passengers—we couldn't
fail and take a delay."

She turned around. "Hey, Joe. Jewel. Pretty exciting,
huh?"

"Or tense, depending on your perspective," Joe said.

"They're going to do great," Jewel assured him,
again with a smile. Nikki and Dixie both kind of
frowned, staring. But Jewel and Joe didn't notice, since
they were busy introducing themselves to everyone present.

Then suddenly the crowd stilled as the flight attendants boarded the aircraft behind the inspectors. The
doors were closed, and the stairs pulled away. The aircraft was still lit within and without. Everyone waited
tensely. Nikki pulled out her stopwatch. Minutes passed.
Inside the plane, the flight attendants would be going
through their preflight duties, explaining safety procedures to their mock passengers, the inspectors. What
seemed like hours actually lasted less than fifteen

minutes, and then the aircraft went dark except for the flashing emergency wing lights.

Nikki clicked on the watch. Everyone in the crowd was mentally ticking off the seconds. Eleven, ten, nine, eight, seven, six, five— A door cracked and slowly began to open. Another door cracked. Then a third. A slide billowed out, and then rapidly, three more followed, all four exploding into view.

Nikki stopped her watch. She was right at ten seconds, but she wasn't sure she had started and stopped with the inspectors. She held her breath and waited with everyone else.

The flight attendants suddenly came into view in the doorways, then shot down the slides, screaming yahoos, arms raised above their heads in victory, and their compatriots charged toward them. The spectators roared, whistled and hugged one another with the enthusiasm of Superbowl winners. Although NCA was not even airborne yet, its founders were alive with the exhilaration of giving birth to a giant.

In the happy chaos, Nikki somehow ended up being bounced up and down in Sam's powerful embrace. It was perfectly natural; people were hugging one another all over the place. But in that moment she was incredibly aware of him, and wished it would never end. When she broke away, she hugged five more pilots with enthusiasm, lest anyone get the idea Sam was someone special.

After people toured the inside of the plane—many of them checking out the trip down the slides—the entire gathering moved from the airport to the Tail Spin Bar and Grill, an establishment catering to airport and airline employees. It was so near the end of the runway that it

periodically trembled as jets passed over on their way
to land.

Dixie and Carlisle went straight to the bar, while
Nikki made a side trip to drop her kids off at home. The
place was already bursting at the seams and rocking with
music and laughter by the time they arrived. A man
Dixie recognized as one of the pilots lifted the pretty
young flight attendant who had taken part in the inspection up onto a table. She took a few bows to the cheers
of the crowd. The waitresses scurried around with heavy
trays loaded with sloshing pitchers of beer. Many a toast
was being raised.

"Great place for a fear-of-flying clinic, huh?" Dixie
shouted.

"I'll get us drinks," Carlisle said. "Find a table or a
lap or something."

Looking around the packed bar, she was pretty
amazed by how many people she knew. Every pilot present had been run by her desk in the application process
and made frequent stops after being hired for everything
from uniform orders to picking up the business cards she
had printed for them. Flight attendants were in and out,
as well, and after several weeks in the office, Dixie knew
all the other executive assistants and secretaries.

She was looking around for Danny when she caught
Jewel's eye. The Gatekeeper was sitting by herself at a
table in the corner, and she extended one long finger,
inviting—or maybe commanding—Dixie over. Dixie actually looked behind her to make sure she didn't mean
someone else. After all, Jewel never came around Flight
Ops. Dixie touched her chest, mouthed "Me?" and
Jewel slowly nodded. Ah, it appeared the ice queen de-
sired her company.

"I don't mean to keep you from your friends," Jewel said. "I thought you were looking around for a spot."

"Yes, I was," she said with fake enthusiasm. She was afraid it would not only bore her senseless to sit with the aloof Gatekeeper, but also keep her from finding Danny.

"No, take this chair," Jewel said, patting the seat beside her. "The view is spectacular."

Feeling a bit odd, Dixie did as she was told. For a split second she feared Jewel was going to make a pass, but then she realized Ms. Goddess wanted her to take in the room from the same vantage point she had. Ah, yes. Airline crews at work and play.

In the corner, Bob Riddle sat at a table with four pilots and they seemed to be having a serious conversation. At the other end of the bar, a sexy young flight attendant was being hit on by a couple of pilots. There was a little swing dancing, a little dirty dancing. And straight ahead was...

Dixie squinted as the woman, a brassy blond in a tight black dress cut low on top and high on the bottom, seemed to be grinding her pelvis against a guy. He wasn't moving away, either. His arm periodically went around her waist as if to encourage her.

But then the most bizarre thing happened. He moved away to the bar and began talking to a couple of people there. The blonde gave her shoulder-length hair a sweep upward, let it fall, and turned to the man on her other side. She spoke in his ear and began grinding *his* thigh.

Jewel leaned toward Dixie. "She is going to have the worst headache."

"Who is that?"

"You can't tell?" She gave a short laugh and leaned back in her chair. "She's been doing shots."

At that moment the woman turned to face them. *"Shanna,"* Dixie breathed. She also sat back. "Great little window on the world."

"I thought you'd like it. Knowledge is power. Remember that."

Dixie watched Joe Riordan work the room. He was at once the big boss and one of the guys, glad-handing and slapping shoulders. He raised his mug and toasted over and over, but the level on his glass never seemed to get any lower.

He walked over to the table where Bob Riddle held court, and all five men sprang to their feet as if the general had just dropped in, each one taking his turn at a lengthy verbal ass-kiss.

"They're up to no good," Jewel said.

"Why do you say that?"

"Just a feeling. They've set themselves apart from the group."

"So have we."

"But we're different." She smiled conspiratorially. "We're gatekeepers."

Dixie was shocked. "You know you're called that?"

"I know everything. By the way, I don't see enough of the chief pilot around Riordan's office."

"Well," Dixie said, a tish uncomfortable at the remark, "she's been out of town, at the simulator. Plus, she works really long hours."

"I know," Jewel said. "But you should know, that one—" she indicated Riddle only with her eyes "—seems to have plenty of time to hang around my desk, looking for information and face time with the boss."

Dixie absorbed this, aware her mouth was slightly open. She clamped it shut. "Thanks."

"Hey. No problem."

Presently Carlisle arrived at the table with two drinks. "Ladies," he said, setting down the glasses. He noticed Jewel's was quite low. "Can I get you anything?"

"Thanks, no. I'm fine."

Carlisle sat down across from them, his back to the room, and the two women shifted slightly because he was blocking their view. After a few moments of being ignored, Carlisle dragged his chair around to their side of the table so he could watch the show.

They entertained themselves like this for a good while. Nikki came in, but she was so busy with the pilots, she didn't seem to notice them. There was some serious drinking going on, but nothing that could keep up with Shanna, who was growing more unsteady by the minute.

"Did you see if she came in with anyone?" Dixie asked Jewel.

"No, but I'm sure she'll leave with someone. Unless there's a person with a conscience at this table."

"Ew. Is it going to be me?" Dixie asked, feeling so much the subordinate.

"Or us," she said.

"But aren't you here with…?" Dixie began.

Jewel tilted her head and peered down her nose at Dixie. "Don't believe everything you hear," she said. "I have my own car here. But I will leave when he leaves."

Dixie stole another look at Shanna. The dragon of HR was smashed and acting so very slutty. "She doesn't really deserve help, you know."

"But she also doesn't deserve what's going to happen to her if we don't help," Jewel said. "At least this once. Who knows where she'll wake up in the morning?"

"I love it," Carlisle observed. "The Bed Cross."

"Okay, then…" Dixie said.

"Your car," Jewel told her. Dixie's head snapped around. "Seniority." She flashed Dixie that rare smile. "Think of how easy it's going to be to work with HR after tonight."

"All right, then. Let's get this over with."

"I'll be saying good night," Carlisle said. "Much as I'd like to stay and watch."

Quite a few heads turned as Dixie and Jewel, both beautiful leggy blondes, each took an arm and walked a confused and dazed Shanna out the door of the bar. After an emergency stop at the trash bin by the side of the building, they loaded her into the passenger side of Dixie's car.

"Well, at least I'm less worried about what she's going to do to the inside of my car," Dixie remarked.

"Sit tight, I have a couple of things in my trunk that could help," Jewel said.

Shanna, butt on the passenger seat and feet outside, her head resting on her knees, moaned miserably. Dixie tsked. The girl was totaled.

"Here," Jewel said, returning with a beach towel and little lunch-size cooler. "Drape the towel around her and place the opened cooler on her lap. Don't bother returning either if they're used."

"She owes you big-time for this," Dixie said. "If it was just up to me, I wouldn't have bothered."

"Everyone has been rescued at one time or another," Jewel said.

"You're actually a very nice person," Dixie drawled.

Jewel put a finger to her lips. "Don't tell. I have a very useful image going."

* * *

When Nikki arrived at the Tail Spin, she didn't notice her friends and Jewel back against the wall. She'd returned not only because she was in a celebratory mood, but because she knew the value of mingling with her people. And her people were pilots. They would definitely be here.

For whatever reason—her performance at the sim, or the fact she knew the 757 inside and out—the men she'd hired had warmed to her. She was greeted enthusiastically, and her hand immediately fitted with a beer. She'd rather have had a glass of wine, but if they were drinking beer, she was drinking beer.

Talk turned to the proving flights, then the schedule for the first month, then where everyone had worked before. By the time a half hour had passed, many of them had made connections with friends or friends of friends from other carriers. With hundreds of thousands of people in the industry, it never failed to shock Nikki how many of them knew one another.

Nikki spied Riddle and his table of pilots at the end of the room. "Save my place," she said to the group she was standing with. She went over to his table. "Bob. Gentlemen." They popped up like fishing bobbers. "No, don't get up. I just wanted to say hello. What did you think of the mini-evac?"

They looked at one another uncomfortably. "We didn't make it to the evac," one of them finally admitted.

"We were here, having a beer, when the party came in," Riddle said.

"Well, it was great. The FAA was most impressed."

Again there were furtive looks, almost as if they'd been caught doing something wrong.

"Ah, work-rules meeting?" she asked. Only Bob connected with her eyes. The others looked away. At that moment she realized she had ignored his animosity for too long. He wanted her out. He'd already taken credit for her work and would do considerably more damage if she didn't figure him out. "Just enjoy your beer," she said pleasantly. "See you later."

That the next day was a workday didn't seem to deter anyone from staying late at the bar. In fact, once Joe Riordan left, the din rose slightly. But by the time a couple of hours had passed, the airline groups began to thin and give way to the bar's regulars. It was about ten when Nikki looked around and couldn't pick Dixie or Carlisle out of the crowd.

"I guess I should think about getting home," she said to Sam, who was standing next to her.

"Don't," he said. "Let's grab a table and have a cold one."

She looked down at her beer, the same one she'd been nursing all night. It was now reduced to a half glass of warm and flat yellow brew. "Ah, to tell you the truth, I don't think I want a beer. I wouldn't fight off a glass of cabernet, though. If you're buying."

"I am. See if you can find a table as far away from the juke box as possible."

"You're showing your age, Landon," she teased.

"Wasn't ever trying to hide it, boss."

She looked around the bar for a table. *Probably shouldn't do this,* she thought. But it was still a public place and there would be no funny stuff. *Probably shouldn't. I don't need this kind of encouragement.* But she did as she was asked—she found a table away from the noise, the music, the crowd.

She watched Sam at the bar, procuring drinks. He laughed as the bartender said something funny. When he wasn't laughing, he had an almost brooding look. When he was in training class, for instance, concentrating, he could look downright angry. But all you had to say was "Anything wrong, Landon?" and that somber expression would instantly disappear and be replaced with a grin. As he turned from the bar, looking for her, she once again admired his handsomeness. For a man of fifty he had such a boyish look, the thick, floppy hair and twinkling eyes. But it was really his smile that got to her; straight white teeth, and a small hint of the devil.

Because she enjoyed watching him look for her, Nikki didn't wave to get his attention. When he finally did spot her, he made a beeline for the table. "Here we go," he said, putting down the drinks.

"There's that diet cola again," she observed. "You don't drink."

"Not much, no," he said. He lifted a glass to her. "Here's to start-up."

"Amen." She sipped her wine. She'd been toasting the company all night but hadn't swallowed much beer. "How is it?"

It was actually pretty bleak—bar-stock cabernet. "Good," she lied.

"I heard we have something in common that I didn't realize. Your husband died recently?"

That took her so by surprise she nearly choked. "Oh, God, Sam!" She covered his hand in sudden sympathy and looked at him so earnestly, forgetting for the moment that she meant this to look to all the world as if they were just having a friendly drink. "He was my ex-husband. We'd been divorced for four years and... Well, I don't know if there's any delicate way to say this. He was a complete jerk, with a capital *J*."

"Oh, man, that's too bad," he said. "Rough divorce?"

"You don't want to hear all that," she warned, giving him a break.

"I do." He leaned toward her, his head on a hand. "I mean, if you don't mind talking about it. It won't go further."

It brought a smile to her lips to think of him keeping a personal confidence for her, even though there wasn't any need. And it felt awfully good that he was interested. "There's no secret about my marriage and divorce, even if I haven't talked about it much. I married Drake on the rebound. He was the first guy who smiled at me after I broke up with a boyfriend I thought I'd marry. He was a difficult, negative, complaining, controlling pain in the butt, but I was pregnant with April instantly. We divorced eleven years later and he sued for custody based on the fact that I left town for a living and he didn't. But he was a lawyer and had a little edge, you see. So for four years I paid him child support while he made life miserable for me whenever I tried to see the kids. Then one morning he had a heart attack. The kids were in school, he was alone, and boom. Gone. At forty-seven."

"Whoa. Young."

She took a sip of her wine. "Very sudden."

"How about the kids?" he asked.

"They loved him, of course, but they'd had a hard time with him, too. He was strict, inflexible and pretty much impossible to please. I don't know if I ever heard him tell the kids he loved them. It baffles me, because he *did* love them. It's not as though he was indifferent. He demanded custody and promised to fight me to his last breath."

"Maybe that was more about scoring one against you than his need to have the kids live with him."

"I've pondered that a lot, of course. But since there's no way of knowing for sure, I'm going with the idea that he loved them a lot and just didn't have the ability to express his emotions."

"Which could certainly be true. A lot of men have trouble with that."

"You? Do you have trouble with that?" she asked before she could reel the question back in.

He gave a chuckle. "Oh, Jesus, boss. I have too *much* emotion. Leanne's death almost took me with her. If I wasn't heartbroken, I was angry, and if I wasn't angry, I was guilty. I was not a sane man for a year. But I think we're all doing well now, the girls and I."

"If you don't mind me asking…?"

"Really, I'm good with this now. You can ask just about anything."

"How did your wife die?"

The look on his face was so shocked, so still, she scrambled for an apology.

"Gosh, I'm sorry, I—"

"No, no, it's not that. I thought it was common knowledge."

"I'm afraid I don't—"

"She was an American flight attendant. She died on September 11."

"Dear God. I had no idea."

"And I thought everyone knew," he said. "The victims and their families were all over the news for such a long time—I think I heard from every military friend we ever had, and then there was the airline community. I honestly didn't think there was a person around who didn't know every detail."

"Do all the other pilots know?"

"Yeah, I think so."

"Amazing. And no one said anything to me. Sam, I'm so sorry for your loss."

"Thanks. It was a tough one. It will always be emotional for me, but because of the way she died, we were forced to talk about it a lot, and I think that actually helped relieve some of the raw pain. You know what's the strangest? She's part of this country's history. She died in a moment of violent history that spawned a war and changed the world."

"How long was she a flight attendant?"

"Years ago we came up with this plan to both have airline jobs by the time I retired from the Air Force. I could retire at forty-two—still young. Leanne's income helped with college for the girls, and our travel benefits would allow us to visit our families and old Air Force friends no matter where we ended up. With all the time off airline employees can get, we figured we'd travel the world."

"Sounds like a pretty good plan."

"Leanne got her job first, when I was in my last assignment. When she died, she'd been a flight attendant for eight years, while I'd just been in my job for three—with Pacific. I got in on the ground floor so I was a captain. I was just getting home from work after a night flight and saw the whole thing happen on the news. This incredible, unbelievable, spectacular event. I remember thinking about how the world had changed forever, how every person in the world would be affected by what had happened. And I didn't know the half of it."

Then the story began to unfold, he said. First that airplanes had been hijacked, then which airlines had been affected. He'd run to the calendar they kept with their flight patterns inked in. He saw Leanne's. Boston to Los Angeles.

"Boston?" she asked weakly.

But he appeared not to notice her shock. "Boston. Still, it took a few hours to find out that was actually her flight. You recall the chaos of evacuating airports and grounding all planes. The fact that she didn't call didn't convince us, because people all over the country were having trouble with communications."

The next year was a nightmare of grief and trauma. "Every time they played that news footage, I lost my wife again. My kids lost their mother over and over. Not only was I widowed, my company went under when it was not granted any federal assistance. The elite committee of three that made up the Air Transportation Stabilization Board decided that air travel would not be adversely affected if my company didn't make it. My airline wasn't big and important enough. Twenty-five hundred employees were suddenly out of work right before Christmas. Most of them couldn't even get medical coverage. At least I had the Air Force retirement program, which gave me time to try to recover from my loss."

"And the girls?" she asked.

"They're incredible. They're like their mother, thank God. Strong and positive and determined not to live in unhappiness. It was a little tougher for me. I used to drown my sorrows a lot, which led me to hang up the cup with very little fanfare before I found myself going to meetings. Somehow, over the next year or two, we began to recover enough to see life would go on in spite of this. Because, really, Leanne was the kind of woman who had raised our daughters that way, to believe that things would work out eventually, and they should have faith in that fact. She was hopelessly, almost infuriatingly optimistic."

"It's because of her that you could get to this place."

"I think so. Let me ask you something, Nick. If you had known, would you have hired me?"

She was taken aback by the question.

"You would have thought I'd be permanently scarred and unable to make sound decisions in a critical situation. Wouldn't you?"

"I wonder if I would have considered that. I'll never know. There was nothing about your interview or résumé that led me to worry about your stability *or* ability."

"Military training doesn't hurt," he said. He gave a deep sigh. "Thanks. I'm glad you didn't know and that I got to tell you. I know it's heavy. The good news is there isn't anything else skulking around in me. That's all the baggage I've got."

"Well, I've got something," she said. "I don't know how you're going to take it. I was sitting in an Aries 767 at the Boston gate, right next to the American jet that was hijacked. I didn't see any of the crew members—but clearly that was your wife's plane."

The surprise registered on his face. He was rendered speechless.

"I wouldn't blame you at all if you wished it could have been me and not her. In fact, I have no idea why it wasn't."

"You can't imagine the number of weird ironies we've learned about since that day. An old neighbor of ours was actually in the World Trade Center when the plane hit! It sure makes you wonder about the grand plan, doesn't it?"

"I wouldn't have planned it that way," she said.

They talked for another hour about family and friends, places they'd lived, planes they'd flown. After a time, the glum cloud of 9/11 began to lift as Sam spoke of his daughters. He was so grateful to be flying again, to get another ten years in the cockpit before mandatory retirement, and he gave Nikki much of the credit.

When Nikki stifled a yawn, Sam laughed and put an arm around her shoulders, resting her head against his chest. It was only then that she noticed most of the airline crowd had left the bar.

"I have to get home," she finally said. "I hate to. I think under different circumstances, I could stay up talking all night."

"I'll walk you to your car."

As she leaned her back against the driver's side of her SUV, he braced a hand over her shoulder and leaned toward her. "Well, thank God that's all the baggage I have," he said. "At least there aren't any surprises ahead for you."

Ahead? So he saw this as a relationship moving forward? Her mouth parted slightly in question, but that question was to go unasked. He leaned toward her and covered her open mouth with his. It occurred to her to push him away, but the hands that rose to his chest just rested there while he moved over her mouth. She felt that light-headed, weak-kneed feeling she thought she'd left behind in her youth, and heard herself sigh. Then, instead of pushing him away, she moved her hands gently over his chest and around to his back, holding him. When he released her mouth, he smiled.

"We shouldn't be doing this," she said.

"Oh, but we should."

"No, Sam. It's a bad idea. I'm your boss."

"Only sort of," he said. "You're in charge of the pilots, true, and I'm a pilot, true, but I'm just going to fly whatever Scheduling gives me, and I doubt you'll ever have any reason to boss me. Except, maybe, on more private occasions.''

''But still, it's bad policy....''

''In most companies,'' he said. ''In the Air Force, for sure. But in the airlines, it's almost standard operating procedure.''

''I don't know about that,'' she said. ''I'm going to have to think about it.''

''Sure. Take your time. And think about this— What weird twist of fate left you sitting at the gate while Leanne was hijacked by terrorists?'' He shook his head. ''At the same airport. On the same day. At the same time. Somehow I don't think I'd have met you if I wasn't meant to.''

And then he kissed her again. And again, she pulled him to her.

Nikki took the drive home slowly. She just didn't want the evening to end, though she was so tired. It was after midnight by the time she turned into her drive. She was surprised to see the lights still on in Carlisle's casita. Instead of going into the house through the garage, she took a detour into the courtyard and saw him through the open blinds, packing a bag. She tapped on the door.

''Hi,'' she said when he opened it. ''You have a trip tomorrow?''

His eyes were red-rimmed, his nose pink. ''I'm going to be gone a few days. My father died.''

''Oh, Carlisle, I'm so sorry!''

''I didn't think I'd care,'' he said. ''But this seems to bring to a close many years of disappointment for us both. I think in the back of my mind I always thought that one day, maybe when he was very old, very ill—''

''Just go for your mother, Carlisle.''

He gave a huff of laughter. "She didn't think it was such a good idea—me coming—what with the whole family going to be there."

Nikki felt the heat of anger in her throat, and was sure steam must be coming out of her nostrils instead of breath. The very idea that a mother could reject her own son, for any reason, was something she couldn't fathom. She'd heard of mothers weeping at death row for sons who had done unspeakable things, something she could understand far better than this. Carlisle was a dream of a man!

"Her loss is unimaginable," Nikki said. "Just go. Go for yourself, then. Put your father and his narrow-mindedness to rest. You are the better man, Carlisle."

He shrugged. "Sometimes it gets so lonely being the better man."

A few neighborhoods away, Dixie was busy trying to clean out her car while Shanna was passed out in the guest room, a bucket on the floor beside her. Of course the towel and minicooler had not been quite enough.

When they had arrived at Dixie's house, Dixie had scooped the soiled Shanna out of the car and dragged her into the guest shower, clothes and all. Dixie stood in there with her until she was stripped and washed, then helped her into a soft, clean T-shirt and left her in the bed.

The next morning Dixie propped up a note by the coffeepot. *Call in sick—I'll be home to check on you at noon. Dixie, your guardian angel, who you owe so-o-o big.*

Fifteen

The first week Opal was in Las Vegas, she relaxed by the pool. "So nice, after that brutal San Francisco rain and fog." The second week she rented a car so she could get around and do some shopping. The third week was the start-up of the new airline, and while Nikki flew the round trip to Los Angeles, the whole family was on board with other employees, dignitaries, politicians and even movie stars.

Buck and the kids rode in coach, but Opal somehow managed a first-class seat for herself and Precious. Joe Riordan reported back to Captain Burgess that Opal had informed him, "This is my daughter's airline, you know. She's running the show."

"Oh, God," Nikki said. "Did she really?"

"Yes, and she said that you'd never be where you are today if she hadn't encouraged you."

"Brother."

"But how does she get that kind of deep purple cast to her hair?" he asked.

"Do I need to apologize for her?"

"Naw, she's very entertaining. I'd eighty-six the dog, though."

"Precious isn't."

"And you can thank me for protecting your reputation."

"How's that?" she asked.

"I let her think you're in charge, when everyone knows it's Riddle."

Indeed, Bob Riddle had spent the inaugural festivities in the gate area, where banners flourished and cameras flashed. He shook hands, took bows, and all the while told everyone that he was the *senior* vice president of Operations, apparently having given himself a little promotion. "I guess you could say this is my operation," he was heard to boast.

The next week Nikki realized with a shock that Opal had been in town, at her house, for three weeks. Jared pretty much ignored her, and April spent a little time with her in the afternoons and evenings, but her circle of friends had widened, and like any fourteen-year-old girl, she spent hours on the phone and computer. On weekends, she was more than happy to shop with her grandmother during the day and go out with her friends at night.

Carlisle was still with his mother in Anoka, Minnesota, but due home any day. Nikki was just gearing up to say something to Opal about her protracted stay when the unbelievable happened. At midnight, just a week before Thanksgiving, the busiest travel holiday of the year, the Aries flight attendants went on strike and the pilots joined them. The world watched, many of them from a line outside a ticket counter, in stunned disbelief.

Aries was the eighth- or ninth-largest carrier in the country, with one hundred forty planes and fifteen thousand employees, less than five thousand of them pilots and flight attendants. The carrier had lost hundreds of millions of dollars and would surely require Chapter Eleven bankruptcy protection after this. The employees on strike were holding the company hostage at the busiest time of the year.

Perhaps they expected the President of the United States to step in and give an order to disallow the strike. But the industry-wide passenger loads had not recovered since 9/11. In fact, they were barely up to fifty percent of the pre 9/11 numbers. The airlines had furloughed many employees, parked their planes, sustained huge losses. Probably the easiest way to let the industry heal itself was to just let it shrink by natural attrition.

The president did not step in. The future of Aries was, at best, dismal.

Nikki went immediately to Riordan, who called Mark Shows. Their number-four airplane could be online in a couple of days, and NCA being a new company, its bookings were not exactly high. They had plenty of available seats. Nikki grabbed Danny and Eric. "Aries has passengers stranded all over the country. Let's go to Dispatch, reshuffle the pilot flying schedule, call in anyone who is qualified and legal, and go mop 'em up."

And so they did. Aries's disaster was New Century's opportunity. With a little humility and apologies from the crews, the passengers were grateful for any kind of transportation that would get them home. "If you'll just bear with us, ladies and gentlemen, we'll give you the best service possible on short notice. Maybe you'll try us again, under less stressful circumstances."

Nikki found herself flying till she was legally out of time, and here it was Thanksgiving week and she had no idea what to do about Opal.

"Has your grandmother mentioned what her plans are?" she asked April.

"Only sort of. She said that since the holidays were

here and she was all alone now, she might as well just stay.''

''Oh, God, she's giving me a brain tumor.''

''You hardly talk to her. You're been gone all the time!''

''I know, sweetheart, but I barely talk to her because she annoys me so, and I've been gone because... Well, because of work, but also because she annoys me.''

''Besides being so into herself, what bothers you exactly?'' April asked.

''Well, for one thing, I haven't spent a holiday with my mother since she left when I was nine years old!''

''Uh-huh. And you're still pissed. So maybe the two of you should get some counseling.''

Nothing, but nothing, sounded more horrible than that. So Nikki went to the source. She found her mother in the downstairs guest room, Buck's room, which had become awfully cozy with Opal's own special touches. She was reclining neatly on the bed, pillows propped behind her, a book in her lap and Precious curled up at her side.

''Well, Mother, you seem mighty comfortable here.''

''Yes, Nicole. Thank you.''

''And your plans?''

''I'm in no hurry to leave, Nicole. Thank you.''

''Mother, you can't stay forever. I need my own space with my family.''

''Oh,'' she said, as if hurt. ''Am I not family?''

Nikki sat on the bed at Opal's feet. ''Please don't force me to be a big meanie. You've been here for almost a month, which is longer by three weeks than any time we've spent together in more than thirty years. We get on each other's nerves.'' To her utter disbelief, tears were welling up in Opal's eyes. Nikki fell silent. Although Opal topped the list of the most manipulative and self-centered people she'd ever known, Nikki had never seen her cry, not even when Mayer Gould died. "What's going on here? What is this?" she asked almost angrily. "Mother?"

"I didn't want to have to say anything," she said. "But I've had a bit of a reversal."

"A what?"

"A setback. I didn't do so well when Mayer passed on. He had those children, you know."

"But he was *rich!*"

"We were comfortable. And when he passed away, what we had was divided between me and the four children. I found I had to make some choices. I couldn't afford the big house."

"What have you done?" she asked slowly, carefully.

"I've sold the big house."

Nikki began to massage her temples. "And you are planning to…?"

"Get something smaller," she said with a sniff.

"When is that going to happen?"

"After Christmas?" she answered with a hopeful question.

Although another month of Opal would probably finish her off, Nikki held out the hope that was the worst-case scenario. "In San Francisco?" she asked.

"I thought I'd move closer to my grandchildren," Opal informed her.

"What about your step-children and step-grandchildren?" Nikki asked, trying to keep the pleading from her voice.

"We're not close."

Get a grip, Nikki told herself. *Say nothing, do nothing and just stay calm. Just get up and slowly leave the*

*room, go somewhere quiet, have a lot of alcohol, and
think clearly until you pass out.*

She walked into the kitchen in a daze, thinking about
that syndrome in the animal world where a female has
no instincts for mothering her offspring. It was a freak
of nature and happened rarely, but maybe it could happen with humans, too. Maybe Opal had that same
syndrome. Complicated by the I-Can't-Think-Beyond-
Myself one.

April was there, biting her lower lip nervously.

"You knew," Nikki said.

"Look, she's old and lonely."

"April, you are fourteen years old. You are not allowed to be more mature than me."

"It's just that I don't have all these issues with her."

"Well, lucky you."

"I think Mayer's asshole kids rejected her."

It was Nikki's turn to bite her lip, because, oh, how
she wanted to launch into richly deserved recriminations.
Wasn't it Opal who'd rejected Buck, and Nikki along
with him?

She said nothing.

"But what if Grandma really isn't well?" April asked.
"What if she really doesn't have all that much time?"

"She looks healthy enough to me," Nikki said.

In Anoka, Carlisle closed the box holding the last of
his father's clothes to be given to the Salvation Army.
He carried the box to the garage and stacked it neatly
with the others for pickup the next day.

"Carlisle, can you come and eat with us now?" his
aunt Julie called.

"Yes, coming," he called back. "Just let me wash
my hands."

After the death of his father, Carlisle's aunts had done a little "coming out" of their own. In typical Midwestern style, they had refused to get into a family brawl over whether Burt's attitude toward Carlisle was appropriate, but the aunts had never favored ostracizing him. Now that Burt was gone, they took serious issue with their sister over that matter.

Carlisle had thought his aunts shared his mother's views because he didn't hear from them all that often. In fact, he didn't hear from them because they didn't hear from *him.* Now it was clear—Burt Bartlett had perpetrated a great conspiracy of misunderstanding.

It remained true, however, that his mother was enormously disappointed that he was gay. She'd rather he be straight, married and the father of several darling, towheaded children. But she admitted she wasn't sure he'd rot in hell for it.

It was sad, Carlisle thought, that his father's death should bring such a reunion. Being with his aunts again reminded him of how much he'd loved their attention when he was small. It was a pity he hadn't known how much they had missed him; he might have spent more time with them over the years.

"There you are, darling," his aunt Jo said. "Would you like a little tossed green salad with that soup, or half a tuna sandwich?"

"Whatever you're having, Jo," he said, taking a seat.

"Give him the sandwich—he needs the bread. He's much too thin," said Rayanne, who was not.

"I beg to differ, Rayanne. He's not too thin, and I'll bet his blood pressure and cholesterol are perfect."

"Very close, actually," he admitted.

"Your father could have taken a lesson from you," Julie told him in a stage whisper.

Carlisle only smiled, thinking of his father spinning like a top in his grave.

He sat at the head of the table, the old oval-shaped kitchen table that had been in his mother's kitchen since Carlisle was about twelve. When Burt was alive, he'd sit at the opposite end, Ethel beside him. But today, like many of the days since the funeral, Carlisle sat at the end, and the four sisters sat two on each side, yammering endlessly and good-naturedly while they ate. Every once in a while they'd draw him into their conversation, but they did quite well on their own if he had nothing to add.

Right after the funeral he had asked the most liberal of his aunts, Julie, if he had been wrong to assume the family wanted nothing to do with him because he was gay. "That was only Burt," Aunt Julie had insisted. "No one wanted to argue with him or try to override him because, well, no one is quite so pigheaded as a conservative fundamentalist, and it just isn't worth the trouble. But it was really only Burt."

"No," Carlisle insisted, "it was my mother, too. She even suggested it might not be such a good idea for me to come home to bury him."

Aunt Julie had tsked. "My sister. I love her dearly, you know I do, but she's never had the ability to speak her mind or stand up for what she believes. She'll go along with the strongest person in the room. She was probably afraid Burt would sit up in the casket and scream at her."

"But she loved him. I know she loved my father."

"Probably." Aunt Julie shrugged. "Still…"

Still… Ethel seemed to be doing very well with Burt gone and her sisters overstaying their welcome. In fact, Carlisle had never seen her so happy.

Carlisle had been in Anoka much longer than he had expected to be. Three weeks. At first it was the embrace of his family that drew him in and made him so comfortable. Then it was the knowledge that Nikki had her mother visiting in Las Vegas, so he knew the kids would have an adult around if they needed one, even if the adult was the rather childlike Opal. Finally, it was the Aries strike that lengthened his stay.

When it happened, Nikki had called immediately to tell him he shouldn't worry about anything; as long as he wanted, he had a place in her home as the resident au pair. Now, even though Opal lingered in Las Vegas, Carlisle was thinking in terms of getting back, and he said so.

"Maybe you should spend some time with your sisters at their houses," he suggested to his mother. "And although Nikki's house can be a bit of a looney bin, I'm sure you would be made welcome if you decided to visit."

"Oh, Carlisle, I don't know that I'd fit in with your friends very well...."

He rolled his eyes.

"You should go, Ethel," Julie said. "If only to see that your only son and his friends don't all dress up like Cher and Barbra Streisand on Saturday nights."

People were always speculating about the influence of strong women on young boys, turning them gay, Carlisle thought. Or the absence of a father figure doing the same. Here he had the salt of the earth mom and pop, strong dad and loving mom, and he could never remember a straight day in his life, and barely a happy one. But if these aunts had raised him away from the bigoted Burt, he was sure his entire life would have turned out differently.

"What do you suppose did it?" his mother asked him late one night as they had a cup of tea by the fire, her voice hushed even though no one was around to hear.

"Stop it, Mother. You can let yourself off the hook. I was *born* gay."

"Thank goodness," she said in a breath that sounded like a prayer.

Danny had taken Dixie out to dinner twice, and twice she had cooked for him. He had asked for her help in looking at houses and furniture so he could squeeze in a few lunches, as well, and even a Sunday brunch, after which he took her to see the Wynn art collection. He didn't see her every day, but he at least talked to her daily. This had been going on since September, and it was edging near Thanksgiving. He thought about backing off soon. His feelings for her were getting so strong, the dreams so disturbing, that he was afraid if he let himself get any more involved, the pain was going to be unbearable in the end. And there would be an end. At some point she would be forced to break it to him that they were, and would forever be, only friends.

He just hadn't thought it would come so soon.

It was late in the day and he decided to run by her office as she was wrapping up work. There were always a couple of things he needed to speak with Nikki about, which made him appear less obvious. The director of training and the chief pilot worked closely together, which was very handy when the director of training had a huge crush on the chief pilot's secretary.

As he neared Flight Ops, the silky sound of her Texas drawl floated down the hall and brought a smile to his lips. He stopped before going around the corner just so he could listen. "Here's your in-processing package," she was saying to a newly hired pilot. "Get measured for uniforms at this address, get your ID and health insurance materials from Human Resources, and training starts for you on Monday. Do you live in the area?"

"I haven't relocated permanently yet, but I plan to. Maybe after Christmas."

"We have a relocation expert with one of the real estate agencies in town and she's very good. She helped me find my house. Her card's in the packet if you'd like to talk to her."

"I might do that. You've been a big help, Dixie. Can I buy you a drink after work?"

Stunned, Danny peeked around the corner. The guy was another one of those tall, dark and handsome types. He had both hands planted on her desk and was leaning toward her.

"I'm sorry, I have to decline," she said sweetly.

"Come on, Dix, make an exception. I just want to show my gratitude, that's all."

"You're very welcome. No thank you."

"You're gonna give me a complex, now...."

Danny ducked back around the wall, out of sight.

"That's real sweet, but I'm sort of seeing someone."

"Aw, damn. I bet he's a pilot."

"No, sir. I can't be hooking up with the pilots I work with, now can I?"

"Lucky fool. Well, if it doesn't work out, you know where to find me."

The unexpected blow struck Danny and he felt an almost physical pain. But he regained his composure quickly, reminding himself that he had been expecting this all along. *Crazy,* he admonished himself, *I was so crazy to let myself become infatuated with someone so stunning, so warm and wonderful.*

Instead of going to Nikki's office or dropping by Dixie's desk, he left the building. He didn't go back to the training facility or to the airport, but got in his car and drove up the south hills a little until he found a spot to park and watch the planes come in. And there he sat for a very long time, berating himself for indulging such delusions of adequacy, until long after the soft rays of the setting sun faded, and the colored lights of the city made a sparkling backdrop for the jumbo jets as they landed. Who was he but a short, dumpy, bald, aging pilot with big ears? Okay, so the rigors of starting up an airline had meant the loss of a pound or two, but he was still just a funny-looking guy. And she was a fabulously beautiful, witty, sexy, unattainable woman.

Not entirely unattainable, he reminded himself. While he was busy being a supportive friend, someone else had "attained" her.

He took out his cell phone and saw that it was dead—not very smart for someone in his position. He rummaged around in the glove box and found the charging connect. As soon as he plugged it into the cigarette lighter, he was rewarded with a couple of beeps. Messages.

There was a response from an instructor he hoped to interview, and a call from Nikki about a check ride she needed him to give a pilot the following week. She also wanted to see him first thing in the morning about some new hires. And then came Dixie's sexy purr. "Hey, Danny, you must be all tied up if your phone's off. I was hoping you'd be able to come over for dinner. Nothing fancy. But I wanted to tell you something so I figured I could feed you, too. Give me a call."

There it was, he thought. She was going to tell him about her lover. Dixie wasn't stupid—she must know by the way he gazed at her like a lovesick boy that he was mad for her. She must want to make sure they understood each other before he lost control and turned into some kind of crazed stalker.

Uncharacteristically, he didn't call her. He just went straight to her house, trying unsuccessfully to get that hangdog look off his pathetic face. When she came to the door he was standing there, staring down, hands in his pockets.

"Hey, you," she said, smiling all over. "Get in here."

He stepped into the house but stayed in the little foyer. "I really can't stay, Dix. But you said you had something to tell me."

"I sure do, but it'll go down better with a glass of wine. Come in."

"Naw, that's okay. Just give me the bullet."

"What's the matter with you?"

He shrugged. "Nothing. I just let myself get a little behind. I have to get back to the office."

"You?" she said with a laugh. "Come on. You're more efficient than anyone over there." She turned and walked away from him and it was pure torture. She wore a pair of snug jeans, a fitted knit shirt that barely reached the waist of her jeans, and no shoes. The rhythm of her hips and the bounce of her golden hair as she moved toward the kitchen almost made him cry. "Well, if you're going to be a spoilsport, fine. But I have a glass of wine calling me, so you'll just have to be a little less rushed."

He followed her. What else was he going to do? He was, if anything, a gentleman. But this was tough. He genuinely hoped she wouldn't drag it out.

"I found out, just before I left work today, that Bob

Riddle went around Nick and hired some Aries pilots—without even goin' through Eric and the hirin' committee. She is so pissed, but wait till you hear *who*."

This was why they were such good friends, he reminded himself. They were equally involved in this whole company and all its people, including the politics and gossip. He could almost forget she was about to break his heart. "Who?"

Without asking him again, she poured him a glass of the wine he liked, which she kept stocked, and handed it to him. "They're all three very active union guys, but one of them is that useless Texan, Branch Darnell."

His eyes almost popped out. He took a sip of his wine.

"Hah! I knew I could tempt you to a drink, at least."

"Dix, don't worry about my feelings. Just lay it on me. Are you seeing Branch again?"

"*Seeing him?* Have you lost your mind? It takes all my willpower to keep from *killing* him. I can't believe that sleazy devil managed to get a job here! If he'd come across the chief pilot's desk, no way. No *effing* way." She took a sip. "But Nick has asked me to try to be mature, because the one we're going to have killed is Riddle." She clinked his glass. "Now, stay for dinner with me. I shouldn't be alone when I'm homicidal."

"Oh, Dix," he said, shaking his head sadly. "I overheard you before. When that guy asked you out. And you told him you were seeing someone...."

"Hmm? You were eavesdropping on me?" She went to the stove, unperturbed, and lifted a lid. Something smelled wonderful.

"Well, I don't want to get in the middle of... You know. I shouldn't be hanging around so much."

She turned back to face him and laughed. "Danny! What are you saying?"

"You have a guy. I need to spend a little less time with you. He's going to get jealous. I mean, I probably would."

She just shook her head, dumbfounded. "So who do you think I'm *seeing,* Danny?"

"I have absolutely no idea."

"I realize that. And frankly, it's getting to be a problem."

"Huh?"

"I thought I was seeing *you.*"

This was way too much for his very small brain. It was simply not possible. "But you said it wasn't a pilot," he ventured, trying to get her to deny it.

"What did you expect me to say? I don't really like being secretive, but I did promise Nikki I wouldn't get involved with any pilots. It's just that… Well, I hope I'm not being an idiot again, but I thought you were different. And this has been moving very, very slowly, which gave me time to really be sure you're different." She walked toward him, took his glass out of his hand and put both their wineglasses on the table. "I think I've been very patient." She laced her hands around the back of his neck, and placed a very sweet kiss on his mouth.

His mind was reeling. "But…" He swallowed hard. "This just isn't possible," he said, shaking his head.

She looked at him in confusion. "Not possible for who? You?"

He began to blink rapidly, nervously. "I…ah…I just can't…" He gulped again, but it felt as if there was a golf ball in his throat. He tried to think. It couldn't be him she was thinking of. He would only disappoint her. Embarrass her. This wasn't what he'd expected at all.

"Danny, are you seeing someone? I didn't think you were—"

"No!" he nearly shouted. "It's not—" His mouth had gone so dry he could hardly speak. He began to sweat. And tremble. Did she noticed the sweating and trembling?

"Are you *gay?*" she demanded.

"Well, no," he said, but he realized he hadn't said it very convincingly. For just a split second it occurred to him that might be a good way to go—tell her he was gay. That way she'd move along to some high-and-handsome dude she'd be proud to be seen with. Because this way, if he caved, she was only going to look at him one day and ask herself what she'd been thinking. But he said, "No, I'm not gay, I'm just not—"

He tried to seize the words. *Right for you? Good enough for you?*

"What *is* it?" she asked, a touch of anger in her voice.

He wiped his sleeve over his sweating bald head and gave an embarrassed chuckle. "You sure took me by surprise."

"I did? How can you be surprised? We've been seeing each other for months. I know we haven't been very physical, and to tell you the truth, that part's been real hard for me. But it was the right thing to do because it gave me time to get to know your heart, without being biased by a lot of great sex."

She laughed—half little girl, half seductress—and came toward him again, her hands reaching for him.

"No!" he said, and he startled her. The look on her face was one of utter shock. And hurt. He wanted to tell her that this wasn't right, wasn't a good decision, but he didn't know how. She was so incredible; she wasn't supposed to get involved with someone like Danny. He was a realist; he knew what his talents were. He was a good pilot, a good instructor, a good manager of people, but he wasn't a good date. He wasn't a great lover, and Dixie deserved a great lover. The truth was, he had barely any experience at all, and the last time he was with a woman was so long ago he could hardly remember it. He didn't want to go along with this lunacy, only to have to live with regrets later. "You're just lonely, Dixie. That's all."

She crossed her arms over her chest and there was a definite scowl on her pretty face. "Well, no, I'm not, but I'm gonna be if you don't stop this nonsense."

He just had to think this through, because the explanations, which were all logical, were not coming to his lips. "I gotta think," he said. And he turned and practically ran out of her house.

He was all the way to the car before the front door opened and she yelled, "Danny!"

"I gotta think," he yelled back.

As he drove out of her neighborhood, he had to slam on his brakes to avoid hitting a dog walker because he was so out of it. "Sorry," he called out his open window.

"Slow down!" the man yelled at him.

"Yes, sorry," he said. He went maybe a half mile before he came upon a small, well-lit dog park. He pulled into the parking lot and stopped. It might be best if he didn't do a whole lot of driving while he wrestled with this.

What am I going to do? he asked himself. He'd been so certain that this relationship with Dixie could never evolve, so sure she'd let him down nicely but firmly as soon as she found a man she wanted to get involved with, that he had never imagined she could be developing feelings for him.

You're always so hard on yourself, his mother's voice said.

"Go away. You're dead."

You love her. She loves you. What's so strange?

"What's so strange is my dead mother talking to me about my love life. My ridiculous love life. Can't you see what a mistake she'd be making?"

I'm not worried about her mistakes. I'm worried about yours.

He was never quite sure whether it was the many years of his mother's wisdom reverberating in his subconscious, or whether she was really not so very far away and still butting in, but as always, he felt the calming effect of her words. *Yes,* he thought, *I need to worry about me.*

He looked at his watch. It had only been a few minutes. He started the car and pulled out of the parking lot, slowly and carefully.

It had been wrong of him to spend so much time with her and not allow for the possibility that she might have expectations. He'd seen the fancy place settings and candles when he came to dinner. He'd brought her flowers, she'd stocked his wine. If she was shortsighted enough to fall for a guy for whom "ordinary-looking" was a compliment, when she could have anyone she wanted, that was her problem. For his part, it was wrong to lead her on and then hurt her.

When he got to her door, he tapped lightly.

"Just go away," she yelled from within.

"Dixie, I'm sorry," he called back. Dixie's next-door neighbor came outside in his bathrobe and slippers with his little dog in his arms and looked over at Danny suspiciously. Danny lifted his hands in a helpless gesture.

"I'm sorry, too," she yelled. "Sorry I was so *stupid!*"

He could tell she was crying. The neighbor was scowling at him. He tried the door and it opened. There she was, her legs curled under her on the living room couch, sniffing into a tissue.

Danny threw off his jacket and went to her. He sat as close as he could and pulled her into his arms. "I'm sorry," he said. "I was shocked. I just couldn't believe it."

"Couldn't believe what?" she asked with a sniff.

"That you'd be… You know… Interested in me."

"Well, why ever not? We've been together as much as possible for about three months." She blew her nose. "I thought you'd noticed that."

He nuzzled her neck. Funny, now that he was this close, all his nervousness was gone. "I noticed," he said. "But I thought you'd eventually come to your senses."

"And I thought you'd come to *yours*." She turned to him, her nose right on his nose. "By three months, I usually have a tennis bracelet and a whole bunch of lies to get me into bed." She nibbled on his lip, and a shudder of fierce desire shot through him.

"Can I pick up the tennis bracelet tomorrow?" he asked, nibbling back.

Her arms went around his neck. "If you do, you're history." She gave him a very serious, very deep kiss. Her tongue played on his; her hands roamed up the back of his neck where there was hair. "I thought I made it clear—that wasn't the life I wanted."

Yes, she had told him about all the men, all the gifts and come-ons and lies; she had told him what it felt like to put your trust in a future with a man, call it love, and come away feeling used. She had told him all that. "I'll give you whatever you want," he said, and meant it.

She pulled away from him just enough to look into his eyes. "Did you know I sold all the tennis bracelets and necklaces and all that meaningless fodder to buy new living-room and bedroom furniture? And I gave all the teddies and peignoirs away. I have nothing sexy to wear when you *finally* get around to taking me to bed."

He moaned deeply and emotionally, his hands seriously caressing her back, sides and, yes, breasts. He claimed her mouth again, unconcerned about her lack of nighties. "You'll have to take me," he said. "All the blood has rushed out of my head."

She giggled the little-girl giggle.

"Is this really happening to me?" he asked as he pulled her to her feet.

Slowly and deliberately she unbuttoned his shirt and slid her cool, soft hands inside. "You bet, bronco. And you just wait. You're gonna be so glad you came back tonight."

"Dixie," he said weakly, "I'm pretty sure I'm not very good in bed."

"That's okay, sport. I am."

Sixteen

It was predawn and chilly in the room. Danny reached down and pulled the comforter over them, then took Dixie back into his arms. She snuggled close, letting him spoon her. He nuzzled the nape of her neck and she purred.

"Hmm. You said you weren't very good," she whispered. "If you were any better, we'd both be dead."

He chuckled. *"Naked Couple Found Dead, Screwed to Death."*

She giggled and wiggled her butt closer. "Uh-oh."

"I know," he said in a tone both prideful and embarrassed. "I guess I just can't get enough of you." He pulled her over, onto her back. Lifting the comforter, he dived underneath so he could suckle her breast, kiss her flat belly, spread her legs. Her moans and wriggles brought his lips to her mouth and the most important part of him inside her. He'd lost count hours ago, but it was safe to say he'd never had this much sex in his life.

Holding one wrist in each hand, he stretched her arms up over her head as far as they would go. Her legs came around his waist and she rocked with him while his mouth covered hers and their tongues played. It didn't take long for the gentle but strong thrusting to bring them both to yet another climax.

"Oh, Dixie," he whispered against her neck.

"You're going to be so exhausted today," she said, tickling his back with a long fingernail.

"I don't think so," he returned, again with a deep, secretive laugh. He rose above her. "I still can't believe it. You and me."

She held his face in her hands so he would focus and listen, despite the fact that he was still inside her. Soft now, but still inside, where she wanted him to be forever. "Danny Adams, I don't ever want to hear that again. You can say you're grateful if you want, because so am I. But you can't say anything ever, *ever* again that gives a question to why I'd want you. I've been waiting for a man like you forever. An honest and good man who wants only me. And you're the most handsome man I've ever loved."

"Dixie, you're such a liar," he said, but he grinned. "I always think of myself as a funny-looking little guy—"

She whopped him on his left cheek, the lower one. "Well, I'll tell you one thing: You're not a little guy where it counts."

Her arms went around him and she wiggled her hips. He was still a moment. "Oh-oh," he said.

And she giggled.

Nikki was headed for the airport long before the sun came up. Sleep had come hard the night before. Bob Riddle's little adventure in hiring had so blatantly undermined her authority, he couldn't have been more obvious if he'd just come out and admitted he was gunning for her. Two of the three Aries pilots were known to Nikki and Danny Adams; they were highly visible malcontents with a long history of causing problems. And the third was Branch Darnell. Riddle knew Nikki would never hire him, and his presence would greatly disturb the chief pilot's office.

She went to the maintenance base where their newest airplane, which was also their oldest airplane, was undergoing an engine change. Since it was a new lease with an insured engine, the cost of this operation would be moderate, but the liability of having an aircraft that worked twelve hours a day out of service was inevitably a hit in the pocketbook. The plane was grounded while the problem was diagnosed, and a new engine found, and then the engine had to be installed.

Floodlights lit the 757. The engine cowling was raised and the old engine sat on a cradle that had been pulled away from the plane. A tug had pushed the new engine under the opened cowling and winches lifted it into place. About six maintenance techs were at work under the lights, and the Wrench stood at the edge of the action, watching.

It was a cold November morning and Nikki pulled her coat tighter. She wore her ID badge on the outside of her coat. As she went to stand next to Mark Shows, he turned his head and looked down at her, raising his eyebrows. "Righty-tighty, lefty-loosey," she advised, repeating Buck's childhood instructions for tightening screws.

"Thanks," he said, which sounded like "tanks" around his cigar.

"How long is she going to be out?"

"We'll have her back on the line by noon. Maybe. But don't get used to it."

"Maybe she wasn't such a good idea."

"Maybe?" he asked mockingly.

Mark had kicked the tires on this one and advised Riordan to pass up what looked like a good deal on paper. He'd have opted for a slightly higher lease payment on a newer, better-maintained plane. In the long run he believed that to be more cost effective, as did Nikki. Especially when the post 9/11 economy was keeping the cost of planes low.

But the price, availability and support had been irresistible.

"I heard Bob Riddle found this plane," she said.

"That's right. He knows someone at every leasing company, airline and manufacturer. Probably because at one time or another, he's worked for them all."

"He's out to get me," she said.

"Of course he is, Nick."

"Before we certified, while I was in Phoenix at the sim, he handed my manuals in to the FAA. And he took the credit."

He took the cigar out of his mouth. "You gotta look out for yourself better than that."

"Is he going to take credit for his plane?" she asked.

Mark put the cigar back in his mouth. "God, I hope so. Piece of shit."

"Got any advice for me, Wrench?"

"Yeah. Get better intelligence on the guy. 'Cause he's got it in for you."

"See, that's the thing, when you're busy *working,* you don't have time to go gathering dirt."

"I don't make the rules, Nick. I just get whacked by 'em every now and again." He pointed his cigar stub at the plane.

"Yeah," she said. She slapped a hand on his back. "Righty-tighty, lefty-loosey."

"Thanks."

She went to her office. At 5:00 a.m. it was barely coming to life; most of the office staff came in after seven or eight or even nine. She liked the quiet; she even liked the dark. Signing in online, she did a quick Internet search of Bob Riddle. There were a few quotes from local papers and magazines and even a couple of national aviation periodicals. *Bob Riddle, who is spearheading the certification effort at New Century Air... The operation of the new carrier is headed by Robert A. Riddle, who brings to the company years of seasoned executive experience.... "We're on schedule with certification," said Riddle, senior VP of Operations. "I've assembled a powerful team to get this done on time."* There was that senior VP again. Nikki couldn't help but wonder if Joe asked him about it, would Bob claim it was just a newspaper misprint?

The references to articles and interviews were so numerous that Nikki found herself thinking, not for the first time, that this guy must have a press agent. She then went to the Department of Transportation Web site and looked at their active-dockets link. This was where the filing for NCA's Certificate of Public Convenience could be accessed. She had never looked at the whole document, more than two hundred pages in length, but the résumés of all the corporate officers were filed in its pages. She pulled up Riddle's. He cited years of management experience at smaller and, conveniently, defunct airlines. He'd certified a number of different aircraft types, set up training programs, introduced policy and been a *senior* vice president a half dozen times. Hundreds of start-ups had come and gone since deregulation in '78; there was no way to check with nonexistent companies to see what kind of job he'd done, but... He had graduated sigma cum laude from the University of Michigan with his MBA. Hmm. Interesting that with all that education, they hadn't taught him how to say *myriad*.

It was too early to call Ann Arbor, so Nikki printed his résumé and stored the copy under her desk blotter.

Looking back at the Internet search engine, she saw a reference to a "pilot's forum" bulletin board for New Century Air. She hadn't known anything about this. Upon closer inspection, it appeared the site had only recently been established. It was less than two weeks old and about ten of their now forty pilots had expressed opinions under handles like LiftOff, SkiMagnet22, LoneStar, GNnTNIK, QBall, Rocketman, Spoiler and Wings69. Boys and their toys, she thought.

She read through some of the postings and became reacquainted with pilots when they were at their best— whining. They complained about the pay, the schedule, the hotels, the meals, the leadership. And then she saw,

How'd we end up with a box office where a cockpit should be?

If you check out her résumé, you'll see that she must have pictures of Riordan in compromising positions with animals to get the job.

The only thing that will bring a union in here faster than a chick chief pilot is one who is dangerous in the cockpit, too.

Is she at least hot?

Hot? No, she's a dyke.

Have any of you dipsticks actually flown with her? Because I have, and there aren't many men I've

*flown with in the last twenty years who are even
close to that skilled. I almost had to throw a towel
in my lap.*

That had come from LoneStar, but the others weren't
about to let him get away with it.

*I heard she's after Riddle's job, and her first step
was to get him to give up the cockpit, which put
her in the #1 seniority position.*

*Lotsa luck, babe—Riddle's next in line for the CEO
position! And when Riordan's gone, pay is up and
dykes are history.*

And to that, LoneStar asked:

What does Riddle do again?

She hit the print button. Dyke? She started to laugh.
"Nothing can be that funny at six in the morning."
She turned to see Sam standing in the doorway. He
wore his uniform and held his hat, obviously on his way
to a flight.
"It's really not funny, but it just struck me as so...so
predictable." She handed him a page. He looked at it,
looked at her. She laughed again. "Dyke? How unimag-
inative."
Sam gave her back the page. "Want breakfast?"
"What time's your flight?"
"Don't worry, Mom," he said. "I'll be on time."
"Do I do that?" she asked him. "Do I mother people?"
"Only me that I know of. Come on."

The printer spit out the last page and she flipped the switch, turning it off. Grabbing her purse and coat, she preceded him out the door. "You drive," she said.

"Wow, this is quite a turnaround—you willing to be seen in the same car with me."

"Well, obviously my reputation is out of my hands. It appears there would be more gossip if I'm seen out with another woman. Besides, I'm starving, and it's going to be a horrible morning." It wasn't until they were in his car that she asked, "How did you know to find me at the office?"

"I'm stalking you," he said.

"No, really?"

"I wanted to get breakfast on the way to work and I took a side trip through the NCA parking lot. I saw your car. I got a crazy notion. I went wild with longing…to see you bent over a plate of sausage and eggs."

Temptation is good for me, she thought. She felt lighter, less burdened, a little more alive.

"Did you know about that site, Sam?"

"I just heard about it. Sounds like a bunch of typical pilot pontificating to me. Plus, it could be one guy, you know, signed on with ten handles—talking to himself, salting the mine, so to speak."

"Hmm. Hadn't thought of that," she lied. She had thought of it, but the one person she suspected wasn't savvy enough to even send an anonymous e-mail. "I wish I could say it didn't bother me."

"I don't think anyone's that tough. But listen, you have a lot of fans out there. You do a good job, Nick. Just keep doing a good job and things will work out."

That was what she wanted to believe, but clearly Riddle wanted her out of her job.

But Sam had been on her side since the beginning,

and that was worth a lot to her on this cold, dark morning. "Thanks, Sam. For insisting. For stalking me."

"Sure. One of these days I'll let you catch me."

"I look forward to that."

At least a half dozen people saw them return to the office building at 8:00 a.m. Eyebrows lifted above sly smiles, for of course no one would believe they'd just gone to breakfast. She was past caring. In fact, she'd made up her mind that as soon as she could get her life in just a little better order, she was going to officially date him. If her children gave her permission, that was.

But first things first. She told Sam to have a good flight and returned to her office. Her first order of business was a call to the University of Michigan's School of Business. She was transferred to the postgrad department, where the dean's assistant informed her that no one named Robert Riddle had a masters in business. There was a Robert Riddle who had an undergrad degree in business, but far from being sigma, he had graduated with a 2.8.

Riddle would know that while airline employers would check licenses, flying hours and violations, they wouldn't bother with the college GPA for fifty-year-old applicants. He was such a liar!

Ah, Nikki thought. Let the games begin.

She called the Wrench with a list of five airlines, now gone, and it turned out he knew executives from two of them. "Two is enough," she said. "Will you find out from them what they know about Riddle's performance while there? He has himself listed as special assistant to the vice president of Ops at one and director of training and standards at the other."

"Where's this going?" he asked her.

"For starters, I'm making up a nice little packet of misinformation. I started with a dynamite résumé registered with the Department of Transportation. Hell, I'd hire him sight unseen."

There was a moment of silence. "Maybe I ought to take a look at it."

"If you do, I'd love to hear your reaction. But in the meantime, I'd like to know if any more of it's fiction."

"Any *more?*" he asked.

"I've taken your advice," she said. She didn't respond to his nudge. "I'm hunting and gathering. For now, I'm just holding."

When she got off the phone, she called Jewel and asked when Joe had time for a brief meeting with herself and Bob. "We have some hiring issues to work out and Joe's input would be very valuable." Jewel set her up for 11:00 a.m.

She looked at her watch. It was a little bit after eight. Rather than trust voice mail, she walked down the hall to Crue's station. She knew it was too early for Bob, but his secretary would be there. Nikki stretched the truth a tad. "Tell Bob that I just spoke to Jewel and she asked me to pass on that there's a meeting with Joe Riordan at eleven that he'd like Bob to attend."

"Will do," Crue said.

The mystery was, where was *her* secretary? Nikki wondered. It was unlike Dixie to be late coming to work, and when she had heard that Branch Darnell had been hired, she had been so angry that Nikki had expected to see her at dawn, spoiling for a fight. There was nothing quite so potent as a Texas beauty queen's pique.

Nikki resisted the urge to call Dixie; the woman worked long, hard hours, and if she was a little slow one morning, so what? She vowed to call her only if she hadn't seen her by nine.

Mark Shows called her within the hour. He had spoken to the former VP of Flight Ops at the now-out-of-business Dolphin Airlines and, remarkably, he had never known Bob Riddle to work in management at that company. He was a pilot, he might have served on an employee committee, but he was never on the payroll as a director or special assistant.

"He's a liar," she said before she caught herself.

"You get fired for that kind of stuff around here," the Wrench said. "Are you going to take it to Riordan?"

Before she could answer, Dixie stuck her head in the open door and gave a little wave announcing her arrival. "Dixie, get your steno pad and come in here, will you please?" Then to Mark she said, "If I decide to do anything like that, I'll let you know. Thanks. You're a pal."

Dixie just stood in the doorway, a perplexed look on her face. When Nikki hung up the phone, she said, "Steno pad?" Dixie didn't take shorthand.

"Please." Nikki smiled sweetly. When Dixie returned with a notebook and pen, Nikki asked her to close the door.

"What is going on?" Dixie asked.

Since her research had turned up Riddle's lies and exaggerations, Nikki had actually felt a little heady with excitement. She showed Dixie the folder and told her about the meeting she'd set up. "And here's what I'd like you to do. You have a favor you can call in down in HR, don't you?"

"I hope to shout," Dixie confirmed.

"Go see our goddess and get her on our team. First of all, no hiring without giving us—you, at least—a heads-up. And second, I'm going to get Joe's permission to do an internal posting for a crew scheduler, and I don't want to bring in anyone from outside if we have a qualified person in the company."

Dixie gave a small huff. "Those aren't even favors," she said. "Those are like *procedures*."

"Great, then here's a favor. See if you can find out how Riddle got Shanna to go along with hiring those three Aries guys without going through the usual process."

"I'll give it my best," she said. "I hope I don't slap her for bringing that slimeball up here." Dixie stood and brushed down her skirt. "What are you going to do to Riddle, now that you have the goods?"

"It'll suit me fine if I can just find a way to get him to stop doing me."

"Amen."

"How come you're so late today?" Nikki asked.

Dixie immediately broke eye contact and flushed slightly. "Oh, just couldn't get going," she said, but she looked away nervously.

Nikki looked at her more closely. After being friends with Dixie for more than ten years, she could read her pretty well. Her cheeks were rosy, her eyes twinkled, and even though she tried to suppress it, she had a cunning smile. "Oh, my God," Nikki said. "Not *Darnell!*"

Offended, Dixie slapped the edge of Nikki's desk with the steno pad. "Don't be obscene. I *despise* him."

This time Nikki squinted a little as she looked at Dixie's face. "Who is it?" she asked. Immediately her hands went to her temples and she closed her eyes. "No! Don't tell me! I don't even want to know!" Her eyes flew open and she leaned again on the desk. "Not a pilot. Tell me he is not a pilot."

"Nikki... I..."

"No, don't tell me! Don't!"

"Nick, I…"

"Dixie, you *promised!*"

"But this is different," she said, her tone a little whiny. "I know what you're thinking, but this is—"

"Damn it, Dix, it's *always* different! But it always turns out the same!"

Dixie straightened indignantly. "I probably deserve that, but eventually you'll see." She lifted her chin. "I'll take care of HR for you." And she left, her back ramrod straight.

Nikki let out a long, tired breath. Dixie was in the saddle again. That "swearing off men" resolution hadn't lasted long, but then Nikki scolded herself for even thinking it would. Actually, she should give Dixie credit—three or four months was a long time for her. Dixie never could go long without a man. And it showed all over her, the pink cheeks, the secret smile, the satisfied twinkle in her eyes. She'd better not screw up her job on account of this; she'd better not let some tall-dark-and-hung talk her into helping get a friend hired or some other inappropriate favor. Brother, when Dixie had a man in her rack, it sure was obvious.

Nikki shook her head in exasperation.

She was *jealous!* She put her head down and groaned in equal parts petty envy and frustration, pounding her fists on her desk.

"Whoa," she heard a man say.

She lifted her head and saw Bob Riddle in the doorway. "What?" she asked impatiently.

"You have any idea what this eleven o'clock with Riordan is about?"

"No, but after we're done with him, you and I are

going to go a few rounds about this little hiring spree you've been on.''

He grinned arrogantly and touched his index finger to his brow in mock salute. ''I'll look forward to it,'' he said, and left her.

Dixie waltzed right into HR like she owned the place. She pulled the chair that faced Shanna's desk right up close. Shanna flushed—she knew she was in trouble. She tried leaning back a little, but Dixie just leaned forward. ''And here I thought we were friends,'' Dixie said.

''We... We *are*,'' Shanna insisted.

''Don't toy with me, precious, because I've seen you with vomit on your shirt. You rear-ended us in Flight Ops. Why'd you do that?''

''What are you talking about?'' she asked, her nose up and the corners of her mouth curling down.

''I'm talkin' about three instantaneous new hires when we don't even have a pilot class starting, and without goin' through the pilot hirin' committee or giving the chief pilot a right of veto.''

''Well, jeez, what was I supposed to do? He's your boss's boss.''

''Only if you look at the organizational chart,'' Dixie said. ''The fact is he didn't hire her and he can't fire her, but that aside, you could have called me. Warned me.''

Shanna looked away uncomfortably, but she twisted her mouth in some kind of annoyance.

''What?'' Dixie asked. ''You want to say something. What?''

''That was part of his deal. He didn't want anyone to know until it couldn't be undone.''

That pushed Dixie back in her chair. The son of a bitch. "Did he say why?" she asked Shanna.

"He said they were friends, good pilots, and that your boss didn't like them. Dixie," she said, a pleading creeping into her tone, "I thought I had to, you know?"

"Boy, you sure didn't think you had to when Nick hired Danny and Eric. You were on her like a duck on a June bug."

"He reminded me of that. He said, 'She gets one, I get one.'"

"Except this time he got me, you know. That long, tall Texan, Darnell? We have some very unpleasant history." She quickly filled Shanna in on the story, the whole story—six months of promises, his wife on the trip they'd planned as their tryst, the scuffle and head wound, the suspension from Aries. And she noticed as she told it that Shanna's cheeks deepened in color and her mouth set in a line. "Oh, God, he put the moves on you, didn't he?"

"It was just a little flirting," she said. "But he did say he was separated."

"Yeah, and by the way, he could use a place to stay when he comes to town to fly," Dixie said. "Oh, he is going to burn in hell. Shanna, girl, take it from a pro— unless you want a standing appointment at the gyn office to get checked for STDs, you'd better not believe much of what they say."

Shanna chewed her lip but didn't speak. Dixie suspected she'd be making an appointment today.

"You owe me," Dixie said. "I have a little favor, and you don't have to do anything sneaky."

"Sure," Shanna agreed, subdued and perhaps embarrassed. She picked up her pen. "Shoot."

"I'm going to call you later today with a job posting,

after Nikki clears the position in Flight Ops with Joe. All I want you to do is let me know who applies. Okay?"

"Okay," she said. "But that's not a favor really."

"Good." Dixie smiled and stood up. "That means I still have one coming." Shanna's lips formed a pout. "Darling outfit, by the way. It looks positively made for you."

The girl beamed in pleasure.

And Dixie thought, My God, this is just too-o-o easy.

Bob Riddle was clearly disappointed that the meeting with Riordan included only him and Nikki. "You said you didn't know what this was about," he accused.

"I lied," she admitted.

From that point on, there was just a lot of spitting back and forth while Riordan sat at his desk and watched, growing more and more annoyed by the minute. Joe didn't like having meetings, much less witnessing them. He avoided board of director meetings if he could. But here he was, observing the chief pilot and VP of Ops dicker.

"You deliberately went around me and the hiring committee," Nikki accused.

"I had good reason for that—I knew you did not approve of any pilots with previous union affiliation and would veto their hire."

"I might have vetoed these hires, but not because of their union affiliations. And you know Branch Darnell has a romantic history with my secretary that ended very badly."

"With all respect, it will be hard to find pilot hires who haven't had romantic history with your secretary."

"Below the belt!"

"Indeed."

"We agreed on a system for hiring and—"

"You hired two management pilots without a word to me that you were even considering—"

"Before we set up a hiring committee and parameters for the interviewing process," Nikki shot back.

"Still in all, you got yours, I took mine."

"Oh, for God's sake!" Joe snapped, a fist hitting his desk. "Is this what the two of you came here to do?"

At that point Bob's cell phone twittered loudly.

"Forgive me, boss. I'm expecting an important call. Can you give me ninety seconds?"

"Thirty," he said unhappily.

Bob stepped out of the office, saying, "Bob Riddle," as he went. But he stood right outside the door, and though his voice was low, it was completely audible. And Jewel was at her desk, guarding the gate, so obviously he meant to be heard. "Yeah, John, thanks for calling back. I only have a second, but I'm afraid the news is bad for your side. I've made a commitment here and I'm going to turn down your offer." Pause. "Yes, that's right, I'm staying at New Century." Pause. "Well, because I believe in this company. We're going to kick some serious ass. But just out of curiosity, since I won't be changing my mind, anyway, what was their final offer? Whoa, Nellie. CEO?" He whistled. "That's three times what I'm making here. That is tempting, but damn it all, I'm here for the long haul. Nope, can't be talked out of it. Thanks again, John. And hey, keep in touch."

Sparks and light bulbs were going off in Nikki's head like mad, but she composed her features. She stood as Bob reentered the room. "Look," she said, preempting him. "I don't see how we're going to work this out to our mutual satisfaction, so I would find an agreement that we won't do this to each other again to be satisfactory. How about it?'' she said, sticking out her hand.

Slowly, perhaps reluctantly, he took her hand. ''All right,'' he said uncertainly.

''All right. I have another matter to speak with Joe about, so I'll stick around a minute. You done here?''

''Uh. Yeah, I guess so.'' He stuck his hand across the desk. ''Thanks, Joe.''

''What are you thanking me for?''

''Uh, your time. Thanks.''

Joe took his hand limply. ''Sure. Get outta here.''

Nikki sat facing Joe, Joe sat facing her. They did not speak as they listened to Bob make small talk with Jewel in the outer office. Very small talk, because Jewel was a tough cookie who didn't suffer fools gladly, and by the nature of her monosyllabic responses, she was letting him know he could move along. Still, for another moment after he'd left, Nikki and Joe sat and just looked at each other.

He broke the silence first. ''All right, that did not appear to go well. It didn't accomplish anything or end nicely, and yet you have some kind of self-satisfied smirk on your face.''

She tried not to grin like the Cheshire cat. ''I'd like your okay to post internal to the company for a job to fall under the chief pilot's office. Crew scheduler.''

''We don't have a crew scheduler?''

''Me. And I gotta have a little help.''

''You think you can find one inside NCA?''

''I don't want to look outside until some of these people get a shot. Huh?''

''Sure.''

''We don't have any kind of lock on positions, do we?''

"Just mine," he said. "Hey, come on, what's up? What happened to make you so happy with yourself?"

"It wasn't me, Joe," she said, getting to her feet. "I was just so goddamn happy to hear that Riddle is committed enough to turn down a $550,000 CEO position to stick it out with us. Damn, that's good news."

He grimaced at her, not buying in at all. "Whatever."

She stuck her hand across his desk. "And thanks for your time."

"Get outta here."

Which she was happy to do, chuckling all the way back to her office.

Seventeen

When Nikki left the president's office, she went directly to Riddle's office. She very quietly told Crue to watch the internal job listings and then asked to see Bob.

Stepping into his office was like stepping into an aviation museum. All he had on his desk that resembled work was one yellow pad on which he'd been scribbling, but the desktop, book shelf, credenza and walls were covered with memorabilia and gifts from aircraft companies and vendors. There was a 757 model in NCA's paint job from Boeing, a crystal clock from a leasing company, a framed picture of a golfing foursome from Rolls-Royce, a model of an engine from GE, to name just a few things. Where and when he'd gotten all this stuff was a mystery to Nikki.

Bob stood from behind his desk and indicated a chair, but Nikki waved him off. "I just wanted to stop by your office and say I'm glad we've put down that problem and I hope we won't have to revisit that issue. And there was another thing." He nodded that she should go ahead. "I couldn't help but overhear your conversation, Bob. It must have been a job offer."

"You heard me?" he asked, clearly trying to look surprised.

"Yes, bits and pieces. I gathered you're very committed to New Century, which is a relief. But I was wondering—if anyone should ask for your résumé, may I have your permission to pass it along?"

He looked genuinely perplexed. "Who might be asking?"

"Not sure," she said with a shrug. "I've tried to stay in touch with other airlines, especially the young and the start-ups, to compare notes on our progress and mutual concerns, and frankly, I've been asked for my résumé a few times. I've also been asked if there's anyone else around New Century who could be persuaded into a better position once the company is established and no longer in need of certification expertise. I've had a couple of tempting offers, as I gather you have, but hell, I just bought a house and got my kids in schools here."

She watched his face. It was as good as a map. She was sure he had set up that phone call to make him appear sought-after in front of the boss. Now it was beginning to dawn on him that there might actually be something out there, something that would put him closer to his goal of having a presidency.

"I'm sure you've been talking to your counterparts at other carriers and have had some of the same experiences."

"Ah, certainly," he said, very *un*certainly.

"Do you happen to have a résumé in your file? Or I could just refer people to the DOT filing on the Internet," she said, and again she was met with his surprised expression. He wasn't aware that his résumé would be there, right in the public documents section. A résumé that was filled with exaggerations and bold-faced lies.

"Just to make things simple, if anyone should ask, just have them give me a call," he said.

"Good enough. See you later, then."

"You'll be sure to let me know?" he asked as she was leaving.

"Let you know?" she mimicked.

"Yes. If anyone should ask about me."

"Oh! Of course!"

Nikki actually *had* been talking to her counterparts at other airlines. She'd called to introduce herself to their chief pilots and found them enormously helpful in sharing some of their work rules and policy, not to mention tips for managing sticky personnel problems. But no one had asked for her résumé, and no one was likely to be asking for Bob's.

He was going to get on the horn now, she knew. He'd not only call the headhunter that got him this job, but start sniffing around airlines to find out what was going on in their management. Here was a guy who looked so good on paper, his carefully fictionalized paper, and could make a positive personal impression as long as you didn't spend too much time with him. Close scrutiny didn't show his best side; he was especially annoying when cooped up in a cockpit for hours on end. But the fact that Joe Riordan had been impressed enough to hire him was proof positive that Bob Riddle could pull off the scam. With any luck, Joe wouldn't be the last to be fooled by him.

It wasn't going to be too long, Nikki believed, before Riddle would find himself a new job. He was much better at getting them than keeping them.

Carlisle called Nikki at the office. "I know this is a lot to ask, and if the answer is no, I will understand, I promise. But it's my mother. She'd like us to have Thanksgiving together. And Nikki, I just don't think I can go back to another day in chilly Anoka, Minnesota."

The other thing that became chilly was Nikki's blood. Suddenly her veins turned to ice. "What are you asking me?" she said warily.

Heavy sigh. "May I invite Ethel to Thanksgiving?"

Nikki's head fell into her hand. Her eyes closed.

"She won't stay with us, because there certainly isn't room for that. I'll be putting her up in one of the hotels, or I might even see what Dixie has complicating her life right now...."

"You don't want to know."

"Oh-oh. She's fallen off the wagon again, hasn't she?"

"Her cheeks are aglow—all four of them."

"Oh, God, the lucky stiff. Anyway—"

"Sure, Carlisle. Ethel can't be any worse than Opal. But with Buck and Pistol here and the dogs constantly snapping and snarling, it might only insure that she'll never be back."

He laughed. "It sounds fabulous. I'm going to tell her to come ahead. She'll arrive Thanksgiving week."

"One thing. I'm not sure where I'll be. It's the busiest flying season of the year."

"Don't you worry about a thing. I'll prepare as many turkey dinners as it takes until you're sitting at the head of your table."

She felt a smile struggle to her lips. "We missed you *so* much when you were away. We didn't eat very well with you in Anoka."

"I'm glad to do what I can. Opal has been fussing over me as if I'm the one dying," he joked.

"She seems to be doing quite well for someone who doesn't have much longer to live, isn't she."

Oh, compassion, Nikki scolded herself. After all, one of these days Opal *would* die, like it or not. One day it wasn't going to be just another of her melodramatic ploys for attention. And then Nikki would hate herself for being so dismissive.

At the end of the day, Dixie stuck her head in Nikki's office. "The job posting is done—it's on the company intranet bulletin board. And if you don't need anything more, I'm going now."

"Dixie, come in a sec." Nikki turned away from her computer. "I'm sorry about this morning. There was a lot of pressure, I was shocked, it was—"

"It's Danny," she said abruptly.

Nikki's mouth hung open. "Danny Adams?" she finally asked.

"Yes, ma'am," Dixie said quite proudly. "The first time it occurred to me how much I liked him was way back at Aries, when we talked at dinner on a San Francisco layover. We talked about him coming up here. And I've been seeing him ever since, but he didn't make the move until... Well, until..."

"I know," Nikki said. "Sex sure does agree with you. I've never in my life known anybody to show the rapture all over her face like you do."

She grinned. "It's always worked for me, that's a fact."

"Well, I have to say, I'm a little surprised."

"I don't know why. He's—"

"He's a wonderful guy. Shy and thoughtful and smart. You usually go for the arrogant, useless types."

Dixie sat down on the edge of the chair that faced Nick's desk and leaned toward her. "Nikki, you just can't believe how wonderful he is. Why, when he takes me into those arms and—"

"Stop!" Nikki said, holding her hand up and closing her eyes tightly. "You cannot tell me anything intimate about him. Number one, he works for me. Number two, I haven't had sex in so long I've forgotten which armpit the vagina is in.''

Dixie giggled. "But it's okay, isn't it, Nick? I mean, boss?''

"Yeah, what the hell. It's an airline. It's almost required.'' Then, facing her friend more seriously, she said, "He won't hurt you, you know. He is a man of high principles—not at all what you're used to. And though I've never known you to treat a man unkindly— even the absolute worst men on record—do not hurt Danny Adams. I mean it. Because I don't know if there's anyone for whom I have greater respect.''

"You know I won't. I'm a one-man woman. Always have been. And so I was just wondering, can I bring him to Thanksgiving?''

That night, a full week before the holiday, Nikki's house was fairly quiet. She should be exhausted, having been up at the crack of dawn to look at that engine change and talk to the Wrench. But the day had been so wildly crazy that she was wired.

She had come home to find April doing homework in front of the fireplace, Jared in his room on the computer, and Opal resting from a rough day at the beauty shop. After a light dinner of soup, salad and sandwiches, everyone seemed to go to their corners except Opal, who availed herself of the big screen in the family room to watch her favorite bug-eating reality shows.

Nikki sat cross-legged in the middle of her queen-size bed and thought about what the next week was going to bring. The reservations had been heavy for Thanksgiving week since before operations started, and although all the flights were crewed, it was possible that someone would call in sick and she would have to take a flight at the last minute. Barring that, she had made a commitment to be at the airport, anyway, to help load bags and serve a turkey dinner to the employees who were stuck at work.

Be that as it may, she was still planning a family holiday. If at the last minute she didn't make it, she'd catch the rerun on the next day or the next.

Her briefcase sat next to the bed and she reached for it. She retrieved the phone log and scanned the numbers, then called Sam. He answered on the second ring. "Hi, Sam. It's Nikki Burgess."

"Boss," he answered.

He was right, she did kind of like it. "Next week is going to be insane, you know."

"I know. But we should do fine."

"Are you planning Thanksgiving with your daughters?"

"Not this time. I'm flying Wednesday, back Thursday afternoon. Not enough time to hitch a ride to Colorado. The younger one will be with her older sister and her husband."

"Well, look. I won't know until I'm actually sitting down at the table if I'll make it, but we're having family and almost-family here. It's quite a group. Would you like to join us?"

He was quiet a moment. "You're going to show me to your family?" he asked.

"Hmm. It's more like I'm going to show them to you. This may finally bring you to your senses."

"Are they scary?"

"Let's see—there are two kids, both at 'that age'— my son is eleven and my daughter fourteen. There's my gay housekeeper-nanny who is bringing his mother. Oh, and there's my dying mother Opal and her six-pound poodle named Precious, who is mean as a snake.''

"She's dying?" he asked. "My God, what's the matter with her?"

"She's not dying. She's been saying that since I was about eleven. She looks quite well and has tons of energy. And my dad will be coming with his dog, who hates the poodle. His dog, Pistol, is a Labra-doodle-cocka-dachsie. If there is a God, he will eat Precious for Thanksgiving. I think that's everyone." She could hear him laughing. "Oh! I almost forgot. My secretary and friend, Dixie, and her boyfriend, the director of training."

"Danny Adams? And Dixie McPherson? When did that happen?"

"They've just come out. I don't want any more details than that. So, what do you think? Want to meet my circus for Thanksgiving?"

"I wouldn't miss it."

Eighteen

After two weeks of operating a drastically downsized airline by using management personnel as pilots and flight attendants, Aries Airlines announced it was suspending operations. The management blamed the unions, insisting they had absolutely nothing more to give in such a bleak economy and airline environment, and the unions complained of a management so inept it couldn't bring their employees above poverty-level wages.

Aries bought a page in the Monday business newspaper listing average wages by employee group. Unions bought a half page in the Tuesday paper with an entirely different set of numbers, considerably lower.

Passengers stood in long lines that moved slower than bureaucracy, looking for transportation on any carrier that would take them. Despite the fact that nearly every commercial airline was willing to honor Aries tickets, this was Thanksgiving week, and there were very few available seats.

The Wednesday before Thanksgiving, which this year was the last Wednesday of the month, was traditionally the busiest travel day of the year. The airport was standing room only and Security was backed up with at least a couple hours' wait. The management of New Century Air had chosen this time of year, this month as their kickoff, for precisely this reason—they were almost guaranteed good passenger loads even as a new and virtually unknown entrant. For a brand-new airline, good loads were better than half-full planes. Under current circumstances, the planes were filled to capacity.

For most of the New Century employees, the strain of this flood of humanity was too much. There were the inevitable delays and oversights. Not the kind of problems that would cause an airline disaster, but the kind that created havoc and pissed people off.

Knowing the potential for such problems, management was very much in evidence around the airport, pitching in, offering advice. The day started under control. Nikki donned a New Century ramp jumpsuit and steel-toed shoes to help throw bags, as did Joe Riordan, the Wrench, customer service and In-flight management, and even Bob Riddle. Predictably, when the demands of Joe Riordan's office called him from the airport, Riddle disappeared. The first couple of flights left the gate on time and were uneventful. Both were going to West Coast cities and would be back by early afternoon. By noon the crush of passengers had at least doubled, as had the impatience of travelers.

And then that phenomenon well known to airline people occurred: when it starts getting crazy, the crazies come out in spades.

It started when a hassled and harried gate agent in Los Angeles boarded a man who was rambling about his mission in Las Vegas to get even with casino bosses. Everyone ignored him. He was a perfect example of a passenger who was going to be more trouble to detain than to turn over to the aircraft crew and let them deal with him.

His rambling became more precise and threatening above ten thousand feet when he asked to use a crew member's cell phone to call Scotland Yard to speak to the bureau chief and turn himself in for the soon-to-be-committed murder of a major casino CEO. He claimed to have weapons and sufficient ammunition in his checked bags to do impressive damage.

It was highly doubtful he had weapons and ammunition in his luggage—unless the security equipment was faulty or some bags had been missed in the wackiness of the busiest travel day of the year.

"Why in God's name did they board him?" Nikki asked.

"What? And give up his revenue?" the dispatcher said with a shrug.

Las Vegas Metro was there to pick him up when he arrived, along with a couple of dogs to do some sniffing around the baggage area, on the off chance.

But a similar thing happened on the inbound from San Francisco. A young gentleman in the gate area was very excited about his Thanksgiving holiday in the gaming city and had had quite a few cocktails. Again, the harried gate agent thought if he could just get him out of the gate area and onto the plane, there wouldn't be a delay. Taking a delay was always a problem, and one that was pursued until fault could be found. The agent figured once the guy was buckled in and under way, very likely he would settle down…or pass out.

He didn't.

Or rather, he settled down until the flight attendants started serving drinks. He was given one, and when his demands for a second were not immediately acted upon, it brought a string of profane insults from his lips. He was warned by the pretty young flight attendant, then by the largest male attendant onboard, after which he slipped into the lav, took off all his clothes and sprinted up and down the aisle of the plane until someone finally tripped him. *Splat*— flat on his face, unconscious and completely naked.

Las Vegas Metro came to get another one, no dogs necessary this time.

The problems weren't limited to NCA by any means. There were fisticuffs on United, and some out-of-control peanut tossing on American, and a flight attendant on US Airways had a drink thrown on her before a little old blue-hair was subdued with the Tuff-Cuffs.

It wasn't always the fault of a gate agent foisting his or her troublemakers onto the aircraft crew. There were problems aplenty at ticket counters, gates and baggage areas everywhere across the United States. A seeing-eye dog expired on a flight, a woman gave birth while waiting in line to check bags, and three unaccompanied minors got on the wrong plane.

But by the end of the day, New Century Air won the prize for the biggest caper of them all.

"Well, Nikki, your number's up," the dispatcher told her over her cell phone. "We have a no-show on the 4:00 p.m. departure to Chicago. It lays over there and comes back tomorrow afternoon at 3:00 p.m."

"Who's the no-show?"

"Jeff Hayden."

"No way. He's so dependable."

"Maybe he'll make it, but it's time to preflight and board."

What the hell, she thought. At least there was no way they could call her to fly on Thanksgiving Day—she'd already be flying. There wouldn't be any flights left after her return the next day.

"I'll call my kids and sitter if you'll have someone

with a ramp vehicle go to the office and pick up my uniform and overnight bag,'' she instructed.

''Done,'' said the dispatcher.

''Oh, and who's my first officer?''

''That would be Captain Landon. He's already on the plane.''

A warm flush passed through her as she thought about a layover in the same city with Sam. It wasn't going to be a sex circus; she just wasn't in that place yet. But it would be fine with her if they managed a quiet dinner together.

''Captain Burgess?''

''Hmm?''

''If you'll go ahead and board, your uniform and bag will be delivered to the cockpit.''

''Thanks. Did Captain Landon get the paperwork for this flight?''

''All set. He's walking around now.''

''Thanks. Tell the gate agent that a last-minute crew change might cause a slight delay, but we'll try to catch up.''

''Uh-uh. All respect, Captain, it's Ms. Pissant up there and I'm not going any more rounds with her today. After two nutballs before dinner, she's wound a little tight.''

''Fine,'' Nikki laughed. ''Leave her to me.'' She went upstairs to the gate area. New Century used only two gates, the first two on the concourse, while a number of other airlines used a total of twenty, ten on each side of the concourse, all the way to the end. It was a coup to get the closest gates, which meant the shortest distance from parking, ticketing and security—very convenient for their passengers. She dialed her phone as she went. The answering machine came on at her house and she hated leaving them a message that she wasn't coming home tonight. Before resorting to that, she tried Carlisle's cell phone.

"Hello?"

"Oh, I'm so glad I caught you. I just got pegged for a flight. The pilot is a no-show. He's one of the most responsible we have, so he might still turn up. But—"

"Nick," Carlisle interrupted. "Turn around."

She made a one-eighty and found herself face-to-face with him. "What are you doing here?" she asked into the phone.

He smiled and lowered his phone to his side, which made her realize what she'd done. "I'm picking up Ethel," he said. "So, you're going out now?"

"Yeah, but the good news is, I'll be back at about three tomorrow and I'm on the ground for turkey. I couldn't have planned it better than that. But like I said, he might still make it. You'll keep an eye on the kids—all three of them?"

"Four. There's Ethel. And Buck called earlier. Said he'd come up this afternoon if he could escape Phoenix."

"Aw. I don't mean to stick you with—"

He put up a hand. "I have a lot to do for tomorrow. I'm going to serve a light dinner tonight and ban everyone from the kitchen. This suits me fine." He cocked his head to listen to an announcement. "That's her flight. You fly safely and we'll see you tomorrow."

"Tell the kids I'll call later from Chicago."

She then spoke to the gate agent, who, though bristly, was fine when handled with extra consideration for the pressure she was under. Nikki told her to give them an additional ten minutes before beginning boarding, and then hurried down the jetway to the plane.

She was already in the cockpit in her street clothes

when Sam finished his walk-around and joined her there. "I must be living right," he said upon seeing her in the left seat.

"You wouldn't have any idea what happened to Jeff, would you? He's a no-show for this flight."

"I can't believe that." He pulled his cell phone out of his pocket and clicked off some numbers, but all he got was voice mail.

"He might be racing toward us as we speak," Nikki said.

"I don't wish him any bad luck, but if he doesn't make this flight, that would suit me fine."

"Just so long as you don't get any ideas," she warned.

"Nick, so far my ideas are all I've had to keep me warm at night," he said. But he got into his seat like a good boy and they began running the checklist.

From that point it was business as usual. The senior flight attendant came up and introduced herself as Karen; Nikki asked Sam to do a crew briefing so she could catch up. The uniform and overnight bag arrived and she made a quick change as the passengers began boarding. The plane filled up with people, the bags were loaded, the fueling was complete.

"Well," she said, "it looks like Jeff missed Flight 909, Sam."

"God bless him," Sam said.

Carlisle had collected Ethel from her Northwest flight out of Minneapolis and was escorting her toward the baggage area when he heard someone shout, "Stop!" Instinctively, he stopped. Holding Ethel's arm, he pulled her to the side of the concourse, which was swollen with wall-to-wall people.

There were further shouts, a few surprised screams, and then Carlisle saw a young Hispanic man in black pants and white shirt fly through the crowd at a dead run. His head was down, but he had a panicked look on his face as he shoved people of every age out of his path. Carlisle gasped as he watched an old woman who walked with a cane tumble to the floor. There, in the man's right hand, flush against his thigh, was a very large black gun.

Since there were no alarms sounding, Carlisle assumed the man had run full speed through the exit side of the security station. As long as he kept going, running inside the crush of people who couldn't see him coming from behind, he had a path to the gates.

"Dear God," Carlisle breathed.

Close on his tail was a man in airport security livery, but he was unarmed. Behind him came the National Guard, brutally serious-looking young men with very scary M-16s, but as Carlisle knew, there would be no shooting by them; the concourse was absolutely packed.

Just as Carlisle thought this, the man darted into the New Century gate, shoved the gate agent out of his way and ran down the jetway. The jetway that led to Nikki's plane.

Now there were screams in earnest from people on the concourse who had seen the gun. A Metro police officer was speaking into his radio as he ran behind the helpless soldiers who trailed the security guard. Immediately, over the airport intercom, Carlisle heard, "Jack Woodson, Jack D. Woodson."

He looked down the concourse. Airline employees sprang into action at the code word for a security breach. They secured the doors to jetways, while at the other end, crew members were closing and securing aircraft doors and pulling jetways back from the planes. Gate agents were moving people out of the gates, directing them down the concourse.

Running against the flow were more Metro police officers, while in the background that tireless mantra kept repeating, *Jack Woodson, Jack D. Woodson... Jack Woodson, Jack D. Woodson.*

The passengers were boarded and the pilots were ready to push as soon as the Ops agent brought the final weight-and-balance paperwork to the cockpit. Karen stuck her head in. "Captain and Captain," she said, smiling. "A miracle has occurred—there are enough meals on board and you will actually be fed."

"Are we full?" Sam asked.

"An ass in every seat and a face in every window. Like you had to ask."

"Do we have a final head count?"

"Any second now, along with a weight and balance, and then we push. Darn close to on time. Have a nice flight," she added, ducking back out.

Brenda was in the forward galley to finish counting her stock. Stephanie and Georgia were in the aft galley, so Karen went to the door, waiting to see if there were any nonrevving crew members or jump-seaters coming on at the last minute. Failing that, she would secure the door.

She smiled when the young man came sprinting down the jetway, happy to see an airline employee hurrying when they were in danger of running late. He must be an airline employee in that white shirt and dark pants, though he had no logo on his shirt. Before she could ponder this, he stuck the muzzle of a very large gun into her waist.

"Close and secure the door," he said, though not unpleasantly.

"Wha—"

"I said, close and secure the door," he ground out nervously.

Karen had a lot of flying experience, having been furloughed from two other airlines before being hired by NCA, and she had been flying at the time of the 9/11 attacks. She did not want to let him on the airplane. "Okay, look, let's just back out of here and—"

He jabbed her harder. "I want you to close and secure the door." Sweat beaded his forehead and upper lip.

She stood in that little area between first class and coach, her toes right at the edge of the doorway, with bulkheads on either side of her. No one but Karen knew this was happening. She didn't want him to take her airplane and she was willing to make a huge sacrifice to avoid that. The problem was, would her sacrifice prevent others?

"No, I can't," she said, and began to walk toward him, pushing him backward. "You have to leave the jetway."

He lifted the point of the weapon out of her belly and whacked her across the face, knocking her off her feet and to the floor of the jetway. Then he walked right on the airplane and headed down the first-class aisle toward the cockpit.

Karen struggled to her feet, holding the side of her head. She leaned against the jetway wall and heard only the normal rustling of a plane filled with passengers. Then there was the click of the cockpit door closing after the gunman, and someone in first class cried, "Gun. He had a gun!"

It began slowly. A woman in first class got out of her

seat and fled the plane, padding down the jetway. Her husband followed right behind. In seconds, all the passengers in first class were rapidly but quietly deplaning while the passengers in coach looked on in confusion. And then they began to follow, having no earthly idea why.

Karen pushed her way back into the plane. She struggled to get to the far side, opposite the door. From there, her cheek smarting painfully, she jumped up and down, waving her arms over the heads of fleeing passengers, trying to get the attention of Stephanie and Georgia. Way at the back of the plane she saw the two startled faces of her sister flight attendants, and with hand gestures signaled a gun and pointed to the cockpit.

As one hundred and fifty people fled off the plane, not sure why, Stephanie and Georgia looked at Karen in confusion.

"Gun," Georgia said. "She's saying there's a gun."

Immediately she headed for the tail door to blow the slide. "Wait!" Stephanie said. "Check the ramp!"

They both looked outside and what they saw scared them to death. About six men, dressed entirely in black and wearing helmets, trained lethal-looking guns on the airplane. They stared at one another. "Are they the good guys or the bad guys?" Stephanie asked.

"Okay," Georgia said decisively. "Blow the slide, disable the airplane so it can't take off, but evacuate out the jetway in case they're bad guys."

Stephanie threw open the door and the rubber slide began to inflate—*galoob, galoob, galoob*— flipping open in huge arcs. Like a tidal wave with a mind of its own, the coach passengers turned and headed out the back and down the slide. At the bottom, two of the armed men moved to the end of the slide and began helping people off, pointing out the evacuation route.

Georgia looked at Stephanie and crossed herself. And then began herding people down the slide.

Nikki and Sam had heard someone enter and close the door. Because the cockpit door was to remain open until they had taxied out to the runway for takeoff, the unusual sound caused them to turn. That was the first indication either of them had that the plane was being hijacked.

He stood a couple of feet behind them. Although he raised the gun threateningly, he didn't point it at them. "I have to go to Ohio," he said. "Right now."

Stunned, neither of them spoke. They were installed in cockpit seats, which were not simple to get in and out of. Facing forward as they were, there was simply no way to defend themselves against a man with a gun. One funny move from either of them and he could shoot them so quickly, they'd never know it happened.

"Oregon! I have to go to Oregon!" he gritted out, agitated and sweating. His teeth began to chatter and he looked as though he might cry.

"Sure thing," Nikki said slowly, soothingly. "I'm your captain, this is your copilot, and we're going to take you."

"Right now," he said more evenly.

"Right now," she said.

He was not a terrorist. He didn't even know where he wanted to go. She flipped a couple of switches with her left hand and slid her right hand down to the console to press the open mike button. "There are just a couple of things to do before starting the engines. Can you, um, sit on that chair? Just pull it down from the side of the wall and have a seat.''

''Are you taking me?''

''Absolutely,'' she said. She glanced over at Sam and saw that his eyes were locked on the young man and he seemed frozen—not with fear, but rather anger. Small wonder, after what he'd been through in the tragic loss of his wife. She hoped he wasn't in shock. ''I'm Captain Burgess. This is Captain Landon, flying as my copilot today. And what is your name?''

He bit his lip and again appeared as though he might cry. He glanced left, right, then back at Nikki. ''Michael. My name is Michael. Michael, Michael, Michael, Michael.''

''Go ahead and pull that jump seat down and get comfortable, Michael.''

She turned back to the front and fiddled meaninglessly with switches and dials, as though getting ready to start the plane. Sam also shifted around in his seat, staring out the front of the plane, his hands on his lap, clenching and unclenching his fists. Nikki had an insane and hysterical thought—Michael, Michael, Bo-bichael, banana-fanna-fo-fichael… She compressed the mike button again. ''And do you have friends or family in Oregon?''

''I have to go,'' he said.

''Certainly,'' she said calmly. Even she was impressed by how calm she was. She had heard the cockpit voice recordings of pilots on their way to auguring in: *Tell Mary Lou and little Jack I love them very much.… We're going down.…* Her dirty little secret was that if it ever got that bad, that close, she'd just yell, *Holy shit! Waaaaaahhh!* And she'd yell it like a girl.

But with a gun behind her and Sam unreadable beside

her, would she cave in to fear? Not unless she were suicidal.

Outside the plane, on the ground, in the terminal windows and on the roof, black-clad men began appearing, pointing guns at the plane.

"Get them away! Get them away!" Michael yelled, standing up again. There were metal runners on the floor for sliding the cockpit seats back and forth and she didn't want him to trip and accidentally discharge the gun. Whenever he got excited, he waved that gun around and did not appear to be too graceful on his feet.

"Take it easy, Michael," she said. "I'll tell them to go away. I'm going to call Dispatch on my cell phone and tell the dispatcher to get rid of them. Okay?" She reached into her brain bag beside her cockpit seat and pulled out the cell. She clicked off a few numbers. "Yeah, Dave. Captain Burgess here, Flight 909 to Oregon. The men in black are making our passenger upset. Ask them to leave, please? Thank you." She put the phone down on the console and left it on, hoping they could hear her in Dispatch.

She looked over her shoulder at Michael and gave him a smile. She called up the kind of smile she had used for April when she didn't make cheerleading, for Jared when his soccer team lost in the finals, a really good mother-smile. But she knew that he was unstable, very likely psychotic, and any moment might be their last for no reason at all. "There," she said. "Better?"

He just looked around nervously, chewing his lip, now and then letting out a whimper.

Sam was still staring straight ahead, the muscles in his cheeks pulsing, his eyes mere slits. What must this be like for him? He must be sitting there wondering if it had been anything like this for his wife. She found herself sending him a mental message. *Hang on, Sam, just hang on.*

Joe Riordan was called immediately. At four-thirty the afternoon before Thanksgiving, the corporate offices were beginning to thin out. He called Bob Riddle's office and was immediately transferred to voice mail, so he slammed down the phone and stormed out of his office. He pitched his car keys to Jewel. "Bring the car up to the door. I'll be out in a second."

She caught the keys and grabbed her purse. This was a command she'd never been given before, and she wasn't going to be asking questions.

Joe was on the other side of the building in no time. He passed Dixie's desk on his way to Riddle's office. "We have a gunman on 909. Jewel's got the car in front." And he kept going.

Dixie could tell by his panicked stride that he wasn't going to wait for her to think about this. She grabbed her purse, her blazer, her ID badge and fled. It was probably the first time she didn't bother to freshen her lips or wash out her cup.

Crue was just returning to her desk from the ladies' room when Joe came bearing down on her. "Where's Riddle? He at the airport?"

"No, he's...ah..."

"He still in town? On his cell?"

"He said something about meeting some of the pilots and then..."

She looked at her watch. He had told her he was going to meet some of his boys for a drink, and then he was going to try to get a hop to Phoenix for the holiday. She was to call him one more time today from the office at exactly four-thirty, and then she could go on home. Her instructions were the same as many times before. She should call from the phone at her desk, he would recognize the number as his own office, and he would take it from there. She was to hang up, but many times she had covertly listened to his scam.

Joe Riordan picked up the receiver from the phone on Crue's desk. "Punch him up for me?"

The large console and keypad faced her. She popped off the seven numbers rapidly. There on her desk, looking back up at her, was her résumé—she was planning to leave it with Shanna in HR before going home. She had already applied for the position of crew scheduler and this would complete her application.

Joe's attention was on his call; he could barely make out Riddle's voice above the bar noise and ching-ching-ching of slot or poker machines. "Riddle," Bob answered. Before Joe could even say hello, Riddle was nearly shouting, "What? She did *what?* She can't make decisions about pilot pay! Jesus Christ, she's just trying to create some political coup because she thinks I'm already on my way out of town for the holiday, but I'll fix her little wagon. I'll see Riordan on Thanksgiving Day if I have to, because we're not going to screw our pilots out of their rightful—"

"*Riddle!*" Joe shouted, cutting him off. "Get back to your office ASAP! And don't leave until you see me, no matter how late it is!" He slammed the phone onto its base. "We have a hijacking," he told Crue. And with that he left the building.

By five o'clock, Nikki was exhausted, but Michael wasn't. He was clearly in some manic state. She had told Michael about a dozen times that they'd be under way as soon as they could get some clearance, but he was growing impatient. Sam, on the other hand, had needed some time to get his head together and come out of shock, but he was back. Cool and in the moment.

"Growing up, I had a dog, a cat and a duck," Sam said. "What about you, Michael? You have pets?"

Nikki shot him a confused look, but he just winked at her.

"Two dogs," Michael said. "Bowser and Glory. They're dead."

"Yeah? Mine, too—but dogs don't live as long as people. What kind?"

And for about ten minutes the men bonded over childhood pets. Apparently this young man had had a pretty decent childhood, a mom, dad, brothers, sisters, and now he was clearly suffering from some mental illness that held him as much a victim as Nikki and Sam. Nikki found herself hoping no one would hurt him—but then she'd think about April and Jared and begin praying that this kid wouldn't kill her.

Her nerves were taut. She began to tremble slightly.

"What's taking them so long?" Michael asked.

"They might be waiting for a new flight plan," Sam suggested. "Captain Burgess, can you radio ATC and ask them if you need to file a new flight plan?"

"You bet," she said. "This is NCA 909, do you need a new flight plan from us?"

"What's your destination, 909?"

"Oregon."

"Affirmative, we'll need a new flight plan and we have current weather for you."

"Michael," Sam said. "The captain usually files the flight plan. It should only take her about ten minutes. Okay?"

"But what if she doesn't come back?"

"Why wouldn't she come back? She said she'd take you to Oregon."

"Ohio!" he yelled.

"Okay, good thing you corrected her now, before she filed the wrong flight plan. Captain? Hurry up on that, will you? I'm getting stiff waiting."

Good old Sam. He was one hundred percent. And how could he manage? When she thought of April and Jared, she imagined his dilemma—two daughters who had already lost a parent to a horrible aircraft disaster. "I'll hurry. Ten minutes. Fifteen tops."

"I don't know if I should let you—"

"Don't worry about it, Michael. You don't really need two pilots to fly the plane. It's just a safety precaution."

She moved very cautiously out of her seat and past the young man. It was a terrible moment, leaving Sam alone with him, but she had the sense that if this went well, it could lead to the end of this miserable ordeal. She glanced at her watch—it had been almost an hour and a half.

She opened the cockpit door and stepped through, completely unprepared for what would happen next. The second she was clear of the door, she was taken down by two SWAT officers who had no idea who was exiting the cockpit. They flattened her to the floor of the plane between the flight attendant jump seats and the first-class galley. Her breath was knocked out of her with a whoosh, but lest she make any noise that might alert the gunman, a hand covered her mouth.

Quickly and quietly she was lifted to her feet and hustled off the aircraft between the two officers. She had a chance to glance at the interior of the plane, now empty of passengers, and saw that SWAT members were scattered throughout, rifles trained on the closed cockpit door.

Once she was down the jetway and in the deserted gate area, she viewed her plane from the windows—it was a surreal vision. Her beautiful NCA 757 was surrounded by armed SWAT officers. It was a sight she hoped to never see again in her life.

When she got to Dispatch, she was hushed with a finger. Her cell phone remained open on the console of the cockpit and the dispatchers had somehow amplified the conversation. Sam and Michael were now talking about Sunday School teachers they'd had as children.

Nikki was led to the break room in the Flight Control area by a SWAT commander. "We've got to get Sam out of there right away," she said.

"Do you think he's in imminent danger?"

"I think Michael is a couple of fries short of a Happy Meal. I'd hate to see him hurt—but I'd hate to see Sam hurt even more."

"We got it. We need your uniform."

A woman stepped into the break room. She was wearing jeans, a T-shirt and a bullet-proof vest. She shook a short wig in her hand, then pulled it over her blond hair. Soft reddish gold curls framed her face.

"Wow," Nikki said. "Amazing."

"Close enough, anyway. Let us change, Charlie," she said to the guy. She was already unzipping her jeans. "Then Captain Burgess can call her family."

Nikki was quickly left alone with the female officer, who kindly handed her a clean police sweatsuit. "The condition of this uniform is…" Nikki began.

"Don't worry about it," the officer said.

"Damp. Really damp."

"I bet it was a little scary out there."

"Yes and no. I'd call him unpredictable and off his bean, but certainly not malicious or vindictive."

"That's good to know. I heard you talking him down. You did a great job."

"If you scare him, he might shoot you. Or Sam."

"I'm not going to scare him. I'm going to go into the cockpit," she said, buttoning Nikki's shirt. "And I'm going to disarm him quickly. And I'm going to have tons of help backing me up." She fanned the shirt a little, grinned and said, "This isn't too bad, Captain. You're my hero."

Nikki handed over the pants. "Get my copilot out of there before I have a heart attack."

"Michael has been identified as a young man with mental problems who is currently off his meds. His father is waiting with the police. We're looking to get everyone out without injury."

The woman pulled the pants on, then the boots, and adjusted the gun she wore around her ankle. Once she'd shrugged into the jacket and put the hat on her head, she squeezed Nikki's upper arm firmly. "Don't worry about a thing."

"Hey. I don't even know your name."

"My name's April Carberreri."

"April," she replied. "My daughter is April."

Officer Carberreri grinned. "No kidding? Cool."

"Yeah," Nikki said weakly. The officer took off at a sprint. "And for the first time in my life I am relieved that April wouldn't be caught dead in anything as ghastly as a *uniform.*"

The hijacking lasted only another fifteen minutes, but the national news managed to milk it for days. Officer Carberreri knocked on the cockpit door, coughed a couple of times, then said with an altered voice, "Got that flight plan filed, Sam." It was Sam who opened the door for her, which made life easy. She shoved him behind it, entered with her head down and slammed Michael's hand with the gun sharply to the right, banging it against the wall. The gun fell to the floor, and with a very slight struggle, Michael was taken into custody.

The man in custody was removed from the plane by way of the air stairs. More than one reporter with a telescopic lens managed to get a shot of a man in SWAT gear on one side of the cuffed suspect, a woman in a pilot's uniform on the other side, a couple of SWAT guys behind him, and sailing past them in a sweatsuit was Captain Nikki Burgess, who jumped into the arms of the copilot.

So much for discretion.

Nineteen

After almost two hours of nerves stretched tighter than drums, the attempted hijacking of a New Century 757 was over. Aside from the flight attendants and ramp personnel who were on the scene when it all happened, Joe Riordan was the only airline employee allowed to stay while the police debriefed the crews. There would be more debriefings with the FAA and NTSB later, but the interviews immediately following the incident were very important. So there were Jewel and Dixie, sitting at the airport waiting, almost limp with the exhaustion of wondering what was going to happen.

Slowly, passengers began to return to the ticket counters and concourse. Even though the threat had been isolated and was not conspiracy or terror related, the presence of police and National Guard seemed to be greatly increased.

"I could give you a lift to the office and come back for Joe," Jewel offered.

"Or I could buy you a drink if the bar isn't too crowded, and we could watch this whole clambake on CNN," Dixie suggested.

"Perfect!" Jewel said. "I need a drink!"

"Now, there's a first," Dixie said.

"What do you mean by that?" Jewel asked as they walked toward the nearest bar.

"You're a little... Well, if you don't mind me saying so, you might be a little on the rigid, perfectionist side. It'd do my heart good to get you just a bit sloppy."

"Ah, payback for putting Shanna in your car?" Jewel asked with a smile.

"Putting her in my car doesn't need no payin' back, Jewel, darlin'. But what she did in there is gonna take you some big-time payin' back."

Jewel laughed, and it almost shook Dixie out of her snakeskin pumps. "Well, where you been hiding that, girl?" Dixie demanded.

She let it go again. And her eyes sparkled wickedly, as if she'd been dying to laugh real hard for a long time now.

"Let's get some liquor in you," Dixie said. "I think you're coming unhinged on me."

They passed two overcrowded bars and kept walking down to the far end of the airport, where several non-scheduled carriers made a couple of flights a day. There was a sports bar, and though hardly vacant on this of all nights, at least the two women could find a booth from which they could see the TV.

Jewel, throwing caution to the wind, ordered a dirty martini. Dixie followed with a Crown Royal on the rocks. They toasted the crew of 909, clinked glasses and watched the denouement of the hijacking about three times in a row. By the time they'd seen Nikki run into Sam's arms three times and their drinks were more than half gone, they were starting to feel pretty good.

"I've always taken a shine to you, Jewel," Dixie said.

"Bull. You hated me, admit it."

"I never did. I hated Shanna, but I now only feel very sorry for her. Looking at her was like looking in an old mirror. But you? I always liked your style. The way you never let anyone know if you're *really* sleeping with the boss.''

Jewel let that wild laugh go again and Dixie started to think maybe it had been a good thing that she'd kept it under wraps this long. But she *still* didn't tell.

"What makes you think it's sex?" Jewel asked, lifting one eyebrow. "Maybe he's hooked on me because I'm the smartest woman who's ever run his office. And when he's away, his company."

"I wouldn't doubt that," Dixie admitted.

"Tell me about that one," Jewel said, pointing to the television screen as Nikki, for about the fifth time, ran into the arms of her first officer while her look-alike dragged away the cuffed perpetrator.

"Nikki? Or the guy?"

"Are they an item?" Jewel asked, plucking her olive out of the glass.

"They couldn't be," Dixie said. "She'd have told me."

"That boss of yours, she's a curiosity." Jewel bit on the little plastic sword that had speared her olive. "When she first stumbled into Joe's office, she was a little on the dowdy side. Not that I pay attention to things like that."

"'Course not," Dixie mocked.

"But look at her now," she said, stabbing the air toward the TV with the sword. "She's turned into a fine-looking woman, hasn't she? It does make you wonder if love did that to her."

"You think?" Dixie asked.

Jewel thought a moment. "No. More likely success. Power and success."

"You would know, oh, my queen."

"They do look good together, though."

"But I bet it was just the tension of the situation. Because they were in danger together, I reckon. Or else—"

Dixie stopped talking a second. She heard a man's voice, speaking softly, quietly. She tilted her head to listen and put a finger to her lips, warning Jewel to be quiet. But in the bar, with all the noise, they weren't likely to be heard.

She recognized the voice but couldn't remember where she'd heard it.

"I was working undercover on another case when the shit hit the fan," the man said.

"Really?" answered a fascinated woman's voice.

"That's right. So I was already on the job, ya might say, and was just outside the cockpit door there, when the SWAT boys came in. After that, it was pretty much routine, if you know what I mean."

Dixie got up on her knees, turned around and looked over the top of the booth to the one behind her. He was sitting there, cozily, with his arm around a young woman and a drink in his hand. "You!" she said. The man promptly spilled his drink down his shirt. "Rocky!"

It took him a moment to focus, and he might never have placed her, his attempts and conquests so many, but he knew he was busted. He nearly dumped the young lady on the floor in his effort to scramble out of the booth and make his getaway.

"Hey!" the woman shouted, stumbling into the lap of a patron at a table across from the booth.

Once Rocky, if that was his real name, cleared the door of the bar, he broke into a dead run. He didn't get very far, however, because running through an airport immediately following a hijacking attempt wasn't the most intelligent move.

Dixie just turned around in her seat and began to laugh.

"Who was that?" Jewel asked.

"Just another of our local aviation nutballs."

Joe Riordan told Nikki and Sam that he wanted them both seen by a counselor before coming back to work, and they readily agreed. Then he got the dispatcher to find a jump seat for Sam to Colorado Springs so he could see his daughters. "Make it a priority," Joe said. "If you can't find him a jump seat, find him a full-fare seat and charge it to me. If you can't get one of those, I'll rent a plane to take him there."

It wasn't hard to find him transportation, once airline personnel knew who the passenger was. During crises like this, all airlines were a part of one family, a family that took very good care of one another. The first airline called said they'd put him in first class and get him home even if they had to bump a passenger.

Nikki walked with Sam from Dispatch to the upstairs concourse, but no farther. She was too recognizable from the news and the Metro sweatsuit she still wore. They stood just inside the door at Gate 1, as alone as they were about to get.

"I'm sorry about what this does to your holiday dinner," he said.

"The least of my worries. I hope everything is all right with your girls." Then she swallowed and said, "With you."

"I have no idea what to expect when I get there, Nick. It's one of those things we might never get past. I mean, they saw their mother die about a thousand times...."

"I know. I can't imagine..."

"I might need more than a few days."

"Take as much time as you need. Doesn't matter. Even if it takes years, your job and seniority number are protected here."

"I'll be in touch, then," he said. He gave her a brief hug and walked away.

She watched him go. It had taken a lot to bring him back to the flying life, and he might just have encountered the one thing that could take him out of it. She knew in her heart she might never see him again. The business had become insane, and she wasn't sure if Sam hadn't just had all he could take.

A hand rested on her shoulder and she turned to see that Joe had come up behind her. "I didn't know about him until tonight," Joe said.

"I didn't know when I hired him. He didn't keep it a secret, though. He thought everyone knew. I mean, he'd been on the news, he and his daughters, along with hundreds of other family members of 9/11 victims."

"I listened to the two of you with that guy. You did a good job, Nick. Both of you did. I couldn't have done that…and I'm fearless."

She laughed.

"Tell me something. Did you think maybe he'd kill you? Did you think you might die?"

"It crossed my mind a couple of times. But it wouldn't have been because he was filled with hate, like terrorists. It would have been because… It would have been because he was totally helpless. I almost feel sorry for him."

"Yeah?"

"Almost," she repeated.

"What if you had to fly again, right now. Could you do it?"

She rolled her eyes at him.

"Seriously," he pushed.

"Come on."

"Like I'm kidding? I don't think I want to go for an airplane ride right now."

"Look, I started flying when I was eleven. I went on a cross-country flight with Buck when I was fourteen. I raced the Stearman when I was seventeen and I almost won. I fly. I might fly a desk sometimes in my job, but in my life I fly. No matter how tough the bastards make it for us, I fly. I love to fly."

Hands in his pockets, he rocked back on his heels, grinning. "Boy, did I know what I was doing when I hired you. Hah! Listen, you interested in the VP job?"

"You have a VP already."

"I heard he was looking around."

"Yeah, I heard that, too. But he's still with us."

"I know. I told him to sit in his office and wait for me till I get back over there, no matter how late I am." He pulled out his cell phone. "I wonder where Jewel went. She brought me over here in my car." He pecked off some numbers and spoke into the phone. "Where are you? Oh, yeah? Sit tight…I could use one, too."

Then he turned to Nikki. "Jewel and Dixie are having a drink at the sports bar down toward the north end. Want to join us?"

"No, I have to get home. My kids sounded fine on the phone, but I know they must be waiting to see me, hear the whole story."

"Okay," he said. He grabbed her in a quick clutch. Grateful. He was probably grateful his plane wasn't shot up, but she knew he was also grateful she was all right. That everyone involved was all right. "I'm going to have a drink and take Jewel out for a big, fat steak. And I'm going to bed early and, by God, sleep in tomorrow."

"You going to the office first?"

"Hell, no. Why would I do that?"

"Tell Riddle the coast is clear and he can go home?"

"Hell, no. Why would I do that?"

It was almost nine o'clock by the time Nikki drove up to her house, and it was lit up like a carnival. When she walked in the door she was greeted by yapping and barking and shrieks from the kids. "You've been on the news all night!" they yelled.

This was good, she thought. They were more wound up about her celebrity than the fact that she'd been held at gunpoint. As long as that was their perspective, they'd get over this pretty quick.

Everyone had to touch her, pat her, hug her. Even Ethel, who had been in tears on and off all evening.

"We didn't want you to come to a boring household for Thanksgiving," Nikki teased.

"Oh, my goodness, we were frightened to death!" she said.

And Opal had genuine tears in her eyes. "My girl, my poor Nicole—are you ever going to get over this? You poor darling! And who was that handsome pilot you had your arms around?"

"That was the copilot, and we were pretty relieved by the time that was caught on film."

It was a full house and she was glad yet again that she'd bought this place. The late-November nighttime temperature was hovering around forty, and a fire crackled in the family room hearth. Nikki sat in the corner of the sofa, legs curled up under her, looking out at the city lights, watching those bright dots that were planes lining up to land in Las Vegas. Carlisle brought her a glass of chilled white wine and everyone gathered around. Opal and Ethel took the love seat beside each other, Jared and April sat next to Nikki on the sofa, Carlisle and Buck turned chairs around from the breakfast nook as they waited to hear the details from beginning to end.

She looked at them and said, "Why do I feel like a kindergarten teacher at storytime?"

Three hours later, story told and retold, she still sat on that sofa, still looked out at the lights and the now-rare beacon of a plane coming in. The house was quiet and dark, except for a dim light glowing in the living room and the night-light over the stove. The fire was the only illumination in the family room and Nikki hadn't moved since she walked in the door. She'd been waited on by Carlisle, who brought her food and served her a cup of tea before he left for his casita, turning off lights as he went. Because of all the excitement, everyone was staying here at the house instead of a hotel. Ethel was upstairs in the spare room and Nikki assumed Buck was bunking in with Jared.

She turned at a noise in the kitchen and heard the refrigerator door open. Her dad was digging around in there for a diet cola, which he pulled out and snapped open. He sat on the love seat perpendicular to her. "You doing okay?" he asked.

"Fine," she said. "I just can't get enough of those lights."

"It must feel particularly good tonight, after the long day you've had."

"It isn't getting any easier in the airlines, that's for sure. Every year it's a little more challenging, a little more uncertain. Isn't it funny—our equipment just gets better and better, our systems safer and safer, and yet it's a tougher job. Funny."

"That guy—Sam Landon. They did a profile on him on one of the stations. His wife died in 9/11."

"Oh, man," she said, annoyed. "I wish they hadn't done that. I think he and his daughters have enough of a load without media, too."

"They say he did a good job with the guy."

"He was awesome," she said. "At first I thought he was stricken. But then he got himself together and he's the one who got me out of the cockpit."

"Was it because you were a girl?"

"No. No, absolutely. He would have gotten anyone out. It was his idea, the new flight plan. He had it working for him with the gunman—he had to do it that way. If he'd volunteered to leave the cockpit, it would have been fishy. Not that our guy knew the difference between fishy and unfishy. *Shew.*"

"I was real proud of you, Nick."

"Thanks, Dad."

"And the kids were. And Opal."

She laughed. She was quiet for a long moment, then said, "He might not come back, you know. Sam. He had just barely come back after two years off. And when he left, he said he didn't know how much time he'd need. It depended on a lot of things. His daughters. And he didn't say…himself. It depends on how much of this shit a person can take."

"That's not always something we're in charge of."

"Huh?"

"How much we can take… How well we do with crises. Trauma. It's like a pain threshold. You get what you get. Some people are tougher than others. You don't know until you're there."

"You think that?"

He shrugged. "Deductive reasoning. Take two soldiers who have a similar war experience. One suffers for years, becomes an addict, can't hold a job, and the other re-ups, can't wait to get back into combat. I don't think either one of them responded the way they did intentionally. It's what they were capable of."

"You don't think you can get better at handling the hard stuff?"

"Within reason."

She smiled. "So you don't think I'm all that tough, just lucky."

"I think you're both tough and lucky. And smart as the devil."

She felt the sting of tears in her eyes. "I like him, Dad."

"Sam?"

"Uh-huh. I thought we... I was resisting liking him because I'm the... Oh, hell, I'd just made up my mind that it would be okay if we saw each other. Dated. You know. And then... This."

Buck considered what she'd just told him. "He's got an awful lot of baggage there, Nick."

"Oh, and I don't!"

"Just the usual stuff. And some of it's real good."

"Some of his stuff is real good, too." She felt the tears on her cheeks and she *never* cried. *Never*. It's just that she and Sam had been so close to getting together. And it had been so bloody long since she'd loved anyone and been loved back.

"I know you haven't had the easiest time, Nick, but you've had some damn good breaks, too."

The list is long, she thought. "Yeah, I shouldn't complain."

"It'll work out the way it's supposed to." Buck's

mantra. She'd heard that all the while she was growing up, through her darkest moments.

And it always had. More or less.

"You don't have to sit up with me, Dad. I'm fine."

"I'm not sitting up with you. You're on my bed."

It was maybe the best Thanksgiving Nikki had ever had, even though Sam hadn't made it. Her mother and her father, not exactly together, but together. Their dogs had to be put in separate rooms, but Buck and Opal managed. Dixie and Danny were too cute for words. "*Ew*, you're making me gag," Jared complained.

Carlisle's mother was such a trip—talk about being from a simpler place. Whenever anything the least bit racy or provocative was uttered, she went completely crimson. Opal said, "Ethel, I'm going to do you a big favor. I'm going to take you to San Francisco for Christmas shopping and introduce you to all my very favorite homosexuals." Everyone standing immediately collapsed to the floor and practically wet themselves while the walls rocked with laughter.

Opal was no tease. She did take Ethel to the gay Bay Area. But unfortunately she said she'd be right back.

Work and school recommenced. Buck returned to Phoenix. Plans were being set in motion for a big Christmas open house—pretty much the same group that had made Thanksgiving plus some New Century employees and their families. Carlisle was in a tizzy of planning, making lists and collecting recipes, when the doorbell rang. He went to answer it, and there stood Alex.

"Thank God," Alex said, placing his hand on his chest. "You were not easy to find, you know."

"I'm sorry. I didn't know anyone was looking."

"When Aries shut down, I immediately called your

house to see if there was anything you needed. That man, Roberto, said you'd been gone for a long time, but he refused to tell me where.''

Carlisle smiled. "He's such a jerk.''

"You're okay, then?''

"Perfectly all right,'' he said. *Better than all right,* he wanted to shout. *Happy, healthy, reunited with family, thrilled to see you standing there.* "Great. And so good of you to think about me, Alex.''

"Why wouldn't I?'' He kind of peeked inside. "Nice place, Carlisle.''

"Yes. Thanks.''

"You don't live alone, do you?''

"No. No, I'm living with someone.''

"Ah. I see. Of course.'' He cleared his throat. "Well, I just wanted to assure myself—''

"You live with someone, as well, Alex,'' Carlisle reminded him.

Alex looked confused. "I…?'' He shook his head. "I'm not in a relationship, Carlisle. I haven't been in years.''

"That young man…''

He frowned again, shook his head.

"The young man who offered to put out wine and cheese when I dropped by your house.''

"Christopher?'' Alex asked.

"My God!'' Carlisle gasped. He had not recognized Alex's son! "I can't believe it! He must have thought me so rude!''

Alex laughed. "He was just spending a couple of weeks. He's full time at Stanford. Has a serious girlfriend and they're threatening to move in together. I think he'll make me a grandfather long before I'm ready.''

"Oh, Alex, you don't know what I thought."

"I do now," he said.

"Oh, my God, come in. Come in, my good friend. I am so happy to see you!"

And so, there was one more for Christmas.

New Century Air benefitted from the unfortunate demise of Aries Airlines. Four months after ceasing flights, a skeleton staff was still trying to get an operation up and running, but labor relations remained strained.

Bob Riddle moved on to a senior vice president position at a start-up in Florida, where, it was rumored, he was making more money than he had at New Century. Joe Riordan admitted he was tempted to call the CEO there and give him a heads-up on Riddle's phone call conspiracy. "But," he said, "it would just create a *madrid* of problems."

No one ever knew how long Riddle sat at the office waiting for his meeting with Joe. It was never spoken of again.

Nikki moved up and Danny Adams moved into the chief pilot's position. Joe Riordan acquired six more 757s, to be delivered over the next twelve months. Of course, every time he found more airplanes, they had to rush to hire and train more pilots, and if they could just slow down a little, Nikki's life would be easier. But why should she want it easy?

Sam called regularly. His daughters were doing fine, he said. They all were. But he didn't make any plans to come back. "I don't want to get ahead of myself," he said. "I'm getting a little counseling. I want to be sure that commercial flying is good for me—and that I'm an asset to the airline."

She told him the same thing every time—his job and

his number were secure, and she would look forward to his return. She didn't push him, didn't tell him she missed him or that she wanted him to come back. If he did return, it had to be because he was compelled to return. But in her heart she assumed he was done. Done and having a hard time letting go.

As she knew would happen eventually, Carlisle went back to Phoenix, to Alex, where he was completely happy. He wasn't working, just keeping the home fires burning and thinking about going back to school for an advanced degree. Dixie and Danny, inseparable outside of work, were edging cautiously toward marriage, and Nikki expected to see a big ring any day. And Opal, kicking and screaming, had been moved into a sweet little bungalow in a retirement community just a stone's throw from Nikki and the kids. She still spent as much time at Nikki's as she pleased, still squawked about not having long to live, and still had more energy than the average teenager.

On one particularly busy day in the first week of March, Joe Riordan stuck his head into Nikki's office. "Are you going to be here awhile?"

She looked at her watch. It was five. "Another half hour. Maybe hour. What do you need?"

"I want to show you something at the airport, but I want to show you after dark. Or at least dusk."

"What?" she asked again, in no mood for games.

He grinned. "You'll see, you'll see. Meet me out front at five-forty-five."

"Is this going to take long?"

"Five-forty-five," he said, and left.

At the appointed time, she met his car at the curb. She got in and said, "You aren't going to blindfold me or anything, are you?"

"You'll thank me for this," he promised her.

They walked into the terminal together, went up the long escalator to the second floor where the concourses were, but rather than going toward the gates, they went in the opposite direction. They came to a restaurant, a bank of slot machines and a bookstore. There were rest rooms to the left and an unmarked door to the right.

Joe took a key out of his pocket and unlocked the door. Inside was a large unfinished room, construction debris scattered around a plywood floor. Wires were hanging from the walls and ceiling, plumbing fixtures stuck out between the studs, and there was no drywall at all. But the entire wall opposite the door was glass, and on the other side of the glass was the Las Vegas Strip. The pyramid, the Sphinx, the beam from the Luxor to the stars, the big green MGM, the gold Mandalay Bay—all of them close enough to touch.

"God," she said. "What a view."

"You like it."

"Yeah, I like it."

"It's our new executive lounge. I'll get you a membership."

"Really?"

"Yup," he grinned.

"When do you sleep?"

"I can sleep when I'm dead."

"If you don't stop buying things, I'm gonna be dead."

"Bitch, bitch, bitch. Want me to give it back?"

"No. This I like."

Joe's phone twittered. He pulled it out and looked at it. "Jewel," he said, and answered. "What? What? Why? All right, yeah, yeah, yeah…" He moved away from Nikki and backed out the door—for better reception, Nikki assumed.

She stood in the empty space, her back to the door, taking in the staggeringly beautiful view.

"Hey, boss," Sam said.

Nikki turned around with a start. "Sam!"

"I'm back." Grinning with that perfect bad-boy smile, his hair floppy from the wind, he stood right behind her, hands on his hips. It sliced through her again, how handsome she found him. She didn't know if he really was, but she sure responded to that square jaw and bushy brows.

"So you are. How're you doing? How're the girls?"

"Everyone is good. You going to let me work again?"

"I told you. Anytime. Are you sure you're ready?"

"I got a note from the shrink. I was sure, anyway, but I wanted good backup."

"You're not scarred from the experience?"

"No. You?"

"No."

"I think we worked pretty well together," he said.

"We did. Mission accomplished, anyway. No one got hurt."

"It hasn't been that long, Nick. Three months. And we were just about to... Weren't we?"

"Seemed like it," she said.

"How do you feel about that now?"

She shrugged. "How do you feel about it?"

"Every time we talked, I kept waiting for you to say something like, 'I miss you.' Or 'Hurry back.' Or, 'Are you almost ready to come back?' But you never did, so I assumed it meant I was welcome to come back as a pilot, but not anything more."

"I didn't want to push."

"You sure didn't."

"Well, you never said anything, either. Like you really missed me and couldn't wait to get back or— Well, I did some assuming, too."

"I didn't want to push," he said. "You never were real comfortable with the idea."

"It was growing on me."

He took two steps toward her and put his hands on her waist. "Then one of us is going to have to push."

"And I guess the other will have to push back," she suggested.

He pulled her closer. "That's what I'm talking about." He held her for a moment and then, holding her away from him just a bit, he asked, "By the way, what did Riordan say that got you to come here, take this on?"

She frowned as she thought. Then her face broke into a grin. "He said, 'Nikki, I think you're going to like this New Century.' And you know what? He was damn straight. It just gets better every day."

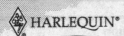 

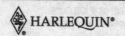 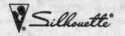

Carnival Elation
7-Day Exotic Western Caribbean Itinerary

DAY	PORT	ARRIVE	DEPART
Sun	Galveston		4:00 P.M.
Mon	"Fun Day" at Sea		
Tue	Progreso/Mérida	8:00 A.M.	4:00 P.M.
Wed	Cozumel	9:00 A.M.	5:00 P.M.
Thu	Belize	8:00 A.M.	6:00 P.M.
Fri	"Fun Day" at Sea		
Sat	"Fun Day" at Sea		
Sun	Galveston	8:00 A.M.	

TERMS AND CONDITIONS

PAYMENT SCHEDULE:
50% due upon booking. Full and final payment due by July 26, 2004.
Acceptable forms of payment are Visa, MasterCard, American Express, Discover and checks.
The cardholder must be one of the passengers traveling. A fee of $25 will apply for all returned
checks. Check payments must be made payable to **Advantage International, LLC** and sent to:
Advantage International, LLC, 195 North Harbor Drive, Suite 4206, Chicago, IL 60601.

CHANGE/CANCELLATION:
Notice of change/cancellation must be made in writing to Advantage International, LLC.

Change:
Changes in cabin category may be requested and can result in increased rate and penalties. A
name change is permitted 60 days or more prior to departure and will incur a penalty of $50
per name change. Deviation from the group schedule and package is a cancellation.

Cancellation:

181 days or more prior to departure	$250 per person
121—180 days or more prior to departure	50% of the package price
120—61 days prior to departure	75% of the package price
60 days or less prior to departure	100% of the package price (nonrefundable)

**U.S. and Canadian citizens are required to present a valid passport or the original birth cer-
tificate and state issued photo ID (driver's license). All other nationalities must contact
the consulate of the various ports that are visited for verification of documentation.**

<u>We **strongly** recommend trip cancellation insurance!</u>

For further details call 1-877-ADV-NTGE or visit www.GetCaughtReadingatSea.com

---

For booking form and complete information
go to <u>www.getcaughtreadingatsea.com</u>
or call 1-877-ADV-NTGE

Complete coupon and booking form and mail both to:
Advantage International, LLC
195 North Harbor Drive, Suite 4206, Chicago, IL 60601

Harlequin Enterprises Ltd. is a paid participant in this promotion.

THE FUN SHIPS, CARNIVAL DESIGN, CARNIVAL AND THE MOST POPULAR CRUISE LINE IN
THE WORLD ARE TRADEMARKS OF CARNIVAL CORPORATION. ALL OTHER TRADEMARKS
ARE TRADEMARKS OF HARLEQUIN ENTERPRISES LTD. OR ITS AFFILIATED COMPANIES,
USED UNDER LICENSE.

Visit us at www.eHarlequin.com

GCRSEA2

ROBYN CARR

66940	JUST OVER THE MOUNTAIN	___ $6.50 U.S.	___ $7.99 CAN.
66839	THE WEDDING PARTY	___ $5.99 U.S.	___ $6.99 CAN.
66704	DOWN BY THE RIVER	___ $6.50 U.S.	___ $7.99 CAN.
66609	DEEP IN THE VALLEY	___ $5.99 U.S.	___ $6.99 CAN.

(limited quantities available)

TOTAL AMOUNT	$_____
POSTAGE & HANDLING	$_____
($1.00 for 1 book; 50¢ for each additional)	
APPLICABLE TAXES*	$_____
TOTAL PAYABLE	$_____

(check or money order—please do not send cash)

To order, complete this form and send it, along with a check or money order for the total above, payable to MIRA Books, to: **In the U.S.:** 3010 Walden Avenue, P.O. Box 9077, Buffalo, NY 14269-9077; **In Canada:** P.O. Box 636, Fort Erie, Ontario, L2A 5X3.

Name:_____

Address:_____ City:_____

State/Prov.:_____ Zip/Postal Code:_____

Account Number (if applicable):_____

075 CSAS

*New York residents remit applicable sales taxes.
Canadian residents remit applicable GST
and provincial taxes.

MIRA®